THE GREAT JACKALOPE STAMPEDE

"A laugh-out-loud randy and rowdy mystery centering around the rabble-rousing Morgan sisters. Add the discovery of a box of eyeballs, suspicious strangers, a silent sexy sheriff, and lots of 'action' of the romantic and suspenseful kinds, and you've got yourself one entertaining read. Ann Charles' complex characters, witty and ribald dialogue, and cleverly intertwined plot twists will keep you turning the pages."
~Chanticleer Book Reviews

"Cool characters, a clever mystery, and a ton of laughs—*The Great Jackalope Stampede* delivers them all! If you haven't read a Jackrabbit Junction Mystery yet, I highly suggest you hop to it!"
~Gemma Halliday, New York Times bestselling author of the High Heels Mysteries

"… an action-packed, sexy mystery loaded with Ann Charles' special brand of humor, including dirty old men, The Shaft, and a beagle. Ms. Charles hit one out of the trailer park with the third offering in the Jackrabbit Junction series. Highly recommended!"
~Jacquie Rogers, Award-winning Author of the Hearts of Owyhee Romance Series

"Sassy, laugh-out-loud funny, and a rollicking romp of a mystery! Ann Charles delivers another sizzling page turner in her highly entertaining Jackrabbit Junction Mystery series!"
~Wendy Delaney, Award-winning Author of the Working Stiffs Mystery Series

"Claire, Gramps and the rest of the gang are at it again. The Great Jackalope Stampede is the best one yet!"
~Diane Garland, Reader

Dear Reader,

Back when I wrote the first book in the Jackrabbit series, *Dance of the Winnebagos*, I had no idea I eventually would be introducing Claire's older sister, Ronnie—at least no more than a mention here and there. But then I wrote the second book, *Jackrabbit Junction Jitters*, and introduced Claire's younger sister, Kate. After Kate came to life on the page, I knew Ronnie deserved some screen time, too.

What I didn't realize when plotting this book was how strong Ronnie's personality would be. She came on stage and took over, sitting in my director's chair, telling me how the story was going to go, just the way older sisters do. (Trust me, I know all about older sisters. I grew up with them, and they taught me lots of things about life and who really was the boss of me. Ha!)

I'll admit I had a blast sitting back and watching Ronnie take command, ruffling feathers but fitting in with everyone else in the story. I really enjoyed the interaction between the three sisters. They are not touchy-feely sisters ready to grace flowery Hallmark cards and family movies. They fight, poke fun at each other, and often drive each other to drink and curse. Their relationships are bumpy, yet much more real to me because of it. Many families don't get along every minute of the day, but like Claire and her sisters, there is a bond between them that holds them together through thick and thin.

This third book in the series completes the introduction of Claire's family—her grandfather, her mother, and her sisters, Kate and Ronnie. I hope you have as much fun experiencing their wacky and often spark-filled family dynamics as I did writing them.

Oh, and if you ever find yourself in southeastern Arizona, pay a visit to the tiny town of Three Way, a junction where three roads come together. That's the real-life town I used as inspiration for Jackrabbit Junction.

When you finish *The Great Jackalope Stampede*, stop by The Shaft for a bit. Drinks are on me!

Ann Charles
www.anncharles.com

THE GREAT
JACKALOPE STAMPEDE

ANN CHARLES

ILLUSTRATED BY C.S. KUNKLE

THE GREAT JACKALOPE STAMPEDE

Copyright © 2014 by Ann Charles

All rights reserved. Except as permitted under the U.S. Copyright Act of 1976, no part of this publication may be reproduced, distributed, or transmitted in any form or by any means now known or hereafter invented, or stored in a database or retrieval system, without the prior written permission of the author, Ann Charles.

This book is a work of fiction. Names, characters, places, and incidents are the product of the author's imagination or are used fictitiously. Any resemblance to actual persons, living or dead, business establishments, events, or locales is coincidental.

Cover Art by C.S. Kunkle (www.charlesskunkle.com)
Cover Design by Sharon Benton (www.q42designs.com)
Editing by the "Grammar Chick" (www.grammarchick.com)
Formatting by Biddles ebooks (www.biddlesebooks.com)

E-book ISBN-13: 978-1-940364-10-0
Print ISBN-13: 978-1-940364-11-7

Dedication

To my stepmom.

You've read my stories and believed in me from the very start, always encouraging, always supporting. I couldn't have wished for a kinder, more loving woman to help raise me. Nobody can write to-do lists, make monster cookies, or chop up poor innocent snakes like you. (Ha!)

You're the best!

Also by Ann Charles:

Jackrabbit Junction Mystery Series:
Dance of the Winnebagos (Book 1)
Jackrabbit Junction Jitters (Book 2)

Deadwood Mystery Series:
Nearly Departed in Deadwood (Book 1)
Optical Delusions in Deadwood (Book 2)
Dead Case in Deadwood (Book 3)
Better Off Dead in Deadwood (Book 4)

Short Stories from the Deadwood Mystery Series:
Deadwood Shorts: Seeing Trouble
Deadwood Shorts: Boot Points

A Short Story from the upcoming Goldwash Mystery Series
The Old Man's Back in Town

Coming Next from Ann Charles:

An Ex to Grind in Deadwood
(Deadwood Mystery Series: Book 5)

A Mayan Muddle
(a novel starring Quint Parker, the brother of Violet Parker from the Deadwood Mystery Series)

Title TBA
(Jackrabbit Junction Mystery Series: Book 4)

Acknowledgments

This third book in the Jackrabbit Junction Mystery series had plenty of help to bring it together. In addition to my critique partners, first-draft readers, and editor, I had an amazing crew of beta readers who volunteered their time and knowledge over the week between Christmas and New Year's Day to add another layer of polish to this book and make it sparkle like a disco ball under the desert sunshine.

In addition to all of these generous readers I want to mention:

My husband, who not only brainstorms with me at a moment's notice, but who is forced to drop whatever he is doing and listen as I read him part of a scene or a few lines of dialogue at any given moment. He helps me find just the right words when I'm stuck, edits my rough draft chapter by chapter along the way, and hugs me time and again while saying, "You can do this." I'm a lucky girl!

My funny kids and mouthy cat who keep me smiling every day with kisses, snuggles, and purrs.

Mimi "The Grammar Chick" (my editor), who gently and kindly teaches me how to improve my writing with every book.

My brother, Charles (C.S.) Kunkle (cover artist and illustrator) for his awesome drawings and constant support.

Sharon Benton (cover graphic artist) for not only her talent, but also for her incredible patience with me.

My sister-in-law, Stephanie Kunkle, for helping me pick which illustrations to include in this book.

My publicists and sales help for all of their time and help promoting my books—my mom and brother (Margo Taylor and Dave Taylor), my aunt (Judy Routt), my sister (Laura Rensberger), and my sister-in-law (Wendy Gildersleeve).

The kick-butt first and second draft crew: Beth Harris, Wendy Delaney, Marcia Britton, Mary Ida Kunkle, Paul Franklin, Renelle Wilson, Sue Stone-Douglas, Marguerite Phipps, Diane Garland, Margo Taylor, and Wendy Gildersleeve.

Diane Garland for her amazingly detailed spreadsheets on all of my books in this series, including this newest book. Never has it been so easy to keep all of the series details straight. I'm so glad you like my books!

Wayne Roberts for letting me bug him out of the blue with law enforcement questions.

Jacquie Rogers, Wendy Delaney, Amber Scott, Gerri Russell, and Joleen James for being some of the best author friends I could have.

My coworkers at my day job who continue to cheer me on even now that I have quit my job and write full time. I miss you guys (but not enough to come back to work there).

My family for their never-ending love and support. I really appreciate that you actually read my books.

My Facebook and Twitter friends who lift my spirits during the hard times, crack the whip when I get lazy, help me promote new books to all of their family and friends, and cheer with me at the top of their lungs when something wonderful happens with my career. I can't thank you all enough for being there day after day (and late night after late night). You make me want to write more stories to share with you.

Finally, my brother, Clint Taylor for never hesitating to explore a mine with me, especially the ones that would have made Mom pull out her hair if she had known we were playing around in them. We probably should have gotten a canary to take along during our spelunking fun. Hindsight is 20-20, right? Ha!

THE GREAT
JACKALOPE STAMPEDE

Cast

KEY: **Character *(Book # in which they appear)—Description***

Claire Alice Morgan (1,2,3)—Main heroine of the series, Mac's girlfriend, Harley's granddaughter

Harley "Gramps" Ford (1,2,3)—Claire's maternal grandfather, Ruby's husband

Henry Ford (1,2,3)—Harley's beagle/dog

MacDonald "Mac" Garner (1,2,3)—Main hero of the series, Claire's boyfriend

Ruby (Wayne) Martino-Ford (1,2,3)—Mac's aunt, owner of the Dancing Winnebagos R.V. Park, Harley's new wife

Jessica Wayne (1,2,3)—Ruby's teenage daughter, Harley's stepdaughter

Chester Thomas (1,2,3)—Harley's old Army vet buddy

Manuel "Manny" Carrera (1,2,3)—Harley's old Army vet buddy

Joe Martino (1,2,3)—Deceased; Ruby's first husband, previous owner of the Dancing Winnebagos R.V. Park

Deborah Ford-Morgan (2,3)—Claire's mother, Harley's daughter

Kathryn "Kate" Morgan (2,3)—Claire's younger sister, Deborah's youngest daughter, Butch's girlfriend

Veronica "Ronnie" Morgan (3)—Claire's oldest sister, Deborah's oldest daughter

Natalie Beals (3)—Claire's cousin from back in South Dakota, Harley's granddaughter

Grandma Ford (1,2,3)—Deceased; Claire's grandmother, Harley's first wife

Valentine "Butch" Carter (1,2,3)—Owner of The Shaft, the only bar in Jackrabbit Junction, Kate's boyfriend

Grady Harrison (1,2,3)—Sheriff of Cholla County

Mindy Lou Harrison (3)—Sheriff Harrison's niece

Aunt Millie (3)—Sheriff Harrison's aunt, leader of the library gang

Ruth and Greta (3)—Members of Aunt Millie's library gang

Steve Horner (3)—Jessica's biological father, Ruby's ex-lover

Lyle Jefferson (3)—Ronnie's ex-husband

Arlene (3)—Waitress at The Shaft, friend of Kate's

Gary (2,3)—Bartender at The Shaft

Chapter One

Friday, September 21st
Jackrabbit Junction, Arizona

In a bone-littered desert bristling with prickly plants and venomous predators, Claire Morgan had forgotten one of the most important rules of survival—to keep her big mouth shut.

"You told Ronnie what?" her grandfather, Harley Ford, asked, his hammer frozen mid-swing as he squinted down at where Claire stood at the base of his ladder.

Was it just her or had the skull-baking Arizona sunshine rocketed the temperature another twenty degrees? Claire fanned the neck of her faded Tijuana Toads T-shirt.

Crud. What had she been thinking? She should have gone to Ruby first, Gramps's much less crotchety better half.

Claire cleared her throat, not letting the glare from Gramps or the sun deter her. "I told Ronnie that she could stay with you guys for a month."

Footfalls on the gravel drive behind her caught Claire's attention. A tall, skinny college kid wearing flip-flops, checkered swim trunks, and a yellow velvet sombrero complete with black embroidery and chin strap smiled at her through a mouthful of braces.

"*Hola, señora,*" Beanpole called to her, pushing his thick rimmed eyeglasses up the zinc oxide that coated his nose.

Claire waved back, trying her damnedest not to rubberneck. Had someone hired a Mariachi-singing lifeguard?

"What in the hell did you tell Ronnie that for?" Gramps didn't wait for Claire's answer before pounding another nail into one of the two-by-sixes making up the skeleton roof of the new bathroom facility.

Claire winced with each hit, glad her head wasn't shaped like a nail.

Up the way, she watched Beanpole open the door of a beige camper and step inside.

Autumn had almost arrived at the Dancing Winnebagos R.V. Park, a dusty slice of paradise beneath a grove of old cottonwood trees that lined Jackrabbit Creek in the southeastern corner of the state. Along with slightly less hot temperatures there was a whole new monkey troop of oddballs. However, unlike the harem of golden-oldie babes who had danced through the park last spring or the pretty flock of summer bird watchers, there were more Y chromosomes in this new bunch.

A couple of weeks ago, the University of Arizona's Anthropology Department had rolled into the R.V. park, filling several camper and tent sites. Since the cave dwellings they were excavating had been discovered in a mine belonging to Ruby, she had given them a discount on their weekly rent. In return, she had a steady income—something the park hadn't seen in a long time.

Unfortunately, the traffic was overworking the plumbing in the only set of restrooms at the back of the campground. That had spurred Gramps to build more, seeming to forget he was more of a crotchety old rooster these days than a spring chicken.

About the time he'd started pouring the cement, Ruby had called Claire. Growing up, Claire had spent summers working for Gramps's general contracting business. A jack of all trades and master of absolutely none, Claire knew enough plumbing and carpentry to act as Gramps's second in command. She also happened to be unemployed—again.

Claire grabbed a handful of nails from the pocket of her tool belt and held them up to Gramps. "I told Ronnie she could stay because she's your granddaughter."

He pointed the hammer at her. "But she's *your* sister. That makes her one step closer in blood to you than me. She needs to stay put right where she is—with you."

Shielding her eyes, Claire glared at the ornery cuss on the ladder. "Ronnie has been staying with me for almost a month now in case you've forgotten." Her older sister had been the source of several rumbles between Claire and her boyfriend, Mac, whose house the three of them were sharing. "It's someone else's turn to chauffeur her around like she's Miss Daisy."

Since arriving in Tucson, Ronnie had been blowing her money on a silly post-divorce makeover. She'd had her salon-blonde hair dyed back to brown and trimmed into shoulder-length curls. She'd even bought vanity contacts to make her 20-20 brown eyes blue, which put the old song by Crystal Gayle in Claire's head whenever Ronnie wore them.

"I'm not sure if you've noticed, Claire, but Jackrabbit Junction doesn't have any of those fancy spa places Ronnie likes to go to."

She snorted. "No shit."

Gramps took off his faded U.S. Army hat and wiped the sweat from his brow. "The last thing I need right now is another pain-in-the-ass female nagging me to take her to town."

"Ruby can take Ronnie to Yuccaville. It could be a weekly girls' day out."

Gramps grunted. "Ronnie is *your* problem. We have our hands full with a teenager whose father is scrambling her brains."

Far from done with her campaign to get her older sister out of her hair, Claire let him change the subject. "Jess is giving you grief, huh?"

Gramps's new wife had come with some hormone-laden baggage—a sixteen-year-old whose biological father had opted to pay child support in lieu of doling out love and attention.

"It's not really Jess's fault." Gramps pounded in another nail. "Her dad is getting her all stirred up."

"Is he still ignoring her letters?"

"It's worse. He's writing back."

"What? Why the sudden interest?" Then it dawned on her. "Jess didn't tell him about the mine stocks, did she?"

Gramps grunted again.

"Damn." When was that red-haired, freckle-faced girl going to learn that talking about cash attracted all sorts of trouble? "Is he trying to get out of paying child support?"

Gramps banged away for several seconds, the echo ricocheting through the arroyo behind them. "He's trying to get Jess to come live with him."

"I thought his other kids were more important than her."

"So did he until his wife left him and decided to sue for custody. Rather than pay two sets of child support, he's set his sights on Jess moving in with him so Ruby has to pay him. Jess is convinced he's finally come around to wanting her in his life, and you know how hard it is to sell her any truths when it comes to that horse's ass."

"How's Ruby taking this?"

"She curses and throws things when Jess isn't around."

Claire grimaced.

"He says he's coming down here soon to spend some time getting to know Jess."

"Wow, he's not messing around now that there's money in it for him, is he?"

"Nope." Gramps pounded in another nail with three hard blows.

Two older women strolled past wearing tan University of Arizona shirts, khaki pants, and Aussie hats with air holes in the tops. Claire recognized them from the campground General Store and waved.

The two dressed like twins, but according to Jess, they were just lifelong friends. They had lobbied Jess to join them at the site to learn all about archaeological digs. Claire had them pegged for volunteers, here to help the university catalog the cave dweller remains. Jess waged her bet on the two being visiting professors partly due to their age, but mainly because they kept trying to teach her stuff she had no desire to learn.

Claire waited until they were out of earshot before turning back to Gramps. "All of these new people around here make me nervous."

"You're paranoid." He held out his hand for more nails. "Too much of that schooling you've had over the years has stirred up your brains."

"No, my schooling has made me more aware of the value of the 'goods' stashed in Ruby's basement. You guys need to be more careful letting strangers in the house."

"That's a little tough since the store is attached to the house, Miss Big Brains."

"Maybe you should install a door between the two. That old curtain has seen its day and the velvet stinks like cigar smoke thanks to you and your army cronies."

"We're not putting a door there." He emphasized his statement with a hammer blow.

"Fine, but you and I know that Joe was up to a whole lot of no good."

Joe was Ruby's dead husband. He had gone out in a blaze of greasy potato chips and cigarettes that had stroked him and his brain into the grave. Asshole that he was, he'd left Ruby in a pile of debt without any life insurance. Earlier that spring, she would have lost everything if it hadn't been for Claire's curiosity, Mac's help, and Gramps's cash cushion.

Joe's lousy leftovers hadn't ended there. He'd spent decades not only fencing antiques and random black market gems but also stealing goods from other fencers. Not just any goods—sweet, pricey pieces that drew trouble, including the killing kind.

Claire's latest concern was a golden pocket watch she'd found in a hidden wall safe in Joe's basement office. Her gut said the watch would bring bad juju down on Gramps and Ruby. What sucked about all of the strangers milling around was how easy it would be for the boogeyman to blend in and sneak up on them.

"All I'm saying is—" A loud, yapping dog interrupted Claire. She knew that bark. "Gramps, your damned dog got loose again."

Gramps's spoiled beagle, Henry, lived for three things—to lick Gramps's feet, eat sour cream and onion potato chips, and to disrespect Claire.

"Catch him before he heads over to that Fleetwood again." Gramps pointed the hammer toward a camper with pink flamingo lights dangling from the porch awning. "That woman has a Shih Tzu the old boy's crazy about."

Claire scrambled around the back of the building frame. When she caught Henry, she was going to go all Shih Tzu on his bony little ass. She headed the ornery beagle off at the pass. "Gotcha!"

Henry screeched to a stop. Then he backed up a couple of steps, pawed the ground, and barked at her.

"Quiet, Henry!" Gramps yelled from his ladder post.

The dog circled and whined, his leash dragging behind him and then barked at Claire again.

She lunged for the leash and missed.

Henry zigged around her and zagged through the two-by-sixes making up the back wall of the structure.

Claire followed, reaching between the boards, coming up empty. She grunted in pain as her shoulder connected with a board.

"Quit horsing around, Claire, and grab him!"

"I'm trying!"

Henry rounded the corner of the building with Claire on his tail—or at least reaching for it. She tried to step on the leash and missed.

"Damn it, girl! You're gonna lose him."

Cursing, she lunged again, sliding up to where Gramps stood on his makeshift watch tower.

"Quit your bitching and grab him."

She caught the leash as Henry dodged under the ladder.

"Got him!"

Henry turned and leapt back between the rungs, wrapping the leash around the foot of the ladder. He tried to sprint to freedom, but Claire held the leash tight. "No you don't, you little bugger."

"Claire!" Gramps's voice sounded shaky.

She looked up as the ladder tilted to the side, teetering.

"Hold on!" Letting go of the leash, she grabbed for the ladder ... too late.

She watched, cringing as Gramps flailed through the air and landed with a crunching sound on the hard, dry ground.

"Oh, shit!" Claire covered her mouth.

Gramps's hammer bounced and came to rest on the dirt next to him.

Chapter Two

Friday, September 28th (one week later)

What was it about the Arizona sunshine that made Claire want to down a cold one?

Or maybe her urge to chug some alcohol had more to do with the surly old man with the broken leg playing drill sergeant from below, rather than the ball of fire high in the sky.

"Claire, where did you put my crutches?"

Glaring down from where she kneeled on the freshly sheathed roof, Claire shoved her hammer in her tool belt. "I didn't touch your damned crutches."

After being "supervised" all day by Gramps, who was sitting under the shade of a beach umbrella with that danged mutt panting at his feet, she wouldn't have minded shoving one of his crutches where the southwestern sun didn't shine so brightly.

Gramps shifted, adjusting his cast on the upturned five-gallon bucket he was using as a footstool. He puffed on his cigar, the smoke billowing toward Claire's eyes, making her fingers itch for a cigarette to make this all better. "That last sheet of plywood looks a little off."

Sweat trickled down her back, seeping into her already soaked underwear. "What the hell is that supposed to mean?"

"It means you screwed up again," Chester answered from his lawn chair near Gramps.

Chester was one of Gramps's old Army buddies. Bristly from the top of his silver hair and scruffy jaw to his hair-tufted toes, he'd rolled into Jackrabbit Junction last spring and had hung around for the most part just like the heat. Over the last six months, he'd had a fair share of women keeping him company. A surprising number of women actually, considering his favorite saying was, "I like my women how I like my nuts—swingin' free and ready for a tickle," which he usually ended with a belch.

"Maybe you should let your cousin finish the roof work," Chester told Claire, grabbing a beer from the ice-filled cooler and cracking it open.

"He's right," Gramps piped up, taking the can Chester held out. "She's better with wood than you."

Chester snickered. "Mac might disagree with that."

She yanked her sweat-ringed Mighty Mouse cap off her head and threw it down at the two ornery geezers.

Henry leaped up and barked at the hat, all two feet of killer guard dog that he was.

"You both can kiss my—" Claire started.

A shrill wolf whistle interrupted her. She knew the whistler all too well.

"What did I miss?" Manny Carrera asked as he unfolded the lawn chair he'd brought with him. He shielded his eyes and grinned up at her. "Besides Claire swearing." His gaze lowered. "And soaking through her T-shirt. Why don't you shuck that shirt, *querida*, and just wear a bikini top?"

"Stop ogling my granddaughter, Carrera," Gramps growled and punched his other old Army cohort in the arm.

Chuckling, Manny took a beer from Chester. "I can't help it—she's wearing her tool belt again. You know how I get around women who know how to handle a tool."

"And wood," Chester threw in. "All you missed was Claire telling us to kiss her ass again. That's the third time so far today, isn't it, Ford?"

Gramps took a swig of beer. "I think it's the fourth."

"I'm game." Manny dropped into the lawn chair. "But she'll have to bare it first."

Gramps socked Manny again.

"What?" Manny chuckled, saluting Claire as he rubbed his arm. "She knows I'm full of hot air."

The old dog was quite toothless—protective even. Over the last few months, Manny had been the leading defender of Claire's lack of a career. Where her mother crinkled her upper lip and called her thirty-three-year-old middle child a misguided wanderer, Manny patted Claire on the head and praised her untethered spirit.

"Besides," Manny continued, "it's your fault your granddaughters came out so pretty. You should have picked an uglier wife instead of stealing the love of my life after we got back to the States."

According to Gramps, back when the three boys had been fresh out of boot camp, Manny was really popular with the girls, wooing them with his Spanish tongue and smooth dance moves. He was still velvet and liqueur, although Father Time had aged him.

The wood sheathing behind her creaked. "I see the third Amigo has arrived," said Claire's cousin, Natalie, sidling up to her. "I'm going to need some tequila to make it through this week with all three of them sitting down there."

"Shots are on me at The Shaft tonight," Claire told her. "It's the least I can do to pay you back for racing down here to my rescue."

After Gramps had received his diagnosis of a broken fibula, Claire had taken one look at the worry creasing Ruby's face and picked up the phone. She'd called back home to South Dakota, explaining to Natalie what had happened and asking her if she and her tools felt like spending a little vacation time in the desert.

Natalie had grown up working alongside Claire and Gramps, building homes, outbuildings, and more. Unlike Claire, Natalie had followed in Gramps's shoes, making carpentry look easy. She still worked as a "handy woman extraordinaire" at one of the resorts just outside of Deadwood.

Natalie hip-bumped Claire, grinning at her from under her old straw cowboy hat. "I owed you one, remember?"

"Oh, yeah. That guy was such a dick." A grimace wrinkled her cousin's brow, making Claire do a double take. "Wait, you're not seeing him again, are you?"

"No!" Natalie's laugh sounded harsh, still laced with anger. "Not after what he did with that tongue-pierced skank." She waved off the past, seeming to avoid Claire's gaze while she took her time pulling off her leather gloves finger by finger.

Claire decided not to pick at what appeared to be a semi-fresh scab. "You should have come down and hung out when you broke your leg back in August."

"I was a little preoccupied back home." Natalie stuck her

gloves in her back pockets, her jaw tightening, lips pressed together as if she were fighting to keep from saying something else. Then she blew out a breath and her mouth relaxed into her usual grin. "When is that man of yours going to show up? I have a bone to pick with him about stealing you away from us back home."

"Tomorrow morning. He's working late tonight."

Mac had been putting in a lot of overtime lately on the job site. While Claire understood some of what his role as a geotechnician entailed, she had a feeling he was spending more time at work than necessary to avoid spending evenings at home with Ronnie always in the background.

"*Dios mio!*" Manny grinned up at them. "Double the pleasure, double the fun." Manny blew a kiss their way. "Natalie, *mi amor*, I didn't know you were coming down to play build-a-bathroom with Claire. How long will you be in town?"

"Just long enough to make you fall in love with me, Romeo."

"I never fell out of love, *bonita*. Where are you sleeping?"

"With Claire in the Skunkmobile."

Henry had chased a skunk into Gramps's ancient Winnebago Chieftain while Claire had been inside grabbing a change of clothes. It had taken several days and a lot of vinegar and tomato juice, not to mention several *Silkwood* style showers, for the smell to wear off her and the rotten mutt. Even after a full detailed cleaning, the R.V. still had a hint of *parfum de Pepe le Pew*, especially after baking during the day in the warm sun.

"I have a big bed if you need more room," Manny said with an exaggerated wink, and then he jerked as Gramps poked him in the ribs.

"I don't think it's big enough," Natalie said.

Chester laughed. "That's what his last girlfriend told him."

"I thought Ronnie was staying in the R.V. with you," Gramps said to Claire.

"No, she's bunking in your spare room up at the house." Needing some breathing space from her older sister, Claire had insisted that Ronnie stay there.

"Where's Katie staying then?" Chester asked.

"At Butch's place." Claire's younger sister had been spending most nights at her boyfriend's house since she had rammed his pickup for the second time and knocked his world on its side. She also worked for him at The Shaft.

"So, if Ronnie is in the house with us, and Natalie is in the R.V. with you, where is Mac going to sleep when he gets here?"

Claire crossed her arms over her chest. "Where do you think?"

"You know what that means, don't you, Ford?" Chester asked. "They are going to be having more of that wild and woolly sex in your old bed."

"We are not going to have sex." Not with Natalie on the other side of the paper-thin walls.

"Why not?" Manny asked.

"I refuse to discuss my love life with you three."

"If Mac is having trouble getting his soldier to stand at attention, I have some leftover Viagra he could take," Chester offered.

Claire's neck warmed. "Mac is doing just fine in that department. No Viagra needed thank you very much."

"Oh, *mi amor*, so it is you who's not feeling romantic anymore. What's wrong? Isn't he taking care of your needs first?"

"I can't believe you opened this door," Natalie said, chuckling.

"I tried to bar it shut, but they kicked it in." Claire shook her head. "Mac's and my sex life is fine and dandy, okay everyone?"

"Ewww, gross!" Ruby's daughter, Jess, joined the three clowns below. Her face matched her words while her jaw worked on a piece of gum. "Can we not talk about you and my cousin getting naked for once? I swear; that's all you guys talk about—Claire and sex."

"I try not to talk about sex at all, especially when it concerns me."

"Not you, Claire," Jess squatted and scratched Henry behind the ears. "I mean these old dudes."

"When were you guys discussing my sex life?"

"More importantly," Natalie said. "Why?"

"*We* weren't," Gramps said. "I'd rather spend a week under fire in a foxhole with your mother than think about that topic."

Deborah and Gramps had a love-hate relationship—he loved Claire's mother living thousands of miles away because she hated his new wife.

"I was," Manny confessed. "But only because Chester thought you were being so pissy last night because you hadn't gotten any in a while."

"Which Ronnie confirmed after you left," Chester said in his own defense.

"What?" Claire scratched her head. True or not, why would Ronnie say that?

"I told Chester you weren't pissy," Manny said. "Just missing Mac. When's he rolling in again?"

"Tomorrow," Jess answered for Claire. "After he picks up my stepsister from the airport."

The Earth stopped on its axis.

Gramps's head spun toward the teenager. "What did you say, girl?"

Claire cocked her head to the side. "Your stepsister?" Please, God, let her be talking about some child from her father's extended family and not ...

"I said Mac will be here after he picks up my stepsister—you know, Claire, your mom." Jess blew a bubble and popped it as if she hadn't just announced the angel of death was flying in tomorrow.

Claire stumbled back a step, feeling like she'd caught a

two-by-four smack dab in the gut. She reached in her back pocket for her cigarette lighter but came up empty, then remembered that she'd given up smoking again before coming back to help Gramps.

"She called a little bit ago and asked Mom to pick her up, so Mom called Mac to come to the rescue."

Mac was Ruby's nephew and had been her knight in shining armor before Gramps came into the picture.

Claire groaned for Mac's sake. First a month of Ronnie, now a two-hour drive with her mother—he was going to need a whole lot of coaxing not to drop Deborah off, then race back home and change the locks.

"Well, shit," Natalie murmured. "If I'd known Aunt Deborah was coming, I would have stayed back in South Dakota."

"Why is the Evil Witch of the North flying south?" Chester asked.

"The Witch of the North was a good one, *idiota*." Manny cracked another beer and handed it to Gramps, whose face looked like it had been slathered with beet juice. Claire checked his ears for steam as he chugged the beer.

"She was sexy in that fancy pink dress," Manny added. "How old is Deborah? She always looks good in pink."

Henry barked at the sound of Claire's mom's name—a trick Chester had taught him since the last time Deborah had come down and had nearly screwed up Gramps and Ruby exchanging vows.

"Don't even think about going near my daughter, Carrera." Gramps crushed his empty beer can on the arm of his chair. "Claire, you're gonna need to fix this."

What? "Why me? She's your daughter."

"Because I can't. I'm laid up, remember?"

Funny, his mouth seemed to be running without a hitch. "What am I supposed to do?"

"Keep your mom from pissing off my wife again."

Veronica Morgan had a cash flow problem. Her ex-husband, Lyle, who had been stashing away their money in a high yield savings account for years, had lied about one small detail—there was no account.

Actually, he'd lied about several things, such as the whole business about owning their five thousand square foot home free and clear, which she found out was mortgaged to the hilt. Better yet was the little fib about being a partner in a prestigious accounting firm. Lyle was a partner all right; only his partnership was in multiple illegal drug activities where he acted as the chief money handler and cash launderer.

But his best whopper of all was the day he had said "I do" to her. It turned out he should have said "I already did," since he was still married to some woman in Wyoming, whom he'd left without even saying goodbye. Veronica had found out that doozy thanks to the Feds, who had dragged her in for a fun-filled interrogation right after hauling Lyle, her *not*-husband, off to jail for his handiwork in the drug trade. There was nothing like trying to keep a calm face while being told everything she'd thought was real was pure fiction, including her shitty marriage.

With all of the deception, outright lies, and continual adultery she'd found out about since that fateful day several months ago, the words spewing from the pawn shop owner's lips this afternoon shouldn't have surprised her at all. But they did, and after she'd caught her breath, she leaned closer to the guy's greasy, stubble-covered face, ignoring the ripe odor of onions that clung to him.

"What do you mean none of it's real?" she asked.

"I don't know how to make it any clearer, babe." He dug in his ear with his pinkie and then pulled it out to admire his waxy find. "This jewelry is all fake."

Ronnie tried to inhale and exhale, but her lungs felt like they were being squeezed to death by a huge anaconda.

The pawn guy pushed her collection of rings, necklaces, and bracelets back toward her. "I even had my pop double-check it—the old man's been pawning gold and gems for half a century. He said it's high-quality fake stuff, if that makes you feel any better, but nothin' more than a bunch of pretty colored stones."

"So, there's nothing here you'd be willing to give me cash for?" she managed to choke out, blinking away the flying black dots that were swarming her vision.

He frowned down at the pile of metal and jewels that she'd figured would carry her through the next few months. Now how was she going to afford that plane ticket to Costa Rica where she'd planned to rebuild her life without having to watch over her shoulder day and night?

"I don't know. We have plenty of costume jewelry already." He plucked her wedding ring set from the pile. "Hmmm. Mindy Lou will probably put out for this. I'll give you fifty for it."

Ronnie had "put out" for that damned ring, too—for five long fucking years she'd put out.

"Sold." She held out her hand for the cash.

The cash register dinged when he opened the drawer, showing slots full of twenties and tens. For a split second, she considered pretending she had a gun and robbing the place, driving Ruby's pickup straight to the Tucson airport, and catching the first flight out of the country, but the vapors of pride she had left kept her in check.

She stuffed the bills into her wallet and scraped the jewelry into her purse.

"If you have any guns to pawn, we're always on the lookout for more." He pointed at the wall of guns behind him. "Trust me, you can't have enough firearms in this part of the state."

Great. There was nothing like waiting for the hit man Lyle had warned her about in a land filled with gun-toting paranoids.

She left the grease ball at the counter polishing her wedding ring set. She hoped Mindy Lou gave him the Clap.

Opening Ruby's pickup door, Ronnie threw her purse inside. It bounced off the bench seat and landed upside down on the dirty floor mat, spilling her worthless jewelry.

"Damn it!" She climbed in and glared down at her purse. "Screw you," she muttered to the worthless jewelry, jamming the key in the ignition. The pickup squealed out onto Yuccaville's Main Street while Johnny Cash sang on the AM radio about everywhere he'd been.

As the city limits sign shrank in her rearview mirror, Ronnie considered moving to Winnemucca or maybe Oskaloosa, wherever that was. Somewhere she could fade into the background and live off the land. It would need to be warm enough to grow a garden but not too warm. She couldn't afford air conditioning.

The sound of a siren interrupted her Farmer Ronnie plans. A glance in the rearview mirror made her heart upend and sink to her toes.

"Oh, come on!" she yelled at the big, black and white pickup riding on her ass. Lights flashed behind its angry-looking grill guard.

Easing onto the sandy shoulder, she shifted into park and shut off the Ford. The engine ticked as she watched the officer taking his sweet-ass time shoving open his door and stepping to the ground. She cranked down the window and waited for the question and answer game to begin.

The crunch of his boots on the asphalt announced his arrival. His khaki shirt filled the window, a brass Cholla County Sheriff star front and center in her face. Criminy, they grew them tall out here in the sticks. Hadn't they heard of water rationing in the desert?

He leaned down and peered at her from under his tan cowboy hat. She stared back at her reflection in his aviator sunglasses, picking up the scent of cloves and cinnamon mixed with something else coming from him. What was that? Some bay rum concoction?

After a good ten seconds of seeing who could stare the longest, she cleared her throat. "Aren't you going to ask me the usual question, officer?"

"What's the usual question?" His voice was all gravel and bass.

"Do I know how fast I was going?"

"Do you?"

She tried to make light of this whole mess. "Not fast enough apparently, because you caught me."

Her smile hit the brick wall that was his face.

Thanks to the angle of the sun, Ronnie could see his narrowed eyes through his dark lenses. She bristled at his glare. After being reminded by the pawn shop guy that she'd been totally duped for half a decade, she didn't need Officer Hardass staring down his nose at her. She gripped the steering wheel to keep from reaching out and flicking him in the chin.

"License and registration, please, ma'am." He looked over his shoulder at a passing Mustang, waving at the driver.

Recent memories filled with guys in suits and uniforms asking painfully embarrassing and personal questions flooded her thoughts, shoving everything else aside. Something cracked and splintered in the wake of the wave.

She was done dancing to the tune of those enforcing the law. "No."

His cop sunglasses whipped back to her. "Come again?"

Oh, yeah, where were her manners? "No, thank you."

He lowered his sunglasses, drilling her with whiskey-colored eyes. "Have you been drinking?"

"Nope." But she could sure use something to take the edges off right about now—all of them. "Has anyone ever told you that your eyes are the color of a shot glass of Southern Comfort?"

He narrowed said peepers, leaning in through her window sniffing. "Have you been smoking pot?"

"Not since college."

His gaze bounced around the cab, landing on her purse on the passenger side floor. "Where did you get all of that jewelry?"

"It's mine. Don't be fooled; none of it is worth diddly, unless you need to get laid." She reached down and grabbed a handful of necklaces, bracelets, and earrings, holding them out toward him. "Give me thirty bucks and this is all yours."

His face seemed to harden.

"The chandelier earrings are especially nice."

His eyes nailed her over the top of his glasses. "Are you trying to bribe an officer of the law?"

"No, I'm trying to sell you cheap-assed jewelry to give to some chick named Mindy Lou. I hear she puts out for the fake stuff."

A muscle in his jaw ticced. "Are you referring to Mindy Lou Harrison?"

"Yep, that's her." How many Mindy Lou's could there be in this corner of the state? "She's quite a catch from the sounds of it. But I'd wear a condom if I were you. How about it?" She shoved the handful of necklaces under his nose. "I'll drop the price to twenty-five."

"Mindy Lou is my niece."

Ronnie noticed the tag on his right pocket bearing the same last name. "Oh. Oops." She grimaced. "You may want to go arrest the guy behind the counter at the pawn shop then, because he's going to try to coerce your niece into some lewd activities tonight, using my wedding set as bait."

The officer's lips tightened into a thin pink line. "Don't move, ma'am. I'll be right back."

Watching him return to his cruiser, she figured any chance of getting out of a speeding ticket was now in the one-in-a-million range.

She looked down at the jewelry in her hand, shrugged, and tossed the bunch on the seat next to her. Scooping up her purse, she dug inside for her lip gloss, and then jerked the rearview mirror in her direction. A layer of shine on her lips made her feel more human. A fluff of her curls helped bolster her spirits even more. She was getting used to these shorter curls, especially since they were her natural brown instead of blonde.

Although she probably could have gotten more money out of that grease ball back at the pawn shop if she'd been blonde. Officer Hardass might have let her off at the toss of her bleached waves, too.

Her vision blurred, her thoughts straying from Officer Hardass. Now it all made sense, Lyle insisting she go blonde. The fake hair was a perfect match for the fake jewelry and fake marriage. Maybe she should write the asshole a letter, listing all of the fake orgasms she'd had during their five non-bliss-filled years.

A shadow blocked the sunlight shining through her window. "According to the South Dakota Division of Motor Vehicles, your eyes are supposed to be brown, not blue, Mrs. Jefferson."

His use of her married name yanked her back to the present. She trained her blue-brown gaze on him. Somebody had been playing Sherlock while she'd been busy daydreaming about her nightmare past. Damned government records! Her new makeover could shield her only so much. She hoped it gave her enough time to escape a hit man's detection.

"Wow, you're good, Officer Hardass."

His head cocked to the side. "What did you just call me, ma'am?"

"Officer Harris ... son." She felt a slow burn at the base of her throat and prayed it wouldn't climb any higher.

"That's what I thought I heard." His lips twitched. "Ruby claims you're her relative." He handed her a piece of paper. "You should thank her."

Ruby? Gramps's Ruby?

"Why?" She took the paper from him.

"Because she saved you a trip to jail this afternoon for attempting to bribe the Sheriff of Cholla County."

The Sheriff? As in the one lawman in charge of the whole damned county? Well, wasn't it just her lucky day?

"I told you it wasn't a bribe, Sheriff." She frowned at the words on the paper, then looked up into his sunglasses. "What's this?"

"That there, ma'am, is a speeding ticket from the state of Arizona." He tipped the brim of his cowboy hat at her. "You have a nice day and drive safely."

Chapter Three

Saturday, September 29th

By the time Mac Garner rolled into the Dancing Winnebagos R.V. Park late Saturday afternoon, his forearms were on fire from trying to bend the steering wheel with his bare hands for the last hundred miles. It was that or cram one of his work boots in Deborah Morgan's big, fat mouth. An air horn blasted through a megaphone would be less grinding on his nerves than Claire's mother's relentless bitching.

He stopped in front of his Aunt Ruby's General Store and killed the engine. "We're here," he said, staring straight ahead while willing her to get the hell out of his pickup.

Deborah peered out the window at the old two-story house that doubled as a store, her upper lip curling with a sneer. "Your aunt really needs to add a fresh coat of paint if she wants to impress customers. Something to make the place look less like a rundown sha—"

Mac slammed the pickup door on her words. His girlfriend's mother or not, he'd had his fill of Deborah's complaints about her father, her two younger daughters, and the state of Arizona in general. He suspected the only reason she'd bitten her forked tongue about Ruby most of the way to Jackrabbit Junction was because she'd known he'd have stopped and kicked her out of the pickup.

She was wrong, though—he wouldn't have stopped, just opened the door and shoved her out. A firm foot to her ass would have done the trick, a washboard-rutted road somewhere down near Cochise Stronghold the perfect spot.

The General Store's screen door swung open as he climbed the porch steps. His aunt walked out, wearing a faded denim shirt with a dishtowel draped over her shoulder.

"Hi, honey," Ruby greeted him in her soft Oklahoma drawl and dropped a peck on his cheek. "I'd ask how you are, but that scary look in your eyes says plenty."

"Only for you," he said under his breath, pointing his thumb at where Deborah was climbing down from his pickup. "Not for anyone else in this world would I spend two hours in an enclosed space with that ... that ..."

"Watch what you say about my new stepdaughter," Ruby whispered while barely moving her lips. "She may be your mother-in-law someday."

The family dynamics resulting from his aunt marrying Claire's grandpa often left him shaking his head. Deborah was now his step-cousin, making Claire not only his girlfriend but his first cousin once removed, and all of that was before he'd even figured out how to get Claire over her commitment phobia and agree to be his fiancée. Some days he felt like he'd walked onto the set of a western rendition of Li'l Abner. Right now his brain was craving some of Mammy Yokum's Yokumberry Tonic.

"I need a beer." He headed inside the store, noticing the strong odor of nail polish in the cool air.

Speaking of Claire, where was she? It'd been too long since he'd had her all to himself without one family member or another interrupting, interfering, and screwing up any chance of getting her alone and naked. With her older sister living under his roof for the last month, sleeping on the other side of the wall from his and Claire's headboard, most of his nights had ended up with the only action under the covers involving Claire's knee ramming into his thigh. He had half a mind to kidnap Claire and drag her to one of the rundown motels up the road in Yuccaville for some R-rated fun.

"Hi, Mac." His cousin Jess sat on the stool behind the wooden counter, painting her toenails pink.

"Hey, kid." He headed over to the wall of coolers and grabbed two cans of beer. Cracking one open, he chugged it down barely tasting the hops. He carried the empty soldier and the second unopened can over to the counter, tossing a few bills down. "Where's Claire?"

"Out back working on the new bathrooms. The roof is almost done."

He should go help her finish it. "How's Harley doing?"

"Okay but he's pretty growly. I overheard him bitching at Mom last night to stop treating him like a baby when she asked if he was ready for his bath."

According to Claire, her grandfather was more than growly. She'd used words on the phone this week like "pissy," "impossible to live with," and "ornery as hell." Unfortunately, with Deborah on the premises, Mac had a feeling that Harley's attitude would only get worse. Teddy Bear Chollas would be less prickly.

He opened the other can of beer. "Jess, I don't think your mom would like you using the word *bitching*."

"I'm sixteen now. That's old enough to cuss."

"I know you're old enough." He'd been swearing plenty by her age. "I'm just saying you probably shouldn't practice it when your mom is within a one-mile radius."

The door banged open. "Jessica!" Ruby's face looked two shades angrier than when Mac had left her a moment ago. "Get out here and help me with Deborah's luggage."

"Why me? My toenails are wet. Can't Mac do it?"

"I don't give a darn tootin' about your nails. Get your hiney out here right now." Ruby's green gaze flashed in Mac's direction. "Mac, will you go find Harley and tell him that his daughter is here and fixin' to have a fit if he doesn't come to the house right now to greet her after she flew all of the way from South Dakota."

Put more space between him and Deborah? No problem. With a nod, Mac grabbed his beer off the counter and pushed through the cigar smoke-filled green velvet curtain that divided the General Store from his aunt's rec room.

He looked around the room and noticed Ruby had bought a new loveseat to replace the green sofa that had been left over from the disco decade. The orange shag carpet was still there, though, along with the faded picture of a ten-point buck that hung on the opposite wall. The long walnut bar shined with a layer of polish he hadn't seen coating it in the five-plus years Ruby had lived in the house. She must have been busy preparing for Deborah's white-glove inspection. Mac would bet his next paycheck that short of knocking down the walls and rebuilding the whole two-story house, no amount of sprucing would be good enough for Claire's mom.

Mac headed out the back door to find Claire and her grandfather. His upper lip was sweating by the time he reached the back of the R.V. park where he found Harley and his two cronies sitting in lawn chairs drinking cheap beer. Henry, Claire's least favorite beagle on earth, lay on his side next to his owner's one dusty sneaker.

Where was Claire? There was no sign of life on the roof of the stud-framed building in front of the three troublemakers.

"What in the hell are you drinking, boy?" Chester said as a greeting. "That stuff won't even put hair on your chest."

"Yours seems to be adding a winter coat's worth to your back," Mac said, grinning at the bristly vet.

Manny chuckled and petted Chester's hairy shoulder. "The women line up to brush his shiny fur these days."

"At least they are lining up for me, Carrera. That caterpillar you wear on your upper lip keeps scaring them away."

"How's the leg?" Mac asked Claire's grandfather.

Harley pierced him with a glare straight out of the old West. "Well, if it isn't the Lone Ranger, here to take care of all our problems."

What the hell? Harley must have his boxers on crooked. Mac ignored the crabby jab and delivered his aunt's message. "Ruby sent me to tell you that your daughter is here."

"Such a good boy," Harley said, "always doing what your aunt asks you, aren't you?"

Mac took a step back. "Are you drunk?"

Harley threw his empty beer can on the ground. "I wish. It would sure make my situation more palatable this afternoon."

His situation? Did he mean his obnoxious daughter showing up for a few weeks or something else? Something to do with Claire or Ronnie or both?

He shot Mac a scowl. "I'm sure everyone will be all giddy now that you're here, though."

Mac had no idea what he'd done to get on Harley's pissy side today, but after the two hours of hell on wheels thanks to the grouch's daughter, he was in no mood to kiss anyone's owies and make things all better.

"When you're done sulking in your beer," he told Harley, "you need to haul your butt to the store and deal with your daughter."

"You're here to save the day, you go deal with her."

"I already did, all of the way from Tucson. Now it's your turn." Mac gulped the last of his beer and tossed the can in the paper bag at Manny's feet. "And get off my ass while you're at it. I'm not here to save anything. I just want to see your granddaughter."

"Naked," Manny added to the end of Mac's sentence and then nudged Chester, who snickered along with him.

Naked would be great, but Mac wasn't about to say that aloud and risk getting the jokes rolling about his and Claire's sex life. He'd had enough ribbing over the last few months to last the rest of his days.

The gravel crunched behind him. He turned, hoping to see Claire, and ended up frowning at her older sister instead. When had she gotten her hair cut? With it brown now instead of blonde, he could see her resemblance to Claire even more. Only Claire was curvier, softer on the edges, whereas Ronnie seemed skinnier, her collarbone showing more than before.

"Hey, Mac." Ronnie shot a worried-looking smile at him,

and then focused on her grandfather. "Gramps, Mom is looking for you."

Harley grunted and swore under his breath. Mac couldn't agree more.

"Where is Claire?" she asked Mac.

"That's the question of the hour," Manny said.

"She and Natalie went to Yuccaville to get another drill," Gramps answered. "Natalie's died this morning."

"It took both of them to go get another drill?" Ronnie's voice held a dollop of disbelief. "I don't think so. Claire's just avoiding Mom."

Mac couldn't blame Claire, but damn it, he had been hoping she'd be here and feel like rewarding him for his pain and suffering. Alone. Some place where these cigar-smoking nosy Nellies and any other family members wouldn't hear them.

Harley struggled to grab his crutches, batting away Ronnie's attempt to help him. "I don't know why your mom's so bent on seeing me."

"She expects you to help her get settled in."

"What's to settle? She's sleeping with you."

"No, she's not." Ronnie crossed her arms.

"Where is she going to sleep then?" Harley scooted to the edge of his seat. "In a tent? I don't think so."

"She can sleep in my rig," Manny offered.

"You keep your mind and paws off my daughter, Carrera. The signatures are still wet on her divorce papers. She doesn't need you messing with her head."

"I'd offer my couch," Chester said, "but she'll scare off those two matching archaeologist babes. They're coming over later to take a look at an 'old bone' in my bedroom." His bushy eyebrows wiggled at the same time his fingers made invisible quote marks in the air.

Mac had to smile at Chester's gumption. Storm or not, the old vet was always determined to find a port.

"Mom is sleeping in the spare room," Ronnie said. "I'll

bunk in the R.V. with Claire."

Harley grimaced. "I don't think Claire is going to be happy about that."

"Claire's not the only one," Mac said.

Ronnie's chin lifted. "I'm *not* sleeping in the spare room with that woman."

Her stubborn reaction seemed over the top. What was her beef with her mom? Ronnie had been acting more and more peculiar over the last couple of weeks. When Mac had asked Claire about it, she'd shrugged as if it were no big deal, muttering something about Ronnie having a history of temporary insanity. That was all the more reason to get her out from under Mac's roof sooner rather than later.

"Claire's happiness is not my concern at the moment. I'm sleeping in the Skunkmobile." Ronnie pointed at Mac. "And you can live a few more days without having sex with my sister."

"A lack of blood flow can make a man's willy fall right off," Chester said. "I'm sure I read that somewhere."

Manny nodded in agreement.

"Where's Mac going to sleep then?" Gramps asked, shooting Mac another glare. "The rec room?"

Forget it. Between Deborah's festering presence and Harley's grumpy bear song and dance, Mac would rather sleep out under the stars with the snakes and porcupines.

"He can sleep with Chester or Manny." Ronnie said as if she'd just solved the problem, end of story.

No, absolutely not. Cuddling up with a *javelina* sounded more appealing.

"I don't think my bed's big enough for both of us." Manny grinned at Mac. "Unless you like spooning."

Mac shuddered. There wasn't enough whiskey at The Shaft to make him even consider spooning with Manny. "No thanks, I prefer the fork."

"I'll sleep on the table bed in Harley's R.V."

"I don't like you sharing an R.V. with three of my

granddaughters. It's bad enough you already snookered one of them without putting a ring on her finger."

Hold up just one damned second. First of all, he'd been sharing his house with two of them for over a month. Second, it was Claire who had "schnookered" him, not the other way around. Third, she was the one who still stuttered every time any talk of *love* came up. Mac didn't even dare breathe the word *marriage*.

Chester slapped his hand on the aluminum arm of his lawn chair. "That settles it then, Mac. You and I will have a stag weekend in my pimp mobile."

"I don't—" Mac started.

"Sounds like a plan to me." Harley crutched over to the golf cart he'd bought a month ago to get around the R.V. park.

That settled nothing. Mac had taken care of his aunt long before any of these people had shown up here; didn't seniority count for anything? He was tempted to crawl into his pickup and head back to Tucson. He shot Ronnie a glare of frustration.

Sorry, Ronnie mouthed to him before crawling behind the wheel and driving Harley toward the store.

Chester joined Mac, holding out a beer. "I hope you don't mind a little cigar smoke in the morning."

Manny joined them, clapping Mac on the shoulder. "Some time away from Claire will do you good, *hombre*. I hear you two are having some trouble in the bedroom. Good ol' Chester and Manny have just the fix for you."

The women's bathroom in The Shaft smelled like sex and men's cologne, all musty with a hint of something spicy. Claire checked under the stall doors to make sure she hadn't caught anyone in the act of a little commode nookie. Nope, all clear. Maybe Butch had decided to try a new air freshener.

She stepped into the third stall. Locking the door behind

her, she lowered her pants and cursed. Aunt Flo hadn't arrived yet for her monthly visit, and Claire was now two days late.

Two days was nothing, she told herself. The stress alone of dealing with Gramps barking at her, as well as her mom coming to town, was probably enough to interrupt her cycle for months, even years. Add that to her middle of the night worries about the possible thieves wandering around the R.V. park pretending to be part of the archeological crew. With that gold pocket watch still tucked away in the wall safe in Ruby's office, and lord knew what other pricey antiques stashed around the house that Joe had skimmed during his black-market romps, Ruby and Gramps were sitting ducks for the kind of strangers who shot first and interrogated later.

Take those two cowboys sitting at the corner table across from the bar. They'd been watching Ronnie a little too intently for the last hour. Now if Natalie had been the focus of their attention, Claire wouldn't have thought twice about it. Nat inspired love-sick looks with her long legs and full lips, especially from drunk cowboys. But Nat had gone back to the R.V. park over an hour ago, before the two had shown up.

Zipping her pants, she ignored the twinge of pain in her lower back that had come from spending too much time bent over on a roof. Yeah, it had to be the stress, mental and physical. With her luck, her period would probably show up about the time she finally got a moment alone with Mac.

She flushed the toilet and headed to the sink, looking past her reflection at the tampon machine on the wall. It mocked her with its two twist-knob eyeballs and slot mouth. The door next to it swung open.

Her younger sister, Kate, burst in, squawking in surprise at the sight of Claire. "What are you doing in here?"

With her wavy blonde hair escaping her pony tail, her face drawn and pale, and her blue eyes underlined with dark half-circles, Kate looked about a decade older than her almost thirty-two years tonight.

"Call me kooky, but I came in here to pee." Claire squirted

soap on her palm. "What else would I be doing in here, nut-job?"

"Why does it smell like sex? Is Mac in here?" Kate walked over to the stalls and slammed one door open after another. "I told you The Shaft is off limits from now on, especially the parking lot. I swear you two are like rabbits sometimes."

Bristling, Claire dried her hands on a paper towel while glaring at her sister's profile. Kate had been working at The Shaft for a little over a month as a bar waitress. So what if she was sleeping with Butch. Shacking up with the guy didn't give her the right to act like she owned the place.

"No, Mac is not in here. And for the record, we were only kissing in his pickup that night, not doing the wild thing." It wasn't her fault she couldn't get a whiff of privacy with Mac these days thanks to Ronnie and everyone else south of the Canadian border. A girl had needs, and cigarettes and MoonPies didn't always fulfill them all.

"That's not what Manny and Chester told me."

Claire didn't justify that with a response. "What's wrong with you tonight, Kate? You've been stomping around with this sourpuss pinch on your face and acting like somebody broke your favorite flying broomstick. Did you forget to add some eye of newt into your boiling cauldron this morning?"

Kate stepped into a stall. The lock rattled closed. "I'm tired."

"Tell Butch to give you a night off."

"I need the money."

"You're sleeping with your boss in his big fancy house."

"Not anymore."

Claire cocked her head at the closed stall door. "What does that mean?"

"I'm coming back to the R.V. park."

"Why would you want to do that?"

"Butch and I had a fight this morning."

"So make up tonight and stay where you are. There's no room for you now that Mom's here."

"I'll stay in the Skunkmobile with you and Natalie."

"Nope. The inn's full. Ronnie's staying there, too."

The toilet flushed. Kate joined her in front of the mirror, frowning at her reflection before her gaze moved to Claire. "Why isn't she sleeping with Mom?"

"She's mad at Mommy Dearest."

"Oh, for Christ's sake, you both are being absurd about Mother. She may be a little bitter and hard to stomach, but she's still our mom."

"Fine, then you sleep with *your* mom in the spare room."

Kate broke eye contact, focusing on washing her hands. "I can't." She shut off the water.

"Can't or won't?"

Kate fixed her ponytail. "Maybe I'll crash on Chester's couch."

"Ronnie told me Mac is sleeping there." Much to Claire's frustration. Maybe she could sneak over there in the middle of the night when Chester was buzz-sawing logs in his sleep and snuggle up next to Mac's warm body. "You could share Manny's bed."

"I'd sooner sleep in a tent. Does Ruby have any spare ones?"

"You're being silly. Just tell Butch you're sorry and stay at his place where you belong."

"What do you know about where I belong? You can't even commit to staying with Mac—where you belong."

Claire gaped at her sister. "Don't be turning this around and taking it out on me."

"Fine." Kate nudged Claire out of the way. "But I'm not staying with Butch. We need a break."

Claire grabbed Kate as her sister pulled open the door. "What are you talking about? You two are gaga over each other. I've watched you watch him. You look like Elmer Fudd does when Bugs Bunny slaps on red lipstick and a blonde wig."

"Yeah, well I'm not so sure that feeling is mutual."

"It's only been a month."

"It's been five weeks since we got together." Kate drilled Claire with a frown. "If it's true love, shouldn't that be enough?" When Claire hesitated, Kate pulled free. "What am I thinking asking the biggest commitment phobe east of the Rockies about love?"

"The Rockies are mostly north of us, Kate."

"Whatever. You wouldn't understand. You've been with Mac for six months and still break into hives when someone even mentions wedding rings." She rubbed her hand over her forehead. "I gotta get back to work."

Claire followed Kate out of the bathroom. "I suppose you could sleep in Jess's room with her, but she'll keep you up all night talking about boys and snogging."

"I'll figure something out." Kate grabbed the wall for a moment, holding her stomach. "Oy."

"Are you okay?"

"Yeah." Kate waved her off. "I ate some fried mushrooms earlier that are now rioting in my gut."

"Why don't you take a seat over in my chair and let me play barmaid for a bit."

"You don't have to do that."

Claire took the order pad and pen from Kate's little apron. "Stop acting like Gramps and go sit down."

After nudging Kate toward the table she'd been sharing with Ronnie, Claire made her way closer to the corner table where the two lookie-loo cowpokes still watched Ronnie. She had a nose for strangers in these parts, and with their pristine cowboy hats and shiny boots, they smelled plenty fishy.

She followed their line of sight. Ronnie seemed to be oblivious to their stares, which wasn't surprising. Ever since her sister had come home from her shopping trip in Yuccaville yesterday, she'd had the attention span of a gnat. Something was up with Ronnie, and maybe it had something to do with these two slicksters.

Claire strolled up to their table, blocking their view of her older sister, who'd been joined by Kate. "Do either of you two need something?" she yelled over Waylon Jennings and Johnny Cash singing on the jukebox about the lack of good in an evil-hearted woman.

Two freshly-shaven faces looked up at her, both smiling too wide too fast.

"We're good," said the one wearing the fancy brown Stetson hat.

"Not right now," said the other, pulling his dust-free, black Stetson lower over his light blue eyes.

"Great." She stuffed the order pad in the back pocket of her blue jeans and crossed her arms over her T-shirt. "Then maybe you can tell me why you're so damned interested in my sister?"

Chapter Four

Ronnie swirled her gin and tonic, her stomach roiling. She needed an escape plan. Something logical and rational. Something that didn't involve fire, a puff of smoke, or a panic-filled scramble out of The Shaft. Some way to sneak out of the bar without the two beady-eyed goons in the brand-spanking new cowboy hats noticing she had high-tailed it into the dark desert before they could grab their guns and give chase. Not that she'd seen any guns on them, but they sure looked the type a mob boss would hire, all pale-faced and slick.

She scanned the bar. Plastic plants swayed in the breeze from the overhead fans, a 1970s looking jukebox lit up the semi-darkness, video games sported plastic rifles to practice killing Bambi and his buddies. The musky smell of sweat filled the warm, humid air, mixed with different notes of cheap cologne and bargain-bin perfume. Butch's multiple no-smoking signs posted throughout the bar undoubtedly saved her from a lungful of smoke on top of it. Behind the bar, a cue-ball wearing glasses with lenses thick enough to view the Horseshoe Nebula tugged on the tap.

Butch, the owner of the place—aka her youngest sister's current heartthrob, was out of town at the moment according to Katie, who had just joined her at the table. A bit pasty-looking with pink blotches on her cheeks and watery eyes, Katie looked like she'd been paying homage to the porcelain god recently. She claimed to be feeling fine, but Ronnie saw the tension lining her lips and fanning from the corners of her eyes. Something was up with her little sister, but she would dig into that later. Right now, goons were waiting to pounce.

She took a rough count of the other patrons, coming up with fifteen women and about twice as many men, including the goons. More men were pouring in as she sat nursing her drink, savoring the hint of lemon along with the sharp bite of gin while contemplating her potential escape options. Maybe there was a window in the women's restroom she could squeeze through, or a back door out of the kitchen. Katie would know.

"Katie, if I needed to—"

"What is she doing?" Katie asked, half-standing up from her chair across the table, her forehead all crinkled like when she'd caught Claire giving their dog a reverse Mohawk.

Ronnie followed her sister's line of sight. *Oh, shit!* What was Claire doing over by the two goons? She was going to get herself hurt if not killed. Those two hadn't been admiring Ronnie's fake Tiffany earrings for the past hour. She'd bet her last two hundred-dollar bills they had been sent by whomever Lyle had stolen from before he was busted by the Feds. Sent for what, she didn't know and shuddered at the idea of finding out.

As she watched, Claire snatched the black hat off one, flipped it over, and pointed at something inside of it before throwing it back at him. The hat bounced off his chest and dropped to the floor. His whole face pinched up, like somebody had wound it too tight.

"Oh, he didn't like that one bit." Katie rose fully to her feet. "I'm going over there before she gets herself into another fight."

Before Ronnie could catch her arm, Katie was gone, zig-zagging between tables on her way over to where Claire now stood on her tiptoes, nose-to-nose with the scrunch-faced goon.

Ronnie stood there, frozen in dilemma. Her instincts told her to use this distraction Claire had created to escape, but she hesitated. Claire didn't understand who she was up against here. These men were hired to break bones and crack skulls, not play patty cake with nosy sisters.

Katie made it to Claire's side at the same time the second goon slid between the two contenders, stiff-arming both. Ronnie took a step toward them, her fists clenched so tight her fingernails bit into her palms. Tugging Claire back by the T-shirt, Katie joined the goon who was playing monkey in the middle; her head bowed slightly, her body language all apology as she shoved Claire in Ronnie's direction.

Claire reached around Katie, blasting the dark haired goon with a middle finger salute. "Next time take a picture, asshole!" Ronnie heard her yell over Glen Campbell starting in on the jukebox about being a lineman for the county.

The goon strained in his friend's hold, his face rippling in fury. Ronnie grinned in spite of the whole mess. Claire had a real knack for pissing people off. A true gift. Just ask their mother.

Her escape window was closing. Ronnie made a break for it. She glanced back as she reached the door, making sure nobody had noticed her flight. All focus was still on Claire, who was threatening something with her fist raised while struggling to pull free of Katie's hold on her arm.

Ronnie shoved open the door and raced out into the cool night air, slamming into a wall of shirt. "Oof!"

Hands grabbed her by the shoulders, peeling her from the chest she'd face-planted into. A row of buttons and a metal star came into focus.

"Hello, Mrs. Jefferson." Sheriff Hardass frowned all the way down at her from under the curled brim of his hat.

Ronnie had forgotten how tall he was. His mama had done well corn-feeding him. She should have entered him into the county fair. He'd have been a sure-fire blue ribbon winner.

"I had a feeling I'd find you inside," he added in that deep, deep voice of his.

The Sheriff of Cholla County was having feelings about her? That didn't bode well. Neither did the grip he still had on her shoulders, as if he didn't want to let go in case she decided to make a run for it.

"You did? Why?" Was he in cahoots with the two goons inside? A crooked lawman down in these parts wouldn't make her blink twice. Jackrabbit Junction might be a tiny town, but it wasn't Mayberry. For one thing, there were too many dirty old men in town ... and too many secrets, according to Claire.

Ronnie matched the Sheriff's squint. Was he waiting for his buddies to come out so they could throw her in the back of a van and drag her off to torture her for information on where her piece of shit not-husband had hidden some skimmed money?

He nudged his head in the direction of Ruby's pickup, sitting under an orange-tinted street light next to the road, looking like a tired old dog. "I saw Ruby's Ford."

She stepped back, slipping out of his grip and away from his sweet and spicy scent. "Well, Sheriff, it looks like your feelings were dead on."

"They usually are."

"Great. Bully for you. Now, if you don't mind, I'm just going to be on my way." She continued back stepping toward the safety of the truck.

"Actually, I do mind." His comment stopped her short.

"You do?" She spoke just above a whisper. She couldn't help it, what with her heart clinging to her uvula for dear life.

He crossed his arms over his chest, his legs taking that wide authoritative stance he probably practiced every morning in front of the locker room mirror down at headquarters. "You and I need to have a little talk."

A semi-truck roared past, giving Ronnie a moment to get a hold of her voice and force it to obey.

"About what?" She cleared her throat, buying more time. "If this is regarding what I said about your niece's promiscuity, I apologize. You know, at her age she's probably just exploring her options." Exactly how old was his niece anyway?

His chin jutted. "You're illegally parked next to a fire hydrant."

She stared at him for a couple of seconds, trying to make sense of his words. Then the bubble of fear that had been lodged in her esophagus for the last half-hour popped and a burst of laughter exploded from her chest, echoing across the parking lot.

"You find breaking the law here in Arizona funny, Mrs. Jefferson? Because I don't."

"No, not at all. I was just thinking—" The bar's door creaked open. She glanced back and locked eyes with the dark-hatted goon from inside. His friend followed on his boot heels. Breath held, she watched as they tipped their hats at Sheriff Hardass and moseyed on out into the parking lot.

"You were thinking what, Mrs. Jefferson? Enlighten me." The Sheriff didn't seem to take any extra notice of the two men.

"Umm, I was thinking you were ..." The goons had made it to their car, which was a late model black sedan with tinted windows. Sheesh, couldn't they at least try to be original? Instead of opening the doors and climbing inside, they leaned against the side of the car. The one in the brown hat fished out a pack of cigarettes, the match flaring in the night.

"Thinking I was what?" the Sheriff pressed.

Damn it, those two were going to wait the Sheriff out. Wait until she was all alone and then stash her in their back seat and take her out to their shanty in the boonies and torture her. Or something worse. The dueling banjos from *Deliverance* played a riff in her head.

Sheriff Hardass nudged his hat brim toward her two hit men. "Those boys friends of yours?"

"No." Were they friends of his? It appeared not.

He watched her, his lips flat-lined. "All right, then finish your sentence."

An idea hit her. A way to keep from ending up tied to a chair tonight with a gun in her face. "I was thinking that you need to arrest me, Sheriff."

She needed him. Well, needed his protection anyway, until

she could shake these two goons. Being arrested solved that problem. She'd worry about how to lie her way out of this with her family later.

"For parking illegally?" He shook his head slowly. "I don't know how things work back in South Dakota, but down here in the desert illegal parking scores you a ticket, not jail time."

"Yes, but this is my second offense in as many days." She held out her wrists. "You should slap your cuffs on me and take me in."

Sheriff Hardass pushed his hat back on his head, scratching his forehead. "Take you in? I'm not even heading back to Yuccaville tonight."

"Where are you heading?"

"That's none of your business."

"Well, it's obviously not a date." She tapped her fingernail on his Sheriff's star. "Unless your girlfriend likes it when you role play."

He stared hard at her, his chiseled face completely still in the orange-tinged light, shadowed in the crags and crevices. "Have you been drinking, Mrs. Jefferson?"

"You used that line on me last time. You need to come up with some new ones. And my name is not *Mrs. Jefferson*." The less that name was spoken the better, especially in front of the two goons who stood watching them—one smoking, the other leaning. She grabbed the Sheriff by the arm, tugging him toward his white, four-door patrol truck with the obnoxious grill.

He didn't budge. "What are you doing, Mrs. Jef—"

"Call me Veronica, please." She pulled again, this time getting his feet to crunch across the gravel after hers.

"Fine. What are you doing, *Veronica*?"

That was better. When she reached his truck, she let go of his arm and hauled open the passenger side door. "I'm arresting myself for multiple infractions."

"Did you hit your head recently, woman?"

"No." She climbed up into the truck, settling herself into

the passenger seat. "Let's go, Sheriff. Take me in and throw away the key."

He filled the door frame, his face a mask of shadows. "What's really going on here?"

"It's simple. I broke the law. You're going to punish me for it."

His shoulders stiffened. "Get out of my vehicle, Mrs. Jefferson."

She pushed her feet into the floorboards, digging in the heels of her sandals. "It's *Veronica*, Sheriff, or *Ronnie* if that is easier for you to remember, and you owe it to your community to lock me up tonight. I could be dangerous."

"Dangerous?" He guffawed. "More like off your meds."

"Exactly. A night in jail would probably do me good." And keep her safe. "You should teach me a lesson while we're at it."

"What in the he—heck is wrong with you?" He reached for her arm but she pulled away before he caught her. "Lady, get out of my pickup."

"No."

"I'm not joking." He reached again.

She dodged. "Neither am I. Arrest me, damn it. It's your job."

"I'm not going to arrest you for illegal parking."

Shit. Why was he making this so hard? Maybe she should just tell him about the two goons. No, he'd think she was even more nuts, paranoid even.

Another brilliant idea hit her. "Fine, if you aren't going to haul me in for my illegal parking, you need to take me home."

"Take you home?"

"Yes. I've been drinking." When he continued to stare in at her without moving, she added, "A lot. Way too much."

"You're not slurring your words."

She thought fast. "I studied linguistics in college." Okay, maybe that was too fast.

"Studied linguistics, huh? That's a new one." He fumbled

with a snap on his belt and then shined a flashlight in her face, making her wince and shield her eyes. "You don't look drunk."

"I've built up a tolerance for alcohol and hold my liquor well, but I'm sure I'm over the legal limit."

He lowered the light, leaning into the cab sniffing. "You don't smell like you're drunk."

When he started to pull away, she grabbed him by the shirt front and yanked him back. "I do, too." She opened her mouth wide and breathed all over his face. "See?"

He recoiled, overacting in her opinion.

"Gin and tonic," she told him. "Now is it or is it not your duty as an officer of the law to transport someone who has had too much liquor and has no way of getting home safely?"

"I wouldn't say it's my 'duty.'"

"Quit splitting hairs. It's a service you are supposed to offer."

"You've been watching too much television. I'm not a taxi driver."

"Of course not. You're an elected civil servant who is paid by taxpayer money. Therefore, I believe that makes me your boss, and as your boss, I'm asking you nicely to drive me home."

He stared at her for a handful of heartbeats. Ronnie could have sworn she heard his back molars grinding away.

"You came here alone?" he asked.

"Not entirely, but she's busy right now."

Sheriff Hardass looked up at the sky and cursed under his breath; then he took on that authoritative stance again, hands holding onto his belt. "Veronica Jefferson, would you please remove your person from my vehicle before I …" he hesitated.

"What are you going to do? Call for backup? Arrest me?"

He closed his mouth, opened it, and then closed it again. It was a great fish out of water imitation. She doubted he practiced that in front of the locker room mirror.

Ronnie checked over the Sheriff's shoulder. The two men had climbed into their car, but remained there in the semi-darkness. She could see the dark outlines of their hats through the windshield.

They sure were persistent assholes. Cripes. She needed the safe passage that Sheriff Hardass could offer, and he was playing hardball. Fine, after the hell she'd been through in the last few months, she could play hardball with the best of them, especially a small-time Sheriff in a dust-bunny county.

She started unbuttoning her blouse.

The Sheriff found his tongue when she made it to the fourth button. "What in the hell are you doing now, woman?"

The fifth button slipped out, then the sixth. Two to go.

She glared up at the big doofus. "If you're not going to arrest me for parking illegally or escort me home after I've had too much to drink, you leave me no choice."

Shucking off her shirt, she threw it at him. It hit him in the face then drifted to the ground.

She reached for her bra's front clasp. "I'm going to get arrested for indecent exposure."

Mac slammed on the brakes, skidding to a stop in The Shaft's gravel parking lot.

What in the hell?

On the other side of the lot, a big white pickup with SHERIFF decaled in black on the side idled under a streetlight, waiting in the orange glow as a semi-truck roared past. Between the streetlight and the glare of his headlights, he could swear it was Claire's sister in the passenger seat.

The pickup rolled out the other side of the lot onto State Route 191. Mac leaned forward, peering through his front window. What would Ronnie be doing in a Sheriff's truck? It'd make more sense if she were in the back seat behind the divider after the cagey way she had been acting lately.

The Sheriff's truck made a right at the junction and sped off down the road toward his aunt's R.V. park. After watching the taillights fade in the darkness, Mac eased into a spot that a black sedan with tinted windows had just left and killed the engine. If that really was Ronnie in the cab, why was the Sheriff or one of his deputies taking her home? Did something happen in The Shaft requiring the law to show up? Something involving a certain brunette he couldn't resist with a cute but prying nose, who had a knack for slugging first and sobering up later?

He climbed out into the cool night air and slammed his door closed, his footfalls loud in the soft copper light surrounding him. Maybe he was seeing things. Maybe Sheriff Harrison had stopped by to talk to Butch and that was all. The two were long-time fishing buddies if Mac remembered right. The woman could have been the Sheriff's sister or a date. Ronnie was probably sitting inside nursing her usual gin and tonic while plotting the next thing she could do to throw a wrench in his sex life.

He glanced around the nearly full parking lot and growled under his breath when his gaze found his aunt's pickup. *Damn it, Claire.* She knew better than to park in front of Jackrabbit Junction's only fire hydrant. He'd have to get the keys and move the truck. It was a wonder Sheriff Harrison hadn't left a ticket under the windshield wiper or had the pickup towed.

Natalie's truck was nowhere to be seen. Maybe she'd left early and slipped by Ruby's General Store. Mac had been stuck inside playing a game of Euchre in the rec room with Manny, Chester, and Ruby while Deborah had been chewing on Harley in the kitchen. Her father's refusal to agree to spend a month with her in Phoenix going through physical therapy with more qualified doctors than "Yuccaville's quacks" had her in a rant-filled tizzy.

A steady thumping bass leaked out of The Shaft's front door. He yanked it open and stood back as a couple of women stumbled out giggling. They smelled like they had been swimming in a vat of perfume and beer.

Mac stepped inside the bar and scanned the room until he locked onto Kate. He dodged an older woman with a mass of platinum blonde hair hay-stacked on her head and carrying two pitchers full of beer and foam, and threaded his way through clusters of bodies.

"What happened to your lip?" he asked when he got a close look at Kate. Her lower lip was swollen on one side, a slice of dried blood splitting the center of it.

Kate leaned back, crossing her arms over her chest. "Somebody clipped me." She glared across the table at her sister, who was just lowering into a chair.

Mac pulled out the chair next to Claire, noticing her right hand had a white napkin wrapped around her knuckles. He put one and one together. "Christ, Slugger. You hit your sister?"

"Not on purpose." She pointed a finger at her sister. "Besides it's Kate's fault."

"How is getting punched by you my fault?"

"You shouldn't have gotten in the way."

"You shouldn't have swung at the guy."

"What guy?" Mac asked, sitting. His gaze lowered to her T-shirt. The faded image of a she-devil with *La Diabla* written under her forked tail was pulled tight across Claire's chest, the fabric strained just enough.

Claire leaned toward him. He smelled the watermelon shampoo she used, flashing back to the last time he'd had her against the wall in the shower, and gulped. "I think they're after that gold pocket watch Joe has stuffed in his wall safe down in your aunt's basement," she said in his ear.

"They?" He looked across at Kate. "There was more than one of them?"

"Katie-girl," a woman spoke from behind Mac, "here's some ice for that lip."

Mac looked over his shoulder. The waitress he'd seen earlier carrying the pitchers of beer handed Kate a bumpy bundle wrapped in a towel. The woman's bright pink lips matched the bright pink checkered shirt tied at her waist, just above the jeans she must have painted on. With the mole above the left side of her upper lip and the extra-long eyelashes she was sporting, she reminded him of a blonde version of Ginger from *Gilligan's Island*. Only her voice had a soft drawl to it, rather than a vixen's purr. Subtract twenty-five years from her face and the Professor and Gilligan would definitely have been putty in her hands.

"You sure you don't want something for your knuckles?" Ginger the blonde waitress asked Claire.

"Nah. I didn't hit her that hard, just scraped over her teeth."

Mac removed the napkin from Claire's hand and looked at the two cuts on her knuckles, whistling under his breath. "You should get some peroxide on that. I have some in my truck."

"Don't we have some in the first aid box Butch keeps on the wall in the kitchen?" Ginger asked Kate.

"I've never looked."

"I'll go see." The waitress picked up a glass from the table that was half-full of clear liquid and a lemon wedge stabbed by a straw and left.

Mac's focus returned to Claire's knuckles. "That was a good graze."

"I think Kate's part shark. Her mouth is full of razors."

Lifting her hand, he brushed his lips over the back of it, careful to skirt her injury. Claire gave him a smile that warmed his cockles and everything below them. She cupped his jaw, leaning toward him, angling for a kiss.

"Oh, my God!" Kate snarled, grabbing Mac's shoulder and jerking him away from Claire. "Knock off that googly-eyed shit, both of you. She punched *me* in the mouth, her baby sister, and you're kissing her owie better? This is all wrong. She's a freaking bully. She was a bully back when she gave me rose-gardens on my arm every other day, and she's a bully now." She hit Claire with a pointed glare. "Wait until Mom sees what you did to me, you big brat."

"You're such a puss." Claire slid over into the chair next to Kate and grabbed her head, forming her lips into an overexaggerated pucker. "Come here, my poor little baby sister, and let me kiss it all better for you."

Kate smacked at her arms and punched her in the shoulder. When Claire refused to be pushed aside, Kate broke into a big grin, and then winced and dabbed at her split lip. "Ow! I can't even smile without it hurting."

After dropping a loud kiss on Kate's forehead, Claire took the bottle of peroxide Ginger the waitress had returned with, along with a handful of cotton balls.

"Where did Ronnie go, anyway?" she asked, unscrewing the cap of the peroxide bottle.

"She left," Kate said. "I saw her racing out the door right before you clobbered me."

Claire's lips twisted. "Typical of Ronnie to run, skirting conflict at every turn. She's never stood up to anyone."

"Especially Mom," Kate smirked at Claire. "And look where that got her—newly divorced."

Mac took the peroxide from Claire, picked up a cotton ball and soaked it. He tugged Claire back to the chair next to him and went to work cleaning her cuts. "I think I saw Ronnie heading down the road in the Sheriff's pickup."

"What?" Kate and Claire both said in unison.

"I'm not one hundred percent certain, but it sure looked like her."

"Is Ruby's Ford still out there?" Claire asked.

Mac nodded. "You parked next to the fire hydrant again."

"Not me. Natalie dropped me off and went back to get some sleep—something is up with her lately, I swear. She'd normally always choose men and beer over sleep." She winced when he dripped peroxide into the deeper scrape on her middle knuckle. "Anyway, Ronnie must have illegally parked and gotten busted by the Sheriff."

"Sheriff Harrison can be a stickler for the law," Kate said, "but he wouldn't have taken Ronnie in for that, would he?"

"They were headed away from Yuccaville, toward the R.V. park."

The waitress stopped by again, her colored-on eyebrows raised. "Can I get you two anything else?" she asked the brawlers.

Kate pushed out the fourth chair at the table with her foot. "Have a seat, Arlene. It's my turn to do a couple of rounds while you take a break." When Arlene hesitated, Kate grabbed her forearm and tugged her down. "I insist."

"Well, my dogs could use a little rest." She dropped into the chair on Mac's left.

"Have you met Mac before?" Kate asked. Arlene shook her head. "Mac is Claire's ... boyfriend. They live together in Tucson. Mac, this is Arlene. Butch hired her about two weeks ago."

"Three weeks," Arlene corrected.

Mac preferred *Ginger*; it fit the older blonde better and was much more entertaining.

"Really?" Kate frowned. "Damn, how time flies when you're pouring beer night after night with no future goals in sight."

Mac would have had to have been deaf not to pick up on the bitterness in Kate's comment, but after living with two Morgans for the last couple of months and dealing with their problems, he wasn't in the mood to take on a third. He was a geotechnician not a masochist.

"I've been meaning to ask where you're from, Arlene?" Claire asked.

"Southern Kentucky, originally. But most recently from Florida where I spent the last ten years or so takin' care of my mama."

"What brought you to Jackrabbit Junction?" Mac asked, spreading salve on a bandage. Why had she left the Atlantic Ocean for a dusty old stage stop in the middle of Arizona mining country?

"I had family here years ago. They lived up Yuccaville way. When my mama passed a few months back, God rest her soul, I was finally free to go wherever I pleased."

Mac covered Claire's scrapes with the bandage. "And Yuccaville was your destination of choice?" The Florida sunshine must have ripened her brain too much.

"I had so many good memories of the town and folks in it that I decided to come back and hang around for a time."

Good memories of Yuccaville? Mac sat back, his brows raised. Maybe she had Yuccaville, Arizona confused with another Yuccaville. One that wasn't filled with dust devils, rusty mining equipment, and rows of decrepit company-owned shacks.

Claire made a fist, testing his first aid skills. "And you got a job here at The Shaft of all places."

"Hey," Kate slapped Claire's shoulder. "Butch runs a respectable business. Don't knock this place."

"You were the one knocking it a moment ago."

"I'm allowed to. I work here."

"Oh, is that what you call sleeping with the owner for money?" Claire's grin took the sting out of her words.

"No, I call sex with Butch a fringe benefit." Kate's smile was ghostly, not quite reaching a full bodied form. "Anyway, Arlene was hanging out here several nights a week keeping me company and asked if we needed some help. With Butch's newest adventure taking up so much of his time and energy, this place needs all of the help we can get."

"Where is Butch?" Mac asked, wondering what she meant by his "adventure."

"In Phoenix. He's starting another business."

"You mean the greenhouse business?" Claire asked.

"No, another one. Buying old cars, fixing them up, and selling them."

"He's a busy guy." Mac wouldn't mind seeing some of the old cars Butch was buying or selling. Harley's 1949 Merc, nicknamed Mabel, made him itch to get some old Detroit steel of his own to polish and stroke.

Kate frowned. "Yeah, you could say that."

"It's kind of ironic," Claire said.

"What?"

"Butch dabbling in antiques. It seems to be a common hobby among the desert dwellers in these parts. He must have picked up the bug from Joe."

"Joe who, darlin'?" Arlene tucked a stray hair into her hive.

"Joe Martino," Kate said. "He used to be married to Ruby."

"Ruby is your new grandmama, right?" At Kate's nod, Arlene continued, "Joe fiddled with old cars?"

"No, just antiques in general. He was fencing th—" Kate jerked in her chair, her face tightening. "Ouch!" She glared across at Claire. "That was my shin, you big dope."

"Oh, was it?"

Leaning down, Kate rubbed her leg. "First you punch me, then you kick me. Keep it up and I'm going to give you a buzz cut in your sleep, brat."

Kate turned back to Arlene. "As I was saying, Joe was fencing stolen—"

"Kate!" Claire leaned across the table, clapping her hand over her sister's mouth. "Arlene doesn't need to know our family history, so ixnay on the blabber-mouthing-aye."

Kate pushed her sister's hand away, wrinkling her lips and nose. "Yuck, where was that hand last? You better have washed after you went to the bathroom."

"It was socking you in the mouth. Now zip it."

"Relax, Claire. It's just Arlene. She doesn't give a rat's ass about Joe and his checkered past."

"She's only been here a few weeks. She could be a serial killer who likes to cut blonde waitresses into bite-sized pieces for all you know." Claire's gaze moved to Arlene. "No offense, Arlene. I've just had bad luck with strangers in the past."

Bad luck? Mac leaned back and crossed his arms over his chest. More like bad decisions with near deadly results.

"Claire's paranoid," Kate said. "She thought those two guys she picked a fight with tonight were here fishing for information about something Joe stole."

Claire looked like she wanted to punch Kate in the mouth again. "Would you shut up, Kate?"

"I'm telling you, Arlene is one of us. Matter of fact, I was thinking about introducing her to Manny. He might be fun company for her."

Mac glowered at Claire, stuck on something Kate had said a moment before. "You picked a fight with *two* strange men?"

"No, I picked a fight with one man. The other got in the way."

"Haven't you learned anything about fighting in bars? In this bar?"

"I didn't intend to get into a brawl, just find out why they were watching Ronnie so closely."

"Maybe they liked her." Kate offered. "Since she cut her hair, she has that sexy, sophisticated woman thing going on."

Really? Mac had trouble seeing her face with the angry frustration blurring his vision whenever she came around.

"I don't think so," Claire said. "It wasn't your typical leering drunk kind of stare. They wanted something from her, I could tell, and when I asked them ever so politely what they were looking for one of them told me to mind my own business."

"Why did you grab his hat?" Arlene asked.

"Because I was making a point."

Mac groaned, scrubbing his hand down his face. "What point?"

"That they were fakes. His cowboy hat didn't even have sweat stains in the rim."

Kate crossed her arms. "Maybe he'd just bought it. Had you thought about that?"

"Along with his brand-spanking new boots?"

"He was dressing up for a night on the town," Kate shot back.

"Bullshit. You don't dress to the nines to come to The Shaft on a Saturday night. You'd go to Tucson and hit one of those urban cowboy bars if you were going to do that. Those two are up to something, and Ronnie came in driving Ruby's pickup."

Huh? Had Mac missed something there?

"What's Ronnie driving the pickup got to do with the two strangers?" Kate asked the question on Mac's tongue.

"They've probably been watching Ruby's place, and figured out that Ronnie was an easy mark. She's always been naïve when it comes to men, never catching on when a guy was giving her a little extra attention."

"An easy mark for what?" Mac wasn't really sure he wanted to hear the answer.

Claire wiggled her index finger for him to come closer. When he obliged, she whispered, "They've come to collect what's theirs—that gold pocket watch."

"Oh, Christ." Mac covered his eyes. "Here we go again."

Chapter Five

Sunday, September 30th

Claire shut the basement office door behind her and locked it. Alone at last.

After a crappy night in the Skunkmobile with Nat and her two sisters, she was contemplating dragging a sleeping bag down here and camping out on the floor. It would be a lot more comfortable than that damned table-turned-torture-bed she'd ended up on, tossing and turning long past the wee hours this morning.

Crossing the olive shag carpet, she grabbed the far side of the floor-to-ceiling bookcase full of first edition classic books like *Treasure Island* and *Moby Dick*. Her back ached at the thought of even trying to lift the sucker to move it away from the wall.

She had started the night sharing the new sofa bed with Kate, but after three long hours of putting up with Kate flopping around, groaning and mumbling, and kneeing her back, Claire had taken a blanket and pillow and curled up on the torture bed. Her left hip still ached from the hours there, counting and recounting sheep.

The bookcase would not budge on her first try, not even with some grunting and a mouthful of swearing. Claire put more of her shoulder into the job for heftier lift and move, getting a close-up whiff of the fumes from the fresh coat of yellow paint Ruby had rolled on the walls last week.

The paint smell did not fully hide the stale odor of cigarette smoke—Ruby's dead husband's signature scent.

Claire had a feeling the only way to exorcise Joe's ghost from the basement office would be to rip up the carpet and sell off all of the antiques he'd fenced or stolen that filled the room from floor to ceiling.

Claire stepped back from the bookcase. She rubbed the ache twanging in her lower back, trying to remember from her Human Anatomy 101 class where the spleen was and how easy it was to rupture it.

Ruby had suggested they buy those furniture moving disks to make the bookcase easier to move, but Claire had told her she would rather suffer from a sore back and shoulder to keep their secret safe—and by "safe," she was referring to the fireproof steel box that Joe had installed flush with the drywall behind the bookcase. The safe's treasures, such as the gold pocket watch and the chunk of Nazi gold Jess had found under the floor in Ruby's closet last month, were better protected thanks to the shag carpet making it harder for some thief in a hurry to move the heavy bookcase.

Gramps was too cheap and ornery to buy a security system for the place. He claimed a couple of shotguns and a guard dog were all they needed. Claire hated to piss in his daily bowl of prunes, but Henry was no guard dog. She knew that from firsthand experience when she'd had to face down a double-barrel shotgun with Henry by her side a couple of months back. The damned mutt had run off with his tail between his legs.

Claire wedged herself behind the bookcase and kneeled down, punching in the combination to the safe. The door popped open. The pocket watch sat on the middle shelf, front and center. As always, its polished gold and enamel casing called to her, but this time she donned a pair of leather work gloves before picking up the watch. She'd cleaned all fingerprints off of it weeks ago, wanting to keep the oils from her skin from damaging it.

Clutching the watch with her gloved hand, she double-checked the rest of the contents of the safe. The derringer still lay on the top shelf jammed in its matching miniature holster. The box of .22 caliber cartridges and the leather carrying strap filled the shelf along with the gun. As big as she imagined Joe had been thanks to all of those years of greasy spoon dives and bags of even greasier potato chips, she had no idea how he had ever managed to get his fat finger in around that little trigger. Maybe he found the whole getup cute; or he stole it from Gulliver after the traveler returned from Lilliput.

The black box on the second shelf next to where the watch had been still held the piece of Nazi gold. Claire could only imagine the shady dealer from whom Joe had gotten it. She'd had a nightmare weeks back about a platoon of Nazi zombies trying to break into the house to get to it. She'd woken in a pool of sweat, vowing never again to chase red velvet cake with peach schnapps.

The bottom shelf where last month she'd found the mummified hand inside a woven bag now held rolled up Copper Snake stock certificates bound by a thick rubber band.

Ruby and Gramps had decided to store them in the safe rather than in a safe deposit box in Yuccaville's only bank. Ever since the vice president of Cactus Creek Bank in Yuccaville had tried to steal Ruby's R.V. park out from under her, she'd had a bit of a chip on her shoulder when it came to financial institutions.

Unfortunately for Claire, Gramps, and Ruby, Jess knew all about the safe's contents. However, she still didn't know the new combination, which was something the three of them made doubly sure not to leak. It wasn't that Jess was likely to steal anything—more that she couldn't keep her lips sealed most of the time.

Claire closed the safe door and dropped into the leather chair behind Joe's antique, Queen Anne style desk, placing the watch on the coffee stained desk calendar.

Her mother had drooled over the desk when she'd first seen it. After years of religiously watching *Antiques Roadshow*, Deborah was a know-it-all about eighteenth and nineteenth century furniture. She had run her fingers over the finely carved legs and edges and gone on and on about the curves and lines like it was a souped-up hot rod.

Claire had an equal appreciation for Joe's desk ever since the first time she'd had sex with Mac—smack dab on top of it.

Just thinking about Mac made her smile. She'd missed sharing sheets with him the last week. On the way to the General Store this morning, she'd passed Chester's old Winnebago Brave and had paused to peek in the windows. Mac lay on Chester's couch with both legs hanging half off the end of it. The sound of Manny's whistling in his Airstream next door spurred her to hurry on her way.

Laying the pocket watch on the desk, she skimmed her gloved fingers over the tiny flowers and ovals that rimmed the gold case. Just as she did every time she held the watch, she paused to admire the workmanship of the artist who had painted the enamel cover. Pale green trees dotted the landscape while small, sixteenth century buildings rose in the distance. Finally, her two college classes on Art History were paying off. She mentally thumbed her nose at her mother, who never stopped making snide remarks about how much schooling Claire had with so little to show for it.

Claire shook off the tension that came each time she thought of her mother's voice and returned to the watch. A carriage was the focal point. The two dark horses hitched to it had tiny, glittering eyes—something Claire had confirmed with a magnifying glass during a previous inspection. The crowds of people filling the foreground gave the appearance of a fair or some festival in progress.

Initially, she'd thought the watch might be a nineteenth century piece. But with what she'd learned recently from an article Kate had found at the library, Claire now suspected it was quite a bit older.

She'd considered showing it to her mother, the expert, but the last thing she wanted was her mom catching wind of one of Joe's felony-inspired mysteries. Not only would it give Deborah more ammunition as to why Ruby was a bad choice as a wife for Gramps, but also it would mean Deborah would have her nose shoved even further into Claire's life and business. Claire would sooner have her colon inspected in front of an auditorium full of pre-med students.

Someone knocked on the basement door. The locked knob turned partially back and forth several times.

"Who is it?" Claire asked, wondering if someone had seen her sneak down here this morning. Ruby had been rattling around in the kitchen when she had tiptoed down the stairs.

"It's Kate. Open up."

"I'm busy."

"Is Mac in there?"

"No."

"Then open the door."

"How'd you know I was down here?"

"You're obsessed with that damned watch. Where else would you be? Now open the door or I'm going to go tell Mom what you're up to."

Claire growled in her throat. Kate always played dirty. She crossed the room and opened the door a crack, peeking through it. "What?"

"I have something for you. Let me in." Kate pushed on the door.

Claire held firm under Kate's muscling attempt, her butt weighing a good twenty pounds more than Kate's scrawny ass at the moment. "Just give it to me."

"No." Kate shoved hard, knocking Claire back several feet.

"Jeez," Claire said, "for a stick insect, you have a mean shoulder."

Kate shut the door behind her. She looked a little pasty around the gills under the fluorescent lights. "Mom is looking for you."

Ah, Kate had been talking to Medusa. That explained why she looked ill. Actual face-to-face conversations with the pinch-lipped woman who birthed her usually made Claire's armpits sweaty and her stomach cramp. "Why me?"

"I didn't ask."

"Well, I'm busy."

"Doing what?" Kate looked at Claire's gloved hands, then over at the desk. "Playing with that super-mysterious pocket watch again, Sherlock?"

"Poke fun, but I'm telling you this thing is way more valuable than you think."

"Like five thousand dollars valuable?"

"I'm thinking like ten times that."

Kate snorted. "I'm thinking you've been smoking some of that happy weed you used to score back in high school from the nude hippie down our street."

"He wasn't a hippie, just an old vet who got confused

after too many joints and thought his invisibility suit hid his bits and pieces from view."

"Thank God Chester and Manny don't smoke weed," Kate said. "They're already 'one toke over the line' without even touching the stuff."

"Thanks, dork. Now that song is in my head." Claire walked around the desk and dropped into Joe's chair. "I need more information on the pocket watch to pinpoint a year. When can you get back to the library?"

After having been kicked out of the Yuccaville library for fighting, Claire was still on their suspended list for another few months. She held firm in her position that the old broad double-tapped her with that damned cane before Claire took it upon herself to push back. Unfortunately, the librarian remained unsympathetic.

"I'm not going back." Kate planted her hands on her hips, her back getting ramrod stiff. "I have a life, you know. One that doesn't revolve around your warped, fictitious world full of criminals and murderers."

"Fine. Calm down." Claire sat back in the chair, frowning up at Kate and her flared nostrils and suddenly pink cheeks. "Jeez, Princess, what crawled up your ass and died this morning? Was there a pea under the cushion of your side of the couch bed last night?" That would explain Kate's restless slumber.

"Sorry," Kate said, waving away Claire's raised brows. "I woke up on the wrong side of the bed this morning. Why were you sleeping on the table, anyway?"

"Because you were kickboxing in your sleep." Claire had the bruises to prove it. "Where did you go at the butt crack of dawn?"

Sleep was a pipe dream when it came to that damned table. A bed of nails would have been more comfortable or at least therapeutic. Kate's attempt to sneak out had been a temporary distraction from the ache in Claire's left hip.

"I felt like taking a walk."

"*You* wanted to exercise early in the morning? Have we made a free right turn into a parallel universe and nobody told me?"

Kate's jaw jutted. "What? I've turned over a new leaf."

"A new leaf would mean a darker shade of lipstick for you, not something that involves the potential to actually produce sweat." Kate was allergic to anything that made her leak from her pores. "Did Butch get you on this health kick?"

"Butch has nothing to do with it." The sharpness in Kate's tone made Claire lean forward.

"What's going on with you two?"

"Nothing," Kate said, her tight lips making it clear she was not going to share a peep.

"Fine, if it's nothing, then you'll help me get access to his home computer so I can get online and do my own research on this pocket watch." Claire tapped the gold casing with her gloved finger.

"I'm not going back there."

"Listen, whatever this fight between you two is about, I'm sure he doesn't want you to move out. You're overreacting."

"Said the kettle."

"I do not overreact to a fight—unnecessary drama is Ronnie's song and dance routine."

"That's right," Kate said. "You just tuck tail and run."

After waking up to another morning with the impending doom of motherhood still a possibility in the forecast, Kate's words struck way too close to the truth. It had taken Claire five minutes of whispering to herself in the Skunkmobile's bathroom mirror and a few self-inflicted smacks to the face not to grab the car keys for Mabel and flee the state. Instead, she had grabbed her hidden pack of cigarettes on her way out the door but then had remembered why she needed a smoke and cursed, stubbing her stress-aid out as soon as she had lit it. She had settled for stuffing her face with Twinkies upon reaching the store.

However, while Kate was dead-on pinpointing Claire's

flaw, she didn't need to stand there looking so damned smug about it. "Do you really want me to come around this desk and sit on your diaphragm until you turn a lovely shade of purple?"

Kate sighed. "No. Sorry, I'm just ..." she flapped her hand in the air as if she were shooing away a fly.

"Okay, crazy, let's move on then," Claire said. "How about you let me into Butch's office at The Shaft? I know he has a computer and internet connection there."

"He has a docking station, but he took his laptop with him."

"Damn it." Claire picked up the watch again, stroking the face with her gloved finger. It was time for Ruby to join the modern world and start offering free wireless internet to her campers. If Claire could only talk Gramps into buying a computer, or shipping the one he had back home in Nemo down to Arizona.

"Claire!" Deborah's voice rang through the closed office door, making Kate jump and Claire cringe. "Open this door. I need to talk to you."

"I'm busy," Claire yelled back.

Her mother was quiet for a couple of beats. "Is MacDonald in there?"

Claire rolled her eyes. "You know Mac hates it when you use his whole name."

"You two aren't doing anything funny in there again, are you?"

Kate snickered into her fist.

"Mac isn't in here, Mom. Just Kate."

"Kathryn? I thought I told you to bring Claire upstairs."

"I'm trying, Mother."

"Try harder. She needs to come get a handle on her new grandmother. Ruby is throwing a silly tantrum."

Claire stormed over to the door and yanked it open. "What did you do, Mom?"

Deborah stood under the stairwell light looking like she'd

dressed for the horse track down in Del Mar, with bright lipstick, a pale pink shirt, dress pants, and a silk scarf with cowgirls lassoing cowboys on it. All she was missing was a feathered hat.

"I didn't do anything." Deborah smirked. "Jessica did."

"What did Jess do now?" Kate asked, looking over Claire's shoulder.

A wicked glint lit Deborah's blue eyes. "She invited her father to breakfast."

Chapter Six

Mac rolled to a stop in front of his aunt's place. Shielding his eyes from the morning rays, he stared at the silver Cadillac sitting in his usual parking spot by the willow tree. Aside from the complimentary coat of dust that came with southeastern Arizona breezes and being a decade old, it looked to be in mint condition. Ruby must have a visitor. From where he sat, he couldn't read the license plate to see if it were a local.

He climbed out of his pickup and stretched, trying to work out several kinks he'd acquired last night thanks to Chester's couch. As if the lumpy cushions and lack of length weren't bad enough, Mac had tossed and turned in a fog of stale cigar smoke that seemed to seep from the fabric and foam.

He shaded his eyes from the sun, which had crested the *Tres Dedos* Mountains to the east hours ago and burned away most of the remaining coolness. The only shadows left were huddling at the base of the large mass of Precambrian granite called the Middle Finger, which jutted out of the northern flank of the range. He grinned, remembering Claire's comment from a couple of months ago that the Middle Finger was Mother Nature's response to the Copper Snake Mining Company's continued blasting and ravaging of the surrounding desert over the last century. She had such a creative way with words.

The screen door creaked open. Claire's cousin Natalie stepped onto the porch, letting the screen door slap shut behind her. When her gaze hit his, she shook her head. "You don't want to go in there."

"I don't?"

"Absolutely not. I'd advise getting back in your pickup and flooring it in the other direction."

Shit. He felt his grin wilt. "Is Deborah dabbling with her evil magic wand already this morning?"

"Not yet." Natalie descended the steps and joined him in the warm sunshine. "Your aunt has a visitor," she said in a lowered voice.

He glanced back over at the Cadillac then walked around the front of it. Natalie followed.

The Ohio plates were plastered with bug guts. Who did Ruby know from … then it hit him. He winced, hissing inwardly through his teeth. "Oh, hell. Don't tell me that's Jess's dad's car."

"Winner winner chicken dinner. Give the man a prize." Natalie crossed her arms over her chest. "From what I've gleaned through all of the yelling and cursing while I inhaled my bacon and eggs, your cousin invited him to come to Arizona for a visit, and he took her up on it."

Had Ruby known about this? She would normally have mentioned something as big and ugly as this to Mac if so.

"Ruby looked like she'd bit into a slab of raw liver when Jess's pop walked in the door."

Mac rubbed his hand over his face, his whiskers making a scratching sound. "Damn it. Ruby doesn't need this on top of Deborah being here, especially with Harley out of commission."

Natalie nodded slowly. "Yeah. Not to mention the situation with the university crew."

"Exactly." *Wait!* Mac frowned at Natalie. "What situation?"

"You know, the conspiracy stuff Claire keeps talking about."

What particular conspiracy stuff this time? He cocked his head to the side, his eyes narrowing. More importantly, he thought, "Has something happened recently?" Something that

Claire had not told him about? Not that he had had any time alone with her since he had arrived at the R.V. park to get caught up with her latest presumptions.

Natalie's cell phone rang. "Didn't she tell you about that weird conversation I overheard?" She tugged the phone out of her back pocket.

"Not yet."

She grinned when she looked down at her cell phone's screen. "It's my other half from back home. I have to take this." She lifted the phone to her ear. "Nat's cat house, head puss speaking."

Mac did a double take. Had he heard her right?

"Violet Lynn Parker, always good to hear your sweet swearing voice." She paused, listening. "No freaking way." She listened some more, her smile widening. "Wait, wait! You need to back the truck up and tell me how this all started."

Mac didn't hang around to eavesdrop on Natalie's call. Ruby was most likely in need of reinforcements by now. He just hoped her shotgun was still resting against the wall up in her closet. He took the porch steps two at a time, wondering if Claire had been inside eating breakfast with Natalie when the devil had walked in, or if she'd escaped before all hell had broken loose.

Inside the store, Mac found Ronnie sitting behind the counter, a half-eaten candy bar and a can of root beer in front of her. It was not exactly her usual grapefruit and granola she had insisted on back in Tucson.

"Mornin', Mac." She tucked away a bunch of loose strands from her crooked ponytail.

A ponytail? He rubbed the back of his neck, trying to remember if he'd ever seen her wearing a ponytail before. Usually if her hair was up, it was secured all tidy and neat in one of those French curl thing-a-ma-jobs.

A cacophony of yelling rang from the other side of the green velvet curtain, sounding like someone had thrown a snake into a chicken coop. For a moment he thought he heard

Claire's voice in the mix. The slamming of a door ended the commotion and all was silent in the other room.

Ronnie grimaced at the curtain and then took a bite of the candy bar. "Did you sleep okay?" she asked.

"I slept like shit." And it was her fault.

"Yeah, me, too."

He had trouble scraping up any sympathy for her. She hadn't had to listen to Chester's grunts, burps, and farts all night long. Mac swore that man lived on canned *chili con carne* and Velveeta cheese. Judging from the sulfur vapors seeping from Chester's bedroom in the back of the Brave, he was dying from it, too.

"Did you have to sleep on the table bed?" he asked. It seemed a fitting punishment since she had caused his exile to the Isle of Chester.

"No, Claire drew the short straw. Kate felt sorry for her, though, and let her share the couch bed."

That didn't surprise him knowing Kate. She had told him once how much she admired Claire and her screw-it spirit, especially when it came to dealing with their mother.

"But she must have hogged the bed," Ronnie continued, "because Claire was sleeping on the table this morning when I got up to go pee."

Poor Claire. On the bright side, maybe she would need some of her kinks massaged ... and then some.

Ronnie nodded her head at the keys in his hand. "Where did you go this morning?"

"To fill up my pickup."

After listening to Chester's wake up routine through the Brave's thin bathroom wall, the urge to put Jackrabbit Junction in his rearview mirror had spurred Mac to top off his gas tank.

He'd almost taken a detour on the way back here to hike up to Ruby's Lucky Monk mine and check if the No Trespassing signs and barriers at the main adit entrance had been tampered with by anyone. With the university's archeological crew accessing their dig site through a back door into the Lucky Monk, he was being extra careful about keeping the front entrance to the mine blocked.

After Natalie's comment about the "situation" with the archaeologists, he needed to talk with Claire. Depending on what "conspiracy stuff" she was whispering in Natalie's ear, he might be paying a visit to the Lucky Monk before the day was out after all.

"Filling up, huh?" Ronnie glugged down some root beer, then slammed the can on the counter, burping into her fist. Two of her fingernails had the paint half peeled off. Another one looked ragged, like it had been torn or chewed.

Mac could not help but gape at her. He had never seen Ronnie anything other than perfectly poised with her hair coiffed, her nails polished, and her smile fine-tuned. It looked like Jackrabbit Junction was working its dusty magic on her, leaving her pucker faced and sour tempered.

"Don't tell me you're planning to leave paradise so soon." Sarcasm laced her tone along with something he could not pinpoint. It almost sounded like a touch of desperation, or maybe fear.

No, it couldn't be fear. That made no sense. What did Ronnie have to fear besides a missed spa appointment? Whatever it was, Mac had no time for this. He needed to see Claire—and Ruby, too. He took several steps toward the curtain, but then remembered something from last night and returned to the counter.

Stuffing the last of her candy bar in her mouth, Ronnie looked up at him with raised brows.

"Did I see you getting a ride from the Sheriff last night?" he asked, watching for her reaction.

Claire had called Natalie before leaving the bar with Mac last night and confirmed that Ronnie had made it back to the Skunkmobile, which meant Mac most likely had been spot on about her leaving in the Sheriff's pickup.

Ronnie's cheeks reddened. "Like I told Claire and Katie,"

she said through a mouthful of chocolate, "he was just doing his duty and taking me home after I'd had a few too many drinks."

"Right." It was his turn to use sarcasm. "Since when does the Sheriff of Cholla County act as a taxi service for drunks?"

She swallowed while shaking her head. "I wasn't drunk, just tipsy."

"Is that why you didn't stick around to help Claire and Kate with the fight?"

Ronnie's mouth opened, but a loud war cry from the other side of the curtain interrupted her, followed by a crash and several thumps.

Mac didn't wait to hear what came next. He rushed through the curtain into the rec room only to stop in his tracks at the sight of Claire and Kate rolling around on the carpet, grunting and cursing as they wrestled for something Kate clutched in her right hand. Ruby's set of four T.V. trays, which usually sat stacked next to the couch, lay scattered across the floor.

Frozen in surprise, Mac watched as Kate rolled on top of Claire and nailed her with a solid elbow in the breadbasket, and then tried to scramble out of her sister's reach. Before Kate could make it to freedom, Claire recovered. She latched onto Kate's ankle, yanking her backward.

His brain finally thawed. Mac barged forward. "What in the hell is going on?"

"Dang it, boy," Chester said from a stool at the bar. "Don't go ruining the match."

"What match?" Mac grabbed Claire's arm, the one that had a hold on Kate, and tried to loosen her grip.

"Kate 'the Ex-Porn Star' Morgan versus her sister Claire 'the Tool Babe.'"

Manny burst through the back door, a can of beer in his hand. His gaze landed on the three of them in the middle of the rec room. "Holy *frijoles*! What's going on in here? Can I join in?"

Chester snickered. "You wouldn't last a round with your trick hip."

"Claire," Mac growled. "Let go of her."

"Fine! Fine! I'm letting go." Claire sat up, rubbing her gut. "She started it, though."

"She's right, Katie did start it," Chester confirmed, puffing on his cigar. "I saw the whole thing."

"Bragger," Manny said.

Chester rolled the ash from his cigar. "I've seen better matches in the mud pen at Dirty Gerties."

Mac turned his glare on the two contenders. "What's with all of the fighting lately? Are you two trying out for the WWE?"

"It's their mother," Manny answered. "Ford has said it time and again. Every time their *madre* comes around, all three of his granddaughters go a little *loca*."

"Or a lot," Chester added. "Like werewolves during a full moon."

Mac got a look at what Kate was holding in her hand—the damned golden pocket watch from Ruby's safe. That explained Claire's temporary insanity.

"What are you doing with the watch?" he asked Kate.

"Keeping it away from her." Kate pointed at Claire. "She's obsessed."

"Would you stop touching it with your bare hands! The oil in your fingers can ruin it."

"See, Mac, like I said—obsessed."

"I told you, I am not obsessed," Claire said. "I'm just concerned about the trouble it might bring our way."

"There's not going to be any trouble," Kate said, her voice higher than normal, her cheeks dotted with red splotches. "Nobody but our family knows about this stupid watch or any of the rest of Joe's stuff."

"I do," Chester said. "So does Manny."

Kate shot them a glare. "You two don't count."

"That's not true," Claire said. "Your barmaid buddy

Arlene knows now, thanks to your big mouth."

"What watch?" Ronnie asked from behind Mac. She stood just inside the curtain.

"Arlene doesn't give a damn about any of this."

After helping Claire to her feet, Mac said to her, "I thought we agreed last night that you were going to take a break from this whole sleuthing business."

"I said I would do my best to keep my nose out of trouble," Claire said, picking up her Mighty Mouse hat from the floor and jamming it on her head. "Not stop researching it altogether." Her eyes challenged his. "There's no harm in just reading about it, is there?"

A scoff came from Kate's direction. "There is when you're trying to blackmail your younger sister into breaking into someone's house or office to get on his computer."

"He's your *boyfriend*, numb nuts." Claire straightened her red T-shirt so the mummy image was back in front. "It's not breaking and entering when you're having sex with him on a regular basis."

"How regular are we talking?" Manny asked.

Chester scratched his jaw. "I thought they were breaking up."

"Let me see the watch." Ronnie sidled up next to Kate, who opened her fist warily while keeping an eye on Claire.

"Mac, you gotta make Claire stop messing with Joe's things," Kate said. "She's starting to get all twitchy-eyed again."

"My twitch has nothing to do with the watch."

"And look what happened last time she got too deep into someone else's business."

"What? I helped Ruby keep her mine," Claire justified.

"You almost got killed," Mac reminded her.

"Only a little," she shot back.

Chester let out a lungful of smoke-filled laughter.

"Damn." Ronnie whistled through her teeth. "That's gotta be worth a few thousand bucks, don't you think?"

"Hand me the pocket watch, please," Mac ordered.

Kate dropped it into his open palm, dusting off her hands like she was finished with the whole mess.

"What are you going to do with it?" Claire asked.

"Give it to you," (which he did) "and ask you to return it to the place you got it from and leave it there."

"I was going to do just that after I took some pictures of it, but Kate blew this all out of proportion and took it from me."

"I did not."

"You did, too," Chester butted in. "You kind of went a little nuts there, Katie girl, getting all bristled up and jaw snapping when Claire mentioned calling Butch."

Claire lovingly buffed the case of the golden watch with her T-shirt, handling it like it was a museum piece. "What's wrong with you lately, Kate?"

"Nothing's wrong with me." She pointed at her oldest sister. "Ronnie is the one acting all weird."

"What?" Ronnie took a step back. "I'm not acting weird."

"Yeah, you are," Claire joined Kate's side. "You cut and darkened your hair, you're wearing colored contacts, and you keep hiding from Mom."

"I'm not hiding from Mother," Ronnie said. "I'm—"

The back door swung open, interrupting her.

In flounced Deborah, wearing a fancy pink getup. Mac almost laughed aloud at her frilly ensemble.

A tall, lanky blond guy in designer jeans and a button-up shirt followed on her sparkly heels.

"Oh, you're such a charmer," Deborah cooed, fluttering her eyelashes at the stranger. Even her lips were painted pink. Pepto-Bismol should have paid her for ad space.

"*Ay yi yi*, Deborah," Manny said. "You are a vision, like a pink rose."

Deborah shot Don Juan a lightning fast glare before returning to her fawning flutter.

Jess bounced in behind them, stars in her eyes as she

looked up at the man that Mac had no doubt was her father.

All right, so Deborah and Jess were accounted for, as well as Claire, her sisters and cousin, and the old boys. That left Ruby and Harley. Mac had a suspicion that one of them was loading shotgun shells into a chamber while the other tried to add some sense into the mix, but knowing Claire's grandfather, Mac was not sure who would be holding the gun.

A blur of movement in his peripheral vision made him look around. Ronnie was nowhere to be seen; the velvet curtain swaying in her wake was the only evidence she had been there.

Deborah's gaze bounced between her two remaining daughters. Her lips pinched into a wrinkled pink blob. "What's going on here, Kathryn?"

"Nothing, Mother," Kate brushed dust off her work shirt and patted down her blonde waves and curls. "It was nice to meet you, Mr. Horner," she said to Jess's dad, all prim and proper. Mac half-expected her to curtsy. "If you'll excuse me, I need to get to work."

Deborah huffed. "Handing out drinks is not work, Kathryn. It's servitude. You need to come home with me and find a decent job. If Butch were a true gentleman, he'd be treating you like a princess instead of his slave."

Kate's face darkened, but she held her tongue. After flashing a glare at her sister, she pushed through the velvet curtain ... to freedom. Mac was tempted to bow and follow Ronnie and Kate's exits, but Claire would hunt him down for leaving her stranded and nail him with a shitload of guilt, pounding it in deep with her hammer.

"Thank you for showing me around, Deborah," Horner touched Claire's mom's shoulder and then let his hand rest there. "You're a lovely hostess."

Deborah tittered, which made Claire cringe visibly next to Mac.

"Steve," Deborah said with a smile so big Mac wanted to slap a Wide Load sign on her forehead, "it's the least I could do after the way Ruby treated you."

"Oh, Christ," Mac muttered, and then realized he had said it aloud.

Deborah turned toward Mac, her smile pulling a disappearing act. "How rude of me. Steve, I don't think you've met Ruby's nephew, MacDonald Garner."

Deborah had a way of saying his name all wrong, sounding like she was spitting something rotten and slimy out of her mouth when she uttered it.

"Jess talks about you all of the time in her letters," Horner said to Mac, offering his hand. "It's going to be hard to live up to your Superman status."

Mac stared at the hand of the asshole who'd jerked his aunt around for years when it had come to child support and broken his cousin's heart with unfulfilled promises time and again. When he gripped Horner's hand, he squeezed hard, following it up with an even harder glare.

Horner's slick grin turned gritty.

"So," Mac pulled his hand away, resisting the urge to wipe it off on his jeans. "What brings you down here to Jackrabbit Junction after all of these years?"

"Hey, where are you going?" Ronnie asked as she followed Katie out the screen door.

Katie didn't pause on her way down Ruby's porch steps. "The Shaft."

Ronnie slipped back inside and grabbed her purse from behind the General Store's counter and then bounded down the steps after her sister. "I'll join you."

"I'm going to work." Katie yanked open the driver's side door of her Volvo. "Not to drink."

"Fine." Ronnie jogged over, joining Katie inside the hot car as the engine growled to life. "I'll drink while I watch you work."

"Really?" Katie shoved on her sunglasses. "Then you must be even more desperate to escape than I am." She wheeled the car around.

Katie didn't know the half of it. Ronnie grabbed the *oh-shit* handle above the passenger side window and held on for dear life when her sister sent gravel flying in their wake. She'd forgotten how crazy Katie was behind the wheel.

"It's Claire's turn to babysit Mom for once," Ronnie added, swallowing a gasp as Katie swerved to miss a jackrabbit crossing their path. Maybe she should have walked to town.

A guffaw came from Katie. "The two of them can find a whole new reason to swap glares." Ronnie would have had to be deaf to miss the underlying animosity in her sister's voice.

"What's going on with you?" Katie was usually the peacekeeper, keeping the white flag waving in the midst of family battles.

"Nothing."

"Then why are you and Claire fighting so much?"

"We're not fighting." Katie tapped her fingers on the steering wheel. "It's just she has this one-track mind, and some of us have bigger concerns than finding out where a stupid pocket watch came from."

Katie must be referring to the reason she had moved out of Butch's place, but Ronnie had a policy of staying clear of her youngest sister's romantic life. Her brief career as a relationship therapist had ended after an ex-con Katie had been dating had wiggled his eyebrows in Ronnie's direction and suggested a *ménage à trois,* inspiring her to accidentally clobber him with a frying pan—twice. Luckily for him, it was made of aluminum, not cast iron.

"You don't think Claire has a point about being proactive after all of the crap she's been through thanks to Joe's illegal shenanigans?"

After seeing the pocket watch that had Claire so obsessed, Ronnie found herself panting and licking her chops, too. That thing would bring a pretty penny even if it was only a century old.

Katie sighed and hit her turn signal, the bar's parking lot ahead on the left. "Probably, but she needs to find someone else to be her research bitch. I don't have time to hang out at the library all day and take turns on the internet with half of Yuccaville's senior citizens. Those old women go over their one-hour limit and get downright pissy when you politely ask them to take turns. Last time I was there, I got my toes crushed by a mean granny with a cherry red walker lined with dingle balls. Then one of her cronies with a cane—who I'm pretty sure clobbered Claire—warned that I might want to bring a bodyguard to the library or I could win a one-way trip to the handicap stall."

Ronnie laughed.

Katie didn't. "I'm not kidding. The folks in these parts don't take kindly to pretty young blondes."

"Oh, yeah?" She grinned. "And how do they treat old platinum blonde shrews like you?"

"Bite me." She flashed Ronnie her middle finger. "This color is the real thing, unlike your bottle job. Why did you go back to being a brunette, anyway? I thought you liked your hair lighter."

Ronnie looked out the side window. As much as she'd like to unload the burden she'd been carrying around since arriving on Claire and Mac's doorstep, she didn't want to endanger Katie.

She changed the subject rather than answering. "What do you mean when you say you're Claire's 'research bitch'? Researching what?"

"Several of Ruby's antiques. Claire is trying to figure out market values."

How many antiques were they talking?

Ronnie had been down in Ruby's basement once, but she hadn't really paid much attention. She had been an errand girl, sent down to tell Claire that Gramps wanted her as his partner for a game of Bid Euchre. He always favored Claire when it came to winning at cards, saying Ronnie was allergic to taking risks. She wondered what he'd think about her if he knew the mess of risks she was facing daily thanks to the piece of shit her mom had convinced her to marry.

"Why doesn't she do her own research?" she asked as Katie pulled into the parking lot.

Claire was busy building the restrooms all day, but the library must be open in the evening.

"She's banned from the library for fighting with that bully with the cane."

Ronnie laughed.

"It's true. Claire claims she was defending herself. She's convinced that the librarians are in the old womens' little beaded pocketbooks. It's probably another one of her silly conspiracy theories, but nobody came to my rescue when I was being threatened. She may be right on this one."

Everything revolved around conspiracy theories in Claire's world. The girl had watched too many Scooby Doo episodes when they were kids. "So you've been looking up information on that pocket watch Claire had in the rec room?"

Katie parked in front of The Shaft and killed the engine. "That and some other pieces."

"Like what?" Anything that Ronnie could pawn for a quick thousand that would help her escape the goons keeping an eye on her? She'd find a way to pay Ruby back after the issues with Lyle's illegal financial activities had settled down.

"Some of the first editions in Ruby's bookcase, a bunch of those antique cameras Joe had, and some stock certificates Gramps found last month, to name a few things."

Stock certificates? How hard was it to cash in on those? She couldn't leave a paper trail, though. She would have to settle for returning to that greasy dude's pawn shop with that pocket watch in hand. "Why don't you let me help you out?"

"What do you mean?" Katie climbed out of the car.

Ronnie opened her door. "Let me borrow your car today and go hang out at the library in Yuccaville, do some research."

"You don't even know what to look for."

"Don't you have some notes already on it all? Pictures?"

"No pictures. Claire's been pretty adamant about not taking pictures before today." Kate's forehead crinkled in thought. "I think I left my notes back at ... no wait. They're in the trunk."

She popped the trunk and pulled out a flowery backpack. "You sure you want to do this? I thought you were boycotting the internet these days."

Which was the excuse Ronnie had used when Claire had offered to help her get her resume up online via a job hunting website. The last thing she needed was to be posting her address online where any Tom, Dick, or Harry-the-hit-man could find it.

"What else do I have to do here? I'm tired of sitting behind the counter and painting my nails with Jessica's glittery nail polish."

"Fine. Have at it." She handed Ronnie the backpack. "But you need to be back tonight to pick me up when we close."

"I'll be here."

"And be careful with my car. I just got it back from the body shop after my last ... uh ... accident."

"You mean after the last time you plowed into your boyfriend's pickup."

"Stuff a sock in it, rubba dub." Katie tossed her the keys and headed into the bar.

Hopeful for the first time since the pawn shop creep had spread manure all over her field of dreams, Ronnie zipped around the back of Katie's car and slid behind the wheel.

Perfect! Now to go find out how much she could snag for that pocket watch.

She pulled out of The Shaft's parking lot and headed toward Yuccaville, cranking up the radio and singing along with a sad Dolly Parton song about a bunch of laughing and drinking going on two doors down. If she could score some quick cash with one of Ruby's antiques, she might be able to get the hell out of Dodge before she ended up polka-dotted with bullet holes. Then she could join the party going on two doors down, too.

After cruising around Yuccaville's dusty streets for twenty minutes, she found the library. Just her luck, it sat kitty corner from the Sheriff's Department building. At least the parking spots were plentiful this morning. She grabbed the flowery backpack and a sunhat from Katie's backseat. Hiding behind her sunglasses, she stepped out into the hot sunlight, careful to keep her head down and face averted in case Sheriff Hardass was daydreaming out the window this afternoon about handing out more speeding tickets to poor, desperate women.

Last night after her initial striptease, the big ape had relented to driving her home. He had thrown her shirt back at her and ordered her to buckle up. They had ridden to Ruby's place with the thump-thump of tar strips on the asphalt and a periodic squawk from his police radio the only sounds breaking the silence.

When she had thanked him for the ride, he had stared across the cab at her. The dashboard lights had added more angles and ridges to his face, the areas not shadowed by the scruff covering his cheeks and jawline, anyway. She had swatted down the urge to reach out to touch his features, to explore the textures with the pads of her fingers.

"I'd suggest you stay out of trouble," his baritone voice had sounded hard and scratchy in the soft glow of the cab. "But you share blood with the Morgan sisters, so I know better."

She had grimaced at him, not liking the tone he'd used when mentioning her maiden name. "You say that like we're descendants of the Clantons or the James Gangs."

"Well, let's see, since you and your sisters rode into town, Cholla County has been flooded with attempted murders, B and E reports, and multiple irresponsible and reckless driving incidents. Add your speeding ticket, illegal parking, public intoxication, attempts to bribe an officer of the law, and threat to run around naked as a jaybird, and you three Musketeers are on your way to a bang up reputation as outlaws."

The back of her neck had bristled at the high and mighty Sheriff with his tin badge and condescending smirk. "And you love the idea of playing Wyatt Earp, don't you?"

His stiff cotton shirt rustled when he shrugged and shifted to face her. "Makes me wonder what dust devils you girls are planning to stir up next. Guess I'd better make room in my jail for all three of you to come spend the night with me this time."

Her smile felt brittle on her lips, but she hid behind it, anyway. "Sheriff Harrison, I assure you that neither my sisters nor I have any such criminal plans on our agendas." *Well, not at the moment, anyway.*

"Sure." After a long stare down, he tipped his hat. "You have a good night now, *Mrs. Jefferson*."

His deliberate use of the name she had previously requested he no longer use had motivated her to slam his pickup door harder than normal. As he drove off across the bridge leading out of the R.V. park, she rattled off a chorus of colorful adjectives that flowed beautifully with "Hardass."

Now with the sun bearing down on her and the potential to get some cash in her pocket so she could possibly escape from Cholla County U.S.A. along with the steaming pile of trouble her lousy not-husband had left, she wasn't feeling so cocky. A light at the end of the tunnel beckoned. She did not need Sheriff Hardass stepping in front of her and blocking it.

She reached the library's front door and pulled on the handle. The door didn't budge. Pushing the sunhat back, she looked up and found a CLOSED sign front and center in the door window.

Damn it! The place was closed on Sundays. No wonder the open parking spaces were so plentiful on the street. She'd have to borrow Katie's car and come back tomorrow.

Turning, she growled and muttered back to her sister's car.

Halfway there, she noticed a black sedan cruising toward her on the street. She was within ten feet of Katie's car when her brain connected the dots and her breath caught. She looked up, gawking at the car's passenger. He was missing his black cowboy hat, hiding behind dark glasses instead today.

Her heart screeched to a stop along with her feet. She tried to think through the panic clanging in her brain. He had not seemed to recognize her, which might save her ass this afternoon.

Forcing one foot in front of the other, she kept walking instead of stopping at Katie's car. If they didn't know what vehicle she was driving, she might be able to give them the slip after circling around the block a time or two.

She glanced behind her. The sedan had pulled into a parking spot two blocks away, the goons still inside. Had the driver figured out it was her under the hat and shades? Were they waiting for the opportunity to hop out and shoot her down? Would they risk it right in front of the Sheriff's windows? She didn't plan to stick around to find out.

At the end of the block, she took a left and started running, looking over her shoulder every other breath. Up ahead, a sidewalk sign advertised fresh sandwiches and sun tea. The bell overhead jangled as she stumbled inside. Trying to slow her huffing, she took several deep breaths while straightening her bohemian skirt and tank top.

The place smelled like fresh baked bread with a hint of pickles. The sign at the hostess station said to seat herself, so Ronnie slid into a chair at a table in a corner that would give her a view of the front window but with a fake cactus to hide behind. With her back to the rest of the deli, her only concern was the two men she expected to burst through the door any minute.

She opened a menu, pretending to peruse it while peeking over the top. The black sedan cruised by slowly, dark sunglasses on the driver, too. Were they both carrying? Did they have a horse's head in their trunk next to their Tommy guns?

"Keep going," she said under her breath, her eyes on the taillights to see if they brightened. When the car rolled out of her view, she pushed to her feet and edged up to the window, watching the sedan pause much longer than three seconds for the stop sign before continuing on down the road.

She sighed in relief. *Jesus, that was close.*

She needed to get out of here before they came back around again and started going door to door looking for her. When she turned back and let her gaze sweep the rest of the diner tables, her knees almost buckled at the sight of Sheriff Harrison sitting in a chair three tables back.

His hat rested on the table across from him, his black wavy hair flattened around the sides. His eyes had a slight squint as he chewed while he watched her. Tomatoes and bacon spilled out of the sandwich on his plate. His tan colored shirt was pressed crisp as usual, the star pinned there all bright and shiny.

As he finished his bite and swallowed, his eyes took a tour from the top of her head to her sandals and back up again, like she was a suspect in one of his line-ups. She lifted her chin, determined not to let him catch her hands or knees trembling. She could handle a small town Sheriff. After all, she had hosted dinner parties with state senators and rich big-time industrialists without a single fumble.

"Well," he drawled, "at least you're dressed today. But isn't it a little early to be hitting the gin? It is Sunday, you know."

She crossed her arms over her chest. "I haven't been drinking."

"You sure about that? Why don't you come over here and let me smell your breath again."

"No, thank you."

"It wasn't a question." He kicked out the seat across from him. "Have a seat, Mrs. Jefferson."

Chapter Seven

Once upon a time there was a man who skimmed treasures from the fenced antiques black market. This thief of thieves hid his stolen treasures in the basement of his house and deep within his mines. One day, he up and died, leaving his unenlightened widow to play caretaker for his horde of hot goods. The End.

But Claire knew better, unlike what Kate and the others in her family believed. It was not the end. It was more like "to be continued …"

Claire grabbed the ladder from inside the unfinished restrooms and leaned it against the side of her work in progress. Another week of plumbing, electrical wiring, and then drywalling, and they should be rolling the final paint on the building.

Natalie had plans of heading home in a week and no amount of begging or attempts at blackmail would convince her to stay longer. Claire hated to see her cousin go. Working next to her had been like old times, including the sweating, swearing, and post-work drinking. The only thing missing had been the men. Mac had changed all of that for Claire, but Natalie's disinterest in the other sex at the moment had Claire scratching her head. Was there a guy back in South Dakota Natalie was hiding, or did she really mean it when she said she was taking a long-term sabbatical from the dating world?

Speaking of Mac, Claire wondered how pissed he was going to be at her for sneaking away in the midst of the drama back at Ruby's, leaving him to handle Jess's dad and Deborah. Well, he wasn't completely alone; Chester and Manny were there to cheer him on, or at least act as a peanut gallery. Claire would have to make it up to him as soon as she could figure out where they could catch a moment without an audience.

She raised the binoculars she had borrowed from Chester and searched the surrounding hillsides, checking for any movement. She wasn't paranoid; she was a realist. Bad men who stole expensive antiques for a living did not just shrug their shoulders and move on when their merchandise disappeared in transit. They came looking for their missing goods ... and the thief who stole them. Unfortunately, with Joe dead, Ruby was left to take his place in the crosshairs.

Claire saw no signs of life. The only sound she heard was the rat-a-tat-tat of a woodpecker echoing down through the canyon behind the park.

Making sure the ladder rested securely against the roof, Claire started up the rungs. She took it slow, not wanting to copycat Gramps's acrobatic routine and end up sharing that hanger he used as a leg scratcher.

Not to mention there might be a baby bouncing around inside of her. She stuffed that little worry back under the rug and returned her focus to Ruby's dead husband.

According to Joe's crazy ex-wife, Sophy, he transported the stolen goods and stored them here in Jackrabbit Junction, aka the dusty underbelly of nowhere, until the law cooled down and stopped sniffing in corners. Then he would deliver the pieces to the eager buyer, collect his substantial transportation fee, and count his wad of bills while whistling all the way home. Claire had adlibbed that last part, but it was not hard to imagine Joe and his fat, greedy, sausage fingers tainting everything they touched, including Ruby.

At the roofline, Claire placed Chester's binoculars on the shingles, making sure they did not tip over or slide. She would never hear the end of it from the old blowhard if she broke his Babe-o-matics, as he liked to call his tool for spying on women from afar.

She stepped onto the roof, staying low behind the apex.

Kate didn't get it. She lived in a world where the worst thing that happened was the heel breaking on one of her designer shoes. Unlike Claire, she hadn't had a gun pointed at her head, hadn't witnessed a man get his brains blown out, hadn't even come close to being shot. Maybe Kate had spent a night or two in jail for a traffic misdemeanor or possession of stolen property, but those were more frustrating than heart stopping.

"I'm not obsessed, Kate," Claire said under her breath, scooping up the binoculars. "I'm just aware." Aware of how valuable the pieces were that Claire kept finding tucked away in hiding spots ever since she'd arrived at the Dancing Winnebagos R.V. Park this last spring.

Claire crouched as she neared the apex of the roof, keeping down enough to remain hidden from the other side.

Dropping onto her knees, her thoughts returned to the stashes of goods that she had found over the last few months. Lord only knew what else Joe had buried around the place. She was not alone in her knuckle chewing, either. Weeks ago, when she had asked Ruby if she had considered that there might be more things hidden, the older woman's brow had knitted into a tight weave.

"I thought I knew Joe," Ruby had said in her soft drawl, "but in the last few months, you showed me an all new, dirty, rotten, no-good bastard."

Ruby had confided to Claire that she was starting to think the safest course for her and Jess and Gramps would be to sell the R.V. park and her surrounding mines and then head north to Nemo, South Dakota and the house Gramps had left behind. "But if somethin' bad happened to the new owners because of Joe's big ol' mess, how could I live with that?"

It was the pinch of fear on Ruby's face, along with the vulnerability in her tone, that had Claire determined not to lower her guard, to keep digging for answers. Ever since that fateful day when Claire had applied for a job at the R.V. park and had ended up fixing Ruby's leaky bathroom faucet, Ruby had demonstrated a faith in her that no one in her family had ever shown. Because of that fact alone Claire would continue to help Ruby, come hell, a shotgun toting bitch, high raging waters, or a pissy sister and grouchy grandfather.

Lying flat, she scooted closer to the apex of the roof and raised the binoculars, searching the archaeologists' compound. Today was the first time the whole crew had caravanned over to the Lucky Monk dig site. Usually one or two of the students stayed back in the head archaeologist's camper. According to Jess, whom Claire had bribed with a ten-dollar bill to knock on the door and play curious kid, they were recording all sorts of "boring stuff" in notebooks and on laptops in there.

Today, after escaping the farce going on up at Ruby's, Claire had taken the long way around to the restroom worksite. She had zigzagged through their group of tents and R.V.s wielding a forked stick while pretending to inspect the patches of dry grass for snakes.

Stealing peeks out from under her Mighty Mouse cap, she had not seen a single curtain flutter or tent flap move, nor had she heard a sound coming from any of the campers or seen any signs of life when peering through the windows. But this time she was going to play it safe. She was damned if she was going to get caught snooping again. The end result last time had almost made her wet her pants.

From her perch on the roof, she scanned the area once more. Double-checking the routes to and from the General Store, she mentally crossed off the list of possible troublemakers. She had left Mac busy pawing the ground around Jess's father up at the house while Manny and Chester watched and Deborah and Jess fretted. On her way out the door, she had run into Natalie, who had been happy to escape the family drama and drive to Yuccaville on a fool's errand. Gramps and Ruby had disappeared from the face of the earth, along with Mabel, so Claire assumed they were off plotting the best way to drag Jess's dad to the edge of town and threaten his hide if he dared set foot in the R.V. park again. Kate's car was also gone and so was Ronnie. Knowing both of her sisters as she did, their running in the midst of a shitstorm did not even make her blink.

With everyone preoccupied elsewhere and the archaeology camp a ghost town, it was now or never. Claire slid back to the ladder and hurried to the ground.

After one last glance around the area, she tugged her cap lower and jogged from tree to tree. That was her first mistake, because by the time she made it to the nearest of the four campers, she was huffing and puffing like she intended to blow their flimsy walls down. She waited a minute for her breath to return to normal, and then inched up to the camper closest to her—the beige one she'd seen the beanpole kid enter several times since she'd first laid eyes on him last week.

The door was unlocked.

She glanced around, her heart hammering away. Was she being set up? She knocked and waited.

Nobody answered.

She opened the door and stepped inside, setting foot in a vast sea of beige. From the walls to the furniture to the carpet, everything blended together like a big pool of oatmeal. The faint smell of baby powder and gardenias added the only pizzazz to the place.

Not wasting any time looking for color, Claire made a beeline to the back of the R.V. and found a bedroom with tan curtains and a matching bedspread. She opened and closed drawers and closet doors full of khaki colored shirts and pants for women, judging from the pleats on both. This camper must belong to the two women who were trying to enlist Jess to help at the dig site.

A quick peek in the dresser drawers came up empty. Hell, even their underwear and bras were beige. Manny would be so disappointed. He was going to lose his bet with Chester—the two women were not sex kittens in disguise, not with those control top bloomers.

Claire moved to the tiny bathroom, frowning at the beige

toilet lid and shower curtain. Sheesh. Their interior decorator must have been allergic to rainbows.

The kitchen cupboards and dining storage area gave away no clues, everything tidy and organized. Too organized. Something was not normal about these women. This place had serial killer written all over it.

Inside one cupboard a map of a section of the Lucky Monk mine had been taped to the door. The main adit with several drift spurs shooting from it was shown. The dig site was circled at the bottom left. Little red triangles and green circles had been drawn on it, indicating what, Claire had no idea. There was no map key listed, not that she'd expected an X to mark any treasures and skulls and crossbones to designate the areas to beware of, but it would have been nice. If she'd been thinking ahead, she would've borrowed Mac's cell phone to snap pictures to study later.

After one last look around the whitish brown wonderland, she slipped out of the camper and re-entered the world of dusty green, burnt orange, and cobalt blue.

Skirting the back bumper, Claire tiptoed to the next R.V. This one had a bright red striped awning—there was hope for it already.

The door was locked this time. Why? Was there something worth hiding inside?

She circled the camper, noticing an open window near the back end. Going for her ladder would take too long, so she grabbed one of the aluminum lawn chairs from under the awning and set it up under the window. She unwound the binoculars from her neck and set them on the ground.

After one more check to make sure the coast was still clear, she climbed onto the chair. The screen had dust caked in the little squares, making it hard to see inside. She pulled the screwdriver from her back pocket and popped it off.

There, much clearer. She shoved the screwdriver back in her pocket. But she could use a little more height. Balancing on the chair's aluminum arms, she stood up on her tiptoes. The flimsy metal contraption creaked under her tennis shoes.

Inside, the bed was a mess of sheets and clothes. A musty, almost rancid smell seeped past her, making her grimace. What was living in this camper? A yeti?

There was a plain, unmarked box on the dresser in front of her, blocking the rest of the room. She tried to move it aside, but it was just out of her reach.

With a small jump, she managed to pull herself up, locking her forearms so she could teeter forward and in. Unfortunately, gravity and the two MoonPies she had inhaled after breakfast weighed on her ass end like the anvil the Roadrunner was always dropping on Wile E. Coyote. She began to teeter backwards.

She tried to get a toe hold on the back of the chair but kicked it over instead.

"Shit!"

Her forearms burned. She made a desperate flail inside with one hand and managed to hook the other edge of the dresser. Grunting, she let go of the sill with her other hand and grasped the dresser with both hands. The sill dug into her hip bones, her bottom half hanging out the window.

One more heave and she would be inside. Taking a deep breath, she started to pull her lower body through the window. They always made this look so easy in movies.

A hand grabbed onto the waistband of her jeans, yanking her backward.

She let out a yelp of surprise. Her grip slipped off the front edge of the dresser, one of her hands bumping the box, sending it crashing to the floor. She flailed, her fingernails raking over the dresser top and coming up empty.

She scraped backwards out the window, her shirt riding up, her stomach and ribs losing a layer of skin. Two hands grasped her by the hips, tugging and lifting. She banged the inside of her elbow on the bottom sill as she lost the battle and rattled out a string of curses that would have made Chester grin.

Then her feet were back on solid earth.

She found her balance and whirled around, her ribs, elbow, and ego all bruised and throbbing. Mac matched her glare with one of his own for several seconds.

"Damn it, Mac." Claire smacked his chest for emphasis. "You scared the hell out of me."

"Good." He caught her hand and held tight. "I hope you replace the vacancy it left behind with some common sense."

"I have plenty of common sense." She tried to pull her hand free.

"Really? Because when I saw your butt hanging out of that window, I experienced some serious doubts."

She tugged again and he let go. Nudging her aside, he picked up the lawn chair and set it back under the awning, and then he popped the screen back into place. Before she could come up with a logical explanation for her previous predicament, he grabbed her by the wrist and dragged her over to the park's drive.

She played mule and dug in her heels, pulling him to a stop. "Mac, what are you doing?"

"Rescuing the damsel in distress before she gets busted for breaking and entering."

"I wasn't breaking and entering."

He snorted. "So you just accidentally ended up dangling out of the camper window?"

"I was checking to see if anyone was home when the chair sort of slipped out from under me."

His laughter echoed across the campground, silencing a mourning dove that was coahh-coo-cooing down by Jackrabbit Creek. "I suppose the screen *sort of* fell off, too."

She crossed her arms over her chest, not liking his smartass tone one bit. "Something like that."

"What about Chester's binoculars?" His gaze zeroed in on where the Babe-o-matics lay in the dry grass below the window. "Let me guess, you were going to take a break from working on the restrooms this afternoon and do some bird watching in the canyon."

"Maybe I was."

"I'm not buying your snake oil, Slugger." He stalked over and scooped up the binoculars.

"What? I took a class on ornithology once. It fulfilled a biology elective."

His brow all crinkled, he handed her the binoculars. "You're something, Claire." Only the way he said it did not sound like he meant a good something.

Before she could ask him to clarify, he crunched off down the drive heading toward the store.

Claire frowned back at the camper she had been checking out. This was her golden opportunity to do some reconnaissance. But to what end? Her suspicions about the archaeology crew were based mostly on her own conspiracy theories, none of which would make Sheriff Harrison lift an eyebrow, let alone a finger.

When she looked back at Mac, he was still trucking along. Growling under her breath, she trotted after him. "Mac, wait!"

He stopped and waited for her to catch up. His hazel eyes were guarded as she approached him, his lips all thin, his jaw clenched tight. She knew that stormy look. It was usually followed by a bolt of frustration from one of them that sparked an argument. Claire tried to blow away the building thunderclouds with some light breezy joking.

"Am I a good something or a bad something?" she asked with a smile.

"I don't know." He did not smile back. "The jury is still out." He started walking again.

"What!" She poked him in the ribs, trying some playful teasing to dissipate the pressure building between them. "Why? Just because you get a little squeamish when I'm investigating a possible crime site?"

"I do not get squeamish."

"Then why were you sweating when we sneaked into Sophy's house last spring?"

Mac flashed her a scowl. "It was over a hundred degrees in there that day."

"More like mid-nineties."

"I was also concerned about getting shot. Trespassing isn't taken lightly in this part of the country. I would've hoped you'd figured that out by now, but your stunt back there at the camper is giving me doubts."

Claire shrugged. "I'm a slow learner."

"No, you're too smart for your own good."

She took that as a compliment and ignored the jab mixed in it. Catching his hand, she laced her fingers through his. "Have I told you lately that I love you?"

"You're so full of shit." His words were edged with laughter, the storm beginning to dissolve.

"What?" She bumped him sideways with her shoulder. "I mean that."

He reached over and pulled her hat brim down. "Then why did you leave me at the house with that asshole?"

She adjusted her hat. "You know Mom's bark is worse than her bite."

He laughed. "I meant Jess's dad."

"Oh, yeah. I'd forgotten about him."

"I guess it's to be expected that he slipped from your mind being that you were in the midst of planning how to commit your next felony."

"It wasn't like that." Well, not completely like that, anyway. She hadn't put thought into the actual act of entering the R.V.s until after she had left the house.

He stopped and swung her around to look up at him. "What was it like then, Claire? Because I'm going home now, and I won't be here to save your ass from landing in jail or something worse next time."

She blinked in surprise. What did he mean he was going home? "You're going back to Tucson?" At his nod, she asked, "Now? Why?"

"There's no room for me here."

"Does Chester have a date tonight?"

"I'm not talking about Chester's couch. I mean in general." He glanced back toward the store. "With your family everywhere, there's no place for me." His tone was matter of fact.

She sighed. "Listen, Mac, if this is about Ronnie ..."

"It's not about Ronnie, Claire." His gaze locked onto hers, all jest gone from his expression. "It's about you."

"Me?" She took a step backward. "What did I do?"

His eyelids lowered, his eyes shifting down to the left. "Nothing. Not a single thing." He pulled his hand free from hers and took off walking again.

She did not let him get far before hooking his arm and dragging anchor until he turned hard a-starboard. "Is this about the pocket watch?"

He extracted his arm from her grip. "Contrary to what you seem to think, not everything revolves around that damned watch." He and Kate could have sung a duet on that subject.

She shoved her hands in her front pockets, trying to read him and coming up blank. "But I don't want you to go home yet."

"You're busy working. I don't need to be here to watch you finish that building. Your grandfather and his cronies are doing a bang-up job of doing that without me."

"I'm not busy all of the time."

"Really?" He crossed his arms over his chest, rocking back on his heels. "I've been here since yesterday morning and seen you how much?"

The undercurrent of frustration in his voice gave her pause. After all of the overtime he had been putting in at his job, leaving her alone with Ronnie evening after evening back home in Tucson, she wanted to stomp on his toes. "What about last night?"

"You mean when *I* went looking for *you* at The Shaft?"

Her jaw jutted. "I called you before that to come have a burger with me, but you were too busy playing cards."

"Not by choice."

"Oh, I see. So Manny had your arm twisted while Chester sat on you and forced your hand."

His eyes hardened. "No, Claire, I stayed because Ruby asked me not to go until your mother went to bed. Since you and your sisters weren't there to help deal with Deborah, I agreed."

Claire grimaced, his words fueling the guilt trip she had been on since she and Natalie had come up with that lame excuse to go to Yuccaville yesterday instead of having lunch with her mother. Stopping at The Shaft on the way home had been a weasel's way out of dealing with her overbearing mother's need to point out Claire's lack of a steady paycheck, and staying until the she-beast had bedded down for the night, a cowardly solution.

"You're right." She blew out a breath, lowering her gaze. "I was only thinking of saving my own bacon. It was selfish and immature."

"Slugger," he lifted her chin, his face not so rigid. "I understand. Your mother takes great pleasure in pecking at you."

"I should carry chicken feed in my pocket at all times."

His lips twitched as he towed her closer. "It doesn't help that you're living with me, her least favorite person on the planet second only to my aunt."

He was forgetting about Claire's father. He trumped Ruby and then some.

"My mother can kiss my ass," she said under her breath.

Mac lifted off her hat and then brushed his lips across hers, flirting. "I love it when you whisper sweet words like that in my ear."

"Stay here tonight and I'll whisper a few more things." She pulled him down, looping her arms around his neck, breathing in the fresh scent of his sun warmed skin. Mac always smelled like the desert, a pheromone-fueled mix of sage and mesquite with an underlying hint of something spicy and erotic. Pushing up onto her tiptoes, she kissed him good and proper, teasing him with her tongue, hinting at what could be.

His hands trailed down her ribs, landing on her hips where they held tight for several seconds before rounding over her bottom. "You play dirty," he said against her mouth and then gripped her through her jeans.

"Yeah, but you like it dirty." She ran her mouth along his jaw and nipped his earlobe. When she finished her seduction attempt, she drew back enough to stare into his eyes, imploring. "Stay with me, Mac."

He placed her hat back on her head. "And spend another night on Chester's couch? I don't think so, sweetheart." He trailed his thumb down her cheek and then pulled away, putting some air between them. "Besides, I got a call from work. They need me to be down at the job site south of Tucson by five tomorrow morning. Tonight, I'm sleeping in my own bed."

Claire snorted. "What's so important about building a freaking wall that you have to be there at the butt crack of dawn?"

He cocked his head to the side, his forehead creasing. "You do realize that my job as a geotechnician entails more than just laying bricks, right?"

"Yeah, yeah, yeah." They'd had this conversation too many times to count. When he continued frowning at her, she added. "It's just that I need you here."

"To drag you out of windows?"

"To help me protect Ruby and Gramps."

"That's what they have firearms for."

"What if that's not enough?"

"If this is about someone stealing that pocket watch ..."

"It's not about the damned watch!" Claire would just as soon throw that thing down a mine shaft and be done with it if that would solve the real problem. "It's about what's behind the stupid thing and all of the other hidden treasures Joe buried in this damned desert."

He rubbed the back of his neck, looking like he was considering the legitimacy of her concern, and then shook his head.

"Mac, you know I'm onto something here."

"Maybe, but I wish you weren't." He grimaced in the direction of the archaeology crew's cluster of campers. "Why were you trying to break into that R.V.?"

She opted to keep quiet about sneaking into the first R.V. for now. What Mac didn't know would not hurt him or give him reason to speculate on her soundness of mind any further. "I have a gut feeling."

He groaned. "I don't like your gut feelings, Claire. They usually get one of us almost killed."

Ignoring that comment, she explained further, "I think one or more of those archaeology students is up to something."

"As in something to do with the pocket watch?"

"No. Maybe." She kicked at a few loose pebbles of gravel. "I don't know."

"Keep talking."

"I think they found something in the Lucky Monk besides the artifacts from the ruins, something Joe left behind."

Doubt rippled over his features. "I've been in that mine many times, Claire. I even mapped it."

"I know."

"Besides the dead guy, some big spiders, and the burial site stuff, there was only porphyry granite, copper, several pockets of turquoise, a few veins of amethyst, some malachite, and rats."

Claire fought the urge to roll her eyes at his detailed analysis. She stepped closer, lowering her voice even though their only audience was the grasshoppers bouncing around their feet. "Natalie overheard one of them on the phone last night."

One of his honey-brown eyebrows lifted. "Was she listening outside the camper window you were trying to crawl into?"

"No. She'd forgotten her socket set at the new building. With all of these strangers around, she didn't want to leave it there overnight, so she walked back to get it and heard someone talking behind the back wall—the one without plumbing that we have partially finished. She was minding her own business, but then she heard him say something about a cache of artifacts being extremely valuable followed by the words 'black market.'"

"Maybe he is in charge of getting the dig site finds safely back to the university and is worried about someone greedy getting their hands on them."

"That was Natalie's first thought, too." Claire shoved her hands in her back pockets. "She's not as suspicious as me."

He chuckled. "Most of us don't have Nancy Drew fantasies."

"Manny and Chester do."

"I said, 'most.'" He crossed his arms over his chest. "So that's all you have on this guy?"

"There's more. He caught Natalie eavesdropping."

"Then what? Did he threaten her?"

"He hung up."

Mac let out a *hmfff*. "Claire, that hardly adds up to a suspicion that he's planning to sell artifacts from the site on the black market."

"Maybe not, but we have no idea what this guy is capable of and now he knows Natalie might be a problem."

His eyes narrowed. "I can see where this is going, Claire, and I don't like it. Promise me you'll try not to get into trouble while I'm gone."

She crossed her fingers behind her back. "I promise."

He tipped his head to the side. "You're crossing your fingers back there, aren't you?"

Claire smiled. "Call me when you get home."

Chapter Eight

In her hurry to escape the two men in the black sedan, Ronnie had stumbled into a bigger problem inside the Mule Train Diner.

All around her, pictures and paintings of mules hung on the walls. Sculptures and miniatures of the stubborn animal lined shelves nailed up high here and there. Even the tablecloths had cute versions of the beasts of burden on them. There were mules everywhere, including sitting at the table in front of her, demanding she sit in the chair he had kicked out and join him.

With his whiskey-colored eyes scrunched into a wary glare, Sheriff Hardass watched her like he thought she might turn tail and bolt at any moment. But the high and mighty lawman did not realize with whom he was dealing. After being grilled repeatedly by a dizzying number of investigators from multiple law enforcement branches of the U.S. government about Lyle Jefferson's many illegal activities, one Sheriff from Po-dunkville, Arizona did not have a chance at winning a standoff against her.

Acting all prim and proper, Ronnie tucked in her skirt and lowered into the seat waiting for her as if she had not recently been playing hide and seek with a couple of boogeymen. She laced her fingers together and rested them on the table, adopting the same stiff-backed stance she had in each interrogation months ago.

She nodded and smiled at an older couple who passed by their table on the way out the door, leaving her and the Sheriff alone except for a grizzled, gray haired old guy at the counter.

Sheriff Hardass's stare did not waver. Was he even blinking? The thought of reaching across the table and flicking him on that slightly crooked nose of his made a giggle bubble up in Ronnie's throat. She coughed it back down and glanced at the remains of his sandwich.

"As eating joints go in this corner of the state," she said, her voice steady, "the Mule Train Diner appears to be a step above the rest. You come here often, Sheriff?"

He nodded once.

She detected a hint of his bay rum cologne over the aroma of fresh baked bread, noticing his freshly shaved jaw. Did he smell that good all over? Her brain digressed, painting a picture of him dressed in only a towel while he rubbed cologne on his skin. *Whoa!* Where had that come from? She blinked away the image before he figured out what she was picturing and arrested her for having lewd and lascivious thoughts.

"How are their doughnuts?" She could not resist a little jab.

"Nonexistent."

"You could threaten the owner with jail time if he doesn't change the menu to accommodate you." She landed a second jab, still sore about his comment last night regarding making room in his jail cells for her family of outlaws.

"I already tried that and it backfired."

Ronnie could not tell if he were joking or not. "Really? How?"

"She told on me to my mother and I got chewed out for harassing my sister."

"Your sister?"

"Yeah. She's the owner."

Behind the rigid smile on her face, Ronnie cringed. Of all of the mule joints in all of the dust-bunny towns out West, Ronnie had stumbled into the Sheriff's sister's restaurant. Damn.

Claire would have laughed her ass off if she had been sitting there next to Ronnie. Then again, Claire would not have hidden in this diner from those two goons. She would have grabbed a baseball bat and chased after their sedan, probably ending up staring at Sheriff Hardass through the bars of a jail cell.

When Ronnie grew up and had untangled herself from this makeshift noose Lyle had wrapped around her neck, she wanted to be as carefree and reckless as her middle sister. She was tired of always being the proper and responsible one in the family. Look where it had landed her—sitting in a diner full of mules with the law breathing down her neck.

"Maybe you should say 'pretty please' when you ask your sister for a doughnut," Ronnie suggested.

"Those two words aren't in my vocabulary."

No shit. She leveled her chin at the Sheriff. "If we're about done here, Sheriff Harrison," she started, enunciating his name for her own sake, not wanting to drag this out any longer with insubordination.

"We're not," he interrupted and leaned forward, resting his elbows on the table.

If he was waiting for her to sit there and sing like a canary for him, his sandwich was going to go stale. She raised her eyebrows. "Well, speak now or forever hold your peace."

His lips twitched. "I always keep a firm grip on my piece, Mrs. Jefferson."

She found his attempt to embarrass her with a double entendre cute at best. But after the humiliation of finding out that Lyle had planted a hidden security camera in their bedroom and some of the federal investigators had taken a peek at several of the episodes starring Ronnie with her favorite intimate massage device, which she fondly had referred to as *Raphael* at the top of her lungs during the filming, this was child's play.

She leaned forward and lowered her voice. "I have a pair of tweezers you can borrow if it will help."

The widening of his eyes showed her that she had hit his battleship. Now to sink the sucker and be on her merry way.

Sitting back upright, she smiled big and bright. "Sheriff Harrison, if you have something you would like to ask me, can we please get to it. I have somewhere I need to be." As in the inside of a glass of gin and tonic while sitting on a bar stool at The Shaft, but he didn't need to know that.

His jaw stiffened so fast she checked his cheeks for stress fractures. "Where is your husband, Mrs. Jefferson?"

Oh, crap. She didn't want him digging up what she had tried so hard to bury since coming down to Arizona. Holding onto her smile for dear life, she used the standard answer she'd been using since she had said, "I do," all of those wasted years ago. "He's away on business."

"What kind of business?"

"The kind involving travel."

He sat back, crossing his arms over his chest. "You pawned your wedding ring set."

There was no use denying it. She had blabbed that on their first meeting. "I did."

"I take it the travel business is not going well for your husband."

"I wouldn't know. I haven't talked to him in a while."

Except for that one collect phone call she had accepted before heading to Arizona when Lyle had warned her about the possible price on her head, she had only spoken to the son of a bitch through her lawyer.

"Surely he has some way of being reached while traveling."

There was a cocky glint in his eyes that made Ronnie want to lean over the table and bite his head right off. "Sheriff, what is the point of these questions?"

He shrugged, his shiny star bobbing along with his shoulders. "I'm just trying to figure out your next move, Mrs. Jefferson."

"I'll save you the trouble." She jabbed her thumb behind her. "I'm heading right out that door." And out of his life, if possible.

"What about that black Bonneville?"

"Bonneville?" She played dumb to buy a moment. Double crap! Of course he had not missed that detail. She must have been as obvious as a cat on the ceiling in her panic stricken state.

"Yes. The one you were hiding from when you ran in here."

"Oh, that black car."

"Yes, that one." When she didn't expound on her answer, he raised both brows. "Well, Mrs. Jefferson?"

"You can call me, Veronica, Sheriff."

"So you've said."

"Yet you continue not to."

"I prefer to keep your current status in the forefront of my mind when in your presence."

"And what status is that?"

"A married woman on the run from her husband."

Her throat constricted, making her cough. She stole his drink, letting the cool water relax the tightness threatening to choke her.

Well, he was right about one part of that. She was on the

run.

"What I want to know is if you are running because of something he did."

She licked her lips and set his glass back down. "An interesting question," she said. He had hit the bullseye with that one, sort of.

"Or was it something you have done?"

The only thing she had done was listen to her mother about marrying a "real gentleman" who would treat her like a queen. In the end, it turned out she was treated more like a high-priced whore that he cowered behind when the devil came calling to collect on outstanding debts.

She squared her shoulders, months of anger and frustration welling up in her gut. "I am sorry to disappoint you, Sheriff, but you're sniffing around the wrong tree."

"I don't think so, Mrs. Jefferson. There is something going on with you that feels not quite right." He dug in his pocket and pulled out his wallet. "You know I thought you had a screw loose when I pulled you over the other day." He tossed several bills on the table. "But then you came running in here today with a look on your face that said otherwise."

"And what look was that?"

"The look of a woman in deep sh—trouble," he corrected at the last moment.

No, he was right the first time, she was in deep shit. Over her head in it, to be truthful. But it was her shit, and he needed to keep his crooked nose out of it.

She stood, slinging Kate's backpack over her shoulder. "You are mistaken, Sheriff."

"About which part?"

"Well, I am a woman."

His gaze held hers, steady as a riverboat gambler. "Yeah, I noticed that."

"It's good to hear that you're not completely comprised of stone."

"You think I'm made of stone?"

"I do. It explains how you can see a woman who you think is in deep shit and yet still give her a speeding ticket and then threaten her with jail time."

"You are hardly a sad, helpless waif, Mrs. Jefferson."

"You're right. That being said, I would appreciate it if you'd let me go on my way and take care of my own difficulties without interfering."

His grin came slow and sat crooked on his lips. "But it's my job to interfere. I believe you mentioned last night that as a tax-paying citizen, you are compensating me to do just that."

Damn, he got her on that one.

He pointed at the bag she was holding. "What's in the backpack?"

"Library books," she lied without a hitch.

"I didn't realize you were a card-carrying member of the Yuccaville branch of the Cholla County Public Library."

"I'm returning them for my sister."

He smirked. "Claire found a way to sneak books out after being banned?"

It figured he knew about that, too. "No, Katie's taken up reading."

"Really? What kind of books does she like to read?"

"Ones with a lot of pictures of the latest fashion designs."

His gaze measured her up and down. She must have added up to the right numbers because he nodded, seeming to accept what she said at face value.

"If you're done with your questions now, Sheriff, I'll be on my way." She started backing toward the door.

"Sure, but don't get too comfortable, *Veronica*." His use of her first name did not go unnoticed, nor his threat. "You and I are far from being done with this subject."

"That's just peachy, *Grady*." She needed to thank Mac for helping level the playing field on the name game. "Because I do so enjoy our little conversations." She glanced down at the table where his belt buckle was in view. "Be sure to let me know if you need to borrow my tweezers."

With a wink and a coy smile, she bowed her way out the door and practically ran back to Katie's car. Her breathing did not slow until she had reached the city limits at the edge of Yuccaville.

"Great," she growled and hit the steering wheel with the heel of her hand. "Just fucking great."

Now she had the damned Sheriff of Cholla County riding her ass, too. Who was next? Jabba the Hutt and his slew of intergalactic bounty hunters?

"Claire," Ruby called from the front of the unfinished restrooms.

Lowering the torch she was using to finish soldering an elbow joint onto a copper pipe, Claire looked over her shoulder.

The older woman leaned against the roughed out door frame, holding bottles of soda pop in each hand. "Why don't you take a rest for the evenin', mosey on out here, and share a drink with me for a spell?"

There was a hardness in Ruby's soft drawl that made Claire take a closer look at her step-grandmother. Maybe it was the brassy orange tint coming from the sun as it sank toward the horizon, or the after effect of staring at the hot end of a blowtorch for too long, but Ruby seemed worn, faded into a dull sepia version of her vibrant self.

Deborah's presence usually had a way of making Ruby spit and sputter, bringing her fiery temperament out. Tonight Ruby's white and blue checkered shirt had deep wrinkles set in it, her red hair spiraled out of the clip she had holding it back, and her smile sort of drooped at the outer edges.

The fact that she had come bearing one of Claire's favorite drinks made her stomach jittery, like it was full of short-horned grasshoppers. Ruby knew she preferred to dilute bad news with heavy-duty carbohydrates.

Ruby held up the bottles. "It's not quite as good as what's on tap down at The Shaft, but I promise not to act like one of those yokels and invite ya out to my truck to diddle with my bits."

Claire grinned and turned off the torch, setting it on the concrete floor. "You mean fondle your drill bits," she repeated one of the many corny pickup lines that she had heard since frequenting The Shaft. "Give me a minute to put away my tools and clean up."

"I'll be sittin' over where the boys usually do."

Gramps and his cronies had grown bored with watching Claire plumb in the warmer than normal afternoon heat and had headed off to the rec room to play some cards in the air conditioning. With the three of them no longer harassing her about the way she was soldering each joint, she was able to make twice as much progress. But she still had another couple of days left of plumbing work before she had the pipes for the showers and toilets ready for final installation.

After doing a quick clean up and stuffing anything worth stealing into her toolbox, she headed out into the evening's warm breeze and dropped onto the lawn chair next to Ruby.

She noticed a dusty patch of flour on her step-grandmother's shoulder. Crud. Ruby had been baking—even in this heat. The older woman had a bad habit of mixing delicious concoctions of flour and butter and sugar when stressed, and Claire had a butt-widening habit of eating at least two of everything Ruby pulled out of the oven. Her jeans couldn't handle another couple of weeks of Deborah hanging around, getting Ruby all worked up into a Julia Child frenzy again. It had taken Claire three weeks to lose the ten pounds she'd gained the last time Deborah had stormed into town.

Leaning back in Chester's chair, Claire tipped up the bottle Ruby handed her. The first mouthful of Coke washed away the taste of solder smoke.

"Where's Natalie?" Ruby asked, taking a sip from her own bottle.

"She had to run to Yuccaville. A couple of the J-boxes cracked while she was nailing them in place. Plus, some of the wire had splits in the casing." Creekside Hardware Store down in Jackrabbit Junction closed early on Sundays, so Natalie had to head up the road to the mining town where a national chain hardware store stayed open until dark every day of the week.

"Do you think someone messed with our supplies on purpose?" Ruby asked.

Claire did a double take. Was Ruby getting as paranoid as she was? "Nah. Extreme heat for a prolonged period can do that to the wire casing and make the plastic on the J-box brittle. Nat figures Creekside had the supplies sitting in the sun for too long at some point, either outside or in their front window."

"Oh. Good."

"Natalie said she'd stop at The Shaft on the way back to eat with Kate during her break, so I don't expect her back until later."

Considering that several of The Shaft's male clientele had been trying to use free drink offers to coerce Natalie into playing pool the last time Claire was there with her, she wouldn't be surprised if Natalie sneaked in with her work boots in her hands and her underwear tucked in her back pocket long after everyone else had crashed. A single woman with Natalie's good looks and long legs drew men like fruit flies to a ripe, juicy peach. While Natalie had been avoiding men since her arrival for some unspoken reason, Claire knew her cousin well—abstinence did not make Natalie's heart grow fonder. It only lowered her scruples and resulted in bad bedfellows and horrible hangovers.

Ruby took another sip, her green eyes creased and somber in thought as she gazed across the campground.

Shifting in her chair, Claire stretched her legs out in front of her, resting one tennis shoe on the upside down five-gallon bucket her grandfather used as a footstool. "Where's Gramps?"

Was he still playing cards in the rec room? Was he smoking a cigar? Did he have something to do with the reason for Ruby's visit?

"He's runnin' the store." Ruby squeezed the back of her neck, but she still held back from sharing what had her all bunched up in the shoulders.

A thought hit Claire, almost taking her breath away. She jackknifed upright. "Is everything okay with Mac? Did he call to say he made it home okay?"

"Yep. He told me to let you know he's fixin' to call you tomorrow night when he gets home from work."

Whew! Claire relaxed back into the lawn chair again. Her world returned to its regular programming. Maybe she would borrow Natalie's cell phone later and whisper some more sweet nothings in his ear.

Ruby sighed. "Claire, I have a problem and I need your help." The dam holding back whatever was bothering her had finally given way.

Just one problem? From where Claire sat, Ruby had a shitload of them. "What's Mom doing now?"

Ruby waved in the air. "Deborah is a pain in my ass, but she's not a threat."

A threat? Had Claire's nightmare finally come true and another one of Joe's not-so-chummy buddies contacted Ruby about wanting his share of the fenced goods back "or else"?

Claire stuffed a sock in the mouth of the panicky voice yelling in her head about the sky falling. Tapping her bottle against her inner thigh she waited for Ruby to explain more about this threat.

"My problem has to do with my baby girl."

Claire's heartbeat returned to its steady chug-chug. What a relief. It was just Jessica again. She wondered what the kid had done now. In the few months Claire had known the teenaged spitfire, Jessica had caused some whopper headaches for her mother.

"I need you to do me a favor." Ruby turned her creased

forehead in Claire's direction.

"Sure."

"You should probably hear me out before you agree, honey." Ruby patted her knee. "I'm not real proud about this, but I'm at the end of my rope here."

Short of killing or dismembering someone, Claire still stood by her "sure" response. Although, using Ruby's shotgun to dismember a few of the vulgar jerks at The Shaft might not be such a bad idea, like that fake cowboy with the fancy new hat and big ugly mouth from the other night. If Claire ran into him again she couldn't be held responsible for where her knee decided to plant itself.

Ruby finished her bottle and set it down on the gravel, staring out at the twilight filled R.V. park. "I hate to ask this of ya, but I need you to keep a close eye on Jessica."

Babysit a teenager? Claire had suffered through worse jobs, like that veterinarian at the dog kennel who'd assigned her the task of expressing anal glands. One dog later and Claire had been sitting back in the unemployment office with a number in her chapped hands.

"Also," Ruby added with a grimace, "I want you to find out what sort of things she's tellin' her daddy."

Claire planted her elbows on her knees, letting her almost empty bottle dangle between her legs. It was her turn to stare out across the campground with a wrinkled brow. "You think Jess said something to him about that stash of cash we found?"

It wouldn't make Claire blink twice if Jess had told. The girl's filter seemed to be permanently damaged, letting secrets leak out here, there, and everywhere. Then again, maybe Jess was too naïve to realize the trouble her chattering could get her family into thanks to Joe's long history of thieving hands.

"That and then some," Ruby said, her voice edged with a growl. "I think the reason that horse's ass is finally visitin' his daughter is because there's money to be swindled. Of course I can't even look at the guy funny or my daughter will crawl down my throat for trying to ruin what she thinks is the best thing since bubblegum was invented."

Claire would have to make sure to keep her mouth shut about Jessica's father when the teenager was within hearing distance.

Ruby continued, "His wife left him, ya know. Then he went and lost his job and pissed away his savings bettin' on dog races."

How did Ruby know that? Who was her source?

"I'm ninety-nine percent certain the lousy rat is here because he caught a whiff of some cheese, and now he's gonna try to take every piece he can get his damned hands on."

"Has he asked you for money outright?"

Ruby shook her head. "He knows better. But it's not my money that I'm worried about with him."

Claire shooed away a lingering fly. "You don't think Jess was silly enough to tell him about what's in the safe, do you?"

"Maybe. Maybe not. I figure that he's fixin' to line up something more long-term." She turned to Claire, her face creased with what looked like a volatile mix of heartache and fury. "I'm worried he's gonna try to steal my baby girl from me."

After years of pretty much ignoring every attempt Jess made to contact him, the ass had some nerve. She remembered her conversation with Gramps last week. "You're thinking this is all about getting child support, right?"

Ruby nodded. "He's not down here out of the goodness of his rotten heart. The way he's buying Jessica clothes and nail polish—did you see the cell phone he gave her? It's one of those smart ones. As if that child needs another distraction from her homework."

Claire could not help but notice the expensive phone earlier this afternoon when Jessica shoved it in her face and danced a jig in front of her.

"The son of a bitch knows I can afford to pay him

support now. If he can buy Jess from me with all of these trinkets, he'll drag me back to court quicker than beer turns to piss. With your grandfather's savings and that money we found, plus the value of my land, I'd bet my momma's lucky toad's foot that Jess's daddy is fixin' to really take me to the cleaners."

"Shit."

Claire had been so busy trying to figure out the history behind the pocket watch and Joe's other fenced treasures that she had not thought about how figuring out their value could screw Ruby financially in this whole other way. Her focus had been on the enemies they could not see, not those standing right in front of them, wooing Ruby's kid.

"Yeah, 'shit' sorta covers it and then some." Ruby lowered her head into her hands. "I can't lose Jessica, Claire," she said through her fingers. "That girl may push me to my limits some days, but she's all I've had for years." Her voice hitched. "During the tough times, when money was as scarce around here as a jackalope and keepin' my head out of the sand took all the gumption I could muster, her little freckled face kept me goin'. She was the sole reason I dragged my butt out of bed each morning and faced off with one creditor after another instead of scurrying down to Mexico for good. The notion of her bein' across the country from me turns my guts inside out."

Claire squeezed Ruby's shoulder, understanding why Mac dropped everything to help his aunt the few times she had broken down and asked. Seeing Ruby hurting like this made her want to grab a cannon and blow Jess's dad to smithereens.

"If he's planning to use Jess for child support," Claire said, "he'll probably revert to treating her like crap after he gets what he wants, too."

Ruby looked up at Claire with watery eyes. "You and I both know he doesn't care one lick about her. All she is to him is a cash cow."

Claire set her bottle on the ground and kicked it over.

"Makes me want to tie up the jerk, slather him in honey, and bury him up to his neck in one of those red ant hills back in the ravine."

Sniffing, Ruby dabbed at the corners of her eyes with the hem of her shirt. "I'd love to fill him full of buckshot for messin' with my kid's emotions like this, but your grandfather keeps hidin' all my shotgun shells." The fire was back in Ruby's voice, replacing the wavering pain.

Claire chuckled. "I'm happy to help you with Jess, Ruby. I don't want to see anything bad happen to her or you."

"There is one more thing." Ruby sniffed again, and then cleared her throat.

Claire picked up one of the other soda bottles Ruby had brought and opened it. "What's that?"

"There is a young man from the archaeology crew who has taken a shine to Jess."

"You mean that beanpole with the glasses and braces?" Claire had seen Jess and the skinny Mariachi lifeguard walking around the R.V. park's drive a couple of days ago, Jess's mouth running a mile a minute while the beanpole smiled down at her like a big goof.

Ruby smirked. "Yeah, the beanpole who just happens to be twenty years old and smokes a pack a day." When Claire shot her a raised eyebrow, Ruby shrugged. "I made him show me his I.D. to buy cigarettes."

Smart thinking. Claire could use a cigarette herself right about now, but she had made a bet with Gramps earlier this afternoon that she could hold out longer than he could for a cigar. Little did he know that she had extra motivation at the moment.

"Jessica thinks they are just friends," Ruby said. "But I've seen him watching her."

"You think he's stupid enough to make a move?" Statutory rape could lose him his pecker out here in a land full of shotguns, power tools, and over-protective old men.

"I don't know. But I think Jessica might be stupid enough

to get herself in a pickle and not have a way out."

After having had to get out of a pickle or two in her younger years, Claire could see that happening. Some boys did not like to be rejected, nor did they take kindly to a fist to the nose or a knee to the groin.

"I could see that happening with her," Claire said and tipped her drink.

What Claire did not bring up for Ruby to also worry about was that the twenty-year-old might have caught wind from Jess about the money and antiques her mom had stashed away in the house. His interest in Jess might go beyond boy-meets-girl. Claire would have to ask Natalie if Beanpole were the same one Nat had overheard talking on the phone last night. Maybe the artifacts he was planning to transfer were not from the Lucky Monk. Maybe they were from Ruby's basement.

Ruby stood and stretched. "I can't thank you enough for helping me, Claire. Jess thinks the world of you."

"She's a good kid."

"If she finds out you are ratting on her ..." Ruby trailed off.

"I know the risks, Ruby. I also know that Jess is a naïve teenager and I don't want to see her hurt—physically or emotionally. The poor kid's been jerked around by her frickin' father for too long. It's bullshit that he thinks he can come down here and steal her from you with a bunch of lies, expensive toys, and jewelry."

"Jess showed you the father-daughter heart necklace he got her, huh?"

She nodded, remembering the bright glow in Jess's eyes at the time and how it had made Claire's throat tight. The kid was so hungry for her father's love it was heartbreaking. "Was that a real emerald?"

Ruby's laugh was harsh. "I doubt it, but your mother made quite a commotion about it, goin' on about how your grandfather never did anything so nice for her."

It was no wonder Gramps's cheek had ticced this

afternoon when Manny asked if anyone knew how long Deborah planned to stay this time.

"Ruby, I'm sorry I left you alone with Mom last night." Claire had wanted to catch Ruby alone and apologize ever since Mac had made her feel like a heel earlier today.

"Honey, you don't need to babysit me when it comes to your momma."

"It's not babysitting. It's more like tag-teaming or forming a collective front."

She shook her head. "Your momma does have a way about her that could test the patience of one of those Himalayan monks. I don't know how your daddy dealt with her all of those years to be honest."

"He didn't. He avoided her." Thinking back, all of the overtime he had worked and late nights with his bowling buddies now made sense. The connection to Mac and his overtime since Ronnie had arrived on the scene would have been similar if it had not made Claire pace the bedroom floor more nights than not until he made it home.

"I suppose that's one thing I should thank Jess's dad for today."

Claire frowned up at Ruby. "What do you mean?"

"Steve and your momma."

"What about them?"

Ruby's brow lifted. "Your grandfather didn't tell you?"

"Tell me what?"

"Steve asked Deborah to dinner tonight. They were both dressed in their finest duds when they left for Yuccaville a couple of hours ago."

Groaning, Claire closed her eyes. Damn it! She should have seen this coming. Deborah had found a whole new way of making Ruby pay for marrying Gramps. She was going to charm the snake who was aiming to sink his fangs in Ruby's throat.

Chapter Nine

Tuesday, October 2nd

Two evenings later, Ronnie held down a bar stool at The Shaft, sharing a scarred wooden table with her sisters and Natalie. On the jukebox, the Dixie Chicks were ready to run. Ronnie knew that exact feeling clear down to her toes. She just needed to scrounge up a little cash first.

Claire and Natalie had wolfed down their burgers in record speed after building big appetites working long hours on the new restrooms for the last two days. They now lounged in their seats across from her, picking at the piles of French fries on their plates.

Ronnie preferred to drink her supper tonight, her worries ganging up on her stomach and pummeling it. She had almost gagged at the scent of cooked beef and fried potatoes when Katie's friend Arlene had delivered their food.

Katie pushed away her supper of peanuts and pretzels, turning down Arlene's second offer to have the cook grill her a cheeseburger.

"I'm not that hungry tonight," Katie explained, wiping the peanut shells off the table with the rag she had snagged from behind the bar.

Claire caught Katie's hand in mid-swipe, scowling at her. "What's going on?"

"Nothing," she said, tugging free of Claire.

"Don't bullshit me, Kate. Your cheeks are pale again."

"You look like you're losing weight, too," Natalie pointed out, grabbing the loose waistline on Katie's jeans. "Without your belt, these would be on the floor."

Katie pushed Natalie's hand away. "I'm fine. I'm just working harder than usual while Butch is gone. Stop making such a production about me."

Ronnie watched Katie from under lowered lids, keeping her lips sealed for now. Not for the first time she wondered if Butch was really in Phoenix "on business" or if something else was keeping him there ... or someone else.

She had a strong hunch that her youngest sister was on the heartache diet, which was an awful lot like the divorce diet that Ronnie had been on months ago and lost twenty-five pounds without even trying. Only Katie's diet cost less money and didn't involve splitting up community property. Or sitting through a series of incredibly personal, humiliating as hell interviews by men and women flashing stupid badges.

Katie wiped off her chair and shoved it under the table. "I have to get back to work." Without another word, she fished her order pad out of her back pocket and rushed over to a table of workers fresh from the Copper Snake mines.

Normally Ronnie didn't give a rat's ass about her fellow barflies, but after her almost run in with the goons the other night, she had scoped out everyone who had stepped through the door so far. The miners' lack of cowboy hats and worn shit-kickers differentiated them from the three small groups of local ranch crews. Pair that with the telltale red dust visible on their clothes and the dirt rings on the backs of their necks and their trade was obvious. Other than that, The Shaft's clientele consisted of two truckers whose rigs sat outside, a big guy in a Tucson Electric uniform and cap wearing a slew of gold chains around his neck, and two older women clothed from head to toe in khaki. Ronnie recognized the last two from her time behind the counter at the General Store. They were part of the archaeological crew.

No goons, no cops, no Deborah. Ronnie should have been whistling Dixie along with the Chicks, but anxiety seemed to be burning its way up her windpipe, and two glasses of gin and tonic were not dousing the flames.

Oh well, it was early; she would just have to keep pouring more down her throat.

"Something is up with her," Claire jutted her chin in Katie's direction.

"Maybe she's just missing Butch," Natalie threw out, grabbing a fry from her plate. "Men can really mess up your guts."

Claire eyed Natalie for a moment before shaking her head. "I don't think this is about Butch being gone. She's pissy as hell, not forlorn and mopey."

"It's probably something to do with Mom," Ronnie threw out to sidetrack Claire. If Katie felt the same as Ronnie a couple of years ago when she had first learned Lyle was having multiple affairs behind her back, predominantly with the young blonde secretaries he kept hiring and firing, the fewer people who knew her world had been turned upside down the better, including family.

"No," Claire pointed at Ronnie, "Mom is *your* problem lately, or at least a big part of it. Kate has something else bugging her."

Pushing aside the urge to lean over and bite Claire's finger, Ronnie shrugged and shared what Katie had told her on Sunday. "Maybe she's unhappy about being your research bitch, but she doesn't know how to get you to stop badgering her."

Claire's brows climbed up her forehead. "My research bitch? Are those her words or yours, Ronnie?"

"Mine," she lied for Katie's benefit. "I'm going to take her place on this one and get you what you need."

Claire picked up a French fry, took a bite, and chewed while frowning across the table at her. "Really?"

"Uh-huh. What's with that look on your face?"

"This look?" Claire exaggerated her expression, scrunching her nose, making Natalie chuckle. "It's my 'I smell something fishy' look."

"Yeah, well knock it off. It makes me want to grab some French fries and cram them up your nose."

"Now you're getting pissy, too. You need to stop hanging around Kate so much. She's rubbing off."

"I'm not pissy, just a little ticked at you."

"At me? What have I done now besides let you live with Mac and me for the last month?"

"Mac let me live in his house." After being in the same boat Ronnie had sailed in for the last five years, Claire had no room to get uppity about her station in Mac's life. "You're just sleeping with him in lieu of rent while you hop from job to job."

"Ouch," Natalie said, squirting ketchup along the length of a fry before eating it.

"Wow. This coming from the woman who has been focused only on herself since she blew into town with her suitcases in hand and has yet to even offer to take out the garbage."

Ronnie didn't really want to fight with Claire tonight, but it felt good to let out some of the anger that kept simmering inside of her and threatening to blow her top off. Besides, of all the people in her family, Claire could take the heat better than anyone. She always had been the fighter in their family, ever since second grade when she took on the fifth grader who kept bullying Ronnie and stealing her lunch.

"Kiss my ass, Claire."

Claire guffawed and shot a fake expression of disbelief at their cousin. "Holy shit, Natalie. Did you hear that? Ronnie just swore twice within a five-minute period. We should check her for signs of electroshock therapy."

"*Ass* is not really a swear word," Ronnie said, stirring her drink. Claire wouldn't be surprised at her language tonight if she had witnessed the multiple meltdowns Ronnie had had in her lawyer's office a few months back. Maybe in time her sister would get used to the "new Ronnie," although she didn't really feel new, more tarnished and jaded than anything.

"Says she who once chewed me out for using the word 'whore' instead of 'prostitute,'" Claire said. "Mom would keel over if she heard you talking like this after all of those etiquette classes she made you take." Her eyelids lowered into a suspicious glint as she chomped on another French fry. "Maybe I should be asking *you* what's wrong, not Kate."

"Stay out of my shit, Claire," she said and emptied her glass in a single gulp.

"That's the gin talking." Claire took the glass away from her. "You're gonna need a ride home from the Sheriff again if you keep it up."

"You're paying for my drinks, so you can cut me off at any time."

Coughing in surprise, Claire sat back. "I'm paying? Why is that?"

"You owe me for time spent researching Ruby's stash."

"Shhhh." She glanced around them before leaning closer. "I owe you? I wasn't paying Kate, so why should I pay you?" Ronnie's stomach roiled from the smell of fried potato on her breath.

"Why weren't you paying Katie?"

"She owes me for a bet she lost."

"What bet?"

Claire shook her head. "It's complicated."

Natalie bit into another French fry. "Complicated how?"

"Complicated because it involved Mom, but I'm not going into it right now." Claire sat back and grabbed another fry, swirling it around in the pool of ketchup on her plate. "All right, Ronnie, I'll pay for your drinks, but you'd better have something good for me."

Yeah, about that ... "I'm working on it."

Yesterday, she hadn't made as much progress as she would have liked because of the gang of senior citizens Katie had warned her about. She had entered the library and found every one of the computers with internet access occupied.

She donned the polite smile perfected during those

damned etiquette lessons and asked how much longer a lady wearing a gaudy flower brooch missing two petals would be online. Immediately, four gray-haired women surrounded her. The ringleader, who led with the red walker bearing dingle balls that Katie had mentioned, pointed out the "dibs" quarters lining the desk next to each computer.

Still smiling Ronnie pulled out several quarters. That was when the rubber foot of the red walker crushed her pinkie toe.

"A warning," the bully said. "Next time you may lose a toenail."

Hopping on one foot, Ronnie looked to the librarian's desk for help and found it empty where moments before two women had sat, stamping books.

In a fast limp, she grumbled all the way back to Katie's car, yanked open the door, and whipped her purse inside. It rolled across the seat, dumping the contents between the passenger seat and door. Such was her luck in this damned town.

When she stopped yelling curses in the hot car, she leaned over to pick up the contents of her purse. Several pieces of fake jewelry had spilled onto Katie's seat. They must have been buried down at the bottom of her purse, because she'd thought she stashed all of that crap back in her suitcase. She picked up the pearl necklace and squeezed the strand in her palm until the pearls left indents in her fingers, imagining wrapping it around Lyle's dick and cinching tight until that sucker popped right off.

That was when she got a brilliant idea.

Ten minutes later, her worthless trinkets in hand, she was back in the library. The pearl necklace was an instant hit. It secured her a solid hour on what she was told was one of the "faster" computers. The necklace with the fake ruby pendant went next, securing another forty-five minutes on an adjacent, slightly slower computer. She went through two tennis bracelets, one ring, and one set of earrings.

Today, she brought out some of her really good "stuff"

and spent half as much jewelry to get twice as much time online.

It was a good thing Lyle had been so obsessed with buying her affection over the five years of their bullshit marriage. It turned out the so-called "worthless" jewelry was worth something after all.

"Earth to Ronnie, come in." Claire nudged her foot under the table, bringing her back to the present and her lack of gin. "You're working on what?"

"Pinpointing the difference between seventeenth and eighteenth century pocket watches." Ronnie held up her empty glass toward Arlene. "Before I can go much further, I need to see the inside of Ruby's watch."

Claire crossed her arms over her Super Grover T-shirt. "Why?"

"To see if there is any signature on the inside painting."

"We'll need to borrow Gramps's fancy light-up magnifying glass."

"I also want to see if there is a certain kind of spring inside the watch itself."

"We can't tear it apart. A single mar on the surface could reduce its value by who knows how much."

Ronnie waited while Arlene set another gin and tonic down in front of her. "Maybe I can find something else that distinguishes it."

"Did you print out anything I can read on it?"

"No. The library was having trouble with the printer."

"That's a bunch of hooey," Claire grumbled, throwing down the fry and wiping her hands on her napkin. "I bet they disconnected it. When I was there, those golden oldies kept hitting the print key and then making a loud commotion about being on social security. They were demanding a senior discount for the prints. It's a scam."

After hanging around with them for two days, Ronnie had no doubt that Claire was right about the scam—one of many goings on with that geriatric gang of thugs. Now that Ronnie and her fake jewelry had been admitted as an honorary member, she had witnessed plenty of penny-pinching shenanigans committed by several of them. She could also confirm what Katie had suspected—they had the librarians in their pocketbooks, too.

"Either way," Ronnie said, "I've only been able to take pictures of different screens with my cell phone."

"Let me see them." Claire held out her hand.

Ronnie reached for her purse and started digging for her phone through the knots of necklaces, bracelets, and earrings.

Claire cleared her throat loudly, purposefully.

"I'll find it, Claire. Don't get your panties in a wad."

Ronnie better not have left it sitting next to one of the computers at the library. The Geritol Gang liked to pawn electronics left behind and pool the money for their gambling runs. They'd invited Ronnie to join them next Wednesday at a casino over on the Apache Reservation off State Route 70. Katie's bully with the dingle balls was pretty sure they could smuggle her on the senior citizen transportation van without being caught. Ronnie had expressed her doubts and as gracefully as possible declined the curly white wig one of the ladies had pulled off her own head and offered on the spot.

"Uh, Ronnie," Natalie said. "I think you have a visitor."

She looked up.

Sheriff Harrison glared down at her. He'd sneaked in through the door while she'd had her face in her purse. He stood across the table, all stiff legged and hard-faced, his brim tugged low. All he needed was a hand-rolled cigarette hanging out of the corner of his mouth and pearl-handled pistol on his hip and he would be ready to draw on her.

"Mrs. Jefferson." He spoke through his teeth. "I need a word with you."

Ronnie closed her eyes. Dear Lord, what crime was Sheriff Hardass going to threaten her with now?

"Good to see you in one piece, Claire," he said, his voice less gritty. "How's that new building coming along out at

Ruby's?"

"Natalie and I should have it ready for the county inspector by next weekend. Have you met my cousin, Sheriff?"

Ronnie opened her eyes, wanting to see his reaction to Natalie. Maybe if he were smitten with her cousin like so many men were, he would cut Ronnie some slack.

"Nope, can't say as I have. It's a pleasure." His smile was all business when he held out his hand for Natalie to shake. After she took it, he cocked his head to the side. "Is your last name Morgan, too?"

"No. Our moms are sisters," she explained. "I go by Beals."

"Good to know." He let go of her hand. "You need to be careful hanging around these Morgan girls." He said it with a hint of jest in his voice, but his eyes returned to Ronnie all joking aside. "They're always getting into trouble."

Claire laughed.

Ronnie did not.

She hoped Natalie had no unpaid parking tickets or other skeletons in her closet. Undoubtedly, Sheriff Harrison would be checking her records later, probably as soon as he finished shaking Ronnie down for whatever had him sniffing in her direction this evening.

His gaze hardened to match his jaw. "You want to step outside, Mrs. Jefferson?"

"Not really." She sat up straight, brushing some lint off of her red jeans, feeling braver here with her family by her side. "What's this about, Sheriff?"

He shrugged as if it were her funeral. Reaching into his pocket, he pulled out a familiar pair of zirconia chandelier earrings and set them on the table in front of her. "Do you know anything about these?"

She chewed on her lower lip. She did. They had bought her thirty minutes today on the computer with the fastest internet connection and three wrapped peppermint candies as a bonus.

"Well, I can tell you that they are earrings." She played dumb, hiding behind raised eyebrows. "Are you asking my opinion on a gift for your girlfriend, Sheriff Harrison?"

His nostrils flared. "I'm wondering if you have any idea who is selling fake jewelry to innocent old ladies down at the library."

Claire choked on a fry. Natalie clapped her on the back, averting her grin.

Ronnie leaned closer, pretending to inspect the earrings Lyle had given her on their second anniversary during a very expensive dinner of caviar, champagne, and white chocolate covered strawberries.

"Innocent old ladies, you say?" she asked.

They might be old, but they definitely were not the delicate flowers he was trying to make them out to be, especially the one she had bartered with using these earrings. Those women knew how to wheel and deal better than most used car salesmen.

The Sheriff nodded once, his sharp gaze practically poking a hole right into the center of her skull.

"Selling jewelry to them?" she challenged. "No, I haven't a clue."

That was the truth, since she was not officially selling anything. Not one dollar had passed between any of them. The whole system was based entirely on bartering. Now the deal they had going with the librarians—that was a whole other story. But it was not Ronnie's tale to tell. Not if she wanted to keep getting time on the internet.

The Sheriff's gaze dropped to her Coach purse. "Would you be willing to allow me to search your purse just to appease my curiosity?"

Ronnie's tongue glued itself to the back of her throat. Her heart spit and sputtered loud enough for the whole bar to hear.

Her gaze darted across the table, where Claire and Natalie sat sipping on their drinks with smirks still stuck on their faces, clearly enjoying the show. Ronnie scooted forward and kicked Claire in the shin, a wave of satisfaction rippling over her when her sister grunted and jerked in pain. That would teach her for laughing it up while Ronnie got the rubber glove treatment for doing Claire's dirty work.

"Mrs. Jefferson," the Sheriff walked around Natalie and turned Ronnie's chair so she faced him without the barrier of a table between them. He pointed at the purse in her lap. "Would you please empty your purse on the table?"

"This isn't mine," she lied with a poker face. "I left mine back at the R.V. park."

His eyes narrowed. "Whose is it then?"

"Katie's."

"You had your hands in it when I walked up."

"I was looking for Katie's cell phone. I needed to make a call and mine is back at Ruby's ... in my purse."

His stiff shoulders said he was not buying the load of horseshit she was selling. "Do you often go into other people's purses?"

"Katie's my sister. It's no big deal. Claire does it, too, don't you?" She challenged her sister with a stare that could have stripped paint off metal.

"Sure," Claire played along. "I borrow Kate's cell all the time."

Actually, Claire was not lying. Katie had complained to Claire just last night about having phone sex on her cell after she had returned from a call with Mac looking all flushed and happy.

Sheriff Harrison sighed, a very harsh, unpleasant, angry sound. "Veronica, would you please step outside with me for a moment?"

Uh-oh, he had resorted to using her first name. This must be serious. When she hesitated, he wrapped his big hand around her upper arm and leaned down, whispering next to her ear. "Right. Now."

"If I don't come back," she started to tell her sister.

"We'll bail you out," Claire finished. "I know exactly where to find you," she glanced up at Grady, "don't I, Sheriff?"

"I've had the beds in your favorite cell deloused and sanitized in case you feel like paying me another visit," he told Claire and touched the brim of his hat at her and Natalie.

Ronnie allowed him to lead her through the bar past the curious stares and out into the cool, star-filled night. Once there he released her arm as if repelled by touching her skin.

"Am I going to jail, Sheriff?"

"I'm still debating."

"For what? I was just sitting in there minding my own business."

"My Aunt Millie was wearing your earrings this afternoon when I stopped in to check on her."

His aunt? Oh, shit! Millie with the red walker and dingle balls. Of course that would have to be *his* aunt. "You can't prove those are mine."

"They are the same ones you offered me the day I gave you a speeding ticket."

How could he remember that? She had been so strung out on emotion that she could barely remember the trip home after he had given her the ticket, let alone what earrings she had in her hand when she had tried to bribe him.

"Maybe there is more than one pair of those in town."

"Veronica, quit playing games. I know it's you. My aunt described the woman she bought them from, including your red jeans and zebra print top."

"Well, for your information, Mr. Goody Two Shoes, I did not sell your aunt a single thing."

"You're saying that you are not committing fraud by selling fake jewelry to little old ladies for a lot more than it's worth?"

Ronnie laughed aloud at his question. "Hell, no. You have your facts all wrong."

He braced his hands on his gun belt, taking that wide, all-confident cop stance that made her want to jump up and down on his toes. "Well then, Veronica Jefferson, why don't you clear this whole thing up for me so you don't end up in my jail cell tonight."

What would it be like to have a conversation with him that did not include at least one threat?

"If you're going to arrest me on some bogus charge, Sheriff, you'd better get my damned name right. It's Veronica *Morgan*."

His head cocked to the side. "If you're concerned about my contacting your husband, don't be. I wouldn't do that to you. My only concern at the moment is fraud."

She crossed her arms over her chest. "Lyle Jefferson was never my husband. Our marriage was invalid because he hadn't divorced his previous wife when he married me." God, it felt so good to get that out in the open. Emboldened by her honesty, she lifted her chin. "Now if you're going to arrest me for fraud, there is something else you need to know."

His expression was still stiff, but his eyes had darkened after her admission, seeming to soften around the edges. Or maybe all of the gin was messing with her vision.

"What's that, Ms. Morgan?"

That sounded much better coming out of his mouth.

"Your poor little aunt is a member of a gang of old women who run a sting at the library, bullying anyone who tries to get on the internet computers without first offering them some kind of monetary or jewelry-based bribe."

He scoffed. "How much gin and tonic have you had tonight?"

"Not enough, trust me." She poked him in the chest, right under that damned star. "Why don't you go back and ask your poor little aunt to show you the pearl necklace and tennis bracelet she wrangled from me in the last two days in exchange for computer time."

He peered at her from under his haughty brim.

"Better yet," she poked him again, "let's go get Katie and

have her tell you about the bruise she got from your aunt's fancy red walker with the dingle balls when she tried to get on the computer without paying up first."

His jaw tightened visibly.

She poked him one more time. "Or we could talk with Claire and ask her about your poor little aunt's buddy with the cane who egged Claire into a scuffle that ended with my sister being unjustly banned from the library."

He grabbed her hand and pulled her against him, not letting go. To be honest she didn't want him to, either. For the first time in a long, long time, she felt alive and kicking. There was something about sparring with Grady that lit her up inside.

"Let me get this straight," he leaned closer, his gaze drilling her. "You're accusing my seventy-eight-year-old aunt of assault, battery, *and* racketeering?"

Veronica matched him glare for glare. "If the walker fits."

Chapter Ten

Wednesday, October 3rd

"It's lunchtime," Natalie called up to Claire, who was busy installing plumbing vents on the roof of the new restroom under a cloudy sky. The lack of the sun's rays was a relief after being cooked up on top of the building day after day last week.

"I need to finish tarring this vent first," Claire hollered back, brushing on the pungent black paste around the edges of the vent's flange.

One more exhaust vent after this one and she could head back down and hide from Gramps and his cackling cronies. They were currently going back and forth between rehashing bawdy stories from their time in the Army and heckling her about her handiwork. Her threat to climb down and tar their lips closed had fallen on deaf ears—seriously, only Gramps's mutt Henry had heard her threat. He had barked at her in response, pawing the ground. The little shit's doggie ego needed to be taken down a notch before his collar got too tight from his swelled head.

The ladder creaked behind Claire, followed by the sound of boots scuffing on the shingles. She looked over her shoulder. Natalie stood near the roof's peak, holding up a paper bag and two cans of soda pop.

"Finish up and join me over here where the crabby apples can't spoil our lunch."

Claire nodded, smeared on the last of the tar, and capped the lid.

"Claire," Gramps called from down below.

"You rang, your highness?"

"Are you sure you got that plumbing vent flashing in there right and sealed tight? We don't need it stretching or buckling in six months. That will be a pain in the ass to fix, and I'm the one who will be cleaning up the mess."

Her knees popped as she stood. Biting back a curse-filled retort, she nailed her grandfather with a long, hard stare. "Have I let you down before, Gramps?"

At her tone, he stopped scratching inside of his cast with his favorite hanger. "You did almost lose Henry back in April."

"But I found him again."

"He kind of found you," Chester butted in. "If I remember right."

"She did go out looking for him with my camera, though." Manny stuck up for her as usual.

"Take it easy, Claire. I'm just trying to help from down here where I'm stuck, grounded like a broke-dick pilot."

"Well, you're pissing me off, so why don't you try *not* to help for the rest of the day."

"You never used to be this touchy when we worked together."

"That's because you were usually working alongside of me, not sitting there like Napoleon shouting orders."

It also had something to do with the fact that her period still had not come, which made her all thumbs on the job. Her lack of ability to focus this morning had resulted in several bruises and cuts, as well as some tar in her hair.

Every time she thought about a baby, her breakfast of a cherry fruit pie, bacon, and orange juice threatened to rocket back up her throat. She was not ready for a kid. Hell, she couldn't even hold down a full-time job for six months, how could she hope to be responsible for another person for eighteen whole years ... or more?

After watching Ruby struggle with Jessica for the last few

months, Claire figured a child of her own would be better off raised by wolves ... or maybe chimps. Wait, make that bonobos—they had a reputation for making love, not war.

"She has a point," Manny said. "You do like to yell a lot more these days."

"That's because she's way up there." Gramps adjusted the bill of his ball cap. "Napoleon was a chump. I'm more of a General Patton."

"I think you both need to light up a smoke and relax," Chester grumbled. "This stupid no-smoking bet of yours is making the rest of our lives hell."

Until Claire knew if she was pregnant or not, there would be no more smoking, Chester's issue with their mutual grumpiness be damned.

Gramps snorted up at her. "Fine, I'll put on my kid gloves for the rest of the afternoon and treat you like I do Deborah."

Manny crossed himself at the sound of Claire's mother's name.

Claire bristled. Gramps's attitude had gone steadily to hell since he'd broken his leg, an accident for which he had blamed her once again this morning while shoving a metal hanger inside his cast to scratch an itch. Ruby had mentioned to her yesterday after their talk about Jess that Gramps was struggling with more pain in his leg than he let on. Knowing that, Claire had a little more patience for his orneriness, but this continual jabbing while she worked on finishing the building he had started was getting old.

The damned stubborn man. Maybe it was time to stop treating him like he had a broken leg. Now that she thought about it, the more Ruby played nurse, the more he stomped around the house and chewed on Claire's ass. Maybe instead of compassion from her, he needed her to butt horns with him, let him burn through some built-up testosterone.

"You want to play rough, Gramps?" She shucked her work gloves, holding them out before her in reply to Gramps's taunt about donning kid gloves and dropped them on the roof. "Fine. Just don't run home crying to Ruby when you get your ass kicked and handed to you."

Manny whistled long and low. "You go, girl!"

Chester shook his head, lighting up a cigar.

"That's more like it," Gramps said, scratching with his hanger. "I'm timing your lunch, so don't be holding hands and singing *Kumbaya* with Natalie for too long."

After an exaggerated curtsy, she joined her cousin on the other side of the roof's apex.

Natalie patted the shingles next to her. A good looking roast beef sandwich and a bag of pretzels sat on the roof next to her, waiting for Claire.

"Thanks," she said, dropping onto her butt and scooping up the sandwich.

"Thank Ruby. She sent Jessica out with it a few minutes ago."

Natalie pulled a small paper plate stacked with homemade molasses cookies out of the bag. More stress baking by their step-grandmother. Lovely. The button on Claire's jeans groaned. She needed to fix this deal with Jessica and her dad, or she'd end up hanging drywall while wearing a muumuu and probably screw her dress to the wall. The old boys would never let her live that down.

Claire bit into the sandwich. Ruby had remembered to slather on the horseradish, too. She licked her chops and looked out across the campground. She caught sight of Jessica, who was taking a detour past the archaeology crew's campers and tents on her way back to the store. The girl was playing peek-a-boo as she strolled extra slowly past what Claire now knew was Beanpole's tent.

A little bit of investigative work yesterday evening had provided a wealth of information about the tall, skinny college junior whose lofty IQ had made Claire blink. Why was such a smart guy taking an interest in a high school girl? The news about his big brain cemented what Claire suspected, that he was up to something. She would bet that something most likely had to do with a leak—or ten—from Jessica's loose lips.

After swallowing her bite, she turned to Natalie. "You know the guy you overheard on the phone the other night?"

Chewing, Natalie nodded.

"Was he tall and skinny, like a beanpole? Wearing glasses?"

"Huh-uh." She took a drink of soda. "He was only about my height. I don't remember him wearing glasses."

Damn. So Natalie's guy and Jess's beanpole were probably not one and the same. Unless maybe the two were in cahoots—Beanpole was the brains and the other guy was the muscle.

Claire took another bite, chewing on all of the questions she had about the crew and more.

After a few moments of silence broken only by the guffaws of laughter coming from the other side of the building, Natalie asked. "You think Kate is doing okay?"

That was one of the questions Claire had been chewing on. She shrugged. "I don't know, but something is off with her. She said she had a fight with Butch before he left for Phoenix, but I have trouble believing one fight would be all it takes for them to split up." She washed down her sandwich with a sip of soda. "She's been all giddy with hearts in her eyes ever since they hooked up. I even caught her tittering like Mother."

"Oh, God," Natalie groaned. "Say it isn't so."

"Yeah, apparently it's genetic. So if you ever hear me titter …"

"You want me to smack you or just take you out back immediately and put you out of your misery?"

"Let's start with the smack down. I've seen you shoot. You're really good at *almost* hitting a target." Claire took a breath then continued. "Every time I ask Kate what's wrong, she blows me off. I'm about done asking."

That was tough talk. Claire wouldn't stop frowning about Kate until she saw the light in her sister's eyes again. Heck, she'd even put up with the tittering if it meant the end of this dark cloud hovering over Kate, pouring buckets down on whoever was near.

A crow landed at the other end of the roof and shrilled at them, wanting his share of meat.

Natalie jumped up and scared it away. She sat back down with a grunt. "What do you think is going on with Ronnie?"

"Well," Claire said with a chuckle, "now there's a question I've been asking myself since she showed up on Mac's doorstep."

She had thought about Ronnie's comment last night regarding the house being Mac's, that Claire was just sleeping with him in it, and realized her older sister was right … again, damn it. Claire had not really adopted Mac's house as hers yet. When it came down to it, the only place that truly felt like "home" at the moment was here in Ruby's R.V. park. Everything at Mac's place was running perfectly. There were no broken air conditioners to repair, no structures to be built, no mysteries to solve.

Day after day she sat around either looking for her next job or trying to figure out how to quit her current job without pissing off Mac. So far he had not joined her family in song about her lack of ability to keep a job, but Claire was not naïve. Their relationship was still relatively new. In time things would change and probably not for the better if she didn't find a job she could stick with for longer than a couple of weeks.

But now was not the time to dwell on those fears. She had work to do and an old man waiting to give her shit about it.

"Ronnie keeps watching over her shoulder," Natalie said, crunching on a pretzel.

"You noticed that, too, huh?" Claire skipped the pretzels and went straight for the cookies. They were still warm from the oven and so soft she practically drooled just holding one.

"Last night in the bar, before the Sheriff showed up," Natalie said, "she insisted on planting herself with her back to the wall."

"Where was I when this happened?"

"In the bathroom." Natalie stole a cookie from Claire and shoved it in her mouth all at once. "Mmmmm, that's so good," she said through a mouthful of cookie. "Just like Grandma used to make."

Her comment about Gramps's first wife, their real grandma, made Claire smile. "Nobody made monster cookies like Grandma."

Natalie nodded, and then she held up a finger. "I bet Ruby could give her a run for her money, though. It's no wonder Gramps married her, huh?"

Thinking about how fun and feisty Ruby was, Claire was glad he had. The old fart needed someone as stubborn as he was to live with his ornery but loveable ass day after day.

Claire grabbed two cookies and scarfed them so fast she almost bit the tip off one of her fingers. "I don't know what's going on with Ronnie since she left South Dakota. Whenever I ask about Lyle and the whole mess that ended with him in prison, she turns dark red and clams up, insisting on changing the subject."

"Hmmm." Natalie snagged another cookie. "She sure got sparky with Mr. Sheriff last night, didn't she?"

Now that Natalie mentioned it ... "You're right. I don't think I've ever seen her be so bullheaded. I guess she really does have Gramps's blood in her after all. And here I thought she was adopted for all these years, her being all perfect in comparison to Kate with her horrible choices in men and me with my lack of ability to finish anything. I wonder why Ronnie is so mad at Mom."

Natalie snorted.

"Other than for the obvious reason of Mother being Mother." Claire swallowed the last of her soda and stuffed the can in the lunch bag. "Speaking of something being wrong, what's going on with you?"

"Me?" Natalie asked, wiping the crumbs from her mouth with the hem of her shirt.

"Yeah, you."

"What do you mean? I'm the most normal one around here lately."

"You've been here for two weeks and have yet to even share a drink with a guy at The Shaft."

Natalie's gaze drifted out across the campground. Her shoulder shrug was so slight that Claire almost missed it. "I have new standards."

"Really? So the long legs, tight ass, and broad shoulders no longer top your checklist?"

"Nope."

"What are you looking for in a guy now?"

"Nothing."

Claire waited for her to say more but nothing came. "You're going to have to explain that more, Natalie, because I'm pretty high on molasses cookies and my detective skills are only so-so even when I'm on my game."

She chuckled, but Claire could tell it was forced. "I'm taking a break."

"From working on the building?"

"From men."

"Like a short break while you're in Arizona or several seasons of no males break?"

"The latter."

"Why? Did something happen back home?"

Natalie chewed on her lower lip as if debating on letting the words out. Then she shook her head. "No, nothing happened, at least nothing worth talking about. I'm just tired of the game—boy flirts, girl flirts back, sex happens, girl thinks she's fallen in love, boy leaves girl for an easy, young slut with one of those tattoos across her ass that says, 'Enter here.'"

Claire blinked, the obvious non-fiction laced into Natalie's story bringing out a mixture of laughter and disgust both at once. "That's a pretty nasty ending to your tale."

"Yes, according to the jerkoff I'd been stupid enough to get involved with that time, the slut did have a pretty *and* nasty ending to her tail, and he liked it. A lot. That's why he left me. I was too much of a prude to swing that way."

"Wait, you mean the slut swung both ways? She was into guys and girls?"

"No, I mean in addition to her unusual sexual preferences, she also was into sex swings and all that fun stuff."

"Oh, wow."

"Yeah, wow." Natalie frowned. "You know, I'm totally up for exciting sex, but I'm getting too old for that acrobatic shit. If I fall off a swing, I could break my leg again—or worse. Then I'm off the job for months. I can't afford it. Plus my health insurance has a huge deductible."

Claire started giggling.

Natalie swatted at her. "I'm serious. Those swings are dangerous, especially when you're butt naked."

Claire laughed harder, falling back onto the roof and letting it roll out. After having a gut-ache of frustration and fear all morning, she couldn't seem to stop. Tears of laughter leaked out the sides of her eyes.

Natalie sputtered once or twice and then joined Claire, their laughter ringing out across the campground.

The crow returned, shrilling at them, making a play for the bag. Wiping at her eyes, Claire snatched the bag up along with the cookies before the bird got purchase. Natalie hopped up and shooed it away again, then returned to help Claire put the rest away.

"What's going on over there?" Gramps asked.

"Nothing," Claire and Natalie said at the same time.

"Jinx!" Natalie said. "You owe me a drink tonight."

"Damn it, between Ronnie and you, I'm going to be broke by Friday."

Natalie held out her hand to help Claire up. "So, Claire," Natalie said. "Now that I've been honest about me and my problems, answer one question for me."

"Shoot."

"What's going on with you and Mac?"

"What do you mean?"

"I noticed while he was here this last weekend that you two seemed a little distant. Are you two fighting like Kate and Butch?"

"No, we're okay."

"Then what has you frowning at the horizon so much these days instead of singing with the radio while we work?"

Claire hesitated. Natalie had been honest with her. She hated to lie to her cousin in return. "Uh, just this small thing I keep worrying about."

"What is it? Spit it out."

Okay. "A baby," she said, her voice mostly breath.

Natalie's eyes widened. She stepped closer. "Come again?"

Claire jammed her hands in her front pockets, pulling her shoulders in tight. "I think I might be pregnant."

Ronnie cruised into Yuccaville that afternoon, staying well under the speed limit and stopping for a full five seconds at each stop sign. After yesterday evening's bare-all confession with Sheriff Hardass outside The Shaft, which had resulted in a warning from him about the punishment that came with falsely accusing others of crimes, she was not going to give him a single reason to grill her today.

There were no open parking spaces in front of the Yuccaville library, which was probably for the best with the Sheriff's Department sitting kitty corner from it. While Grady had not actually seen her driving away in Katie's car Sunday after she ran into him in the Mule Train Diner, she figured he would have his radar set to sound the alarm at any sight of her or her family, including their vehicles.

She found a spot two blocks away, but it would have required parallel parking between two big diesel trucks that were both hogging the white lines at either end. Ronnie's insurance company had dropped her last month. The last thing she needed was to dent up her sister's car and get stuck in town longer working off the cost to repair it.

Taking a right, she found a spot under a gnarled mesquite tree and cut the engine. She grabbed her purse along with the cowboy hat she had borrowed from Natalie and stepped out under the cloud-filled sky. Just in case the Sheriff or one of his deputies was running surveillance from their front window, she had dressed in faded blue jeans, a plain white T-shirt, and a pair of flat-heeled sandals. Her goal was to blend in with the locals—hide in plain sight.

With her cowboy hat pulled low on her forehead, she opted for the long way around to the library, staying as far from the Sheriff's building as possible. Behind her sunglasses, she kept watch for any government vehicles, hugging the buildings as she walked along, ready to dart inside if needed.

She made it to the library's front doors without incident. Inside, the cooled air held the usual smells she had come to associate with the place—musty books, dusty carpet, and rose water perfume. The latter of the three answered the question that had crossed her mind several times on the way here. Sure enough, Grady's Aunt Millie and her gang of grannies loitered. Only today, instead of filling the seats in front of the internet computers, they lounged in the green padded chairs nearby with bags of yarn at their orthopedic shoes. Their knitting needles clicked in the hushed room.

Ronnie approached slowly, unsure if the Sheriff had talked to his aunt since learning about her racketeering operation. Even though the computers appeared open for business, she followed protocol and waited next to Aunt Millie's red walker.

"Good afternoon, girls," she greeted each with her well-practiced smile. She focused on Aunt Millie. "I brought you some lovely gifts today. Is the library's internet connection up and running?"

Which was code for: *Here's a bribe to score some computer time.*

Aunt Millie nodded while her needles continued to click away.

Ronnie took a step toward the one with the fastest connection.

"What kind of lovely gifts, sweetie?"

Ah, that answered her question. Grady had not returned to his aunt's place, which meant he probably didn't believe a word Ronnie had said. That didn't surprise her really, but it still stung a little.

Damn him for not believing her.

Damn her for caring one way or the other.

Reaching into her purse, she pulled out more chandelier earrings, this time with zirconia stems leading down to pear-shaped, faux yellow sapphires. "I believe these would look just darling with that green paisley scarf you have on today. What do you think?"

Aunt Millie eyed the earrings warily, then smiled and stopped knitting. "Yes, those would look just gorgeous, don't you think so, Ruth?"

Ruth's needles stopped clinking. From what Ronnie had gleaned over the last two days, she was the second in command. Ruth also had a cane she sometimes used, which made Ronnie assume she was Claire's nemesis.

Lowering her rhinestone studded glasses, Ruth inspected the earrings Ronnie held out. "Oh, definitely, Millie. Those are lovely."

"Wonderful." Ronnie placed them on the table next to Grady's aunt. "Now if you don't mind, I need to look up a few things online."

"Sure, darlin'," Aunt Millie gave her blessing.

Ronnie glanced around the library to make sure she had no onlookers, as in lawmen or goons. All clear. Lowering onto the padded chair, she rolled up to the long table filled with monitors and keyboards, moving the mouse to wake up the computer. She pulled out her cell phone, opening the picture of the pocket watch that she had taken this morning down in Ruby's basement office with Claire.

They had sneaked down the basement stairs while the rest

of the house was asleep. Claire had locked the door behind them "to be safe."

Ronnie tried not to roll her eyes at the whole cloak and dagger act. Her sister needed to relax. It was just a pocket watch and they were not in enemy territory.

"Where is it?" Ronnie had asked, checking out the antiques on the big desk in the middle of the room.

"In the safe. Give me a hand, would ya?" Claire stood on one side of the bookcase motioning Ronnie to join her.

The bookcase had snagged on the carpet as they pulled it out, almost tipping the cameras, books, and wooden boxes of who knew what onto the floor.

"Next time, Ronnie," her sister had said, her voice tinged with sarcasm, "could you actually put some muscle into it?"

"I'll put some muscle into you."

Claire snorted. "That doesn't even make sense coming from a girl."

"Whatever. Why are we lifting this thing?"

"The safe is in the wall behind it."

Ah, a wall safe. This was just like the movies.

They lifted the bookcase away from the wall enough for Claire to squeeze in behind it. She pulled a pair of gloves from her back pocket. Dropping onto her knees, she typed in a combination. Ronnie leaned against the side of the bookcase, watching her sister's fingers trip over the keypad.

The door popped open. Ronnie caught a glimpse of a tiny gun holster before Claire started backing out. She walked over to the desk and waited for Claire to join her with the watch.

They had not pried open the back of the casing to check if the power were delivered by a spring-and-fusee mechanism or via a spiral spring balance, but the watch did have two hands rather than one. From what Ronnie had read, that pretty much date-stamped it as a seventeenth century or later piece.

With the help of Gramps's magnifying glass, they had been able to find what was probably the watchmaker's signature. It could have been the casemaker's scrawl, but

Ronnie doubted it since she had read that the signature of a watch's enamel artist was rare. Not that Claire or she could read the swirly letters on the name they found, except for "R"—the first letter. Or maybe it had been a "P."

While Claire was looking at it through the magnifying glass, Ronnie had pulled out her camera.

"What are you doing?" Claire asked, covering the watch with her gloved hand.

"Taking a couple of pictures, so I can compare the real thing to what I find online. You didn't expect me to draw the thing, did you?"

"No, I guess not." Claire didn't sound convinced though and kept her glove over the watch.

"You know I'm not the greatest artist."

"True." She lifted her glove. "Your stick people come out all bent and wavy."

"I told you, those were his knees and elbows."

"I'm talking about his neck."

"He had an Adam's apple."

Claire *harrumphed* but held out the watch.

Ronnie took pictures of the outside of the case with its embossed picture of a carriage and then the inside painting on the face. She took another one of the inside of the casing. Zooming in, she got a slightly blurry shot of the signature, too.

... Now as she stared down at her cell phone under the library's fluorescent lights, she tried to figure out how to zoom in on the picture. When she figured it out, the picture only got blurrier the more she zoomed in. Damn. She should have brought Gramps's magnifying glass along with her.

Wait a second! She swiveled in the chair. "Do any of you happen to have a magnifying glass on you?"

Ruth shot her a glance over the barf-colored scarf she was knitting. "What's it worth to you?"

Ronnie had just the thing. She unzipped her purse and fished out a stickpin with an amethyst in the center, the heart surrounding it supposedly made of sterling silver. Lyle had brought it back for her from one of his many trips to Texas, where he claimed one of his company's satellite offices was located. According to the Feds, he had been down there helping a so-called "client" launder drug money coming over the border.

"How about this?" She held up the stickpin.

Ruth looked at it over the top of her glasses. Then she pulled a magnifying glass out of her knitting bag and offered it to Ronnie.

One stickpin later, Ronnie was back in her chair, holding the magnifying glass over her cell phone.

She typed in the name of the artist, or something close to it, since the last four letters all flowed together in a sort of squiggly line, and the word "Pocket Watch." She clicked on the Search button and waited.

The screen filled with possible links. Skipping over the ads for watches, she scanned down the page. She clicked on one link from a museum, but the painting on the watch was a different style. She returned to the Search screen and looked further down the list.

In the middle of the list of links on the fourth screen of her search she found a link to a German newspaper article from over a decade ago that had a name in the details similar to the one on the watch. The rest of the title was in German of which she knew enough to get her a mug of beer and directions to the train station. She hovered the cursor over it and clicked. A black and white picture of a gray stone, turret topped castle appeared on the right. Several paragraphs written in German filled the left side of the screen.

Highlighted in the third paragraph was the name she had entered in her search criteria. She stared at the signature in the blurry picture on her phone again. It could be the same name. She scanned the article, sounding out the words under her breath in a German tongue so rusty it practically creaked out of her throat, looking for words she sort of knew. There was nothing in there about beer or the train station, dang it.

Scrolling down, she saw several pictures of watches. One of them in particular seemed to match the one on her phone.

"That's weird," she said under her breath.

She went back and forth between the computer and her phone several times. Could it be the same pocket watch? No, there was no way it could be. Or was it? It wasn't like they mass produced pocket watches back then.

She needed to know what the article said.

The clicking of needles behind her made her swivel around. "Do any of you ladies know how to read German?"

"Greta does," Ruth said.

Ronnie dug in her purse and came out with an oval shaped emerald pendant on a gold chain. She held it up. "What do you say, Greta?"

"*Ja, Fräulein. Ja.*" Greta set down her knitting needles and grunted her way up onto her feet. She waddled over on her extra wide hips and took Ronnie's offering, petting the emerald stone with a big smile. "*Es ist wunderschön.*"

Ronnie took it that meant they had a deal. "Would you like to sit?" Ronnie started to stand and offer her seat, but Greta put a hand on her shoulder and pushed her back down.

"No. I need to stand for a bit. My sciatica was starting to give me pains while I was knitting."

Aunt Millie joined them, looking over Ronnie's other shoulder. "What's it say, Greta?"

Greta grabbed the reading glasses hanging at the end of a chain around her neck and leaned closer to the screen.

"Let's see." She started to read aloud in German.

"Greta," Aunt Millie interrupted her. "I mean in English."

"Hold on to your bloomers, Millie. I'm not so good at translating word for word."

"Just give me the gist," Ronnie said.

Greta read a couple of lines under her breath. "It's an article about a castle in Germany, some of its history." She read more under her breath. "There were several battles held outside its walls and you can still see the scars in the stone from the trebuchet attacks." She pointed at walls on the screen image.

Ronnie scrolled down the page a little, pointing at the watch. "What's it say about this?"

Greta's lips pursed. She leaned closer. "It's giving a list of items that were stolen from the castle two years before this article was written, along with pictures of several of the pieces. This pocket watch," she touched the screen, "was stolen."

Ronnie's heart took off like a dragster at a green light, reverberating in her ears for a moment. Her hand on the mouse began to shake, making the cursor jiggle.

Aunt Millie touched Ronnie's shoulder. "Are you okay, honey?"

Ronnie gulped the swell of nausea that pulsed up her esophagus. "Yes," she whispered, then cleared her throat. "I'm fine." This time she sounded a little less wishy-washy about it. "Please read on, Greta."

Greta did, and Ronnie took notes on a piece of scrap paper. She wrote down the name of the painter, the watch style, the estimated value back when the article was written, along with the names and information on the other pieces, too. Her handwriting grew more stable as they went, her heart returning to its normal cruising speed.

When Greta finished, Ronnie thanked her and held up her phone to take pictures of the article since the printers didn't seem to be working again when she tried to print. She scrolled up and down, taking photos of the article, the website address, and the author of the article. Then she went back to the pocket watch and zoomed in, taking a vertical shot.

Was it the same pocket watch? Had Claire been right all along and this thing was as valuable as Greta had read? If Joe had managed to get his hands on this watch, where were the rest of the missing items? Stashed somewhere else in the house? Or was this the only piece he had skimmed from the thieves when he moved the stolen goods from one place to the other?

She flipped her phone sideways and zoomed in again, this time with a horizontal shot. The camera sound on her phone clicked. She stared down at the picture. It certainly looked a lot like the pocket watch Claire had locked back up in the wall safe after they had finished looking it over this morning.

What if ... she sniffed. What was that smell?

Bay rum aftershave.

"Hello, Veronica," Sheriff Harrison said.

Oh, no!

"I was right, that is your sister's black Volvo parked over on Ore Street."

Damn. She should've parked further away. Ronnie fumbled to hit the power down button on her phone, but she was too slow.

"That's quite a fancy pocket watch you're looking at." He grabbed the back of her chair and swiveled her around to face him. "What are you up to today, Veronica?"

She opened her mouth and waited for her voice to come out of hiding.

"She's learning how to knit, Grady," Aunt Millie said to her nephew.

The Sheriff frowned, his gaze warning Ronnie he was not done with her before traveling over to his aunt. "Why is she not sitting over there with you ladies then, Aunt Millie?"

"Because we're also teaching her how to speak German," Ruth joined Millie on Team Alibi. "She's an apt pupil."

"Oh, I bet she is," Grady said, his voice deep and full of mirth.

Ronnie's arms went all rubbery with the fear of being busted for withholding information about a very expensive stolen antique. They were like garden hoses with hands on the ends. She wanted to spin back around and exit the screen showing the article, but Grady still had a hold of her chair.

"Darn it, Sheriff," Greta scolded him with a sweet smile, "you looked so big and handsome when you walked in wearing your spiffy uniform that I got all flutter-pated and dropped a stitch."

Grady's cheeks darkened slightly. "Well, I guess I need to offer my apologies for interrupting, ladies." He tipped his hat at them.

When he turned back to Ronnie, his eyes were dark, promising trouble and something else, something that made her skin warm for a whole different reason. He leaned close enough for her to see a small patch of stubble on his jaw that he'd missed this morning with his razor.

"*Ich habe mein Auge auf Sie, Fräulein*," he whispered, the German flowing off his tongue with ease.

Ronnie didn't have a clue what he'd said but managed to lift her right garden hose and make the hand at the end wave goodbye at him.

"*Auf Wiedersehen*, Sheriff," she said, using a line she remembered from watching repeats of "Hogan's Heroes" on television with her dad back when she'd been in elementary school.

After he left the building, Greta waddled up to where Ronnie still sat trying to convince her heart to slow down before the Sheriff nailed it for speeding, too.

"Way to cover your backside," Greta said.

"Thanks. I owe all of you some more jewelry for covering for me."

"Nah," Aunt Millie said over her shoulder, her needles clicking away again. "That one was on the house."

"Thanks." Maybe these old gals weren't such bullies after all. Ronnie's gut twinged a little with guilt for ratting them out to Grady last night. "I have a feeling he'll be back."

"I know," Greta said. "He's *very* interested in you."

Ronnie gaped at her. "He is? How do you know?" Had Greta seen the look in his eyes that had gotten Ronnie all hot under her collar?

"I know because he just told you in German that he has his eye on you."

Oh. That kind of interest in her. "Son of a *Fahrvergnügen*!"

Chapter Eleven

The Shaft smelled like the inside of a well-used cowboy boot, sweaty with a hint of secondhand cowhide.

Ronnie sat at the bar nursing a drink, her back to tables crowded with ranchers, miners, and truckers. They were all whooping it up about the rodeo being broadcast on the two flat screen televisions Butch had mounted high on the walls.

Tonight she didn't want to watch the door or monitor every man or woman who walked through it. Partly because she was tired of worrying about strangers but mostly because she did not want to see a certain Sheriff or his stupid shiny star. She wanted only to drink her gin and tonic and forget about the ugly truth that she had dug up this afternoon at the library and its possible consequences.

She stirred her almost empty glass, ignoring the cowpoke who slid onto the bar stool next to her and brushed her elbow on purpose. He reeked like he'd been brined in whiskey for a couple of days before being hung out to dry.

"What will you have?" Arlene asked Ronnie's new neighbor. The older woman was playing bartender tonight, filling in for Gary, who Katie said had Wednesday and Thursday nights off.

"I'll have what she's having," Ronnie's barstool buddy said with a definite slur. "And I'll buy her another one since she's almost empty."

Ronnie took out her stirrer and gulped the last of her drink down, sliding the empty glass in Arlene's direction.

Arlene raised her eyebrows, looking toward Ronnie's new friend and then back. "You sure you're interested, sweetie?"

Ronnie shrugged. "Why not? It's free and Claire isn't here to cover my tab."

Arlene complied, placing a full glass in front of Ronnie.

"Who is Claire?" the cowboy asked, trying to rub his leg against her outer thigh and kneeing her instead. "Sorry 'bout that," he apologized at her flinch.

"*De nada.*" She leaned further away from him.

Scooting closer, he asked, "So is Claire your girlfriend?"

He waggled his eyebrows at Ronnie. They looked like two blonde caterpillars inching along his forehead when he did that. She contemplated slapping at them.

"If you're going to sit here next to me and drink," she said, "I advise you not to continue upon the path you are traveling."

He let out a roar of laughter that was as obnoxious as it was loud. The pair of truckers at the other end of the bar glared at him from under the bills of their hats. "Oh, you're a smart one. I like that in a filly."

His hand slid under the bar and landed smack dab in the middle of her upper thigh.

Ronnie shot him a sidelong glance. If he did not remove his palm soon, the doctors down at the ER were going to need to take an X-ray to figure out how to remove her gin glass from his mouth.

"This thing here you're hoping to achieve," she reached down and picked up his hand like it was something dead she had found under the porch, dropping it onto his own thigh. "It isn't going to happen tonight."

He drew up close, a strong waft of whiskey blowing her hair back. "Come on, baby," he said above a wave of groans from the tables after a rider on the televisions didn't make it to the eight second mark. "You've got more legs than a bucket full of chicken, and I'll bet my lucky cowboy hat that every inch of them is finger-lickin' good."

Ronnie looked across her shoulder at him. The idiot must have been kicked in the head by a bull more than once. Why couldn't he shrivel up and blow away in the breeze like the tumbleweed she had almost hit on her race here from the library?

Years of etiquette classes had taught her to be polite when she rejected a man's advances. Years of practicing what she had learned in that class had left her broke, alone, and at risk of getting killed ... or something worse, according to her piece of shit not-husband. This cowboy had picked the wrong woman to get all grab-happy with tonight.

Those blonde bushy eyebrows wiggled at her again, followed by a wink. "Bring this Claire babe along for the ride, if'n you'd like. There's plenty here to share." He pointed both index fingers south of his huge, brass belt buckle that sported bull horns.

Ronnie picked up her gin and tonic, holding it out as if to toast him.

"Is that a yes, baby?" His hand was back and inching up her thigh.

She leaned in close as if going in for a kiss. "Cowboy, you're not gonna make it for the full eight seconds."

His eyelids lowered, his gaze on her lips. "What was that now?"

She lifted off his hat and emptied her glass over his head.

He came up sputtering and cursing, reaching for his hat.

She tossed it on the floor. "One gin and tonic does not give you the right to trespass, idiot."

"You stupid cow!" He lifted his hand, aiming the back of it at her cheek.

Ronnie reacted without thinking. Her hand snaked out, catching him by the wrist and twisting as she stood and threw her weight into the take-down move she had learned long ago during a series of private self-defense classes Lyle had insisted she take. Her momentum caught the cowboy off balance. The whiskey in his blood made him slow to counter, and she dropped him face-first onto the floor with a quick kick to his ankle. Before he could figure out what had happened, she straddled him and jerked his arm up behind his back, making him cry out in pain.

"Is this what you meant by riding you, jackass?" She yanked on his arm, making him squeal like a rutting pig. Months of feeling helpless and frustrated as strangers took potshots at her fueled her meltdown, causing an internal combustion that exploded in red hot anger. "The next time you buy a drink for a girl," she yelled, "keep your damned hands to yourself!"

"Uh, Ronnie?" Katie's voice cut through the rage roaring in her head.

Ronnie looked up from where she rode on the cowboy's back. All eyes were no longer focused on the rodeo, at least not the one on the television.

Ah, hell. What had she done? The flames crackling inside of her blew out in a single blast of cold realization. The last thing she needed was someone calling the cops on her. How was she going to ease her way out of this without making a bigger show of it than she already had?

She glanced back down at the cowboy. Thinking back to her teen years when she had lusted over several local rodeo stars, she remembered the vernacular she had picked up while hanging out behind the chutes with the other much less dignified buckle bunnies.

"Does anybody have a piggin' string?" she called out to the crowd of onlookers. "I'm gonna hogtie this bastard."

The room drew a breath.

Then the hooting and cheering filled the void.

"It's your lucky night." Patting the drunk cowboy's back, Ronnie stood, bowed, and returned to her barstool.

The Shaft in turn went back to its previous dull roar.

Arlene poured her a fresh drink. "This one's on the house, wildcat."

Ronnie buried her burning face in her hands.

"What in the hell was that?" Katie hissed in her ear.

Looking up from her palms, Ronnie grimaced. "He pissed

me off and I wasn't thinking straight."

"You weren't thinking ... " Katie rolled her eyes up at the ceiling. "You've been hanging around Claire too much. Next thing I know you'll be trying to create a mystery out of thin air and clobbering your suspects."

"I am not like Claire. She hits first and asks questions later. I just hit, plain and simple." At least the new Ronnie did.

"Since when do you even risk breaking a nail?"

Since Mrs. Veronica Jefferson found out her highfalutin fancy life was all a highfalutin fancy lie.

Ronnie picked up her gin and tonic, sending a sideways glance at her youngest sister. "People change." Then to redirect their conversation, she added, "Look at Claire. She's never stayed with a guy more than a couple of months, nor even made mention of 'love' in regards to anything other than MoonPies and cigarettes. Yet she's still nuts about Mac after all of this time."

"True."

"And look at you."

Katie frowned, pulling back. "What about me?"

"You fell for a guy who has no jail record. That's a first for you, isn't it?"

Katie punched her shoulder. "Shut up before I knock you down and sit on *your* back." She tucked some loose strands back up in her crooked ponytail. "I still can't believe you took down that big ol' cowboy."

"He was whiskey drunk." Katie did not need to know about Ronnie's self-defense classes. It might raise questions as to why they were needed. The same questions Ronnie had asked Lyle when he'd insisted on them. She'd have to come up with some lies to tell Katie for answers, just as Lyle had done with her.

"I know, but you moved so fast."

Ronnie needed to change the subject pronto. "I found some sweet Jimmy Choo heels today while I was on the internet at the library," she said. It turned out she was going to lie about something tonight, but at least it was not about her past.

"How in the world did you convince that gang of old women to let you have some computer time?"

"I know how to sweet talk the worst of them. After all of those classes Mom forced me to take on how to set the table and the proper way to curtsy, those old women didn't have a chance against my charm."

Arlene joined them, setting a glass of water in front of Katie. "You look hot, honey," she pointed at Katie's pink cheeks. "You'd better drink that up before you keel right over."

Katie thanked her and took a long drink. She wiped her mouth with the back of her hand. "Did you find out anything about the watch?"

"No," Ronnie lied again.

"You mean that pocket watch your other sister was shushin' us about last time she was here?" Arlene asked, wiping down the bar in front of Katie.

"Yeah. Ronnie is helping Claire and me look into it more."

Ronnie shot Katie a zip-it glare. She did not need Arlene blabbing to Sheriff Harrison about the stolen pocket watch. He would put two and two together and come up with four letters: J-A-I-L.

"Oh, jeez," Katie said in reply to Ronnie's unspoken shush. "Don't tell me Claire and her hush-hush mantra has rubbed off on you about this pocket watch, too."

"No, of course not." Well, maybe a little.

If the Sheriff started digging, he might just tunnel right on past China and surface in Germany at a certain castle missing a particular pocket watch. Then the Feds would come, along with the threats and interrogations. Ronnie had lived this nightmare already. The last thing she wanted was a repeat, and she definitely didn't want her family to experience the humiliation of being tied to crimes they hadn't committed.

Not to mention what the Feds would do to Ruby's R.V.

park and mines, searching for the rest of the loot. The R.V. park would be shut down or worse, taken from Ruby. *Eminent domain* and all of that bureaucratic crap. Ronnie could hear it now. She had to keep this all under wraps until she figured out what to do.

Katie glanced toward the door, smiling and waving. "Natalie's here."

Ronnie followed Katie's gaze. Their cousin led Chester and Manny her way.

"Your eyes look a little bloodshot," Natalie said, sliding onto the seat on the other side of her. "What number are you on?" She pointed at the glass in front of Ronnie.

"This is only my third." She had dumped most of her second one on a cowboy's head.

"Which explains why she looks three sheets to the wind," Chester said. "We're grabbing a table," he told Natalie and headed for an open one back by the pool table.

"Are you okay, *chica*?" Manny squeezed Ronnie's shoulder.

"Yeah, sure."

Katie stood. "No, she's not. She just dropped a cowboy to the floor, twisted his arm around his back, rode him like a freaking horse, and threatened to hogtie him."

"No shit," Natalie said, chuckling.

Ronnie shot Katie a what-the-hell look.

"What? This is Jackrabbit Junction. Better they hear it from me now than tomorrow morning when the news of your takedown has made it clear to Yuccaville and back."

Manny leaned toward Ronnie. "Did Kate just say you rode a cowboy like a horse?"

"Yeah."

His smile widened under his salt-and-pepper moustache. "With or without a saddle?"

Ronnie elbowed him lightly. "Go sit with your buddy before I drop you to the floor next."

"Okay, but I have my own saddle. Custom made."

She stuck her tongue out at the old flirt. He laughed and

patted her on the head, and then followed Chester.

"Where did you learn a move like that?" Natalie asked.

Here we go again, Ronnie thought, more dodging and weaving. "From Claire. What are you doing here with those two troublemakers?"

"Escaping your mother's wrath."

"Oh, God, now what?" Katie asked.

"Just your normal fun times with Aunt Deborah," Natalie answered. "The three of us took the opportunity to run when she had Gramps pinned in the kitchen, chewing on him about not taking physical therapy seriously." She grinned over at Manny and Chester. "Well, make that limp. Chester's hip is hurting tonight."

"His hip?" Ronnie frowned. "He didn't fall did he?" Gramps's bad luck seemed to be spreading to each one of them.

Natalie smirked. "No. He had a woman over a couple of nights ago and she got a little too frisky for him."

"He should have borrowed Manny's saddle," Katie said. "Speaking of the old boys getting frisky, I'd better go over there and save Arlene."

Ronnie looked around at where Chester and Manny were sitting. Arlene was at their table, her hand in Manny's, his smarmy wooing smile firmly in place. As she watched, Katie rushed over and pulled Arlene's hand free, scolding the old lover boy with her order pad. Manny grinned and nudged Chester, saying something that made Katie jam her hands on her hips and stalk back into the kitchen, her nose and forehead red. Arlene followed in her wake, grinning.

Turning back to her gin and tonic, Ronnie asked Natalie, "Where's Claire?" She wasn't looking forward to answering her sister's questions about the pocket watch, but she knew Claire well enough to know there would be no avoiding her. In the dictionary next to the word *Relentless*, Webster had Claire's picture and bio posted.

"We left her back at Ruby's."

"Really?" It wasn't like Natalie or the boys to leave Claire behind, especially with their mother on the prowl.

"Yeah, she told us to escape while we could, she'd run interference."

"Claire said that?" Ronnie paused in the midst of lifting her drink, surprised.

Natalie nodded, and asked Arlene for a shot of tequila.

Lowering her glass, Ronnie shoved her drink away. All of a sudden she was thirsty for something more sobering. Wallowing in her fears no longer appealed, especially now that she had made a scene. She had a feeling Grady would somehow get wind of her actions and make an appearance before long.

"Claire's taking one for the team tonight," Natalie said.

"She's probably hiding out in the Skunkmobile, smoking a pack of cigarettes."

Natalie took a breath. "No, I don't think so. Not this time." She glanced at the door and did a double take. "Well, well, well. Look at what the cat dragged in."

Ronnie didn't want to look. She already knew who it was and wasn't in the mood to face off against his shiny star again. "Is he coming this way?"

"Unfortunately, yes."

Ronnie risked a glance over her shoulder. "Is that Jess's dad?"

"In the flesh." Natalie grinned. "I think you should throw this one down and hogtie him for real."

"Life is like a hand of Bid Euchre," Claire said, repositioning the cards she had been dealt by Gramps.

"Oh, yeah, Socrates," Gramps said. "Please enlighten us."

Claire ignored Gramps's sarcasm. She doubted he could help it at the moment what with Deborah being his partner tonight.

"Sometimes you're flush with trump." Which she wasn't, damn it. Not an Ace to be seen, either. "And sometimes you can't score a single trick to save your soul."

"Knock off the table talk," Gramps said, figuring out her game.

Ruby, her partner across the table, winked at her and bid a conservative. "Three."

"Four." Gramps outbid his wife without hesitation.

Deborah's lips tightened into that little pink, pinched circle that Claire knew too well and had grown to loathe during her teenage years. Chester was once on the receiving end of that pissy look until he'd told Deborah that her mouth reminded him of a cat's asshole. Some days Claire wished she had Chester's balls.

She replayed that sentence in her head and grimaced. Or maybe just his guts.

"I hope you're not bluffing this time, Dad." Deborah shuffled a few cards around in her hand. "You're going to lose the game for us again if you keep showing off and outbidding everyone at the table just because you can."

"He's not bluffing," Jessica said from the couch, where she had a clear view of Gramps's cards when her nose was not in the copy of Jane Austen's *Emma* she was reading for her English Lit class. Claire wondered if Joe had a first edition copy of that book stashed away somewhere, too.

"Is Jess on your payroll?" Claire asked Gramps.

"Isn't everybody around here?" Deborah asked, a sly grin curving the edges of her mouth.

"Meaning what?" Gramps took Deborah's bait and tossed a Jack of hearts out on the table. "That's trump."

Deborah shrugged, her cream silk blouse making a slight swishing sound as she repositioned her cards. Her flowery perfume was extra strong tonight, which Claire figured had something to do with Jess's dad being in the general vicinity earlier. "Just that you seem to be doling out a lot of money lately. It reminds me of when you owned your contracting business, what with everyone standing around with their hands held out for more."

Ruby's cheeks sprouted two bright pink flower-sized spots.

Claire threw down a nine of hearts, one of two trump cards she held in her hand and then aimed a frown at her mom. "It's your turn, Mother." *So shut up and play.*

Eyeing her cards like they contained complicated calculus problems, Deborah took her sweet damned time picking out one to add to the pile. "I can understand bankrolling Claire. After all, she is going out of her way to help you build that restroom since you're on the gimpy side currently." She pulled a card and dropped it on top of the other two—the Ace of hearts.

Claire had a feeling she should throw in her cards now and call it a night. Deborah seemed to be building up to something, and Claire would rather not be sitting at ground zero when she dropped the bomb. She glanced across at Ruby and puffed her cheeks with a breath, remembering the vow she had made not to leave Ruby's side, especially when Deborah seemed to be arming her torpedoes.

Gramps growled in his throat. Claire was not sure if it was because of what Deborah was insinuating about his state of health, or lack of it at the moment, or because of her bad choice in card play. It was probably both.

Ruby threw out a ten of clubs, apparently flush out of trump. "How was dinner last night, Deborah?" she asked. "Jess tells me Steve took you out dancing afterwards."

"She said Dad's a smooth dancer," Jess spoke for Deborah, her nose in her book. "They did the two-step and some other foxy dance."

"The Fox Trot," Deborah supplied with a wistful smile as Gramps collected the pile of cards he had won this round and threw out the Ace of spades to start the next. "Steve is so charming." She sighed like she was a poodle-skirt wearing teenager all over again. Claire half-expected her to rest her cheek on her hands and smile with love struck cow eyes. "His moves on the dance floor just took me away."

They had Ruby, too—right to the bedroom almost seventeen years ago and then left her pregnant with Jessica.

"Too bad his moves didn't take you right back home to South Dakota," Gramps muttered.

Claire grinned and hid behind her cards. She peeked over the top of them at Ruby, catching the quick squeeze she gave Gramps's wrist.

"Aren't you the funny one, Dad." Deborah's snippiness said she thought otherwise. "I can't believe you let Steve slip through your fingers, Ruby. He's a real keeper."

"You think so, huh?" Ruby stared hard at the Ace Gramps had tossed out like she was waiting for it to move so she could whack it.

"With those long eyelashes and wonderful cheekbones," Deborah fanned the flames, "he would have been a real trophy."

"I'd like to put him on a shelf all right," Gramps said.

Claire tried to focus on the cards in front of her, but she could not stop watching the mix of emotions rippling across Ruby's features. She trumped Gramps's Ace with the ten of hearts, her only other trump card.

"You have no spades at all, Claire?" His blue eyes looked more bloodshot than normal, even though neither of them had lit up tonight and the alcohol had been poured only into Deborah's wine glass.

"I know how to play the game, Gramps."

He grunted his doubts.

Deborah touched the top of her cards, pretending to consider each one. Claire knew better and worried her lower lips about her mother's next move—with Ruby, not the cards.

"Not to mention ..." Deborah pulled the Queen of hearts trump card and placed it on top of Claire's ten with a haughty smile. "Steve is much closer to your age."

Claire had been expecting her mother to bite onto Ruby's

hindquarter; instead her teeth had sunk into Gramps's hide with that one. She checked his ears. They were red but not smoking ... yet.

"Dad is actually five years younger than Mom," Jessica said, her wistful smile a mirror image of Deborah's earlier one. She turned to her mother. "Does that make you a cougar, Mom?"

"It makes me wonder what I was thinking at the time."

"You had your beer goggles on that night," Claire reminded her.

"More like beer blinders." Ruby slapped down a ten of spades. "I'll follow your lead, honey," she said, reaching over to pat Gramps's cheek.

He watched Deborah rake in the cards, her sharp pink nails scraping across the card table. "Right," his voice sounded tired, a tad wheezy. "Pushing my wheel chair as you go."

Ruby's brow wrinkled. "You'll be back on your feet in no time, Harley."

"I hope you're not rushing him, Ruby. I know you need him to clean up this place, but he's not exactly a spring chicken, anymore." Deborah wrinkled her nose when she said that last part. Claire thought about rolling her cards into cigarettes and cramming them up her mother's nostrils. "Maybe you can see if Steve could help out."

"He's leaving," Claire reminded her mother.

"Not soon enough," Gramps said.

Jess sat up, placing her book facedown on the couch. "He told me today that he's thinking about sticking around for a few months so he can get to know me better."

Ruby's eyes widened. The hand she was using to hold her card lowered, her cards on display for the whole table to see. "He said what?"

"Perfect." Deborah said. Or maybe she purred. She was being so catty tonight that Claire half-expected her to lift up her arm and start cleaning herself. "He can help Claire when Natalie goes home next week."

"Mother," Claire said, "having a penis does not automatically mean you can build shit."

Deborah narrowed her eyes. "Watch the language, Claire."

"What? I used the 'p' word." She shifted her cards around. "Where is Jess's dad, anyway? I thought you three were going to go to a movie tonight."

Ever since Steve had shown up, Deborah had been fawning all over her stepsister, aka Jessica. Normally, her mother could not stand to be in the same room as the teenager. Now Jess seemed to do no wrong, something Claire had never experienced. Ever. She had been a constant screw-up since birth in Deborah's eyes.

"He said he was tired and went back to his hotel room," Jess answered.

"Claire doesn't need any help," Gramps said.

He was wrong. Claire did need help, especially with some of the finishing touches like the crown molding Gramps wanted hung. Those compound miters were a bitch, especially in the corners where she would have to cut upside down and backwards. But she was smart enough to keep her mouth shut at the moment.

"If Claire needs help," Ruby stepped in, "Mac will be here."

Gramps's face darkened into a ruddy shade, his back stiffening visibly. "Your nephew has done enough for you," he said to his wife. "He should focus on tending his own garden a little more before the dandelions go to seed."

Ruby gaped at him for a moment before snapping her mouth closed and glaring down at her cards.

Deborah looked at Claire, her brows raised. "Dandelions go to seed, huh? Are you and MacDonald having some relationship problems?"

"Uh," Claire was caught off guard with the sudden shift of focus. Relationship problems? Honestly, she was still stuck on what a baby could mean to her own future. She hadn't made it to analyzing how it could affect her relationship with Mac yet.

Earlier today, after her admission about the subject to Natalie, her cousin had tried to talk her into buying a pregnancy test. Claire had crossed her arms and dug in her heels. For one thing, she was not ready to face pregnancy head on if it were a done deal, let alone wait for that little stick to show its pink or blue lines. Her breathing grew raspy at just the thought of peeing on it. For another, she was on a first name basis with all of the employees who worked at Creekside Hardware Supply in Jackrabbit Junction, and they knew she was related to Ruby and Gramps. She might as well stand on the corner at the one junction in town with MIGHT BE PREGNANT on a sandwich board if she bought a test there.

In the end, Natalie had driven into town and bought the pregnancy test. She had returned with a nondescript paper bag, which she handed to Claire on the sly when the boys were not looking. Claire had hidden the unopened box still inside the bag under the sink in the Skunkmobile's bathroom, burying it in the back corner behind the drain cleaner and rolls of toilet paper.

Jessica joined them at the table, standing over her own mother's shoulder. "I heard Manny say Claire and Mac were having some problems in the bedroom." She leaned down and pointed at one of Ruby's cards. "Play that one next, Mom."

Ruby shooed Jess's finger away.

"Mac and I are ..." *possibly pregnant*, "... doing fine," Claire announced, dealing cards around the table.

"Are you angry with Mac for some reason, Harley?" Ruby asked Gramps, her gaze locked onto her cards. "Did he say something to upset you?"

Claire watched Gramps, waiting with all ears to hear his answer. Mac had not mentioned anything to her about a problem with Gramps, but he had been less than thrilled with the idea of sticking around the R.V. park an extra day, which was not normal for him. He usually wanted to stay at his aunt's as long as possible, especially when Claire wasn't going home to Tucson with him.

"You're doing 'fine,' huh?" Deborah collected her cards. "Boy, have I heard that before. It was your father's favorite response when I'd ask if everything was okay. Turned out he was fine, especially since he was sleeping with another woman."

"Mom, that's enough," Claire warned, nudging her head in Jess's direction. Jessica soaked up sordid tales of debauchery like a new chamois.

"I know, I know," Deborah crossed her arms over her chest. "You don't like it when I bad mouth your father. I was just making a point."

"How about you just button your lips instead," Gramps said, "and focus on playing cards?"

Deborah rolled her eyes at him and then returned to Claire. "I couldn't help but notice the way you were avoiding MacDonald this last weekend."

"I wasn't avoiding Mac." *I was avoiding you.*

"Before you start your denial routine, Claire, let me finish."

"You probably shouldn't," Gramps said.

Deborah continued, ignoring her father. "If things don't work out with MacDonald, you can always come home and live with me. I have plenty of room in the house. You can even have your old bedroom back if you'd like."

Claire recoiled at the thought of living with her mother again.

"Why would Claire leave Mac?" Jess asked. "I saw them kissing before he left on Sunday."

"Claire tends to have a problem with commitment, Jessica dear," Deborah said, patting Claire's hand. "I don't think MacDonald—or any man out there—has what it takes to get her to settle down and focus on building a successful career. She needs a man who will tame her spirit, not let her run free as MacDonald seems to do." She pulled her hand away and tucked a strand of blonde hair back into her French knot. "I blame her father for her lack of steadfastness. He insisted I leave Claire be, claiming I'd already spoiled Veronica. But I ask you, which of my daughters has been the most successful in life? Certainly not Kathryn or Claire."

"Are you done now?" Claire asked Deborah, bored with the subject. She had heard this all before, too many times to care anymore what her mom had to say on the subject, and had long ago given up trying to prove her wrong.

"For now," Deborah said. "But I won't truly be finished until you stop hopping from one job to another and settle down to make a life for yourself."

Claire turned to Gramps. "Did you adopt her?"

"I'm beginning to wonder about that."

Ruby snorted, reminding Claire of a pissed off bull minus the ground pawing. "After the last couple of days, I'm startin' to think she's a chip off the old block."

Deborah arched one plucked eyebrow. "What are you insinuating, my dear stepmother?"

"Can't we just play a goddamned game of cards?" Gramps asked.

Everyone quieted, focusing on their cards.

Deborah placed the King of clubs in the center of the table.

Jessica pointed at a card in Ruby's hand. "Play that one."

"Would you two stop cheating?" Deborah asked with an unladylike snippiness in her voice.

"Jessica," Ruby warned.

"What? I'm just trying to help. You never let me help, only Mac."

"Ain't that the truth," Gramps said.

Ruby threw down her cards. "What is your problem with Mac?"

"Nothing. He's perfect. Just calm down so we can finish this game and go to bed."

"Don't you tell me to calm down, Harley Ford. You've been pokin' at me about Mac all night. What is going on between you two?"

"Isn't it obvious, Ruby?" Deborah said. "He's jealous."

"Of Mac?" Claire asked.

"No, of Steve. He's just taking it out on Mac."

"Why's he jealous of Dad?"

"I'm not jealous of that horse's ass," Gramps said.

"Dad is not a horse's ass. Take that back!"

"That's enough, Jessica," Ruby said. "Go to your room."

"What? Why? What did I do? He's the one calling names."

Ruby reiterated her order with a point. Ranting, Jess grabbed her book off the couch and stomped up the stairs.

"Jealous," Deborah sang, moving her cards around.

"You," Ruby snatched Deborah's cards away, "go to your room, too."

Deborah's mouth fell open. Shock, disbelief, and outrage reeled down her face like triple sevens on a slot machine. "What gives you the right to—"

"You're in *my* house. That gives me the right to kick you out if I want. For now, I'll settle for you goin' to bed."

Deborah let out a huff that blew Claire's hair back. "Your hostess skills are lacking to say the least."

"Wait," Gramps said as she stalked toward the stairs. "We're not done with the game yet."

"Oh, we are definitely done." Ruby shoved away from the table and slammed out the back door.

Claire dropped her cards on the table. "Gee, that didn't go so well."

Gramps sighed, scrubbing his hand up and down over his whiskers, making a rasping sound. "Nothing has been lately. Not since I fell off that damned ladder. What do you say we end this bet of ours and go have a smoke?"

Hell, yes! "Not tonight."

His hand stopped. "Why not?"

"I'm not really in the mood," she lied.

"First you didn't want the beer I offered and now you don't want to smoke." Gramps blue eyes narrowed. "What's going on, girl? You're not pregnant, are you?"

Chapter Twelve

Thursday, October 4th

Ronnie needed a big favor. One that she figured would cost more than any of Lyle's knockoff sterling silver necklaces or costume jewelry.

She pushed in through the Yuccaville library's glass doors, sniffing the air for bay rum aftershave. All she smelled was stale paper and a hint of rose-laced perfume. She scanned for Grady or any of his deputies, double-checking that the coast was clear before making a beeline over to Aunt Millie and her cohorts, who were knitting in the sitting area next to the computers as usual. Without saying a word, she took out a pair of real tanzanite studded hoop earrings from the front pocket of her knee-length paisley skirt and placed them on the end table next to Grady's aunt.

Aunt Millie whistled through her teeth. Dropping her knitting needles, she scooped up the earrings, lowered her glasses, and took a closer look at the purplish blue stones. Her drawn-on eyebrows lifted, along with her gaze. "Something tells me we're not playing for computer time today, Veronica."

"I have a problem." Ronnie kept her voice low in case the Sheriff was hiding behind a bookshelf waiting to pounce. "I need your help."

"You do, huh? I'm not sure I can offer enough help to cover the cost of these beauties." Aunt Millie set the earrings back on the table. "Maybe one of the other girls can help you."

Ronnie shook her head. "Nope. You're the only one for

this job." She glanced at Ruth, Millie's second in command, whose lower lip jutted a little. "It's about her nephew," Ronnie said, trying to soothe any ruffled feathers.

Ruth tucked her lip back in and returned to the long-necked sweater she was knitting.

"Well, I'll say one thing, you sure know how to get my attention." Aunt Millie reached for her walker. "Why don't we move this conversation somewhere a little more private in case we get visitors. My office will do."

"Your office?"

Aunt Millie pointed toward the women's restroom.

"Oh, gotcha."

The dingle balls on her walker jiggled as she stood, the metal contraption creaking when she leaned on it. "Ruth, you're in charge. Greta, keep an eye out for Grady and run interference if he comes through those doors."

Both women nodded without looking up from their needles.

Ronnie followed Aunt Millie into the women's restroom and checked under the stall doors to make sure all three were empty. She leaned against the door to keep it that way.

"Okay," Aunt Millie placed the earrings on the counter. "What is so gol-durn important that you're willing to exchange an expensive pair of real tanzanite earrings for my help?"

"You know your gemstones." Ronnie's face warmed as the realization hit her that Aunt Millie and her friends must have known all along that her jewelry was fake.

"I wasn't born yesterday, dear."

"But you let me buy time on the computer with the other stuff."

"Your costume jewelry is some of the best we've seen in a long time."

"Oh. Thanks, I guess." Lyle would be so proud. Then she remembered how Grady had dragged her outside of The Shaft and chewed on her about the chandelier earrings. "Wait. Does the Sheriff realize that you know the pieces I've given you are fake?"

Aunt Millie's smile lifted her jowls. "There are some things that my nephew doesn't need to know even though he thinks he does. I let him assume all sorts of things when it comes to taking care of me. It's easier that way." She winked at Ronnie. "Easier to hoodwink him, too."

She needed to take a few lessons from Aunt Millie. So far, all she had managed to do was set off his radar at every turn. "I'll have to remember that."

"Well, let's hear it, dear. What's got you digging deep in your jewelry box for the good stuff today?"

Ronnie clasped her hands together, wondering how much she could trust Aunt Millie, if at all. "I have a little problem."

"Is this about that castle over in Germany?"

Yes, but she did not want to drag Aunt Millie into that mess. Her family was already at risk. Grady would throw her in a cell and swallow the key if he found out she put his aunt in danger, too.

"No," she lied. "It's about your nephew."

Aunt Millie's eyes narrowed behind her glasses. "You aren't in cahoots with his ex-wife, are you?"

"Grady—I mean Sheriff Harrison—has an ex-wife?" Ronnie had trouble picturing the hardass relaxing enough to wine, dine, and bed a woman, let alone marry her.

"Yes siree, and she is a real dandy, too."

Dandy as in beautiful with big blue eyes like the blonde Lyle had been screwing around with behind Ronnie's back?

"I'd have taken that bitch down a notch if I were ten years younger," Aunt Millie told Ronnie, lifting her walker and shaking it at an imaginary villainess. "No man deserves to be treated the way she did my nephew."

Ronnie wished there had been an Aunt Millie standing up for her when the shit had hit the fan in her happy little world and sprayed out the other side, coating her and everything she had owned. "What happened?"

Aunt Millie snorted, disgust curling her upper lip. "She

ripped out his heart, tossed it out the window like a cigarette butt, and then backed over it for kicks."

"That's tough," she said, comparing her heartbreak to Grady's. While she had not really loved Lyle, Ronnie had thought they had a mutual respect for each other. That was before she'd found herself facedown with a set of tire tracks running down her backside.

"Did she have an affair?" Ronnie asked.

"Not just one."

"How did he find out?"

"She told him after the baby was born."

"The baby?" Ronnie blinked in surprise. Grady was a father?

"Yep." Aunt Millie slapped her hand down on the sink counter. "The painted strumpet waited so that the birth was covered by Grady's insurance because her boyfriend was unemployed at the time. After she left the hospital, she told Grady that the baby wasn't his and filed for divorce. The blood test proved she wasn't lying before a full-fledged child custody battle could get rolling."

Ronnie grimaced. Damn, no wonder the Sheriff was such a hardass. The poor guy must have a hollow, broken shell where his heart had been. At least there had been no kids caught up in her mess.

"How long ago was this?" she asked. Guilt filled her, making her gut heavy. She probably should have taken it easy on Grady instead of being so quick to argue with him.

"It's been about five years since the divorce was final. She packed up and moved to Nevada with the baby's real daddy as soon as the papers were official."

"So Grady hasn't seen the baby or her since?"

Aunt Millie shook her head. "It's a subject his momma, sister, and I talk about only when he's nowhere around. Grady once told me that as far as he's concerned, his ex-wife and her kid never existed. I think that's his coping mechanism for losing the baby boy he had thought was his for nine long months."

Ronnie thought of the Sheriff, how cold and hard he had seemed since they first met. It all made sense. "The poor guy."

"Yep, yep." Aunt Millie tapped on the counter. "After the dust settled, he dove headfirst into his job and he hasn't come up for air since. His momma figures work was all he had after she left him knocked flat on his ass like that."

She knew that ass over tea kettle sensation quite well. Her head was still spinning from Lyle's lies and betrayal. "That really sucks." Both for her and for Grady.

Ronnie had something in common with him now, both having been royally screwed by their exes. Truthfully, she would rather they just cut their thumbs and shared a little blood and a matching scar. Not that they would ever swap ex stories over a couple of drinks or anything like that. Grady was broken; she could see it now.

She was, too, for that matter. Two broken lives added together equaled a visit on a Jerry Springer type talk show where someone usually ended up throwing a chair, not a two-hour movie on one of those romance channels with a sap-happy ending.

Veronica Jefferson had died of humiliation in that interrogation room months ago while the government sponsored suits snickered around her, leaving Ronnie Morgan to pick up the pieces and keep going. She would not trust so blindly again or maybe ever trust at all. Life would be much safer that way.

"You nailed it, dear," Aunt Millie scowled across the small room at Ronnie. "It sucks donkey dicks."

Ronnie blinked out of her empathy-filled meanderings. Did Aunt Millie just say *donkey* ...

"But we don't get to choose the cards life deals us. We have to decide whether to stick with what we have or risk going bust by asking for another hit or two."

Had Gramps been whispering in Aunt Millie's ear? That sounded like something he'd say in between puffs on his cigar.

After *sticking* with what life had dealt her during the first thirty-five years of her life, Ronnie was ready to risk going bust.

"Are you ever going to tell me what you need from me that's worth parting with these here earrings, or am I going to die of old age before then? Because if I keel over first, I want you to bury me in these earrings." Aunt Millie waved her liver spotted hand over the tanzanite hoops. "They'll look good with my favorite periwinkle dress."

"I need you to keep a secret for me."

"You're buying my silence?"

"If your nephew asks you anything about that castle article we pulled up yesterday, I want you to tell him we stumbled across it by accident in our search for an article written in German."

"And why were we looking for an article written in German?"

"Greta is teaching me the language, remember?"

"Oh, right." She frowned down at the earrings for so long Ronnie wondered if she had drifted off while standing there. When she looked up, her forehead was tight with what looked like concern. "Are you in trouble, Veronica? Because you've kind of grown on me and I hate to see something bad happen to those I like in this town."

That Aunt Millie cared enough to ask warmed Ronnie's lonely heart, making her want to share every little detail about Lyle and the mess he left her mixed up in. But she kept the lid sealed tight on Pandora's box. No matter how much it rattled, the chain needed to stay locked tight. "Not any more than the normal amount."

"Is there anything we can do to help? Besides keeping quiet about that article?"

Ronnie shook her head, crossing her arms over her chest, holding in the truth even tighter. "No, but thanks for the offer."

"I don't feel right taking real jewelry in exchange for keeping my lips shut."

"Please take them. Your silence on this means a lot to me. I don't want your nephew digging into my business." Actually, it was Ruby's business, but Ronnie preferred to have Aunt Millie and the girls thinking she was the one tied up in something shady.

Aunt Millie pocketed the earrings. "What German article, my dear nephew?" She pretended, talking to the mirror in the sweet old aunt tone Ronnie had heard her use with certain library visitors, like yesterday with Grady. "Oh, that one? We found it and thought it would make great practice for Veronica since she is so interested in learning the language."

"Thank you," Ronnie said, holding open the door for Aunt Millie to shuffle-roll out.

"My pleasure." She paused as she drew level with Ronnie. "And I expect you to keep your lips zipped about my nephew's history."

"You got it." Ronnie pulled her finger across her lips.

"You are welcome to the computers, honey," Aunt Millie said as she and her walker led the way back to the other ladies.

"Thanks, but I think I'm good for now." She didn't need to risk Grady sneaking up on her again and peeking over her shoulder at another article about a stolen artifact "Here's my phone number," she wrote down her cell number on a piece of scrap paper from one of the computer desks. "Give me a call if anyone starts asking any questions, if you know what I mean."

"This is so cloak and dagger like." Aunt Millie grinned. "I haven't had this much excitement since Ruth and I got booted from the senior center last year."

Why had they been booted? Ronnie shook the question from her thoughts. That was not important at the moment.

After making sure Aunt Millie made it back to her seat without a problem, Ronnie gave her farewells to each of the ladies. She handed out a holiday themed brooch to each one and told them she would see them again soon.

She stepped out into the warm sunshine, feeling less like

slipping into flight mode for the first time since she had found out the pocket watch had been stolen and realized the risk it meant to her family. She whistled as she walked the four blocks to Gramps's 1949 flame-painted blue Mercury, which she had borrowed since Katie had needed her car to run errands this afternoon.

When she turned the corner of the building she had parked behind, she stumbled to a stop at the sight of Sheriff Grady Harrison leaning against the front quarter panel of her grandfather's car. His long legs were crossed at the ankle, but his shoulders were stiffer than the Tin Man's after a downpour.

Come on! Now what had she done? Had Aunt Millie called him as soon as Ronnie left the library, singing like a canary? No, she would not have done that. He must have seen her entering the library from his cop shop window.

He stared across the parking lot at her from behind his sunglasses, his mouth molded into a flat line.

Lowering her forehead, she readied herself for more head butting. There would be no getting around him, so she might as well take him straight on. She crossed the lot, fixing a fake smile on her face.

"Hello, Sheriff. How are you doing on this fine afternoon?"

"Cut the chit chat, Veronica." He stood up straight and tugged the brim of his hat lower. "We have a problem."

So much for feeling sorry for the jerk about his ex-wife scandal.

"Really, Grady?" Her lips pursed. "What is it now? I can hardly wait for yet another threat from you."

"You lied."

"About what?" She had lied about so many things since coming to Arizona that she knew better than to engage in any denial without knowing where to start.

"Your husband."

"I told you our marriage was invalid."

"I'm not referring to that particular admission."

"Okay, so what exactly did I lie about when it comes to Lyle Jefferson?"

"You withheld the fact that he is currently in prison, for one thing."

Someone had been doing his homework. Ronnie had figured it was a matter of time before he stumbled across Lyle's prison sentence. "I don't remember saying he was a free man these days."

"You insinuated that he was traveling."

"No, you misunderstood and assumed he was traveling. He used to travel weekly until he ended up in prison."

"You lied by omission, then."

She wagged her finger in front of his rock hard jaw. "*Au contraire*, Sheriff. You're very good at twisting things to make me look shady and suspicious."

He captured her finger in a steel grip, his palm hot to the touch, and yanked her close enough to step on his toes. It was a replay of the other night, including her speeding heart. "From what I read, Veronica," his voice was low, dangerous, "you've done a good job of doing that to yourself."

He was looking down his nose at her again, both figuratively speaking and for real. God, she ached to knock that crooked appendage off his face. Ronnie pulled her finger free and stepped back, clenching her fists. "Be careful assuming things about me, Grady. The truth might sneak up and show you for a fool, along with the rest of your friends with their fancy suits and search warrants."

"What are you doing here, Veronica?"

"Visiting my family."

"No, I mean here in Yuccaville. Today. You're digging for something in the library. What? Something to do with that article with the pictures of pocket watches?"

Shit-sticks! This guy did not give up, did he? Good thing Ronnie had already bought his aunt and her gang's silence. She mentally patted herself on the back for being one step ahead of the busybody staring down at her from behind his dark glasses.

"Your aunt and her friends explained it all yesterday, Grady. I'm learning how to knit and speak German."

He shook his head, barely letting her finish before visibly rejecting her explanation. "Christ. You're a real professional, Veronica Morgan."

"Thank you, Sheriff." She deliberately misunderstood his insult.

"You stand here in broad daylight, blowing my hair back with your lies without showing a single twinge or twitch of guilt. It's been a long time since I've come across someone as smooth tongued."

A long time as in five years ago when his wife pulled her whammy on him? He must kick himself daily for not seeing the truth on her face day after day for nine long months.

"You've had a lot of practice perfecting your craft, I'm betting." The glower he was wearing spoke volumes about his feelings for her at the moment.

His disdain burned, darn it. The resulting sorrow floated up toward the surface, but she caught hold of it and jammed it back down deep before he could see how his opinion affected her.

Why in the hell did she care what a small time sheriff thought of her? He was just one more authority figure treating her like she was something that fell out of the back of a manure spreader.

But she did care, damn it. Maybe it was because of the camaraderie she had felt after hearing he, too, had been royally screwed by his ex. Or maybe it had less to do with the Sheriff himself and more related to the fact that the stink Lyle had marked her with was still hovering around her. It was something she could not shake even a thousand miles away from South Dakota.

She squared her shoulders. The Sheriff wasn't going to be her best friend anytime soon. So what. Life would go on as it had for the last few months. He was just one more person to keep an eye on as she figured out her next move.

"Are we done here, Sheriff?" She hit a button on Gramps's key ring. The Mercury's door unlocked with a clunk.

He stepped aside, letting her open the door and crawl inside. "I don't know that we'll ever be 'done,' Veronica."

She flashed him a sideways glance. "Then you'll need to get in line."

"And what line is that?" He gripped his belt with both hands, the butt of his gun brushing his wrist.

Mabel rumbled to life, her V-8 growling under the flame-covered hood.

"The one filled with other badge-carrying assholes like yourself."

Ronnie slammed the door shut in his face, shifted into gear, and rolled away. Her eyes found him in the rearview mirror as she paused before pulling out into the street. He still stood there stiff-legged, watching after her.

"Fuck." Ronnie said, slamming the heel of her palm on the steering wheel. Every time she tried to untangle herself from the law, the web tightened further. At least he had not threatened to slap her with an assault charge for her rodeo ride on the drunk cowboy last night.

She checked for traffic. Other than an older, red two-door pickup idling curbside with a cowboy smoking a cigarette behind the steering wheel—like every other Jimmy Don and Billy Bob in the region—the road was empty.

She turned, hit the gas, and waved goodbye to the Sheriff. For now.

"Did you take the test yet?" Natalie asked Claire. She'd just returned from Ruby's shed where she had been searching for something to secure the hinge on the ladder Gramps had bent when he had fallen. The makeshift fix Claire had made to it had broken during the night when it somehow had fallen over onto the new concrete floor. Claire suspected foul play; Natalie pointed out some dirt tracks that looked very much like a raccoon had come calling. Such was the difference in their perspective on life in Jackrabbit Junction.

"Shhhh," Claire nudged her head in the direction of the three musketeers sitting in their lawn chairs on the other side of the newly wired restroom wall. They had spent the afternoon drinking cheap beer and talking smack. She could only imagine the gossip her possible pregnancy would fuel.

Natalie pointed a pair of wire cutters at the wall separating them from the boys. "They can't hear anything above shouting level with all of that hair in their ears and you know it."

Claire walked away from her, trying to put some distance between herself and the pregnancy mess in general.

Natalie followed. "Well?"

"It's the same answer I gave you the last three times I came back from the bathroom."

"Why not? What are you waiting for? You either are or aren't. Waiting only delays finding out a fact."

Claire planted her hands on her hips. "Don't you have some wiring to do in the other room?"

"Fine," Natalie grabbed her tool belt and slung it around her hips. "You can put me off, but I'm not going to stop bugging you about it."

"Claire!" Gramps shouted.

"Saved by the crotchety bell." Natalie shoved Claire toward the entryway. "Take the damned test, chicken shit."

Claire flipped her off over her shoulder and walked out into the afternoon sunshine. Across the park, the two older ladies in khaki everything sat at the picnic table next to their ultra-beige camper, hovering over what looked like an unrolled poster or map from this distance. Jess's beanpole was nowhere to be seen, which meant he was probably with everyone else at the dig site. So why had the khaki club-ettes not gone with the rest?

She crossed the raggedy, mostly dead grass to stand in front of Gramps. "What do you want?"

He glanced down at her stomach for a split second. "I think you should sit here by me." He pointed at the ground next to his feet.

"I think you've confused me for your lousy mutt." Henry, his ever faithful companion, growled up at her from behind wrinkled black lips. "How much beer have you had this afternoon?"

"I know you're not a damned dog, Claire. I just think you should take a break for a bit."

Oh, lord. She never should have come clean with him last night after the card game fiasco, but she couldn't help it. She had felt bad for him after Ruby left, especially when she had seen the flashes of pain on his face as he had tried to stand.

After some badgering, he had let her help him to the couch where he figured he'd be spending the night. She had sat next to him like she had when she was a kid, leaning her head on his shoulder. After several minutes of silence, he let it leak that he was concerned about Ruby's future. He did not want to leave her in a mess like Joe had. Claire had recognized his need for a partner in commiseration, and the only thing she had going for her was possibly being pregnant and what that might mean in the grand scheme of her screwed up life.

Gramps had promised after their bitchfest not to tell Ruby until Claire gave him the green light. However, if he did not stop babying her as he had been all morning, insisting she stay off the roof and let Natalie do the brunt of the work, telling her to take breaks every hour, Manny and Chester would be planning her baby shower by supper time. Strippers would undoubtedly be included on the guest list, with mud wrestling being one of the games for all to play.

"I'm fine," she told Gramps.

"What in the hell is going on?" Chester asked, speaking around his cigar. "Yesterday you were barking at the girl for not moving fast enough. Today you're wiping her brow and asking her if she needs more peeled grapes while you fan her with a palm frond."

Claire liked the picture Chester painted. Only switch out Gramps for Mac, who had not called her yet today but who was supposed to be back to the R.V. park later tonight.

"She caught you smoking, didn't she, *viejo*?" Manny elbowed Gramps. "You lost the bet and she's making you pay in kindness and *amor*?"

"Maybe I'm just taking care of my granddaughter."

"What about Natalie?" Chester asked.

"What about me?" Natalie joined them, stealing a beer from their cooler and cracking it open.

Chester's scowl stretched from the beer can up to her face. "Why isn't Ford telling you to take breaks like he is Claire?"

Claire shot Natalie a warning look. Her cousin knew Claire had spilled the beans to Gramps, but one wrong step in front of these two old badgers and they would lock their jaws on tight. No amount of tugging would free Claire from having to tell them the truth.

Natalie shrugged and took a drink of beer before answering. "Probably because I took my breaks on the way to and from Yuccaville. Claire has been here working straight through, putting up with your sorry asses all afternoon. She deserves a break or ten."

Chester's wrinkles around his eyes deepened. His wary expression said he was not buying their song and dance. "Something fishy is going on here. I can smell it."

"That's just the fumes coming from your boxer shorts," Gramps said, making Manny sputter.

"Now sit, Claire." Gramps pointed at the ground next to where Henry sat, his tongue hanging out even though they were in the shade. "Please."

Claire gave in, lowering to the ground next to him, leaning back against his good leg.

He patted her head, making Henry whine and squirm.

Claire stuck out her tongue at the mutt.

Manny grabbed a beer from the cooler and held it out to her. She waved it away, grabbing the bottle of water Natalie handed her.

One of Manny's bushy salt-and-pepper eyebrows lifted, but he sat back without saying anything.

"How are things in the house?" Natalie asked Gramps. The fact that Ruby was still pissed at him was no secret from Natalie, who had told Claire earlier that she had walked in this morning and found him on the couch where Claire had left him last night.

"I don't know." He took the beer Manny had intended for Claire.

"He's too scared to risk Ruby's wrath," Chester explained with a shit-eating grin.

"Damned right I am. She has a wicked swing. I don't want to end up kissing the hard side of that cast iron skillet she uses to cook my bacon and eggs every morning."

"Did either of you two wiseasses tell Gramps about last night?" Natalie asked Chester and Manny.

"Tell me what?"

Chester winced. "We were trying to avoid that name for the rest of the year."

Manny chuckled. "*El stinko* here thinks if he says the word 'Deborah,' he'll turn into a pile of salt this fast." He snapped his fingers.

"A 'pillar of salt,' you Latin loser," Chester shot back.

"What happened last night?" Claire wondered what she had missed while staying back at Ruby's and dodging her mother's barbs.

Chester pulled his cigar from his lips. "Jessica's daddy showed up at the bar."

Snorting, Gramps said, "So he likes to drink—so do we." He reinforced his comment with a gulp of beer.

Sitting forward, Claire picked up a couple of pieces of gravel and tossed them into the drive where they belonged. "I thought Mom told us he was going home after he dropped off her and Jess."

"He probably changed his mind when he drove past The Shaft." Gramps seemed to have taken up the role of devil's advocate for some reason today, the polar opposite from last night.

"The horny toad tried to get into Natalie's pants," Chester added.

Gramps ramrodded up, his knee nailing Claire in the back. "I'll kill that cradle-robbing bastard."

Jeez! Gramps left rubber on the asphalt from that u-turn. Kneading where his knee had jabbed her, Claire scooted forward.

"I'm no longer cradle-robbing material, Gramps." Natalie squeezed his shoulder. "But thanks for making me feel younger."

"I don't give a rat's ass what age you are. He's old enough to be your ..." he paused, doing the math on his fingers.

"Much older brother," Claire said, wondering if he had forgotten about his and Ruby's age difference.

"He hit on Ronnie, too," Natalie added. "More than he hit on me, actually."

"That's because she was already drunk," Chester said, shoving his cigar back in his mouth.

"No, she wasn't." Natalie handed Manny her empty beer can. "She was only on her second glass of gin and tonic by then."

"You mean third, *chiquita*," Manny said.

"No, second. She dumped one glass over that cowboy's head for getting too grabby."

"What cowboy?" Claire and Gramps asked in unison.

When Ronnie had made it home last night, she had been stuck on MUTE, claiming exhaustion, holding up her hand in Claire's face when pressured for any information on the pocket watch. This morning, she had upped her syllables per sentence to one, claiming a hangover, avoiding Claire's questions to the point of locking herself in the upstairs bathroom and cranking on the bath faucet. Claire had slammed her fist against the door and left, muttering all of the way to the back of the R.V. park, kicking gravel at grasshoppers along the way.

Something was very wrong with her older sister, and Claire had a feeling the volcano inside of Ronnie had lava bubbling up its throat. She had gone totally off the "weird" scale and was now existing somewhere in the lower realms of "temporary insanity."

Kate thought Claire was blowing things out of proportion, looking to find problems in everyone's lives rather than focus on her own, and Kate was probably partially right. This possible pregnancy was fucking with Claire's head. But she had been watching their oldest sister closely this last week, and every time someone asked Ronnie about her ex-husband or brought up the whole divorce shambles, she found some excuse to leave the room. Now add Ronnie dumping a drink over some stranger's head, which went completely against all of those etiquette lessons she had been force fed, and Claire was pretty damned certain the volcano was about to go *ka-boom*!

"Kate said he was some drunken cowboy that Ronnie shoved to the floor. Then she rode him like a stallion," Manny said, his moustache curling with his lips. "*Ay yi yi*, I love a woman who likes to buck."

"She did what?" A vein in Gramps's forehead throbbed.

"She didn't ride him like a stallion," Natalie clarified. "What Kate really said was that when the cowboy tried to backhand Ronnie, she did some fancy jujitsu-like move and knocked him to the floor, sat on his back, and yanked up on his arm until he bawled like a baby. Arlene's story matched Kate's, except she mentioned something about Ronnie asking the crowd for a piggin' string."

Hot damn. Claire grinned. Of all of the nights to skip going to The Shaft. She would have loved to see Ronnie take down a frisky drunk. Who knew her sister even had that in her?

Natalie looked down at Claire. "Kate said the move reminded her of something you would have done. Actually, now that I think about it, Ronnie told me it was something you had taught her."

Oh, really? That was even funnier, as in a load of hogwash funny, because Claire did not remember ever teaching Ronnie such a move.

She tossed another piece of gravel toward the drive. Her older sister was lying for some reason, and one way or another, even if it involved doing some hogtying of her own, she was going to get to the bottom of it.

"So, Jessica's father tried to pick up both of you girls?" Gramps asked, returning to the point at where the conversation had derailed.

Natalie nodded.

"I guess he's not nearly as taken with Mother as she is with him," Claire said to Gramps.

"It appears not." He shifted in his chair, his face scrunching in pain for a moment or two. "And while that makes me happy for several reasons," he grimaced, "I don't think it's going to go over well with your mom, which is going to make life even more of a pain in the ass for Ruby and me."

"Your daughter needs to get laid," Chester said to Gramps.

Natalie and Gramps both groaned.

"Curse your tongue, old man," Claire said.

"What? You have to admit she could use some mellowing out. I was hoping Jess's dad would take one for the team and save us all from her sharp teeth. She could spend some time draining good ol' Steve Horner-toad dry while we figured out how to get rid of her ass again. I don't think dumping a bucket of water on her will work this time."

"Are you guys talking about my dad?" Jessica asked, stepping out from the spindly grove of mesquite trees behind them. She had her *Emma* book tucked under her arm, but it looked thicker, the pages more wrinkled. A piece of paper acting as a bookmark fluttered in the breeze along with wisps of her red hair that had escaped her ponytail. Her shorts were rolled up so they were way too short and her mouth glistened with a thick coating of lip gloss.

Claire knew exactly who Jess was out to impress. Unfortunately for the freckle-faced teen, Beanpole was at the dig site.

Rather than try to deny what Jess had probably already overheard, Claire said, "We were talking about my mom going with him to dinner again tonight."

"Oh, right. I think he might be busy though." Jess held out a handful of dollar bills and change toward her.

"What's this?" Claire asked.

"It was in your pants' pocket. Mom had me do the laundry this afternoon."

"Thanks." She tucked away the change from the pregnancy test.

"What happened to your book?" Gramps asked.

"It fell in the washing machine. I fished it out before it got too wet."

He sighed. "You need to take better care of your school books. Your mom had to replace the last one you brought home and dropped in the tub."

"I know. I know." Jess blew some hair out of her face. "I was being careful, but it slipped." She looked over at Natalie. "Will you let me borrow your cowboy hat tonight?"

"What do you need her hat for?" Gramps asked.

"I have a date."

"With who?" Manny asked.

"My boyfriend."

Claire did a double take. So they had moved to that level now, had they? "You mean the tall skinny kid who works for the college?"

"He's not a kid. He's a man." Jessica's voice was all

breathy when she said that last word.

Claire looked away to hide her grimace.

"You are not borrowing Natalie's hat," Gramps said.

"Why not?"

"Because you are not going out with a boy that much older than you."

Jessica's face puckered, turning several shades pinker. "I am, too. Besides, Mom already said I could go."

"Yeah, well she's going to change her mind after I talk to her. He's in college, kid."

"I know. That's why I like him. He's way more mature than the boys my age." She crossed her arms over her chest. "I'm going whether you like it or not, Harley."

"No, you're not."

"Yes, I am, and you're not my dad so you don't get to tell me what to do." She turned on her heel and stormed off.

Gramps pointed at Claire. "This is your fault."

She sputtered. "What? How is that my fault?"

"You and Mac are sleeping together without any talk of commitment. You're setting a bad example." He crushed his beer can and threw it on the ground. "Next thing you know, she'll be pregnant, too."

Claire covered her face and growled out several of her favorite swear words.

"Ha! I knew it, *chica*." Manny clapped.

"That explains the no smoking bet," Chester said. "And all of your bitchiness."

Claire glared at Gramps from between her fingers. "So much for keeping a damned secret, huh?" She parted her palms when she spoke. "What's next? The combination to the safe?"

"I'm sorry, Claire." At least he had the decency to look sheepish. "At least your mom doesn't know about it."

Lowering her hands, she turned a gunslinger glare on the other two troublemakers. "Well, let's all make sure it stays that way, got it?"

Chapter Thirteen

Claire sat alone on Ruby's front porch step, leaning against the post, listening to the bullfrogs croaking to each other down by Jackrabbit Creek. The sun had taken its final bow before sinking behind the purple shrouded mountains to the west, its fading salute painting the sky with pink and lilac brush strokes.

She checked Ruby's cordless phone for the fifth time in as many minutes, making sure yet again that the batteries were still working.

Where was Mac, damn it? He was supposed to have called before supper. She thought about leaving another voicemail, but really the previous three would probably get her point across when he finally checked his phone. Grunting in frustration, she set the phone on the step next to her and watched an airplane contrail cut eastward through the sky until it disappeared into a pink cloud.

How was Mac going to react if she were pregnant? Would he insist on marriage? She squirmed on the hard wood step, every instinct in her reacting as always to the thought of marriage and its long term, breath-constricting bonds. Would he be willing to continue the loosey-goosey arrangement they'd had since Claire had started staying with him? Would he insist his baby have his last name?

"Gah," she shivered in the warm evening air.

How in the hell could she be pregnant? She had been so careful with not missing a pill ... well, most of the time. There was that week where she couldn't find the pill packet. And then there was the time she had missed two days in a row, but she'd popped both pills as soon as she had remembered.

Damn.

Shit.

Fuck.

This was heavy stuff, not just another job to quit or a college class to drop or a bad date to slip away from out the bathroom window. She was the last person in this family capable of taking care of a baby or raising a kid. Her mother had not designated her as the number one screw-up by randomly drawing names from a hat.

She picked up the phone again, squinting down at the dark LCD screen, trying to force it to ring through telekinesis. It sat lifeless in her hands.

The screen door opened behind her, the floor boards creaking after it slapped shut.

Claire jammed the phone in her back pocket like it would start talking on its own at any moment and spill her deep, dark worries.

"On evenings like this," Ronnie said, standing over her, "I understand why Grandma was so enamored with this place."

"We sprinkled her ashes back by the creek. You remember that old cottonwood tree where she scratched Gramps's and her initials in the heart?"

Her grandmother's love of the place was one of the reasons Claire was so attached to this corner of the state in the first place. It was part of why she had fought so hard to help Ruby keep her R.V. park last spring and the surrounding land and mines. The other part had everything to do with Ruby herself and the faith she'd had in Claire from the start.

"Katie and I hiked to the spot last week. It's perfect." Ronnie seemed to hesitate. "We need to talk, Claire."

"Damned straight we do." It was about time Ronnie stopped avoiding her. "Have a seat." Claire scooted over to make more room for her sister.

"Not here." Ronnie walked down the porch steps and hesitated at the bottom. "Let's take a walk."

Claire raised one eyebrow. "Who are we keeping secrets from?"

"I'll explain if you come with me."

She stood to follow and her butt cheek rang. She tugged out the phone.

It was Mac. About damned time. "I'll catch up in a minute, Ronnie. I have to take this."

"I'll wait," her sister said, coming back to the porch steps and sitting down.

Dang it. There was no way she could talk to Mac about a possible pregnancy with Ronnie right there.

She tapped the button to accept the call. "Hello?"

"Hey, Slugger." His voice was static-laced, which usually meant he was out in the boonies somewhere. But he was supposed to be home by now, packing to come to the R.V. park later tonight.

"Where are you?"

"Uh, well, there was a setback ..." *crackle* "... the job site."

"But you're still coming tonight, right?" She really needed to see him right now, not wanting to take the pregnancy test until he knew what was going on.

"Yeah, about that. I'm still ..." *hiss crackle* "... won't make it home until after midnight."

"You mean home here?"

"No, home, as in where you and I share a king sized bed in Tuc ..." *hiss*.

"Shit."

"I'm sorry, sweetheart," his voice grew fainter. "I will call ..." then he was gone.

"Mac?" She waited to see if he would come back to her.

Silence issued from the phone, not even a single spurt of static.

"Mac, can you hear me?"

Still nothing.

She held the phone away from her and put an evil curse on it.

"Maybe he'll call back," Ronnie said, pushing to her feet. "In the meantime, there is something I need to tell you."

Claire set the cordless phone down on the porch. If Mac was not coming here tonight, he might as well not bother calling again. She did not want to spend another evening steaming up the phone's screen. She wanted him there with her in the flesh, partly because he had such great flesh, but more importantly because she missed him and his level-headed, logical, stubborn ass.

Sighing, she adjusted her Mighty Mouse hat lower on her head. How had she come to this ... this ... pathetic inability to go for a week or more without her boyfriend around? Next thing she knew, she would be howling about her lovesickness under the nearly full moon. Chester would never let her live that down. Manny would probably join her for kicks.

Time to focus on the pocket watch and tuck her Mac-plus-baby worries away for another night. She joined Ronnie's side. "Let's go over by the bridge. Jessica's hearing radar rivals most species of bats."

They had not made it two steps when the screen door slammed open so hard it practically shuddered on its hinges.

"Leave me alone!" Jessica yelled back into the General Store, making the bullfrogs down at the creek swallow their tongues. The whole desert seemed to suck in its breath, waiting for her next outburst.

Claire shot Ronnie a questioning frown, and her sister shrugged, shaking her head.

"Jessica Lynn Wayne!" Ruby appeared in the doorway at the same time her daughter ran down the porch steps with tears streaming down her cheeks. She rocketed out the screen door after Jess. "You get back in here right now and explain this!" She held a white strip of paper in her raised hand.

The fury in Ruby's voice made Claire's neck hair stand on end. What in Hades was going on?

Deborah filled the doorway next, her expression smug as she watched the scene on the other side of the screen door.

"Look at Mom's face," Ronnie said to Claire, her tone doused with an extra dose of venom. "She's used her evil powers to unleash another tornado on someone's life and is reveling at the flattened aftermath. One of these days I'm gonna rain some of my own destruction on her miserable world."

"Wow." Claire hit Ronnie with a set of raised eyebrows. "Bitter, party of one, your table's ready."

"You would be, too, if you knew the half of it." Ronnie glared hard at the screen door, as if she were trying to burn a matching set of eyeball-sized holes into the mesh.

What was Ronnie talking about? Did it have something to do with why she seemed to be staying as far from their mother as if she were carrying the ten plagues of Egypt in her fancy Coach purse? "You're starting to sound like a grade-A whack job, Ronnie."

She turned to Claire, her gaze shuttered. "Maybe I am psycho. That would explain a few things."

Like what?

"Jessica Lynn, you stop right there." The threatening tone in Ruby's voice snagged Claire's attention. Jess had almost made it to Ruby's old Ford, the keys jingling in the girl's hand. "If you take another step, you're grounded for the next month!"

Stopping in her tracks, Jess turned, her arms crossed, her back stiff as a two-by-four, her green eyes flashing at her mother in the pre-twilight.

Ruby stormed toward her, a cloud of dust practically billowing in her wake.

The bravado holding Jess up seemed to deflate. She cowered before her mom. A whimper escaped her lips and then she crumpled to the ground. "I swear, Mom," she held her hands together as if praying for Ruby's mercy. "We didn't do anything more down in the basement than kiss on the lips. We wanted a little privacy to talk, that's all."

Alarms clanged in Claire's head. Jess took Beanpole down

in the basement where all of Joe's valuable antiques were stashed? What was the dang kid thinking?

"Then explain this." Ruby shook the strip of paper over Jessica's head.

"I found it after I dropped my book in the washer. I needed a bookmark when the clothes were done and grabbed it. That's it, I swear."

"Bullshit." Ruby ticked off numbers on her fingers. "For one, I saw that hickey on your neck that you were trying to hide with my scarf the other day. Two, you have been wearing your shortest shorts and peek-a-boo tank tops a lot lately. Three, Deborah said you were implying something about going all the way."

Okay, hold the phone, Claire thought. That was old school speech, not the way teens talked these days. Claire took a step toward Ruby. Something was all bungled up with this picture. Claire's mother had to be setting Jess up for a fall, but what she had to gain was yet to be seen.

"Ruby." She held out her hands to calm the red haired fire starter. "Jess may be flirting heavily with Beanpo ... I mean her boyfriend, but I don't think she is the type of girl to throw away her virginity on any old boy."

"Why not? You did," Deborah said from where she now stood at the top of the steps, her chin held high. Slap a crown on her head and unroll the red carpet at her feet and they would have a new queen. *Off with her head!* would be written in Latin on her royal coat of arms.

Ronnie moved closer to Claire, speaking under her breath. "Don't look directly into Mom's eyes. You'll lose your soul."

"What was that, Veronica?" Deborah's focus lasered onto Ronnie. "You know better than to mutter after all of the money your father and I spent trying to correct that overbite of yours."

Their father had had nothing to do with what Kate and Claire had for years jokingly called the Beautification of Veronica Morgan refurbishment project. Ronnie had been their mother's Frankenstein's creation. Their father had given up long ago on saving his oldest from Deborah's clutches, focusing instead on protecting Claire and Kate from receiving the lobotomies and neck bolts.

Ronnie opened her mouth to say something, or maybe to spew a lungful of flesh-eating scarab beetles.

"It's not worth it," Claire told her sister before Ronnie lost control and caused mass destruction.

Deborah's glare bounced back and forth between the two of them, reminding Claire of one of those cat wall clocks with the bulbous eyeballs. Tick tock, tick tock.

"You can't trust teenage girls, Ruby," she turned her clock eyes back on Ruby. "They have one thing on their minds—making babies."

Making babies? Ha! Claire wished she could go back to the time when having sex was … wait! Claire looked closer at the slip of paper in Ruby's hand. Her vision tunneled. "Can I see that, Ruby?" She reached for the paper.

Behind Ruby, Gramps and his merry men rolled up in the golf cart he used to tool around the park. "What in the heck is going on?" He asked his wife. "We could hear you two yelling clear back at Manny's camper."

"Yuccaville called to complain about the racket," Chester added.

He grunted when Manny jabbed him in the ribs. "*Cállate idiota.*"

Deborah sniffed. "Ruby is upset because she found out that my sixteen-year-old stepsister appears to be having sex."

"What!" Gramps turned on Jess, his face reflecting disbelief and then disappointment.

"It happens to the best of us," Manny consoled, patting Gramps on the shoulder.

"Those teenage hormones are hell bent for leather." Chester puffed on his cigar, shaking his head. "I remember my first time. She insisted on me strapping on this—"

"That's enough, you two." Ruby cut in, silencing the two

troublemakers with one glare.

"Ah, Jessica," Gramps struggled to push to his crutches. "What were you thinking?"

"She was thinking about getting pregnant," Deborah said.

"No, I'm not!"

Deborah continued, her soap-box tall and sturdy. "I saw this documentary last month about teenage girls being too lazy to go out and get jobs, so they get pregnant and spend the next eighteen years living off the government, abusing the system."

"Remind me, Mother," Ronnie said. "What was your job for the last thirty-five years?"

"I had three children to raise, Veronica. And I wasn't living off welfare."

"That's been your excuse for not going out and getting a job since I was conceived."

"And what was your excuse, Veronica?" Deborah threw back. "Your resume isn't exactly overflowing with legitimate employment for the last five years."

"You're the one who—"

Claire grabbed Ronnie's arm and yanked her sister back to her side. "Get out of the ring," she told her, "this isn't your fight. Not tonight."

Ronnie growled but submitted, kicking at the gravel instead of their mother.

"Ruby," Claire still held out her other hand. "Please let me see that piece of paper."

Ruby shoved it into Claire's palm, huffing yet. Her eyes darted around, as if she were looking for a neck to snap. Deborah would be wise to keep her trap shut.

As Claire tried to read the piece of paper in the growing darkness, a pair of headlights splashed across the small crowd, a familiar engine growl crossing the bridge toward them.

They all looked over as Kate skidded to a stop and practically fell out the door. "What's going on? Is Henry missing again?"

Henry barked his greeting to his second favorite person in the world. He raced over to lick Kate's fingers, like so many other testosterone-filled suckers had over the years.

Before Kate shut off the headlights, Claire held up the piece of paper and read the evidence being used to sentence Jess to a severe tongue-lashing.

"What's wrong?" Kate stood frozen in the open car door. "Why are you all standing out here? You're not waiting for me, are you? Did Arlene call you?"

"Call us about what, Katie?" Ronnie asked.

"Jessica bought a pregnancy test," Deborah tattled to Kate.

"A test?" Kate's voice fluttered. Her hand flew to her chest as she fell back against the door jamb. "Oh, God, no!"

Claire glared across at her. *Overreact much?* "You trying out for a soap opera role over there?"

"Bite me, Claire." Kate bent over to catch her breath or maybe get a closer look at her shoes, Claire wasn't sure which.

"Your sister has the receipt for the test in her hand," Deborah added.

Claire was going to cram said receipt down her mother's throat if Deborah did not shut her flap soon.

"Mom, Harley," Jessica said, sniffing. "I ... I swear it's not mine."

"It was in *your* book, Jessica," Ruby reminded her. "If it's not yours, why are there little flowers doodled on it?"

Gramps cleared his throat, his knowing look aimed at Claire. Chester and Manny were taking their cue from him, all three of them had her locked in their sights.

Claire sighed. *Son of a bitch.* So much for waiting for Mac to talk about this. She lowered the receipt. "Ruby, Jess is telling the truth."

"She is?" Kate's voice sounding strangled still. "How do you know?"

"Yeah, how can you tell?" Ronnie peeked over Claire's shoulder at the receipt.

Gramps gave Claire an encouraging nod.

She squeezed Ruby's forearm, drawing the woman's gaze. "This receipt belongs to me. I'm the one who bought the pregnancy test."

"You bought a pregnancy test for a teenager?" Deborah guffawed. "Did you buy her a case of beer and a pack of cigarettes while you were at it?"

"No," Claire answered her mother, but her eyes stayed locked on Ruby's. "I bought the test for me. I may be preg ..." *Gurg!* She could not get the word to pass over her tongue. "I'm late."

"You're pregnant?" Kate asked. "I thought you were on the—"

"I don't know, Kate." Claire did not want to discuss aloud in front of everyone in her family the worries that had been clanging around inside of her head for a week. Well, everyone but Natalie. Where was her cousin anyway? This whole mess was her fault for buying that damned test.

"What do you mean you don't know?" Deborah bit out each word. So much for her being happy about being a grandmother. Oh, well, her cookies were always too dry, anyway.

"She hasn't taken the test yet," Natalie said, coming out the General Store's screen door with a candy bar in her hand.

There she was. Excellent. Now this warm and fuzzy moment felt complete. Call Hallmark, someone needed to take notes.

"What are you waiting for?" Ronnie asked.

My period to quit playing hide and seek. "The right moment."

"Wow! Claire's gonna have a baby." Jess's focus bounced back and forth between Claire's stomach and her face.

"Or not," Claire said.

"I bet your belly is gonna get huge."

"Jessica, that's rude." Ruby patted Claire's arm. "You should have told me. I never would have let you up on that roof if I'd known."

"We don't know that I am pregnant yet." Why did everyone keep forgetting that fact?

"Take the test, you big chicken and we will." Natalie polished off the candy bar in one bite.

"Don't you have some bags to pack, mouth?"

"I'm not leaving until Sunday. Things are too entertaining down here to rush back to an empty house."

"Mac is going to be a dad." Jessica smiled wistfully, still adding limbs to her family tree.

"The baby is MacDonald's, right?" Deborah asked.

This time it was Ronnie holding onto Claire to keep her from launching at their mother.

"What?" Deborah exaggerated a cowering stance. "You've never been one for sitting still long, Claire, and he does travel an awful lot."

"Back and forth to a day job, Mother," Kate shut her car door and joined her sisters. "Not overseas to a ten-year war."

"If you say so, Kathryn. I still think Claire should have played hard to get." Deborah nodded, as if agreeing with herself on the matter. "Now he's never going to make her an honest woman."

"I'm still standing right here in front of you, Mother."

Chester snorted. "Who wants Claire honest? I certainly don't. She won't be any fun anymore."

"*Es verdad*," Manny confirmed. "I love the trouble that follows her around. It's what makes her beautiful brown eyes sparkle."

"Why will she have to get honest if she's married?" Jess asked Ruby.

"Who says I'm not honest now?"

"What do you know about Mac, Mother?" Kate's tone had gone up a note, now stronger than before, Claire's virtue seeming to be her new cause all of a sudden. "He's kind and sweet and smart and handsome and strong and yet gentle and very supportive most days and has a good amount of money and—"

"Are we still talking about Mac?" Ronnie asked.

Kate glanced down, brushing something off her black work shirt. She cleared her throat and raised her chin again. "Of course we are. Who else would we be talking about when Claire is having his baby?"

"We don't know that I'm pregnant everyone, remember?"

"Why don't you go take the test now?" Gramps asked. "Then we can stop speculating about this kid and move onto the next step."

"Planning the baby party," Chester agreed with a grin. "Let's keep it co-ed. I vote for bikini mud wrestling."

"No, no, no, *hombre*. You don't have mud wrestling at a baby shower. We'll save that for Mac's bachelor party." Manny wiggled his thick eyebrows at his fellow old coot.

"Where's that pregnancy test kit?" Chester asked. "Let's get things rolling."

"How do you test for pregnancy with a kit?" Jess asked. "The ones in the store have white sticks on the box."

"What are you doing even looking at those, Jessica Lynn?" Ruby grabbed her daughter and pulled her into a hug, dropping a kiss on her head. "How about I explain some of this stuff to you another night when we're alone?"

"Sure, but can I watch Claire take the test?"

"No!" Ruby and Claire said at the same time.

"Whatever." She pulled out of her mom's arms. "I might as well go inside and finish reading my book then."

"Good idea." Ruby looked around. "We all should go inside and leave Claire be for the time. She'll tell us when she knows for certain one way or another."

Thank you, she mouthed to Ruby.

The old boys grumbled on their way past Claire and her sisters, Manny pausing long enough to pat Claire on the head. "Let me be the godfather, *por favor*. Stinky Shorts is way too hairy for the job."

Deborah looked at her watch, then frowned toward the road to town.

"Let's go, Deborah," Gramps said. "Give your daughters a break for a while and play some Euchre with us."

"For your information, Dad, I have a date tonight."

"With whom?"

"Jessica's father. He's picking me up and taking me out for a nice evening."

"And some hot love?" Manny asked.

Deborah sniffed. "No, Manuel. Unlike my daughters, I am not that type of girl."

Ronnie coughed out a *bullshit*.

"I heard that, Veronica."

"Dad's not coming here tonight," Jessica said, her hand on the screen door handle.

"Yes, he is," Deborah countered.

"No, he's got a date."

"With me."

"I don't think so."

"You're mistaken, then."

"Nuh uh. I met her this morning."

"What do you mean, kid?" Gramps asked. "Met who?"

"Dad's new girlfriend."

Ruby frowned down at her daughter. "New girlfriend?"

"Yeah, that's how she introduced herself when she came out of his bathroom in her bra and underwear."

Deborah gasped out a breath. Everyone else seemed to be holding theirs.

Jess continued, oblivious of the blow she had struck. "She showed me this fancy diamond ring on her right hand that she said her last boyfriend gave to her. She even let me try it on. It reminded me of the ring Ronnie is wearing in her wedding picture with her old husband. You know, that picture you guys put on your dresser when Claire called to say she was coming, too?"

Deborah screeched, silencing Jess. "You're a lying little—"

"No!" Jess returned to the defensive, high pitched tone she had been using with her mom. "I swear, I'm not. Her name is Mindy Lou Hair-something. They met at Butch's bar. Do you know who she is, Kate?"

"Ohhh," Deborah let out another shriek before Kate could answer.

Claire winced.

"Men are all rotten, stinking, cheating bastards."

Ah, misty water-colored memories. Her mother's outburst took Claire back to her high school years when she used to listen to her parents fight from the other side of her bedroom door.

Ronnie let out several squeaks of laughter. When Claire gaped at her, Ronnie covered her mouth and turned her back toward the crash scene, her shoulders shaking. What was so damned funny? Claire hit Kate with a questioning glance. Kate shrugged back.

"Jess," Ruby grabbed the cordless phone off the porch from where Claire had left it and pulled open the screen door. "Go inside." She shoved her daughter in, not giving the girl a chance to buck. "Harley, come on." She held out her hand toward her husband, who crutched inside after Jess faster than Claire had seen him move in days. Ruby waved Chester and Manny to follow.

Manny hesitated. "Deborah," he reached for her hand.

Deborah jerked away. "No! Don't touch me." She spun on her high heel and slammed past Ruby, bumping her back a step.

Claire could hear her mother's shoes clonking across the General Store floor, probably heading toward her bedroom where she would hide until she had regenerated and could return to her cool, calm, bitchy self again.

Without looking back, Manny and then Ruby followed her inside and closed the door behind them.

"Wow!" Natalie came down the steps, joining them.

Kate blew out a breath. "That's going to make life hell for the rest of us."

"Where have you been?" Ronnie returned to the

conversation, no longer leaking squeaks. "Hell has come and gone. We're in Hell's basement now dynamiting deeper by the day."

"Jesus," Claire rubbed her eyes with the heels of her palms. "I could really use a cigarette and a beer."

"How about a Shirley Temple?" Natalie squeezed her shoulder.

"I could smoke and you could smell my breath in between puffs," Ronnie offered.

Sighing, Claire shook her head. "I don't want to be pregnant."

Much to her surprise, Kate pulled her into a hug. "Sometimes we don't always get what we want."

She must be referring to Butch.

"But lucky for you," Natalie tugged her free of Kate's hold and led her toward her sister's car, which was still ticking in the darkness. "You have a wonderful, warm, and loving mother to support you in your time of need."

That made all of them laugh, especially Kate, who really cackled until Ronnie asked, "Katie, are you flipping out?"

Kate nodded and then shook her head. Her laughter stopped on a dime.

"Wait!" Claire said as her cousin shoved her into the back seat. "Where are we going?"

"You're going to watch me get soused for my going away party."

"But you're not leaving until Sunday."

"It's a three-night extravaganza." She pointed at Kate. "Jeeves, take us to The Shaft. Let's go find Ronnie a man."

"Why?" Kate asked.

Natalie grinned. "So she can beat him up."

Chapter Fourteen

Friday, October 5th

The grocery store in Yuccaville was crawling with shoppers. Ronnie dodged heaped carts in every aisle. With their paychecks still warm in their bank accounts, the mining community en masse appeared to be stocking up for another week of living the glamorous life of digging for copper.

Ronnie grabbed the barbecue sauce scrawled on Ruby's list and dropped it into her grocery basket. She scanned the slip of paper—*refried beans, bacon, bananas, BBQ sauce, beets, brownie mix*. Apparently, tonight's feature film was going to be "Dinner at Ruby's," brought to viewers by the letter B.

Standing in line behind a sweat-ringed guy who looked and smelled like he had spent the day eating the dust billowing off a mega-huge mining truck, Ronnie searched the sea of heads. She was looking for a familiar patch of ginger red in the crowd.

Jessica was supposed to meet her in line with her own basket full of the other half of Ruby's list—dish soap, liniment rub for Gramps's leg, three packs of low-energy lightbulbs, and a box of tampons. They had split up to save time, but now Jess was nowhere to be seen.

She was probably still sulking about Ronnie being the one to pick her up from school today instead of her new boyfriend, whom Gramps had waylaid back at the R.V. park. The silly boy should have known better than to ask the old man running the General Store counter directions to the high school in Yuccaville. He must have left his brains back in his dorm in Tucson and packed his dick instead.

"This is so embarrassing." Jessica spoke from behind her.

Ronnie turned. "What? Being seen at the grocery store?" She was clueless as to what was cool these days on the teen scene.

"No, hanging out in the tampon aisle. I can't believe you made me pick those out."

If she thought that was embarrassing, she should try having a handful of Feds explain that the video camera Lyle had hidden away in the master bathroom had a clear shot of the shower—the one with the handheld massaging shower head installed behind the clear glass shower door. Ronnie had nightmares about the stag parties in the evidence room for weeks after learning that detail.

Ronnie emptied her basket's contents on the black motorized belt. "They're for you, kid, not me. Why should I have to carry them around?"

"Mom always buys them for me so I don't have to be seen with them."

"You know," Ronnie grabbed the box from Jess's basket and tossed it on the belt. "If you move in with your dad, you're going to have to buy embarrassing stuff like tampons all of the time."

"Who said I was thinking of moving in with Dad?" Jess's voice had an equal pinch of suspicion and defensiveness. "Is Mom trying to get rid of me?"

Ronnie shook her head. "Nobody said anything. I figure that with your dad in town buying you stuff left and right like that necklace you showed me, taking you to the movies and all of that jazz, you're probably thinking life with him would be a lot nicer than staying with your mom and Gramps."

The teenager's cheeks darkened as she unloaded her basket onto the belt. "Dad said he would let me go out on dates, but Harley thinks I'm too young, and Mom keeps listening to him instead of me. It's not fair. Harley is so old-fashioned. He wants me to wait to date until I'm eighteen. Can you believe that? They might as well send me off to some nun school."

Deborah had made Ronnie wait until she was seventeen to start dating, and then insisted on being present during the first date. In the meantime, Claire and Kate had been sneaking under the bleachers with boys during football games and playing tongue tag with whomever they felt like. Which of the three of them was more well-balanced was up in the air, but only Ronnie had ever sought counseling from a professional.

And a lot of good that had done.

The therapist had strongly suggested Ronnie stay with her husband. That she try harder to break through their communication barriers and give him yet another chance to show his devotion to the sanctity of their marriage vows. A few years later they had a new communication barrier—a thick plate of Plexiglas, and their marriage had turned out to be a steaming pile of lies. These days, her therapy came in the form of gin and tonic, which was much easier to swallow and cost a hell of a lot less per hour.

"Gramps is trying to protect you," she told Jess. "There are boys out there who act very nice at first, buy you all sorts of pretty jewelry and designer clothes, take you on weekend trips to Paris or London, put you up in a huge fancy house with all kinds of expensive appliances ..." *Shit, where was she going with this?* Oh, yeah. "But then they turn around and hurt you in ways you never thought about and were not even close to being prepared for mentally or financially. Gramps doesn't want to see that happen to you is all."

Neither did Ronnie, not to Jess or any one of her family members. Well, except for her mother. Deborah could use a little comeuppance for her part in Ronnie's now screwed up life.

"Yeah, but it's my life," Jessica said. "If they don't let me try a few things, how will I ever learn anything?"

Good point. "You should talk to Claire about this." Ronnie wiped her hands clean of the matter and dumped it on her sister's doorstep instead.

Claire had always been much better with kids. That was why it had not made sense when Katie had gone into teaching. Her youngest sister could barely stand being around one kid, let alone a roomful of them. Ronnie was surprised Katie had stayed in the teaching field as long as she had. She suspected it had more to do with Deborah's firm hand in the matter and Katie's inability to lie her way out of her mother's grip.

They made it through checkout with Jess hiding behind Ronnie until the tampons were stuffed in a bag.

On their way out the door, Jess moved up beside her. "Claire's lucky."

"Why's that?"

Jess swung her bag like she had not a care in the world. Oh, to be that young and bitter-free again, Ronnie thought.

"She doesn't have to buy embarrassing stuff at the store anymore since she's pregnant."

"I don't think Claire is feeling too lucky at the moment. If she is pregnant, I'm sure she'd rather be buying a box of tampons right about now. Raising a kid is hard work."

They turned up the row of vehicles where Ruby's old Ford sat near the end next to a red pickup. She had seen that truck before somewhere, but she couldn't remember where. Then again, pickups were thick as plastic bags stuck on barbed wire fences in these parts. She had probably seen ten red pickups just like it in the last few days.

The Ford's windshield glinted in the afternoon sunshine. A warm breeze ruffled Ronnie's curls, along with a piece of paper stuffed under the pickup's windshield wiper.

Jessica headed around the back of the truck. "How do you know kids are hard work? You don't even have any."

No, but Ronnie had daydreamed about having two or three of them for years, waiting for her husband to agree the time was right. Thank heaven that time had never come for them.

"I've read a lot about kids." She had also watched Ruby

enough over the last couple of weeks and observed how raising a teenager could wear a person down to a throbbing nub.

She unlocked the pickup door and popped the lock so Jess could get in. Setting the grocery bag in the middle of the bench seat, she settled behind the wheel. The piece of paper flapped against the outside of her window, partially blocking her view.

Darn salesmen and their stupid fliers.

"I bet Claire would make a great mom," Jessica said. "She'd be a lot more fun than my mom is."

More fun than Ronnie's mom, too. Hell, the bloody Queen Mary would have been more fun. She reached out through her open window and grabbed the flier, tossing it on the seat next to her.

"I think you're being too tough on Ruby." Ronnie started the pickup and shifted into reverse, backing out of the parking spot. She glanced over at Jess, who was looking at the flier. "Raising a child on your own is no easy job. It seems like she's worked hard to provide a roof over your head, food to eat, and clothes—"

"What's with this castle?" Jessica asked.

Teenagers these days had the attention span of a gnat. She finished backing out before looking over at Jessica. "What castle?"

Jessica held up the flier. "This castle? I can't read this. It's in some funky language."

Funky lang ... Ronnie nearly choked on her tongue. She swiped the flier from Jessica. Only it was not a flier, but rather a copy of the German article about the stolen watches.

"Rudeness!" Jessica said, trying to take it back.

Her pulse pounding in every finger and toe, Ronnie held it out of reach. "Knock it off, Jessica. This belongs to me."

"It doesn't have your name on it."

Yes, it did. Her name was written all over it, and she knew exactly who left her this little present. He had not stopped at meddling in her past, now he was nosing into her current business. The intrusive son of a bitch! Just because he had that damned star did not give him the right to harass her like this.

A horn blared behind her, making both her and Jessica jump.

Jess leaned out her window, "Honk again, butt face, and

we'll—"

"Jessica!" Ronnie grabbed the girl by the waistband of her shorts and tugged her back inside. "Buckle your seat belt."

"But ... " Jessica sputtered.

"Now!" Ronnie shifted into gear and stomped on the gas, burning rubber out onto the side street. She slammed to a halt at the four-way STOP sign. Then she gunned it again, keeping an eye out for a certain Sheriff's pickup, jerking the wheel right and left, locking up the brakes in a controlled skid when a dog ran out in the road.

Jessica reached for the dash and screamed like the reaper had swung his scythe at her neck, making Ronnie grit her teeth.

As soon as the dog cleared her path, Ronnie slammed on the gas pedal and roared off again. When she hit State Route 191 leading back to Jackrabbit Junction, she slowed to the speed limit and did several breathing exercises she had learned in her yoga classes years ago.

Jessica still clung to the dash. She gawked at Ronnie. "You are a crazy driver!"

"That was fun, wasn't it?" Ronnie laughed, trying to make light of her *Dukes of Hazzard* performance through the streets of Yuccaville.

"No! Not fun at all."

"Baby," Ronnie said under her breath.

"You're a worse driver than Kate."

"Nobody drives worse than Katie. We didn't get in an accident, did we?"

"Okay, then you're a close second." Jessica sat back, covering her heart.

"I had control of the vehicle the whole time."

"Wait until Claire hears about this."

"She won't. If you tell anyone about my driving or this paper, I'll tell your mom you told me you are going to go live with your dad."

"What?! I didn't say that I was going to do it. I'm just

considering it."

That would be a huge mistake if Jess took him up on it, but it was not Ronnie's place to interfere. "Did he ask you?"

Jessica nodded.

"That's good enough for me. You tell about me and I'll tell about you."

"Claire was right."

"About what?"

"She said you were kind of nutso."

"She did, huh?" Ronnie grinned. Only 'kind of nutso'? "My sister knows me well."

But not as well as Claire thought. She didn't know the new Ronnie. The one who would do whatever was necessary to make sure her family didn't have to go through the hell she had at the hands of nosy federal investigators or murdering thieves who wanted back what had been stolen from them.

"You're lucky you didn't hit that dog."

"I'd say it's more like he's lucky."

Ronnie's luck had run out the day she'd landed on Sheriff Grady Harrison's radar. One small attempt at bribing a lawman and now he was all over her like a hungry flea on a fat cat. He might think slipping that copy of the article under her windshield wiper put him in the checkmate position, but he was underestimating her queen.

"Where did you learn to drive like that?"

"Gramps taught me."

"Really?" At Ronnie's nod, Jess looked back out the front window. "Maybe I need to ask him for some help prepping for my driving exam instead of my dad."

"I can teach you." Ronnie glanced over at Jess. "For a price."

Saturday, October 6th

Claire brushed purple nail polish on her big toenail, using long, smooth strokes. Maybe she'd add one of Jess's little white flower nail stickers to top her pedicure off. Mac might think it was cute, even sexy, and right now she was desperate to butter him up before he found out her situation. She thought about slathering herself in actual butter since he was so fond of the creamy stuff, but she would have slipped right out of his fingers every time he tried to grab her.

She looked out the General Store's screen door, searching for a dust cloud coming up the road. He should be here soon. The thought of looking into his hazel eyes and coughing up her current predicament made her tongue feel thick and heavy in her mouth. Lord, she needed a cigarette. She imagined the feel of the soft stick of nicotine in her fingers, the taste of tobacco on the back of her throat.

She held up the bottle of nail polish and sniffed, desperate for any kind of mind-altering toxin. What good was having a laundry list of vices if she couldn't enjoy them. Pregnancy was going to be a long-suffering, washboard road weaving through Sobriety County.

"Ugh," she groaned aloud. She had to think of something else. Blowing on her wet nails, she focused on Mac again and how she was going to tell him.

Since last night after he had called to say he would not be able to make it to Ruby's until today, she had hashed and rehashed his many possible reactions to her news. Some ended with him twirling her around like the ending to a happily-ever-after romance, others ended up with her living all alone in a trailer in the desert with Sheriff Harrison delivering her baby while his idiot deputy puked into a bucket behind him.

Claire heard the velvet curtain swish and then the creak of a pair of crutches.

"What in Hades are you doing, child?" Gramps asked. "Have you been possessed? Is this gonna turn out like that *Rosemary's Baby* movie?"

Capping Jessica's nail polish, she set the bottle of Grape

Fizz next to her bare foot, which rested on the counter next to the cash register. "I'm painting my toenails."

"Why?"

"Because I want them to look pretty."

Gramps crutched over and placed his hand on her forehead for a moment. "You don't feel feverish." He tipped up her chin, spreading one eyelid wide, then the other. "Your pupils don't appear to be dilated. Have you and Kate switched bodies today?"

After batting his hand away, she gingerly touched one nail. Not dry yet. "I feel fine. I just want my feet to look sexy for Mac when he gets here."

He snorted. "I don't think that boy is gonna care one iota about your silly feet when he sees you."

"It doesn't hurt to stack the deck."

"What are you doing running the store this morning? I thought Ronnie was supposed to be filling in so that you could help your cousin get the rest of that drywall taped and another layer of mud on it."

Natalie and Claire had spent yesterday hanging drywall, with help holding the gypsum board from Chester and Manny and a lot of supervision from Gramps. As Natalie and Claire took turns hanging drywall, the jokes flowed in abundance about women and screwing, studs and mudding. By the end of the day, Claire was not sure which hurt more, her ears or her arms.

"Ronnie left early to take Jessica to Yuccaville to see her dad," Claire told him, grabbing the latest teen queen magazine Jess had stashed under the counter to fan her toes.

"Why would she do that?"

"Because Jess wanted to spend the day with him and Ruby told us that if she saw the 'rotten son of a bitch today,'" Claire quoted with a smile, "she might clobber him with her frying pan."

"That woman has one hell of a swing." His eyes shined with pride.

Claire had no doubts about the redhead after having witnessed her temper erupt now and then over the last few months. "I think he's taking Jess to a double-feature."

"That asshole is sure determined to buy the kid's love."

"She's eating it up, too."

So far, during Claire's tenderfooted attempts to find out what Jess was thinking when it came to her future living arrangements, all she had gotten was a series of wary looks and I-don't-knows from the kid. Ruby should have picked another spy to work on Jess because Claire had a feeling she had already been made.

The rumbling sound of an engine rolled through the screen door.

Claire leaned forward to look outside, watching as Mac parked his white pickup in front of the porch and cut the engine. Her heart sat up and wiggled like a dog, smacking its tail against her ribcage.

Excitement and fear tingled through her, spurring a herd of goosebumps up her arms. This was the real deal. She could no longer pretend this whole pregnancy test was a work of women's fiction … or horror. There was no more delaying it. She was finally going to find out if there were a baby coming or not. Shouldn't she be feeling something other than the need to vomit at this moment?

"The white knight has returned." Gramps's sarcasm cut through her cacophony of emotions. "You ladies can go back to pretending to faint as he walks past."

She frowned at him. "You really need to grab a beer and wash down that sourpuss pill lodged in your gullet."

Mac shut his pickup door, shielding his eyes and frowning off toward the eastern horizon. In his faded brown T-shirt, blue jeans, and work boots, he could have come straight from the job site. Maybe he had. Some days she wished she had a career she loved so much, something she was willing to pour her heart and soul into until well past quitting time.

Scrubbing down his face, he wiped away whatever had

given him pause and headed her way. He took the porch steps two at a time. His gaze locked onto hers through the screen and his eyes lit with a wicked gleam. Then he was inside, rounding the counter, and bending her over backwards with a kiss that would have knocked her socks off had she been wearing any.

When he tipped her back upright, the room spun a little. Most of her blood had packed up and headed south, pulsing out an SOS beacon to lure Mac closer. "Holy crap," she whispered, all flowery words blasted clear out of her brain. "What was that?"

He cupped her jaw, dropping a kiss on her nose. "I missed you, Slugger."

Gramps cleared his throat. When Claire looked over, he said, "I told you he wouldn't give a shit about your toes."

"What's wrong with your toes?" Mac asked, stepping back while keeping a warm hand on her lower back.

"They're painted."

"They're cute."

"They're supposed to be sexy."

"You know the fodder for my fetishes lies to the north of your toes." His hazel eyes traveled up over the hills and dales of her faded green Dancing Winnebagos T-shirt, stalling on the hills before returning to her face. "You're getting tan, Slugger. I hope you're taking plenty of breaks while you slave away on that building."

Her breath wheezed. Did Mac know her secret? She shot Gramps a wide-eyed look. Had somebody blabbed before she'd had the chance to tell Mac herself? "Why do you say that?"

"Because I know how much your grandfather and his cronies like to watch the fairer sex work."

Gramps grunted. "Manny and Chester like to watch; I'd rather be up there with her."

The curtain to the rec room swished open.

"Mac!" Ruby's lined face relaxed into a big smile. She held

her arms wide. "Boy, I am happy as a dung beetle in an elephant pen to see you back here."

A harrumph sound came from Gramps's direction, but when Claire looked, he was straightening the cans of pork and beans on the camp store shelf.

"Are you hungry, darlin'?" Ruby asked as Mac gave her a squeeze. "I'm fixin' to make Harley some breakfast. I can throw together an omelet for you with your favorite stuff." She pinched his side. "You're getting' skinny working so hard day and night. How about a double with some bacon on top?"

"I never say no to bacon," he dropped a kiss on her cheek. "How are things going here?"

Ruby let out something that sounded like a snort and a guffaw mixed together.

"That bad, huh?"

"It's been tryin' at times." She seemed to be avoiding Harley's eyes. "I could use your help with the archaeology folks."

She could? Was Ruby planning to put the fear of God in Beanpole if he even thought of touching Jess again with a threat for a neck wringing from Mac?

"They giving you trouble?" Mac's raised brows included Claire. "Claire mentioned a couple of suspicions before I left."

She would have clapped her hand over his mouth had Ruby not been watching her. Claire had mentioned her suspicions, but they were slightly unfounded and partially illogical yet. More just hunches than anything. But that beige camper still gave her the heebie jeebies, along with the khaki twins. The way they were always showing up everywhere together in matching clothes reminded her of those dead twin girls on *The Shining*. She kept waiting for them to show up next to her bed in the middle of the night whispering, "REDRUM!"

"No trouble." Ruby cast a quick frown in Claire's direction. "No suspicions, either, on my part yet." Her focus back on Mac, she said, "The head archaeologist, Dr. García, stopped by the other evenin' and asked if you were around to look at somethin' they found in the mine and discuss options. I told him that you'd be back this weekend."

Shit! Claire glanced away to hide her reaction to Ruby's news. What had they found? More of Joe's hidden stash? This was exactly what Claire had been pacing the floor about since she had heard they were up in that mine. Thirty years of stealing from thieves could account for a ton of loot, and Joe was an ace at burying treasures.

"I'll look him up this afternoon when they come back from the site," Mac told his aunt.

Her features schooled, Claire looked back to see Ruby drop a kiss on his cheek. "Thanks, darlin'."

"Happy to help out. Last weekend I felt like a fifth wheel around here." His focus lingered on Gramps's averted face for a moment, then he turned to Claire, rubbing his hands together. "So what's the deal?"

"The deal?"

"Yeah, you mentioned you needed to talk to me about something last night on the phone but wanted to wait until I got here. What's going on?"

"Uh ..." she glanced from Ruby to Gramps. "It's sort of private." Yet everyone in this freaking place knew but him. A voice cackled in her head at the irony.

Gramps pointed a crutch toward the rec room. "You two go catch up. I'll cover here until Ronnie gets back."

Holding back the curtain for them, Ruby said, "You can use our room if you'd like."

"Come on." Claire grabbed Mac by the arm, wondering if he noticed how sweaty her palm was. "We'll be in the basement," she informed Gramps and Ruby. *So stay out and leave us alone*, in other words.

"Keep it PG!" Gramps hollered after them. "That room isn't a honeymoon suite, you know."

Mac followed her across the shag carpet in the rec room and down the stairs. "What's going on, Claire? Did you find something else Joe stole?"

Nope. This had nothing to do with one of Joe's expensive leave-behinds, more like Mac's. If there were a baby, she reminded herself. It was still an "if" for a little longer.

She pulled him inside the office and locked the door behind him. He crossed his arms and frowned down at her. "Okay, Slugger, what in the hell is this about?"

Pacing in front of him, she squeezed the back of her neck. How to start? Just blurt it out? Or should she ease into it?

"Mac, we have a little situation." She turned around and tried to smile but could not quite muster one.

He sat on the edge of Joe's desk. "Why do I have the feeling it's not so little?"

At the moment, it might be just a speck.

"Uhhm," Claire glanced past his shoulder at the book case. Something seemed odd about the way the light was hitting the row of Kodak box cameras lined across the top shelf. The shadows were different than normal, hiding half of them like they had been pushed to the back.

"Spit it out, Claire."

She slid her gaze back to his, trying to swallow over a tongue that felt like the alkali salt flats in Desert Valley. "I ... uh ..."

Her gaze darted back to the bookcase and it hit her what was wrong with the picture. The cameras had not been pushed back. It was the bookcase that had been moved. Someone had pulled it forward and not shoved it all of the way back.

Claire's breath got hung up. There was only one reason to pull out that bookcase—to get to the wall safe behind it.

"Claire," Mac urged.

She held up her index finger. "Hold that thought."

"What thought?" He followed her over to the bookcase. "What are you doing?"

"Help me pull this further away from the wall."

He nudged her aside and lifted the case with none of the grunting that she usually employed. As soon as he had moved it far enough, she slid onto her knees behind it.

"Is this big build up for something about that damned pocket watch you're obsessed about?"

"Huh uh." She punched in the combination to the safe. The door popped open.

Oh no. Her gut fell out from under her.

"What's the problem then?"

"The watch," her words flew out in an exhale.

"Claire," his tone was terse. "I thought you said—"

She looked up at him. "It's gone."

"What?"

"The pocket watch." She pushed to her feet, almost head butting him in the chin. "I think somebody stole it."

Chapter Fifteen

Wherever Claire went, bedlam followed, whirling behind her like a dust devil. Having witnessed this firsthand too many times to count, Mac should not have been the least bit surprised that he'd gotten caught in her updraft within the first half hour of being back in Jackrabbit Junction.

"You're jumping to conclusions again," he told Claire, who was doing her damnedest to wear a path in the shag carpet in front of Joe's desk. "That gets you into trouble every time."

"Not every time." She jammed her hands on her hips. "Have you been taking notes from Gramps?"

"He has a valid point."

"So do I."

"Which is what? That the golden pocket watch has been stolen by the evil watch goblin, who is hoarding them kingdom-wide in order to build a time machine so he can return to the future, conquer the rebel forces, and rule the universe with his despotic power."

Claire stopped pacing. "Have you been reading those sci-fi fantasy books again before going to bed?"

He shrugged. "I've had trouble sleeping without you next to me, Slugger. It sucks when you're not there."

She rewarded him for his honesty with a stolen kiss, her lips soft, tempting, sweet with a hint of chocolate and marshmallow. She must have had a MoonPie for breakfast again. He grabbed her by the hips, pulling her closer, breathing in the fresh fruity scent that always seemed to surround her, even after a day working under the hot sunshine. Her shirt and bra were in his way.

He kissed her back, taking his time.

This was the reason he had busted his ass on overtime all week. Well, this and the fact that he would rather keep busy at the job site day and night than go home to a house without her in it. All the long, tiring shifts had paid off, buying him an extra couple of days off here with her.

Her fingernails trailed up his zipper, clicking against the metal teeth, making him ache for a whole lot more. Her hands slipped under his shirt, scraping along the skin below his ribs. Way too soon, she stepped back, her cheeks flushed. "We're not supposed to screw around down here anymore. It's one of Gramps's new rules."

He growled in frustration and adjusted his inseam. "Since when do you follow rules?"

"Since they are followed up with threats to tell my mother some of my deep dark secrets."

"Your grandfather knows your secrets?"

"He's in on a few of my humdingers."

"Do I know any of them?"

She smiled at him, her eyes flirty. "Not yet. You'll have to work them out of me."

"That sounds like a challenge."

She swirled her index finger down his chest, hesitating at his waistline. "I think you'll be up for it. You *usually* are."

"Usually?" He chuckled and knocked her wandering hand away before they digressed into breaking the rules again. "So, what's your valid point about the missing watch?"

She returned to wearing a footpath in the carpet. "If it's not stolen, where is it? Only Ruby, Gramps, and I know the combination to open the safe. At least I think we're the only three." She rubbed her chin, as if contemplating other possible usual suspects for her police lineup.

"Maybe Ruby took it out for some reason."

"She would have told me."

"What are you, the guardian of the safe?"

"Yes. Yes, I am, smartass. Ruby and Gramps both know my concerns about that watch and who might be coming for it. They wouldn't have removed it without telling me first."

"Concerns? More like paranoia." He softened his words with a grin.

"You say to-may-to, I say to-mah-to. In the end, the watch is gone and my fears are justified."

"Remind me again what exactly you think is going to happen next?" He did not want to second guess her. The last time he had done that, shots were fired.

"Well, we know we have a thief in our midst."

"We're assuming this, but we don't 'know' anything concrete yet."

"If you're going to keep being logical about all of my suspicions, this is going to be slow going." When he mimicked sealing his lips, she continued. "I highly doubt he will stop at just a pocket watch when there is so much more to be had."

"He?" Mac wondered who it was she had already strung up for the crime in her head.

A knock thumped on the door.

Mac looked from the door to Claire, who was busy imitating a department store mannequin.

"Simon didn't say, 'freeze,'" he whispered.

"You're a funny guy." She strode over and unlocked the door. "Don't quit that day job of yours, baby. We need to eat." She opened the door.

Kate stood in the doorway, her eyes squeezed tight.

"What are you doing?" Claire asked.

"Are you two dressed?"

"Yes, spaz. What do you want?"

Kate pointed at Mac. "Ruby wanted me to tell you that your omelet is ready."

Claire clamped on her sister's arm and pulled her inside, locking the door behind her.

Rubbing her arm, Kate's grimace started with Claire and then moved to Mac. With her blonde hair pulled back in a

French knot and that pinched expression on her face, she reminded him way too much of her mother, only thinner. Much thinner. Was she trying to lose weight? If so, why?

"What's going on in here?" she asked. "Are we having a secret clubhouse meeting?"

"Did you take the gold pocket watch out of the safe?" Claire did not mince words. Mac often admired her for that, except when she was insulting someone holding a gun pointed at her ... or him.

Luckily, the only thing Kate was holding was a set of car keys. Judging from the words The Shaft embroidered on her black button up shirt and her tan high-water pants, he figured she must have been on her way out the door for work when Ruby had sent her down here.

Kate's brows lifted. "Someone stole the watch?"

"I didn't say that." Claire eyed her sister up and down. "What makes you assume someone stole it? Do you know something about this?"

"No."

"Then why would you think it's stolen?"

"Because you're acting like a freaking nutjob, you big doofus."

Claire's gaze narrowed. Mac couldn't tell if it was suspicion-driven or a pissed off response to Kate's name calling.

"And if the damned watch was just out for cleaning," Kate continued, "you wouldn't be all up in my shit, now would you?"

"I'm not up in your shit."

"Mac?" Kate looked to him for a ruling.

He raised his hands. "No comment based on the fact that I'm sleeping with the opposing party." Or at least he would like to sometime soon before his *cojones* turned into raisins and fell off the vine.

"Have you seen anyone down here who shouldn't have been?" Claire asked Kate.

"When am I ever here, Claire?" Kate's tone got louder, making Mac cringe. He debated moving behind the desk before she blew up in Claire's face.

"I don't know, but you're here right now."

"Yeah, just to tell your boyfriend about his breakfast. That's it. I don't come down here and hang out like the rest of you. Some of us are busy working our butts off to make ends meet since we don't all have sugar daddies."

"Whoa! Why are you being so defensive, Kate?" Claire asked. "I'm just trying to figure out where the watch is, not fight with you."

Kate sighed, rubbing the back of her neck. "I'm sorry. It's just I ..." She looked at Mac, then back to Claire. "Never mind."

"Besides, you're working for your boyfriend, who is a sugar daddy of sorts. I, on the other hand, work for my boyfriend's aunt, who now also happens to be my step-grandmother."

"I said never mind."

"When you look at it that way, I've regressed to working for my grandparents again, just like high school and college. Damn. It's a vicious circle."

"Are you done, Claire?"

"I think so." She shoved her hand through her hair.

"Good, then shut up so I can think." Kate walked over to the bookcase and looked at the books lining the shelf. "Jess's dad was down here that one time looking around, but you know about that."

Claire nodded; however, that was news to Mac. Why in the hell was that asshole down in Ruby's office?

"Beanpole was down here with Jess," Claire added, joining Kate by the bookcase.

"Who's Beanpole?" Mac asked.

"Jess's boyfriend."

"Jess has a boyfriend?" Jesus, how long had he been gone?

"Arlene was down here with me," Kate said, "but I don't

think she was in here for more than a minute or two before I came down."

"You mean that waitress from The Shaft?" Mac asked. The older, blonde version of Ginger from *Gilligan's Island?*

"Why was Arlene down here?" Claire asked. "She's a complete stranger."

"Arlene is not a stranger. She brought me home to change my clothes after I accidentally spilled that nasty runoff juice from the grill's grease trough down my shirt. Ronnie borrowed my car that day to go look up something for you."

"Fine, you two are good-time pals. But why was Arlene down *here*?"

"Jess was showing her the house while I showered. Have you ever smelled that grease runoff? It stinks like vomit and spoiled meat mixed together." Kate shuddered.

"Okay, so we have Arlene," Claire ticked off her fingers. "Jess's dad, Beanpole, Jess, and who else?"

"You're including Jess?" Mac asked.

"I don't think she stole the watch, but I'm not putting it past her to have figured out the combination and borrowed the watch for lord knows what reason. Maybe just to show it off at school."

"I don't think you should include Arlene," Kate said.

"It's my suspect list. I can include whoever I want. You can take her off your list if it makes you feel better."

"If you're going to include Jess, then you might as well include Mom," Kate told her.

Mac grimaced. "Your mother is still here, huh?" So much for the wish he had made on a falling star the other night. Maybe it was time to take the voodoo doll route. Did hit men ever just relocate someone rather than snuff them out?

"Mom was down here? Why?"

"Ronnie said she's been cataloging Joe's antiques."

"What?" Claire blinked several times rapidly. "Why would she be doing that?"

"Ruby asked her to. According to Ronnie, Ruby figured it

would keep Mom out of her hair for a while."

Claire fell back in Joe's chair. "Yeah, but at what cost? Letting Mom see all of this means we may have another source of leaks. I'm going to have to talk to her. If Mom goes around running her mouth, she could bring a lot of attention to Ruby and Gramps. The killing kind."

Kate groaned. "You've watched too many conspiracy theory movies."

"Uh, who in the room has almost been killed twice?" Claire asked, raising her hand.

Mac raised his hand, too. "Make that three times for me since hooking up with you."

Claire's gaze moved from his hand to his eyes. "What doesn't kill you makes you stronger."

"Another couple of months at your side and I should be able to take down Godzilla."

"You can thank me later when we're alone." She focused back on her sister. "I'll talk to Mom and see what she knows."

"How do we know Ruby or Harley doesn't have the watch and all of this angst is for naught?" Mac asked.

"Kate, go ask Gramps if he's been in the wall safe lately. I'll ask Ruby when we go up to get Mac's omelet."

"Yes, boss." Kate headed for the door. "Then I'm heading to work. Stop by later and let me know what you figure out."

"Wait!" Claire sat up in Joe's chair. "When you ask him, don't let on that anything is wrong."

"What am I supposed to say? 'There's a chance of rain today. Speaking of possibilities, is there a chance you have taken the golden pocket watch Claire has been obsessed with for months from the safe?'"

Mac chuckled.

"You make a lousy Watson," Claire told Kate.

"You're not exactly ringing with endorsements as Sherlock." Kate unlocked the door. "I'll think of something and yell down a Yes or No." She left the door open in her wake.

Mac walked over and closed it, leaning back against it with his arms crossed.

Claire held up her palm. "I know what you're going to say."

"What am I going to say?"

"That I'm going off half-cocked again."

"Actually, what I was going to say was that I missed you this week."

"Oh." Her face relaxed, her smile spreading. Then her eyes seemed to cloud over and she looked down at her fidgeting fingers.

"What is it, Claire?"

"I need—"

A fast staccato roll of knocks on the door behind him stopped her short.

"Mac?" Ruby called through the wood. "One of the members of the archaeology crew is here."

Mac opened the door for his aunt to join them. "What's going on?"

"It's Jess's beau. He says Dr. García wants to see you as soon as possible about the situation they have up there at the mine."

"What situation?" Claire asked.

"The kid didn't say. I don't think he knows. I suspect he's just the messenger."

"Okay, I'll head up there now."

"I'll wrap your omelet in a tortilla and you can eat it on the way." Ruby turned to leave.

"Ruby," Claire called to her, stopping her. "Have you been down here lately?"

"No. But your momma has. Why do ya ask?"

"It's no big deal. I noticed some books were moved around. I bet it was Mom."

Ruby smiled. "It's been a slice of heaven. She stays down here for hours, too busy fiddlin' with the antiques to pick at me. But don't worry. Harley talked to her about keepin' quiet about it all. She swore to keep her lips sealed."

Mac started to follow his aunt up the stairs.

"Mac, wait." When he turned, Claire had rounded the desk. "Keep your ears open."

"Claire," he said, leaning against the door jam, "I highly doubt the head archaeologist would risk his career to sneak down here and steal something."

"I'm not talking about the watch."

"Really?" He doubted that.

"Okay, not just the watch. Someone on that crew is up to something. I've been too busy working on the new building to figure it out, but I think this watch is an indicator of something more."

"More what?"

"More trouble."

Claire had nobody to blame but herself. She had let her guard down, all caught up in building the new restroom, lulled by the daily tasks that came with helping to run the Dancing Winnebagos R.V. Park. Not to mention her whole possible pregnancy insanity. Now the pocket watch was gone.

How could she have been so stupid? She, who had witnessed the results of Joe's thieving first hand, should have at least encouraged Ruby to padlock the office door, if not barricade it. She owed it to her step-grandmother to set things right.

Before Kate left for The Shaft, she confirmed what Claire already knew—Gramps had not moved the watch.

Claire doubted her mother would remove it from safekeeping, knowing the value of antiques as she did, but Claire was still keeping her on the list as a person of interest. Over the years she had witnessed her mother acting out in peculiar ways more than once, especially when under stress. She would not put it past her mom to do something like this in order to get some attention, especially now that Jess's dad had pretty much kicked her aside.

Jess herself might be guilty by association—with either her father or her boyfriend. Both were apt to be using the girl to achieve financial gain, and she was naïve enough not to realize it.

Then there was Arlene. She needed to be watched, even more so after seeing how defensive Kate was of her fellow waitress. When it came to choosing honest friends and crime-free lovers, Kate's gut instincts were as trustworthy as a *javelina* with a sore tooth. The only reason she had ended up with the likes of Butch was because she had pinned him as a criminal and fallen head over heels in spite of it. Fortunately for her and the rest of her family, he had turned out to be an honest businessman, innocent of every crime Kate had assumed him guilty of.

That left the archaeology crew, who were in and out of the R.V. park so much each day that nobody paid much attention to them anymore. Several of them even had tabs going at Ruby's. Any one of them could have had access to that basement room several times a day, what with Gramps and the boys preoccupied with watching her build the restroom and Ruby avoiding staying inside her house because of Deborah's constant sharp-tongued presence. A nimble-footed thief could be in that back door and down those stairs in seconds, especially since Ruby never kept the doors locked.

Maybe it had been the same guy who had been out behind the new building that night a week ago whispering on his cell phone when Natalie went to grab her tools. Or one of the khaki twins slipping downstairs while the other one ran interference. Or somebody else from the crew who she had not noticed yet because she had been too distracted with pregnancy worries and plumbing prep.

But Claire was paying attention now. She had spent the last fifteen minutes keeping a wary eye on their campers and tents while pretending to spray the weeds around the perimeter fence and fix loose boards. In that time, not a curtain had moved, not a footfall had been heard, not a soul had come or gone. The place was a temporary ghost town, and Claire knew exactly where she planned to start searching—the stinky R.V. that Mac had found her climbing into last time.

Only this time, Mac would not be around to stop her. Neither would Gramps or Ruby since they were busy up at the house. Chester and Manny were helping Natalie sand and mud the drywall while Claire took a break to "rest." She figured that if she were going to be treated like a pregnant woman, she might as well take advantage of the down time.

She unbuckled her tool belt and draped it over the back fence, not wanting to clink and creak while tiptoeing through the tulips, or rather weeds and thistles as was the case in Jackrabbit Junction. She grabbed a flat-head screwdriver and then crunched through the partly dead grass toward the camper she had been busted window shopping in last time, pondering why the archaeologists required Mac's presence ASAP. Had they found something besides the long dead and their pots and tools? Diamonds? Waddesdon's gold boxes that had gone missing long ago according to an article in Joe's files? Shrunken heads of some exotic Amazon tribe? It had been about five hours since Mac had left to find out, and she had pretty much been counting the minutes since his dust trail had disappeared down the road.

The afternoon breeze ruffled her shirt, cooling her skin and the surrounding desert from the sun's heat. Autumn had finally come to Arizona with its cooler nights and comfortably warm days, a nice reward for those beings large and small who had survived the cruel beatings delivered by the sun's brutal rays the last few months.

She slid along the back of the camper, pausing at the corner to listen for any sign of life. Somewhere in the R.V. park, wind chimes tinkled and pinged. A few bullfrogs down by the creek were warming up for the evening's croak-fest. Blue-winged grasshoppers clacked in flight here and there around her ankles. Up by Ruby's place a dog barked several times. It kind of sounded like Henry, but it must be some other dog because Gramps had been keeping Henry by his side during the day to keep the horny mutt from running off to hang out with his furry girlfriend.

From the sounds of things, it was now or never—at least for today. Claire sneaked around the side, grabbed a lawn chair from under the awning, and set it firmly on the grass below the camper's open back window. Using the screwdriver, she popped out the screen. The chair groaned and squeaked a little but didn't keel over with her standing on it. She shoved the window all of the way up, making sure it latched. On the count of three, she would jump and hoist herself inside.

One.
She shook the tension from her hands and arms.
Two.
She grabbed the sill.
Three.
She bent her knees and ...
"Hey! What do you think you're doing?"
Claire screeched in surprise at the sound of her sister's voice. She whirled toward the R.V. park's drive, almost careening out of the chair.

Ronnie stood there in a white jean mini skirt, blue tank top, and cork heeled sandals with Henry in tow. Actually, it was the other way around. Henry was dragging Ronnie with every muscle in his little body seeming hell bent on reaching Claire.

"Damn it, Ronnie. You scared the shit out of me."
Ronnie let Henry drag her closer to Claire. "What are you doing up there?" Her gaze lowered to the screen lying on the grass. "Are you climbing in the window?"
"Shhhh!"
"Why are you breaking into this camper?" Ronnie whispered a little too loudly for Claire's comfort when she drew near.

Henry tugged on his leash, now anxious to get away from Claire. Either his interest had shifted to something underneath the beige-infested camper, or he remembered the last time he had joined Claire on a heist and the double-barreled, lead-filled ending to that adventure. Then again, maybe he just needed to take care of business.

"I'm doing a little investigation," she explained to her sister.

"Baloney. I know breaking and entering when I see it. If Gramps sees you, he'll skin your hide."

"Well, let's keep this our little secret then."

Henry whined and strained, pawing at the dirt and grass.

"He probably needs to go to the bathroom," Claire said.

"He marked every other numbered post on the way here."

"Marking doesn't count. He's very private about his doggy needs."

"Fine," Ronnie let go of the leash.

Henry took off like she had fired a starter pistol, dragging the leash behind him.

"Now tell me what's going on here." There was an unspoken *or else* in Ronnie's tone.

"Someone stole the pocket watch from the safe. I think someone from the archaeology group may be behind it, so I'm going to take a quick peek around and see if I can find it."

"That's a bad idea."

"Why?"

"Because you're going to get caught. You *always* do."

Claire was getting tired of everyone thinking she was incompetent in the ways of sleuthing. "I don't always get caught."

"Name a time you haven't."

She could not come up with one at the moment. "I don't have time for this; I have a watch to find." She pointed toward the drive. "Keep an eye out for anyone else."

Ronnie's forehead wrinkled. "I don't think the watch is going to be in there."

"Last I heard, Madam Oracle, your psychic abilities were nonexistent." Claire gripped the window sill. "Now give me a boost."

A burst of barks rang from behind the khaki twins' camper.

Damn that loud-mouthed dog. He was going to get her busted.

"Henry!" Ronnie called.

"Would you be quiet," Claire covered her sister's mouth.

Ronnie knocked her hand away, wiping her mouth with the back of her wrist.

Henry raced under the khaki twins's beige camper at a full run, chasing after something in the grass, probably a mouse. "And get that dang mutt before his barking brings everyone in the park over here."

The barking continued, only muffled, as he zigzagged in and out from under the camper. He circled around one of the jacks and then yipped to a stop.

"I think his leash is caught," Ronnie said.

"Go get him then."

"I can't go under there. I'm wearing white."

"Just lift your skirt a little and grab him."

Ronnie's gaze dropped to Claire's pants. "You go. You're already dirty."

Henry barked several times, then yipped and growled.

"Criminy." Claire climbed down off the chair. "You owe me one."

"No, you owe me for saving you from getting caught today." Ronnie followed her over to the camper.

"I am not going to get caught." Claire dropped onto her hands and knees, reaching under the camper for Henry, who was trying to slip out of his collar.

"Just pull on the leash."

"You forgot to lock the handle. He has the leash completely extended and wrapped around both jacks now." She yanked on the leash, but Henry dug in all four paws and pulled in the opposite direction.

Déjà vu, she thought, remembering Gramps's fall off the ladder.

"Henry, come here." She smacked the ground, then coughed when dust flew up her nose and coated the back of her throat. He barked twice at her before returning to his stubborn mule imitation.

"Go under and get him." Ronnie put her sandal on Claire's hip and pushed.

"Do that one more time," Claire called from under the camper, "and I'm going to put my footprint on your precious white ass when I get out of here."

"Sorry, I couldn't resist."

Claire crawled further under the camper, inhaling the dust Henry was kicking up in his struggles. "Would you just hold still, damn it."

She grabbed the leash and dragged him closer until she could reach his collar and unhook him. The dog wasted no time thanking her for her efforts and raced off toward Jackrabbit Creek again.

"Why did you let him go?" Ronnie's feet and ankles stood there at the camper's edge while she chewed Claire out. "He only comes for Gramps and Katie when they call."

Ignoring Ronnie, Claire began unwinding the leash. She turned onto her side to knock away the rock that was grinding into her ribcage and bumped her elbow on the underside of the camper.

"Son of a bitch!" she said through gritted teeth.

She rubbed her bruised joint, glaring up at the camper's underbelly, and noticed a box tucked up under the back bumper.

"What's that?" she asked aloud.

"What's what?" Ronnie asked, her ankles moving around to the back of the camper, closer to Claire's head.

Claire pulled free the pencil-long box and shook it. Something rattled. She shook it again. Make that several somethings rattled.

"I found a box." Claire's heart was now rattling, too. "There's something in it."

Ronnie's bared knees appeared, followed by her head.

"Oh, now you can hike up your precious white skirt to take a look."

"Quit your bitching and open the box."

"Are you sure the coast is clear?" Claire tried to peer around to the front of the camper, looking for more feet and ankles, this time on the gravel drive.

"Yes, it's clear. Open it."

"It's probably just some spare keys." Or a golden pocket watch and other stolen treasures.

"Oh, for crissakes. Just give it to me and I'll open it."

"Hold your dang horses!" Claire scooted around so she could get a good grip on the box lid. "I found it; I get to open it."

She shimmied off the box lid and lifted her chin to take a look inside.

"Holy shit!" She dropped the metal box in surprise.

The contents bounced, several spilling out and rolling every which way.

"What are those?" Ronnie asked, squinting into the shadows. "Marbles?"

"No," Claire's arms were covered with goosebumps as she plucked one up and held it close. "They're eyeballs."

Chapter Sixteen

The Shaft pulsed around Ronnie, loud and throbbing with life. The Saturday night crowd was rowdy and sweaty, filling the bar with pocketed smells of beer, perfume, cologne, and body odor. Katie had cranked up the volume on the jukebox twice now for the music to be heard over the racket of talking and periodic cheers for the college football team playing on the bar's televisions.

Out on the dance floor, couples were kicking it up to Sawyer Brown's version of George Jones's old hit, "The Race Is On." Natalie had finally given in to the bar's male population, agreeing to one of the numerous dance requests she had received throughout the evening.

"What the hell?" she had told the tall, blond cowboy with a sun-weathered face. "It's my last night in town," had been her reasoning. "Let's have some fun."

Natalie was laughing while whirling around the cowboy, who kept sneaking glances at her chest. Ronnie knew her cousin well—the guy was allowed to look but not touch. Natalie's right jab was legendary back home. She had not earned her nickname the Kangaroo for her ability to hop.

Ronnie watched her cousin flirt with her body. It sure would be nice to shake this cornered badger feeling and enjoy twirling around on a man's arm for a night. She hadn't danced with anyone for years, not even her husband. His idea of fun was a bottle of expensive wine, classical music, and a thick book on the history of French warfare. It was no wonder she had taken up gin—the drinking kind, not the card game.

"You found what?" Katie asked over the din, cutting

through Ronnie's woe-is-me thoughts.

Claire leaned over the bar, closing the distance between her and Katie, who was filling drink orders while Gary the bartender took his break. "A box full of eyeballs."

Their youngest sister grimaced while she topped off Claire's soda. "Please tell me they weren't real."

"Of course not. I didn't say eyeball raisins, did I? The desert would dry a real eyeball up in a day or two at most, even in the shade."

"So, like dolls' eyes? Little glass marbles?"

Ronnie covered the rim of her glass when Katie grabbed the bottle of gin from the shelf behind her. Two drinks were her limit tonight. Even though Claire was playing designated driver, Ronnie wanted her wits about her if trouble came storming through the door looking to ask her about a watch.

"Bigger than doll eyes," Ronnie told Katie.

"Were they prosthetic human eyeballs? Like what kept popping out of that pirate's head in *Pirates of the Caribbean*?"

"Prosthetic eyes are just lenses, not full spheres," Claire told her and took a sip of soda pop. "These were glass balls a little smaller than the human eye. Maybe they're mannequin eyes."

"Why would someone hide a box of eyeballs under their camper?"

Claire scoffed. "I'm more concerned about why someone would have a box of eyeballs at all. That's way creepy." She made a show of shivering in revulsion, which looked a lot like the real deal had when Claire had crawled out from under that camper this afternoon.

"Did you keep them?"

"She stuffed one in her pocket," Ronnie piped up. "But she had to put the rest back before we could get a good look at them because Gramps came looking for Henry."

Claire had been right about that dang dog—the barking got someone's attention ... Gramps's. Luckily for them, while his golf cart moved quickly, he was slow climbing off of it. By the time he got to the back end of the camper, Claire and Ronnie had popped the screen back in place and were standing there pretending to discuss the work Claire planned to do in the canyon behind the R.V. park before winter arrived.

Suspicion had creased Gramps's eyes, but he hadn't voiced it.

"Do you have the eyeball on you now?" Katie asked Claire.

"No," Ronnie answered for her. "We left it back in the R.V. park in a safe place."

Which was really the inside zipper compartment in Ronnie's suitcase stuffed in the Skunkmobile's bedroom closet. It was the only spot onsite that Ronnie could think of in the few minutes she had to hide it while Gramps waited outside in his golf cart to take her back up to the General Store. They had dropped Claire off at the new building, where Chester had greeted her with a bucket of drywall mud and a trowel. Before stepping off the back of the cart, she had slipped Ronnie the eyeball with a whispered, "Hide it."

So, hide it Ronnie had ... for now.

But she planned to move it to a safer place as soon as she told Claire about her other hiding spot—the one where the gold pocket watch now rested, safe and sound. If Sheriff Harrison came nosing around, or any other Feds after he told them about that stolen German artifacts article, Claire and Ruby could say the watch was not at the R.V. park without lying.

"I want to see it," Katie told them, pushing wisps of blonde hair back from her glistening face. The poor girl was working extra hard tonight since Butch was held up out of town for another couple of days.

"Why?" Claire reached in front of Ronnie and grabbed a handful of leftover potato chips from Natalie's plate. "Take our word for it, there isn't anything special about it, just weird."

"Are you sure it's made of glass and not ceramic?"

"Well, Kate, when I used my x-ray glasses," Claire's lips were crooked with a half grin, "it appeared to be a solid glass bead."

Katie aimed the tap spray nozzle at Claire. "Keep it up, wiseass, and I'll give you a pair of beer goggles to replace those x-ray glasses."

"Kate," the cook called out from the door heading back to the kitchen. "Phone call." He held up a cordless phone. "It's Butch."

"I'll take it back there." She looked at Claire. "Cover for me for a second?"

Claire nodded.

Katie paused halfway to the door. "And don't get into any fights while I'm gone."

"You're only going to be gone a few minutes."

"That's all it takes for you."

Claire stuck out her tongue at their youngest sister's back and then circled the bar, taking Katie's place at the taps.

"I need to talk to you about something," Ronnie told her. With Natalie still dancing and Katie in back, now was her opportunity to fill Claire in on the mess Ronnie had created with the pocket watch and how she had fixed it for the time being. Claire needed to be in on her secret before Grady showed up on Ruby's doorstep asking about the watch and this all blew out of control.

She thought about how she had bribed Aunt Millie and her crew and smirked. Make that even more out of control.

Holding up her index finger in Ronnie's direction, Claire leaned over and listened to Arlene's drink order. Then she grabbed a pitcher from under the counter and brought it over to the taps.

"If you're going to tell me not to make a big deal about the box of eyeballs," Claire said pulling on a tap, "I don't want to hear it."

"I don't know what to make of those eyeballs. That's just

serial killer kind of weird shit, so I'm not even going to go there."

She scraped the foam head off the pitcher and topped it off. "What's going on then?"

"It's about the missing watch."

Claire carried the beer pitcher down to Arlene, rubbing her lower right side under her ribcage as she returned. She frowned, still massaging. "What about it?"

Leaning forward, Ronnie mouthed more than said, "It's stolen."

"That's what worries me. Who figured out how to get into that safe? They must have somehow gotten the combination."

"No, I mean it was stolen from somewhere else."

Claire's gaze narrowed. "You found something at the library on it, didn't you?"

Nodding, Ronnie unzipped her purse and pulled out the article. She spread it out on the bar in front of her.

"Put it away." Claire did not look at it and instead shoved it back across the bar toward Ronnie.

"Wait, I need to show you—"

"We have company," Claire said through a forced smile and wadded up the article, tossing it on the floor behind her. "Hi, Mom. What are you doing here?"

Ronnie's back stiffened so fast her lower vertebrae cracked. Oh, God, no! The Sith Lord had found their rebel base.

Deborah slid onto Natalie's bar stool, her lips wrinkled as she pushed the half empty glass of beer in Ronnie's direction.

The notes of sandalwood and jasmine in her mother's Chanel No. 5 perfume was extra strong tonight, burning the back of her throat. Ronnie wished upon her empty gin glass to be beamed anywhere else but The Shaft.

"I'm here for a drink."

"Why?" Claire did not hide her shock.

"What do you mean why?" Deborah looked around. "Isn't this where you go if you want to get happy?"

"That depends on who you are," Ronnie said dryly. She suspected finding happiness was impossible for her mom, since the doctors had removed her funny bone at birth according to Gramps.

"Don't get snippy with me tonight, Veronica," Deborah warned. "I'm in no mood for it." She turned back to Claire. "I'd like some cognac on ice."

"Mom, don't you think—" Claire started.

"I'm tired of thinking, Claire. Just give me the damned drink." She slammed her fist down on the bar.

"Okay, okay." Claire held up her hands and scanned the bottles lining the shelves behind the bar. "One cognac on the rocks coming up."

"Cognac was your grandmother's favorite drink," Deborah said as Claire poured.

"I remember." Claire winced and rubbed her side again. "I remember a lot about her."

"So do I." Deborah's tone was not reminiscent. It matched the wrinkle in her lip.

"Listen, Mom." Claire capped the bottle. "If this is going to turn into some Ruby versus Grandma contest, I'm not in the mood to hear it."

"There is no contest." Deborah sipped from her glass.

"Mother," Ronnie cautioned. "That's enough." They all knew that Claire had been Grandma's favorite. Attacking their grandmother was a very shitty way of hurting Claire, and Ronnie was not going to let that happen tonight. She needed Claire to focus on the watch, not their screwed up family politics.

Deborah snorted. "Ruby wins."

"Why's that?" Claire took the bait in spite of Ronnie's head shake. "Because she's still alive?"

"No." Deborah grabbed a stirrer stick and put it to work, dragging this out, which Ronnie suspected was all part of her show tonight. "Because she's a hell of a lot nicer than your grandmother was."

"Mother, you're cussing." Ronnie leaned closer and sniffed. It was like burying her head in a bouquet of extra-scented flowers. "How many glasses of wine did you have before coming here?"

"None. I don't mix wine with hard liquor; it makes me do irresponsible things." Deborah's pink lips pursed. "How do you think I ended up pregnant with you while I was still in high school?"

That gave Ronnie pause. She had not heard this version of her story of conception before. Previously, the tale had involved variations of romance, not booze.

"What do you mean she's nicer?" Claire asked, giving a customer at the other end of the bar the one-minute finger. "Grandma was very sweet."

"Sure she was—to her grandchildren. But not to her daughters."

"You're just trying to get me back for something by insulting her."

"No, Claire. This isn't about you."

"Hold that thought," she ordered and went to fill some glasses of beer, leaving Ronnie alone with their mother.

"What are you doing here really, Mom? You know how close Claire was with Grandma. Why are you trying to hurt her? Just to pull her down into that miserable shithole you're living in?"

"You shut your mouth right now, Veronica Lee. I don't know what has gotten into you since your marriage went sour, but judging from the way you've been giving me the cold shoulder, you're placing the blame for your failure on me when you are the one who stood up at that altar and said, 'I do.'"

A lightning bolt of anger seared through her, making her fingers and toes tingle, her gut burn. "You nudged me all of the way up there, Mother."

"No, all I did was show you what Lyle looked like on paper—all dollar bills and expensive assets. You're the one who was bitten by greed and overlooked his tendency to flirt with younger women at parties. Especially blondes." Her lips twisted in chagrin. "He really had a thing for pretty young blondes, didn't he?" She took another drink of cognac.

Ronnie gaped. "You knew about the other women from the start and you didn't tell me?"

Her mother shot her a sideways glance. "It was right in front of you, Veronica."

"What do you mean?"

"He tried to get Kathryn into his bed a week before he asked you to marry him."

Come again? Talk about giving good jabs, Deborah's words hit Ronnie smack in the throat.

She coughed and swallowed. "Why didn't either of you mention this before I agreed to marry the jackass?"

"You were there at the party. You saw it and looked the other way. I figured you knew what you were doing—marrying for money." Deborah covered Ronnie's hand with her own. "There's no shame in that, Veronica. No shame at all. We women have to look out for our futures. Look at me, I married for love and now I'm old and penniless with no prospects for a solid future."

Ronnie's tongue fainted dead away in her mouth. She tried to remember back to the time prior to their engagement, but could only remember Lyle and all of his fancy gifts, the expensive restaurants, the weekend trips to Paris and Rome. God, it was all so cliché, and yet she had fallen for it 'hook, lies, and stinker,' as Grandma used to say.

Katie pushed out through the kitchen door, her eyes glassier than normal. She blinked several times as she joined Claire behind the bar, straightening loose wisps of blonde hair. Her eyes widened when they zeroed in on Deborah.

"Mom, what are you doing here?"

"Drinking." Deborah cocked her head to the side. "Kathryn, have you been crying? Your mascara looks a bit smudged. I told you to buy that waterproof kind. I know it's more expensive, but sometimes—"

Ronnie pushed her empty glass toward Claire, who had rejoined their merry little soiree, pointing down at it for more gin to be added. Then she turned on Katie, "How come you never told me Lyle tried to get you into bed?"

Katie turned three shades of pink before going full red. "Mother! Why did you tell her that now? It's ancient history. No good can come of it being voiced. They're already divorced."

"She wanted to make Ronnie feel as shitty as she does," Claire said, still holding onto her side. She filled Ronnie's glass and added a splash of tonic. "I'm not buying it, Mother. Grandma was not a bad mom. I've never heard Aunt Mary talk bad about her, nor Aunt Jilly."

Natalie danced up between Ronnie and Deborah, stealing her glass of beer from between them. "You talking about my mom?"

Ronnie sloshed her drink around. "Yep. Mother here says that Grandma was not a nice mom to her own kids."

Deborah did not deny Ronnie's replay of her words. Instead she nodded.

"Oh, wow." Natalie took a step away from them. "You guys are talking about some serious therapy shit here and we're supposed to be having fun. It's my last night in Jackrabbit Junction, remember?"

"Natalie's not disputing it," Deborah pointed out with a tight, humorless smile.

Claire's gaze narrowed, bouncing between Deborah and Natalie, settling on the latter. "Nat? Tell the truth. Has your mom mentioned anything like this about Grandma?"

"She was a great grandmother," Natalie confirmed that part of Deborah's comment. "But I've heard stories."

"What?" Katie balked. "About Grandma?"

Nodding, Natalie said, "She had her kids way too young is what my mom always says. She didn't have the mom thing figured out until Ronnie was born."

"You're full of shit." Claire glowered.

Natalie shrugged. "You were always her favorite, Claire, like her in so many ways. You couldn't help but see her good side." She finished her beer and glanced longingly out toward the dance floor. "She was a wonderful grandma. That's what my mom always says. We were lucky to have someone so warm and doting."

Holy fuck bucket. Ronnie finished her gin and tonic in one long gulp. She had come here tonight to unload her secret to Claire and instead a heap of truths had been dumped down on top of her like a bucket of pig's blood; only this shit would not wash off anytime soon and she was rusty at hurting others through telekinesis.

"I need to use the bathroom," Claire handed an empty set of beer mugs to Katie. She took two steps and then turned back, hitting her mother with an icy glare. "Now I get it, Mother. That's why you've done nothing my entire life but point out everything that's wrong with me. You see her in me, don't you?"

"No, Claire Alice. You're wrong. I love you in spite of you being just like her."

"Then why? Why have I never been good enough for you?"

Deborah poked at a bobbing ice cube with her fingernail. Her eyes grew watery. "Because she thought you were perfect in every way I never was."

Katie gasped. "She never would have said that."

"She didn't have to, Kathryn. She showed it to me every time she held Claire in her arms and told her how smart and beautiful and funny she was."

"Fuck this shit." Claire stormed off toward the restrooms. Ronnie debated on following her to make sure she was okay, but she knew Claire. They were the same when it came to emotions, shoving the world away so they could lick their wounds in private. Ronnie wished everyone at the bar would go away so she could salve her newest lashes alone with her gin.

"Kate," Arlene bellied up to the bar, an order slip in her hand. "This is for the corner table." She handed it to Katie and turned to their mother. "Are you Deborah, by chance?"

"Who's asking?"

"Romeo over there in the corner. He said to tell you that when you wear that color of blue, your hair glows like an angel's halo." Arlene pointed at the sheet of paper in Katie's hand. "He bought Ms. Angel here another cognac."

Ronnie looked over her shoulder at the same time as Deborah. Manny waved from the corner. Chester sat opposite him shuffling a deck of cards. A woman Ronnie recognized from the archaeology crew shared the table with them, her back against the wall.

"Kathryn," Deborah scooted off the edge of her bar stool. "Have my next drink delivered at Manuel's table."

"Watch out," Arlene warned Deborah. "They are rowdier than usual tonight. Must be something in the air."

"Must be." Deborah gave Ronnie a cool stare. "You're lucky you got free of Lyle when you did. You're still young enough to start over."

Ronnie watched her mother cross the room and take the deck of cards from Chester before dropping into the empty fourth chair between the two old boys.

"That was a slick way to get a fourth player," Katie said, fixing Deborah's drink.

"Thank God she took the bait." Ronnie had had enough of her mother for the time being. Her face burned again just thinking about how stupid she had been about Lyle, how blinded she'd been by all that glitter to see through his games. "Fill me up one more time, please, Katie."

Her sister measured her up with a glance. "Okay, but you're not driving."

"No problem. Claire's driving. If she leaves me here, I'll pass out in Butch's office until you finish for the night and catch a ride home with you."

Katie set a full glass of gin and tonic in front of her. Ronnie reached for it, not feeling her fingers when they embraced the glass. Ah, here it came, the numbing nothingness. This last hit would push her over the edge to where none of it mattered until the sun came up again. She lifted the glass off the bar.

Someone jostled into the seat next to her, a knee bumping into her thigh, making her drink slosh over the rim.

"Damn it."

"Sorry about that, Ronnie," Mac said. "Where's Claire?"

"I'm not pregnant," Claire told the brown-eyed woman in the bathroom mirror.

Her reflection stared back, speechless.

The sharp twinges in her lower abdomen that she had been feeling over the last hour were actual, monthly cramps, not just gas bubbles like she had figured after chowing down a bacon and mushroom cheeseburger and chasing it with a side of French fries dipped in vinegar.

There would be no baby.

Life would go on as it always had.

She didn't need to get married, "to do the right thing."

She should be happy as hell.

Why wasn't she happy as hell?

She pumped a pink glob of fruity smelling soap into her palm and rubbed her hands together, thinking about the heavy weight that had moved from her shoulders to her heart.

This was good news. "It really is," she told her reflection, who did not look very convinced. "You're a lot like Grandma."

All of these years, she had held that fact near and dear to her heart, warmed by it, proud of it. But after learning that her grandmother had not been the best mother to her daughters, and knowing how miserable her mom turned out in part because of that, Claire would have run screaming into the hills if that pregnancy test had turned out positive. Undoubtedly, she would have screwed up the whole mothering business and produced another Deborah ... only smaller and cuter. A sweet, pudgy version of her mother, one without the pinched lips and judging eyes. Maybe the baby would have had Mac's hazel eyes.

She shook off the thought and cranked on the water. It didn't matter. There'd be no baby now. Nobody's life to screw up. Nobody to tie her down. Nobody to love her unconditionally when Mac grew tired of her.

Her reflection frowned. "Are you done wallowing yet?"

"Cram it," she told it and shut off the water right as the door swished open.

Ronnie stumbled into the room. "Mac's out there looking for you." She ricocheted off the wall into one of the stalls and slammed the door hard enough for it to bounce back open. "Damn it, door," her sister slurred.

Speak of the hazel-eyed devil. Claire's chest loosened at the thought of Mac right outside, waiting.

Grabbing some paper towels, she checked her reflection one last time and tried to blink away the confusion she felt swirling behind her eyes about her non-pregnancy and her mother's tales of the past. Other than a scrape over her right cheek that she'd received somehow in the midst of drywalling earlier in the day, she looked pretty good. Her teeth had nothing lodged in them and her T-shirt had no ketchup stains. "Bonus," she whispered.

Should she go out there and tell Mac about the baby now? Would it do any good for him to know? Did she want to see what his reaction would be after worrying about it for the last week?

"I'm crazy for loving you," Ronnie sang from the stall, her Patsy Cline impersonation decent considering Ronnie's condition.

"Aw, isn't that sweet," Claire pinched some color into her

cheeks. "I love you, too, you two-bit drunk."

"Why are you still," *hiccup*, "in here with me?"

Good question. Mac was waiting, and now that she was baby-free, she had a watch to find—make that a stolen watch to find according to her gin-tipsy sister.

And the story behind a box of glass eyeballs to figure out.

And an archaeology crew to spy on.

The toilet paper roll thump-thump-thumped, then something crashed onto the floor in the stall. "Oh, crap," Ronnie said and then snort-cackled. "I think I just violated the toilet paper holder. Someone better call Sheriff Hardass."

"No more gin for you, ya lush." Claire pulled open the door to the bar.

It was time to stop screwing around and get back on the case.

Chapter Seventeen

Mac was not sure where he'd gone wrong.

After Ronnie had left to go find Claire, Kate had come over and asked if he wanted a beer.

"Sure," he'd said. "Whatever you have on tap is fine."

When she slid the glass of beer his way, he thanked her and asked, "How's life treating you these days?"

That was when everything had gone to shit.

Kate's eyes welled up without warning, tears spilling onto her cheeks.

He lowered his beer. "Kate?"

She broke out in sobs, something he had not seen her do before. Hiding behind a bar towel, she ran into the backroom and left Mac sitting there, his jaw unhinged.

"What did I say?" He stood, hesitating as the bar went on with life around him. Should he follow her? Should he wait for Claire first?

He glanced around the crowded room, looking for answers. The sight of Deborah playing cards with Chester and Manny at the back table made him do a double take. What was she doing here? This place was below her station, wasn't it?

He watched as Deborah poured herself a glass of beer, the foam pouring over the rim and onto the table. Manny grinned and picked up her glass while she mopped up the mess with some napkins. He took a sip before handing it back to her. She playfully slapped Manny's arm while laughing. Then she stole Chester's cigar, stuck it between her lips, and dealt out a round of cards.

What in the hell was going on? Had someone slipped

Deborah some roofies?

A loud cheer from the other side of the room pulled his attention away from the corner table. His focus locked onto the backside of a brunette on the dance floor who had some blonde cowboy's arm twisted behind his back. For a moment, Mac thought maybe this was some new dance move, but then she swept the cowboy's feet out from under him and dropped the guy face first onto the floor. Before the crowd of onlookers swallowed them from his view, he caught a glimpse of Natalie's profile as she leaned over the cowboy and yelled, "You lose! Pay up, sucka."

The crowd roared.

Mac dropped back onto his stool, feeling like he had tumbled down a rabbit hole after swallowing a handful of pink and blue pills.

Movement over by the doorway pulled his attention in that direction. Sheriff Harrison stood there in plain clothes, his white cowboy hat in hand. He might be dressed incognito, but the way the Sheriff's gaze searched the crowd, measuring and suspecting, gave away his secret. Mac thought about trying to warn Natalie, but a glance her way showed her laughing and dancing with the blond cowboy, no grudges to be seen.

What the hell was going on? He grabbed blindly for his beer but his hand came up empty. Instead, he found Claire sitting on the stool next to him, chugging down his drink.

She slammed the nearly empty glass down on the bar, burped into her shirt, and then winked at him. "A big drunk birdie in the bathroom told me you're looking for me."

Mac reached out and pinched her arm.

"Hey!" she slapped his hand away. "What was that for?"

"You're real."

"No shit."

"For a minute there I thought I was having a dream." Or a nightmare.

"You're supposed to pinch yourself if you think you're dreaming, not me."

"You're more fun to pinch." His gaze drifted down her snug blue T-shirt with South Dakota State University Jackrabbits plastered in yellow across her chest. "More fun to touch all around."

She sat up straight, rounding out the words below her v-neck shirt even more. "No touching allowed until you tell me why Dr. García needed you up at the mine. Did they find something?" She leaned closer, her brown eyes narrowing. "Something of Joe's?"

"Relax, Slugger. He wants to check out some other areas of the Lucky Monk that he thinks may have been used by the people who were living in the cave before it was mined. Back when they first got rolling, I'd told him much of that mine isn't stable. Today, he wanted to show me where they want to dig, make sure I was okay with it, and if so, see what I thought the danger level would be."

"Why was he in such a hurry?"

"One of his crew found some pot shards in one of the off-limits areas. Before word got out that they were digging in unauthorized areas, he wanted to okay it with me."

"I don't like it."

"It's just a chamber and a short drift that is partially collapsed. With some shoring, it should be safe."

"I wasn't thinking safety." She grabbed his arm. "You know Joe liked to play hide-the-stolen-treasure in those mines. What if they stumble onto something big that he hid, talk it up in the papers, and someone else puts one and one together and comes to Jackrabbit Junction to double-check their addition?"

She had a point, but tonight he was more interested in her other, not so paranoid points; and the curves partially hidden by her T-shirt and jeans. He looked down at her hand on his arm. "You said no touching allowed."

"You're not allowed, but I am."

"That doesn't seem very fair."

"Yeah, well you don't stop at just one touch."

"I see no problem with that."

"It gets distracting. Before I know it, my shirt and underwear are on the floor and I'm on the road to Shambala."

"Shambala is a nice place to visit. It neighbors Shangri-La, I believe. Follow me out to my truck and I'd be happy to take you there right now for a quick visit."

Claire laughed. It was a sexy, throaty sound that made Mac's skin tingle. "Is that a pickup line you've used before?"

"No, and I didn't say a thing about my pickup, just my truck." She poked him for the pun. He caught her hand and wouldn't let go. "How about it, Slugger? I parked around back in the shadows. You feeling a little daring tonight?"

While it was far from the romantic scene in which he would prefer to undress her, the dark offered more privacy for them than any place they seemed to be able to find at his Aunt Ruby's place these days.

She raised one eyebrow. "Do you realize that the Sheriff of Cholla County is sitting three seats down from you?"

"Desperation can make a man do stupid things." He grabbed a fistful of her T-shirt and pulled her toward him. "You have no idea how desperate I am right now."

She hesitated.

He lifted his gaze from her lips to her eyes and tried to read what was going on in her head. "If you don't want to take a chance in the parking lot, we can drive somewhere instead. Find a back road maybe. Or hike in the moonlight out to your favorite spot like we did last month."

"You'll get sand in your pants again."

Cupping her face, he angled her lips for easy access. "Trust me when I say I don't give a damn about sand at the moment."

He kissed her slowly, savoring. The taste of his beer on her tongue made him thirsty for more of her. So much more. She sighed, leaning into him, giving in with her mouth while her hands inched up his thighs, her nails scraping over the thick denim.

God, he loved it when she succumbed. But taming Claire was always a temporary win, and losing to her was just as much fun, especially since it usually meant she was on top. Just thinking about watching her move over him made his pants tight.

He pulled back, his breath rasping. "Come outside with me."

"We shouldn't."

"Yes, we should." He stood and pulled her up with him. "I'm not in the mood to take you on the bar in front of everyone tonight, including the Sheriff." He wanted her alone, all his to touch without interruption or audience.

She let him lead her toward the door. The Sheriff nodded at them as they passed. Mac wondered what he was doing here on his night off. He'd have thought a noisy, rowdy bar was low on the list of Top 10 Places to Relax for a cop.

Outside, the moon sliver split the western horizon with a comma. The pleasant aroma of the desert lavender growing along the banks of Jackrabbit Creek sweetened the air, but it could not compare to his memory of the musky scent of Claire's skin when he got her nice and sweaty. The glow from the orange streetlights lit most of the parking lot, so he led her behind the building into the dark.

His pickup waited in the thick shadows. It was no 1970s Dodge van with carpeted interior, but it would do until he could take her somewhere roomier and enjoy exploring her from head to toe again.

He pulled her to his side, draping his arm over her shoulder. "Your love chariot awaits, my lady," he joked.

"Oh, how my heart beats in anticipation for your touch." He could tell she was trying to keep from laughing, but then ruined her act by pinching his butt.

They were almost at his back bumper when she pulled to a stop. "Shit. I forgot my purse. It's in Butch's office."

"You can get it tomorrow." He tugged her toward him, catching her by the hips and backing her up against the tailgate. "Please tell me you aren't wearing any panties."

"They're green satin with a little heart sewn on the front."

He knew exactly which ones. Those would do. "I'll improvise." He pulled her tight against him, his hands finding and squeezing her soft curves. "You know how long it's been since I got to feel you around me, Slugger?"

She looped his neck with her arms and pushed her breasts into his chest. "You missed me, then?"

"Every inch of you." He stroked down her sides, his thumbs brushing over the words on her T-shirt, drawing a sexy moan from her. His body throbbed in response.

She kissed his collarbone, and then teased his earlobe with her tongue. "I missed every inch, too."

His hands cradled her bottom while his lips slid across her jaw and down the cord of her neck. "Let's get in the pickup."

"I can't."

"You can. You've done it before. I promise to massage away the Charlie horse again."

"I'm on my period."

He growled against her skin. What were the chances timing wise? It was as if the goddess Aphrodite had a grudge against him.

Claire unbuttoned his pants. "But that doesn't mean we can't take care of this little problem of yours."

God, he loved this woman, except ... "Little? It's not a *little* problem."

She slid his zipper down one tooth at a time. "You sure? Maybe I need to measure it with my hand."

His whole body shuddered in anticipation.

She stopped mid-zip.

"Don't tease me, Claire." He caught her bottom lip between his teeth, then kissed the nipped spot better. "It's been too long."

"Shhhh." She leaned back from him. "Do you hear that?"

The only thing he heard was the blood rushing from his ears and heading south of the border.

"Someone's crying," she whispered.

He held his breath, listening. The sound of a sob reached his ears. That reminded him of something he had meant to tell her. "Kate was crying earlier when she got me a drink. What's going on with her?"

Claire's sigh had frustration and disgust mixed together in it. "Mom dropped a bomb on us tonight. Maybe Kate was upset about that."

"What bomb?" Claire started to answer and he stopped her with a quick kiss. "Never mind. I don't want to think about your mom when I'm standing here in the dark with my pants unzipped."

"Really? You don't want me to slip my hand inside like this," she demonstrated, "and then tell you all about Mother's childhood trauma?"

"You're twisted." The thought of Claire's mother added to the sound of sobbing was the equivalent of someone packing his dick between two bags of ice. He pulled her hand out and zipped his pants. "We'll finish this later."

Claire grabbed Mac by the shirt sleeve and pulled him along after her. "I think it's coming from over here."

They crossed in front of the shed that sat behind the bar. The sobbing turned to hiccups.

"Back here," she whispered, holding his hand as they circled behind the shed and trespassed into the deeper shadows. "Kate?" she called out. "Is that you?"

"Go away, Claire."

Yep, it was Kate all right. Mac hesitated. He would rather wrestle a rattlesnake in the dark than console a sobbing female tonight, even if it was Kate.

Claire tugged him with her around the back of the shed in spite of his dug-in boot heels. "What's going on?"

"Nothing," Kate said, and then a sob slipped out.

"Bullshit. Stop playing games with me and just tell me what is going on with you lately. Is this about Butch?"

Hiccups and sniffs were Kate's answer.

"Kate, I can't see you nod back here."

"Yes," Kate spat out. "It's about Butch, okay? Now go away and leave me alone. I'll be fine as goose feathers in a minute."

"He'll be back soon." Claire said, soft and gentle. "I know he's been gone a while, but this is only temporary."

"No, it's not." Kate's voice was acidic, reminding Mac of Deborah.

"It's his bar." Mac spoke up, trying to think of something uplifting. "I'm sure he's coming back."

"Of course he's coming back," Kate said. "But my problem isn't just temporary."

Claire nudged Mac.

What? This was not in his comfort zone. Not even in his comfort arena. "Can I get either of you something to drink?" he asked.

He caught an elbow in the ribs for that one. "What?" he said to Claire. "I'm trying here. Maybe I should wait in the truck."

Claire's grip tightened on his arm. "You two will work this out, Kate. Butch really likes you."

"There is no working this out, either."

"Why not? Because you're stubborn like Ronnie?" Claire jested.

"No. Because I'm pregnant, and Butch doesn't want kids."

Mac sucked in a breath through his teeth. Poor Kate. That was a doozy of a situation.

"The only thing to work out," she continued, "is if I take him to court for child support or go back home with Mom and raise the baby on my own."

Claire let go of Mac. "Come here, spaz." He heard clothing rustle. "You're not going home with Mom. We'll work through this together."

"Thanks, Claire," Kate's voice was muffled. "I knew you'd understand more than anyone. I'm so glad I'm not alone in this pregnancy shit. We can do this together."

Mac frowned. The way Kate had phrased that seemed a little off. Then again, Kate was pregnant. He had heard horror stories from his co-workers about their wives' crazy range of emotions and weird cravings when they were expecting. Maybe this was Kate's example of temporary insanity showing itself in the form of schizophrenia.

"Shhhh," Claire said. Thumps followed. She must be patting Kate's back. "We'll take this one day at a time."

Mac debated on backing out of this family moment step by step. He would try to catch an hour or two with Claire tomorrow. Maybe drag her up to a mine with him under the guise of looking for one of Joe's hidden treasures. Sex or not, he wanted time alone with her.

"Mac," Claire caught his hand and squeezed it, not letting him go. "We need to take her home."

"No," Kate spoke up. "I can't leave. Gary went home feeling sick, and I told Butch I had everything here under control."

"You do. I'll finish your shift tonight. Mac will run you home and then come back and help me close up."

Mac fished his keys from his pocket. "Come on, Kate. Let's get you back to the Skunkmobile." He led the way back to his pickup and held the door open for Kate.

Claire grabbed him on his way around to the driver's side and gave him a soft kiss. "Thank you."

"You owe me." He returned her kiss more thoroughly, exploring her mouth with his tongue until her knees softened. "I'll be collecting on that debt soon. Your tool belt will be required."

Ronnie staggered on her way out of the bathroom, reaching for the wall to steady herself. She shouldn't have downed that last drink so fast.

After spending five minutes trying to fix the toilet paper

roll dispenser with no success, she'd washed her face with cold water from the sink and taken several deep breaths to stop the bathroom from tilting sideways. The gin was trying to wash her out to sea, but she didn't want to be caught in its riptide anymore. All she wanted was to sit in The Shaft and watch the world move around her while she picked up the pieces of her life and started the reassembly process.

The jukebox was playing The Dukes of Hazzard theme song when she walked out from the restroom. Maybe she would dance some first. She watched her cousin go twirling by and her stomach gurgled out a warning at that silly notion after so many drinks.

Or maybe she would shoot some pool. She always played better while tipsy, something to do with being willing to take more risks, probably.

She pin-balled her way through a cluster of dancers over to the busy pool tables, skirting wide around her mother and the old boys so they didn't try to pull her into their card game. One of the pool players scratched on the eight ball as she closed in on them. Perfect timing. It was as if this were meant to be. Ronnie smiled with a feeling of purpose.

She pulled a bill out of her back pocket and slapped it down on the table edge. "I'll play the loser next," she said and then snorted at the irony. She had been playing the loser for over five years. Hell, for most of her life while her mother ran her world.

Correction, make that while Ronnie let her mother run her world. Those days were over, though, and tonight she was going to win, damn it.

The actual loser looked her up and down, his wide face draped with brown bushy hair and sideburns. His even wider smile had a crowd problem with too many teeth jostling together, knocking some of them crooked. *Louie* was embroidered across his bowling shirt. With arms that seemed to hang longer than normal and hands like giant fleshy pancakes, he looked straight out of a cartoon. *The Jungle Book* came to mind, making her chuckle under her breath.

"Well, lookee what we have here." He chalked up his pool stick with those huge hands while his eyes crawled up, down, and inside her tank top. "It must be my lucky day."

Ronnie plucked a pool stick off the rack and hefted it between her hands, liking the feel of it. "Don't get too excited there, King Louie." She half expected the guy to jump up on the table and slap the green felt several times while breaking into a hip jungle beat. "We're only playing for bananas here. There'll be no monkeying around."

"Ah, come on, baby. There's no fun in that." His tone seemed friendly enough. His eyes weren't doing any weird rolling about or twitching, but they were pretty red-rimmed and watery. Judging from the crowd of empty bottles sitting on the closest table, she figured Louie's own party was well under way.

She just hoped he remained friendly enough or she'd be breaking the pool stick over the big orangutan's head before the night was over, and then running like hell. She doubted one hit would do more than make him scratch his thick skull.

"Trust me, you don't want any of this," she warned him and racked the pool balls. "I'm damaged."

"You got you some of those vaginal yeast sores, do ya?"

Ronnie stopped racking and blinked across at him. Really? He took "damaged" and turned it into vaginal yeast sores?

"'Cause I'm okay with sores. They don't slow me down. I just push on through."

She cringed, her stomach bucking at the picture he had painted. Dear lord, she hoped he had washed his hands after using the restroom last.

"Well, thank you for sharing that, King Louie, but I was talking about emotional damage." She rolled the cue ball his way, and then held onto the edge of the table while the world tilted for a second before returning to its normal horizontal position. Ugh, there was that gin again. "Are you familiar with what emotions are, you big monkey?"

"More than you know." He bent over to line up the break shot, but then his lower lip began to quiver. Before Ronnie could fully register what was happening, his whole face convulsed into pain and tears.

"What the …" She came around and patted him on his sweaty back with one of her fingertips, her nose wrinkling at the body odor wafting from his shirt. "I was just kidding around, Louie. Are you okay?"

He rubbed one of his huge pancakes down his wet cheeks. "My girl left me today and she ain't coming back."

Ronnie grimaced, feeling like she should give him a hug but not anxious to embrace the hot, smelly ape of a man. She found a dry spot on his back and patted him with her whole palm. "I'm sorry your girlfriend left you, Louie."

A fresh round of tears filled his red-rimmed eyes. "Not my girlfriend, my baby girl. She got shipped off to boot camp and I miss her already."

"Oh, Louie. I'm sorry." She reached her arm around him, ignoring the wet spots, and gave him a half-squeeze. She was going to need more gin to dull her senses if this therapy session continued. "I'm sure she'll come home."

"Maybe someday but not for a long time." He lifted the tail of his shirt and blew his bulbous nose into it.

"Oh, dear," Ronnie said, hoping he would not come looking for a bigger hug. As much as she wanted to make the big monkey stop crying, she drew the line at snot.

He sniffed and dabbed at his leaky eyes. "Do you mind if I try to call her again and not finish our game?"

"Not at all, Louie. You go and talk to your kid."

He reached out to hug her and she captured his hand and shook it instead. It was damp and sticky, but she managed not to recoil or let go. "I hope you hear from your daughter soon."

"Thanks." He pulled his hand free and leaned his pool stick against the wall. "I hope you get those sores taken care of," he said a little too loud for her comfort.

She watched him lumber over to the payphone, shaking her head at the crazy play of events tonight, including King Louie. "I hope I get these sores taken care of, too."

Turning back to her game, she leaned over and took aim at the racked pool balls. A pair of blue jeans filled the background behind them.

"What sores?" Sheriff Harrison asked.

Only he wasn't dressed like a sheriff. He was missing his official hat and star and everything else tan. The transformation was mesmerizing, especially while her guard was down thanks to the gin buzz. Out of uniform, he looked human—and holy-shit handsome in a rugged, pickup truck commercial sort of way. All he needed was a flannel shirt over his white Henley, all tucked into his well-fitted jeans, and a horse trailer to pull. The white cowboy hat he set on the corner of the table finished his ensemble to perfection.

Shaking off the temporary lust blindness that had hazed her vision for a moment, she searched for sarcasm—her shield of defense. "The emotional sores that I have from constant harassment by a certain local lawman."

She took her shot, scattering the balls around the table, dropping the three ball in the pocket on Grady's left. "If you're here tonight to threaten me some more, Sheriff, I'm not in the mood to dance."

After her mother's heart-to-heart earlier, Ronnie wanted to float around in a tipsy haze for the rest of the night and that was it. She'd face the fact that she was responsible for her own fuck-ups in the sober light of day tomorrow.

"Harassment from me?" Grady crossed his arms over his chest. "You're the one who just drove poor Louie off in tears. What did you say that made a three hundred and fifty pound miner bawl like that?"

Her cheeks warmed. "It was an accident."

"An accident?" he grinned. "I'd hate to see what you could do to a man on purpose."

"Is that a challenge?"

His gaze slid down over her tank top, jeans, and boots. "No."

The heat in his eyes said the opposite.

Emboldened by the gin, she sauntered over to him, circling, admiring his ridges, bulges, and lines up close. He grunted when she tapped his thigh with the butt of her pool stick, but held still for the rest of her inspection. Nice and brawny with broad shoulders. Not too many donuts judging by his waistline. She sniffed at his neck, showing her approval of his aftershave with a brief wiggle of her eyebrows. He needed to shuck the badge more often.

"Good answer, Sheriff." She turned her back on him and bent over to line up her next shot. "I'm not sure you could handle me when you're not hiding behind that tin star." She hit the cue ball hard, ricocheting it off the bumper into two striped balls, which rolled into opposite corner pockets. "I am a Morgan sister, after all. We're nothing but trouble."

He came up behind her as she was chalking the tip of her pool stick, leaning down so that his breath warmed her ear. She tried to hide her shiver of attraction. This was Sheriff Hardass brushing up against her backside. She needed to keep her head on her shoulders and not let this game she was playing get out of control. Besides, he was probably trying to knock her off her guard before he dropped his bomb about him knowing all about the stolen pocket watch.

"I could handle you, Veronica, with or without handcuffs—your preference." His deep voice held either a promise or threat. She couldn't tell which and itched to turn around and find out.

Instead she stepped away, rounding the pool table to take another shot while putting some much needed distance and a solid table between them. "What did I do tonight to deserve your special attention, Sheriff?"

"Nothing."

She aimed to hit the six ball into a side pocket. "So you came here to mess with me for fun then?" Was this part of his plan for getting her to give up the truth? Follow her around until she caved?

She tried to keep her hands steady, not wanting him to see how much he was making her sweat and shake. She wished she'd grabbed that copy of the article Claire had wadded up and thrown behind the bar and tucked it safely away. As unlikely as the chances were of him finding it, the way her luck was running, he would.

"You have nothing to do with the reason I'm here."

"Then why are you standing there watching me?" The six ball missed the side pocket and rolled back into the center of the table. Darn.

"I have a question for you."

Her heart fled to her toes and pumped out SOSs in fast motion. "Oh, yeah?" She grabbed the blue chalk and rubbed it on her cue tip, trying to act cool and relaxed. She was a cucumber, an ice cube, a penguin … were penguins actually cool? Or did they just live where it was cool? She held his gaze, steady. "Is it personal?"

"Yes, it is." He came around the pool table as she lined up her next shot and leaned on the edge of the table close to her, the seam of his jeans only a forearm twitch away.

Her mouth felt like she had eaten a bowl of sand pudding. She put her energy into focusing on her shot, not his hip, thigh, or groin, which were all right there for her to admire. Her shot went wide, the twelve ball hitting the edge of the corner pocket and bouncing off. He was screwing with her concentration, and the flirty look in his eyes when she stood upright confirmed it.

She glanced at his Adam's apple, wondering if he would like it if she licked the skin covering it. A hot bolt of lust tore through her. She placed a hand on the edge of the pool table to steady herself. The thought of tasting his skin left her gulping.

Holy hell, she really needed to lay off the gin when Grady was around.

Get ahold of yourself, Ronnie. A voice sounding way too much like her mother's said in her head, tossing her libido out the front door onto the porch and locking the deadbolt behind it. *If he asks you about the watch, you are going to have to play dumb.*

"What's your question?" she asked.

"Did you have sex with a lot of men—other than your husband—before you were married?"

Ronnie gasped. Had she heard that right? "What?" She cocked her head to the side, trying to figure out his angle. "Are you trying to add 'prostitution' to my list of crimes, Sheriff?"

"No. Wait." He shoved his hands in his pockets, hunching his shoulders. "That didn't come out right."

"No, it sure didn't. You want to try again?"

His brow wrinkled. "Did you ever go through a period in your life when you acted a little uninhibited?" His gaze darted toward the jukebox. His body language, which usually broadcasted authority and control, showed his discomfort clear as the desert sky. Then he looked back, his focus lowering to her chest for too long to be misconstrued as anything other than interest, before lifting above her chin. "Like you are right now with me."

She laughed. It came out sounding a lot sultrier than she had meant it to and blamed him for it. He needed to quit sending her mixed messages, especially while alcohol was polluting her bloodstream. "You think I'm acting uninhibited tonight for your benefit?"

One of his dark eyebrows lifted. "Aren't you?"

"Nope. I was minding my own business trying to play a game of pool when you came along."

"You keep bending over in front of me."

"I can't shoot standing upright, now can I?"

"You have to realize I can see down your shirt when you shoot opposite me."

Actually, she had been too distracted by him to think about her cleavage. "I assure you that flashing my breasts at you was the farthest thing from my mind while I was shooting pool." She placed her palm over her chest. "Besides, I have a bra on." It was not like her boobs were hanging out for a National Geographic cameraman to capture on film.

"I know. It's white satin with a lace edge that has a little orange flower in the center where it clasps."

She pulled open her neckline and checked. The son of a bitch was spot on. Her face was hot when she frowned at him. "Shame on you for looking that closely."

Amusement danced behind his amber eyes. "Contrary to what you may think of me, Veronica, I'm made of flesh and blood."

"Yes, well contrary to what *you* may think of me, Sheriff Harrison, I am not an uninhibited sort of girl." She stepped closer to where he leaned against the table, facing him eye-to-eye. "And while we're discussing me and my bra, let me make it clear that I am not promiscuous or wanton or easy either." She did have some pride left after all of the interrogations, damn it.

His eyes crinkled at the corner. "I'm glad to hear it. But you do hang out at this bar a lot, so you'll have to forgive me for my confusion."

Was he having her watched? "My sister works here."

"Right. Your sister."

She lifted her chin. "You know she does, Grady. I come here to keep Katie company while she works, certainly not for the men."

"So the clothes you choose to wear here have nothing to do with snaring anyone's attention?"

"There's nothing wrong with the clothes I wear."

A pair of vertical lines divided his eyebrows. "Are you actually going to stand here and tell me that you don't realize how you look in that tank top and those jeans?"

He had no idea how soured she had been on men since her world had fallen apart. "I wore the jeans because they were clean, and I chose this shirt because it's always hot and humid in here by the end of the night."

"Yes." He traced the strip of cotton fabric that rounded over Ronnie's shoulder. "It is very hot."

A lightbulb flashed on in her head. She cocked her head to the side. "Is all of this your way of asking me to sleep with you, Sheriff?"

He laughed low and husky. "No, Veronica. You are the last person in this county who I should get involved with."

Was he trying to convince her of that? Or himself? She planted her hands on her hips, glaring at him. "Then what's with the questions about being uninhibited and my clothing choices?"

"Hell. I'm going about this all wrong." He plowed his fingers through his dark, wavy hair. "I knew I wasn't the man for this job."

"What job? Trying to find prostitutes at the local bar?"

His gaze held hers. "Let's get something straight between us. I suspect you are many things, Veronica Morgan, but you are no prostitute. Just because I thought you were being uninhibited tonight does not mean I believe you sell your body for sex."

Good to know where he stood on the subject of her livelihood. "My records state that clearly, do they?"

"They don't need to."

"You haven't seen the home videos then, I take it." Her bitterness seeped into her tone. It always did when she cut through the layers of humiliation.

"Home videos of what?"

"Never mind." She sat next to him on the table edge, shoulder to shoulder. "Grady, why are you here asking me about my sex life if you don't want anything to do with it?"

"I never said that, Veronica." He leaned closer, his shoulder actually touching hers. "I came looking for my niece," he said for her ears only.

"Mindy Lou?" Ronnie asked.

He nodded. "Ever since her fiancé told her she was too fat for him and then left her for another woman, she keeps searching for her self-confidence in strangers' beds. My brother's wife begged me to come here tonight and try to talk some sense into her."

"Your sister-in-law sent you to help with this?" That made Ronnie grin and then laugh.

"Yeah. Why is that so funny?"

"You're like a robot when it comes to emotions."

His eyes grew steely. "I'm not a robot, Veronica. I just don't wear my emotions on my sleeve like you."

She shrugged off his observation. "For that reason, Grady, I try not to wear sleeves. And I wish you'd stop calling me Veronica."

"It's a nice name."

"I like Ronnie better." Although, she did enjoy the sound of her real name when it rolled off his tongue. "You're probably not going to be able to help Mindy Lou."

"Why not?"

"She needs to feel like she's attractive, and she's searching for that confirmation from a man who isn't related to her." Like the pawn shop dude and Jess's dad. "Her uncle telling her she's pretty isn't gonna cut it."

"You really think so?"

"I know so."

He drilled her with his gaze. "From experience?"

"Something like that." She pushed away from the table and rounded to the opposite side, bending over to line up the fourteen ball in the pocket under Grady's very nice ass.

"Don't look down my shirt, Sheriff," she told him as she focused on her shot.

Ronnie might not have been overweight in the past, but she had been a brunette instead of a blonde. The few times she had been hit on since dying her hair back to her natural color had done wonders for her confidence after years of feeling like she had to pretend to be someone else, someone blonde, to be noticed by any man, including her husband.

"I'm not a robot, Veronica Morgan."

She had hit a nerve there. When she looked up, his eyes were on hers, not her chest. She took the shot and sank the fourteen ball. "Okay," she stood up, stretching her lower back. "How about a cyborg?"

He came around to her side in a few determined strides and pinned her butt back against the pool table. His thighs were pressed hard against hers, along with another very noticeable part of his anatomy. "Your ex-husband was an idiot."

Suddenly, there seemed to be a lack of oxygen in this corner of the bar. She tried to catch her breath. "He was?"

He angled his head like he was going to kiss her. She peered up at him from under her lashes, wishing like hell he would hurry up and do it. As much as she didn't want to find Grady attractive and tempting, she did. Plain and simple. Seeing him tonight without the reminder of what he did for a living only cranked her interest in the man behind the star even more.

"I appreciate your advice," he said, inches from her lips.

She pushed up on her toes, lining up with his mouth. "It was my pleasure," she whispered, licking her lips in anticipation.

He stared at her mouth for a long moment, and then grinned. "You'd want me to use the handcuffs, I'm betting."

Before she could figure out what that meant in relation to her jumping his bones right there on the pool table, or vice-versa, he grabbed his cowboy hat and walked away, leaving her aching for more.

Chapter Eighteen

Sunday, October 7th

"Where's Mom?" Claire asked Kate, who was sitting behind the counter in the General Store, apparently holding down the fort. Her face looked paler than usual, especially against the black collar of her work shirt. Her blonde tendrils hung limp around her cheeks, and her blue jeans looked baggier than ever on her thighs. Pregnancy was beating the crap out of her inside and out.

"Good morning to you, too, Sunshine." Kate lifted a spoonful of white creamy stuff to her mouth, plugged her nose, and then gagged it down like she was self-medicating with castor oil.

"What are you doing?" Claire picked up the plastic container from the counter in front of Kate.

"Eating yogurt."

"I thought you liked yogurt."

"I did before morning sickness hit."

Claire set it down on the counter. "How long have you been dealing with this?"

"About a week."

"You weren't really going on walks early in the morning, were you?"

"Well, if you count the distance to and from the bathrooms, then sort of. Thank God Ruby takes pride in keeping her campground's toilets clean."

Claire grimaced. "I don't envy you."

"I don't envy me, either. When are you going to tell

everyone you're not pregnant?"

Claire held her finger to her lips. She had told Kate the no-baby truth late last night when she had returned to the Skunkmobile without Mac in earshot.

"What? We all know about the baby. Well, what we thought was a baby."

"Mac doesn't."

"What?" Kate frowned at her. "Why haven't you told him yet?"

"I wanted to talk to him about it in person, not over the phone." Claire walked over to the packaged fruit pies display and grabbed a blueberry pastry from the shelf. "But I never got to it yesterday with everything else going on." She tore the wrapper open and returned to the counter, throwing some money down for the food. "Then I started my period, you were crying about being pregnant, and Ronnie got totally wasted." She took a bite out of the pie, the glazed crust sweetening the sugary globs of blueberry filling perfectly. "Jeez, my life sounds like one of those reality T.V. shows. I wonder if there's any money in letting them come follow me around with cameras day and night."

"I'd opt out. They always focus so much attention on the one whose life is the most screwed up, and right now I think I'm out in front of you and Ronnie."

Claire nodded, happy as hell to be dealing with cramps today instead of morning sickness. "When are you going to tell Butch?"

Kate dropped her spoon on the counter and pushed the container of yogurt away. "I don't know. I should probably wait until he gets back from his road trip."

"Does he have any idea what's going on with you?"

She shook her head. "I told him I was staying out here because I felt safer around my family while he was gone." She hugged herself, clearly uncomfortable with the subject. "I just couldn't bring myself to break up with him over the phone."

Claire agreed. Phone breakups were right up there with

Dear John letters and walking in on your boyfriend having sex with your best friend, but still ... "So he's going to come back and find out you're pregnant and you've moved out?"

"Yeah, pretty much."

Claire shook her head. "That's not going to go well. Are you sure this is the best choice?"

"No, Claire. Right now I'm not sure about anything other than the fact that I am pregnant with his child, and that he told me face-to-face weeks ago that a child would mess up his plans for the future."

"What did you say when he told you that?"

"I agreed. I didn't know I was pregnant at the time, and you know how much I don't love being around kids. A life with Butch and only Butch sounded like nirvana."

Claire could see Kate in that lifestyle, traveling the world with Butch, no children slowing her down. Kate never had taken much interest in other children. When they were in elementary school, she always hung out with the much older kids. In junior high and high school, she had delivered newspapers for extra money instead of babysitting like Claire and Ronnie.

"Well," Claire searched for the silver lining and grinned when she found one, "at least you know who the father is. And as a bonus, he isn't in jail or prison, unlike a few of your exes."

Kate tried to hold onto her frown and failed. She reached across and poked Claire hard in the shoulder. "Not funny, smartass."

Chuckling, Claire rubbed the spot Kate had poked. "It is, too. I made you laugh." Then she sobered. "Seriously, Kate, it could be much worse."

"Worse than having a baby on my own with no job to support us after I quit working at the bar? Don't even get me rolling on my inadequate health insurance nightmares."

"There are plenty of places around here to get a job, and you won't be on your own. I'm here."

"You're in Tucson."

"So come live in Tucson with me." Claire bit her lower lip. She probably should've run that by Mac first.

Kate stared out through the screen door, her forehead lined. "I'll think about it."

"Good. Just remember, you're not alone. You have Ronnie and me."

Her eyes flooded with tears. She pinched her lips together and nodded.

"Don't start crying again, you big bawl baby. You got mascara and snot all over one of my favorite T-shirts last night."

A half-sob half-laugh leaked from Kate's not-so-sealed lips. She dabbed at the corners of her eyes with a tissue. "I can't help it, damn it. The stupid hormones have me all messed up."

"I'm going to leave you here now to have a nice little blubber-fest while I go find Mom."

Kate sniffed, straightening her shoulders. "You're not going to start a fight with her, are you?"

"No." Claire was not in the mood to go head to head with her mother this morning. Her wounds from last night were still too raw. "I want to ask her if she has seen any strangers down in the basement over the last few days while going through Joe's antiques."

"You're still fixated on that watch, aren't you?"

"Of course. I have to have something to obsess about until you have that baby." Especially since she no longer had a baby of her own to worry about 24/7.

"Tell Jess that I have to leave in an hour. Her shift is next."

"Will do." She started toward the curtain then paused. "Who knows about you know what?" She pointed at Kate's belly.

"You, Mac, and Natalie. And that's all who needs to know for now."

"What about Ronnie?"

"I'll fill her in when she drags her hungover ass out of bed."

Claire nodded and then slipped through the curtain into the rec room. The smell of eggs and toast teased her stomach—the blueberry pastry merely an hors d'oeuvre. She detoured to the kitchen and found Mac and Jess sitting at the table eating with Gramps, the newspaper in his hands. Ruby looked over from where she stood breaking eggs into a cast iron skillet.

"Good mornin', sugar." Ruby held up an egg. "Hungry?"

"Famished." She flicked Gramps's paper as she passed in front of him.

He grunted something that sort of sounded like it had the word "morning" in it and turned the page.

Patting Jess's head, she said, "Kate says you need to take over behind the counter within the hour so she can head to work."

Jess smiled up at her. "Dad's taking me to see that new movie tonight about the zombies who fall in love while on the run from vampires. You want to come with us?"

As much as Claire wanted to see that film, there was no way in hell she was going with Steve Horner.

Wait.

Then again, if he was the one who had stolen the pocket watch, this might be the perfect opportunity to interrogate him and watch his body language to see if he was lying. What was that rule? If the person looked up and to the left, then they were lying? She once had a pilot for a boyfriend who diddled with his sausage and biscuits every time he lied. One face-burning visit to Gramps's house had marked the grounding of that relationship before it had left the gate.

"Maybe." Her answer made everyone except Jess frown in her direction. "What time does the movie start?"

"Eight fifteen, I think."

"That's too late for you to be going to a movie on a

school night," Ruby said, beating the hell out of Claire's eggs in the pan. Today's special: Eggs—Murdered with a splash of blood and a side of butchered pig.

Claire walked around Mac and gave him a hug from behind, wondering how Manny's couch in the Airstream had treated him last night. Mac certainly looked well-rested and smelled desert fresh with his hair still damp from the shower. Unlike Claire, who had yet to rinse off the dried beer mess from last night. Silly drunken knucklehead. That was the last time she'd let Ronnie help behind the bar when she was four gin and tonics to the wind.

"Morning, Slugger." He scooted back and pulled her down on his lap, getting handy under the table until Claire elbowed him. She shot him a warning glance, nodding toward Jess.

Mac shrugged and tried to look down her skull-and-crossbones T-shirt.

"Dad said I could spend the night in his hotel room," Jess continued. "He has two beds in there, and if I bring a set of clothes, he said he can take me to school in the morning."

"Oh, he did, did he?" Ruby said through gritted teeth. "He's fixin' to be a real standup daddy these days, isn't he?"

"Yeah." Jess seemed oblivious to the sound of Claire's eggs being brutally slashed and slain via blunt force trauma. "That would save us driving back here after the movie and give me an extra half hour to sleep in tomorrow morning before school starts." Jess slurped on her orange juice. "Can I go, Mom? I promise to go to bed right after the movie is over. Please, please, please?"

"Why don't we ask Harley what he thinks." Ruby smacked Gramps's newspaper with her deadly spatula.

"I'll finish my homework this morning while working in the store," Jess added to try to sweeten the deal.

"If Claire goes," Gramps said from behind the paper, "then Jess can go. But Claire needs to bring her home tonight."

"But—" Jess started.

Gramps lowered the paper. "Jessica, it's Sunday. You know the rules about curfew on a school night. If I were you, I'd keep my mouth shut and appreciate that your mother is letting you go when you have a full week of school in front of you."

Ruby was back to hacking into the eggs, apparently not happy with Gramps's answer.

Ah, good times with the family, Claire thought and wrapped her arm around Mac's neck, wiggling her eyebrows at him. "What do you say, McStudly? You want to go watch some vampire zombies tonight with Jess and me and her pop?"

"Please, Mac," Jess pressed her palms together, begging.

His muscles tightened under Claire and not in the way she preferred. He avoided looking at Jess and picked up his fork. "I'll think about it."

Claire kissed him on the smooth-shaven cheek. "How'd you sleep?" While they were discussing sleeping arrangements last night at The Shaft, Manny had offered his couch to Mac along with a promise not to bring any women home, whereas Chester had watched Arlene's hips as she walked away and given no guarantees.

"Good. I didn't even hear Manny come in." Under the table, Mac's hand crept up her thigh until she clamped her hand down on his fingers.

Mac, she mouthed, trying to frown, but ruining it when she broke into a grin.

What? He feigned innocence yet shifted his hips deliberately under her derriere.

"Hey," Jess said, giving them her version of the stink eye. "If you guys are going to spend the movie sucking face, I'd rather stay home and paint my nails." She looked over at her mom's back. "They're always making out when you guys aren't looking."

"As long as they aren't doing it in my car again," Gramps said, "I don't give a rat's patootie."

Claire's cheeks warmed, remembering how close they had come to being caught in the midst of car sex by Gramps and his buddies—twice. She was not going to go for a hat trick on that one. Manny had plans to bring his digital camera along for the next peep show if she did. She knew that old dirty bird well enough to believe him when he said he would post the pictures on the internet, too.

"Stayin' home to paint your nails sounds like a good idea to me," Ruby piped in. "I bought ya some new pink polish when I was at Creekside Hardware store the other day."

Cutting off a square of his omelet, Mac held his forkful of eggs and meat out for Claire. She took him up on the bite, moaning in her throat over the maple cured bacon mixed with melted cheddar cheese. Next to that, her murdered eggs were going to taste like ketchup covered cardboard.

Mac's hazel eyes were glued to her mouth, watching her chew and then lick her lips. His Adam's apple bobbed. "Claire," he paused to clear his throat, "I need you up at the mine with me today."

Really? That was weird. Last time she had wanted him to take her up there, he had talked her out of it. "I don't know if I can. We're doing the final touches on the drywall. I hope to get a layer of primer on some of the walls before I clean up for the movie tonight."

"I can help you with the drywall and painting," Mac offered. "Then we can go take a look at things up at the mine."

Did he mean the Lucky Monk? Where the archaeology crew was snooping around? Maybe he had remembered something suspicious during the night that he needed to tell her in private.

"No." Gramps's paper rustled as he folded it and tossed it on the table in front of Mac. "I'll finish up the sanding and help her with the painting so she can go with you. The new restroom is *my* project."

Sensing an upcoming pissing match and not wanting to

hang around for either male to mark her as his territory, Claire hopped off Mac's lap and made for the rec room. "I need to talk to Mom quick before breakfast. I'll be right back."

She was halfway across the rec room when Ruby called her name.

"Claire, hon. Could you hold up a sec?"

She paused with her foot on the first step and waited for Ruby to join her.

Wiping her hands on a dish towel, Ruby glanced behind her before asking, "Will you do me a favor?"

"Of course," Claire said, wondering if this were going to be about Jess and her dad or Gramps or all three. "What is it?"

"Your momma's birthday is comin' up."

Oh, shit, that was right. Her mother took to getting older like a cat to a bath. There was always lots of hissing, growling, screeching, bristling hair, and biting—and then her actual birthday arrived.

"Will you order her favorite cake from the grocery store in Yuccaville when you head into town? I'd make the cake from scratch, but she probably would suspect me of fillin' it with a laxative." Ruby's lips curved upward. "And I just might, too, if she was in one of her pissy moods while I was makin' it."

Claire squeezed Ruby's shoulder. "Sure. I'll order her favorite. That should make her happy for a whole two seconds."

"Thanks, sweetie." Ruby glanced once more at the kitchen. "I'd appreciate it if y'all kept quiet about this. Your grandfather thinks I'm a fool for throwin' her a party."

Gramps knew his daughter well. He was probably right, but Ruby's heart was too big for her own good. Claire would join in on the birthday fun, even if she had to get vaccinated for the rabies virus after the party was over.

"My lips are sealed," Claire said and took the stairs two at a time.

She hesitated outside of her mom's bedroom door, listening for any sounds coming from inside. Her mother had been very happy last night when Chester and Manny had pretty much carried her out of The Shaft. The sight of her wide smile was as rare as a giant squid sighting, and Claire could not help but gawk as the old boys had fun making her mom laugh.

However, in the light of morning, Claire was ninety-nine percent certain that the Deborah who was crashed on the other side of this door was not nearly as sugar tempered. All Claire needed to do was get a couple of answers about who her mother might have seen down in the office and find out if she had discovered any pieces of extraordinary value in Joe's collection that Claire had missed. Pieces that Claire should be concerned about someone not-so-nice coming to take back. Then she would head out to start spying on the archaeology crew in between sanding drywall and rolling on primer. Something weird was going on there, especially with those creepy glass eyeballs under the khaki twins's camper. A box full of eyeballs was no blood-covered weapon, but hiding them like that was definitely not normal behavior.

Claire lifted her knuckles to knock and heard a long, shuddering moan come from the other side of the door. It almost sounded pain-filled. Yep, Deborah was hungover. Rather than provoke her mother with knocking, she grabbed the knob and turned it, quietly pushing the door open.

"Mom? Are you okay?"

She stepped over the threshold and froze at the sight of a bare, hairy male ass smack dab in the middle of the bed. The smell of liquor and sex and something sweet slapped her in the face. Her gaze darted to the bottle of tequila on the nightstand next to a red and white aerosol can of whipped cream and a can of refried beans with a spoon sticking out of it. Her tongue recoiled to the back of her throat.

Holy fuck!

Manny rolled onto his side, the morning sunlight shining through the curtains and spotlighting him. Her mother popped up next to him like a whack-a-mole. She grasped the sheet and pulled it up over her naked chest. "Claire," she gasped. "You should have knocked!"

"OH! MY! GOD!" Claire yelled, stumbling backward out into the hall.

"*Hijo de puta*," Manny cursed, starting to stand up. The sheet slid down below his navel. Way below, the image burning into the backs of her eyes.

With a screech, Claire grabbed the doorknob and yanked the door closed. The scene she had witnessed replayed in her head in high definition. The memory of the smells and that can of refried beans made her stomach heave and buck. She covered her mouth.

"Oh, shit, no!" She stumbled down the hall to the bathroom and upchucked her blueberry pastry into the sink.

Ronnie stumbled out of the Skunkmobile, shielding herself from the mid-morning sunlight. She needed Manny's sombrero to block the UV rays that were passing right through her cheap sunglasses and stabbing her behind the eyes with sharp sticks.

She kept her head down as she passed in front of the archaeology crew's campers. Several of them were sitting outside at a cluster of picnic tables, sorting, sifting, and brushing off their finds or pieces or whatever they called them. She wondered why they weren't up at the mine, but then remembered it was Sunday, their sort-of day off. Most of them still made the climb to the mine on Sundays from what she had witnessed in the past, but some stayed at the R.V. park and enjoyed a more relaxed schedule.

The two ladies whose camper had the box of eyeballs tucked under the back bumper were lounging in lawn chairs under their awning. One of them waved at Ronnie. Ronnie waved back, wondering if either or both of them knew the box was there, or if someone else had stuck it there for safe hiding, like what she had done with the watch. In their matching khakis, photographer vests, and safari hats, they seemed friendly enough to be selling Girl Scout cookies. Could Claire be right in suspecting them of something dark and menacing?

The smell of sausage cooking at one of the fire grates made her nauseated. She had overmedicated with gin last night. During the wee hours, her stomach had waged a rebellion, but this morning she had managed to keep it all down with the help of some antacids on top of a glass of baking soda and water. By no means was she up for a breakfast buffet though. Even a dry piece of bread made her mouth water like she was about to imitate Mount St. Helens.

It was a good thing Grady had left when he had. If he'd stayed, she might have done something she really regretted, *besides* making a super huge ass of herself by almost kissing him. The lack of his star and uniform had thrown her off. She needed to remember that he was the law, cast from the same mold as those who had torn her world to shreds, smirking all the while.

After Grady had disappeared, she had returned to the bar and allowed Claire to refill her glass. That last one was the clincher, finally pushing her beyond the ability to think at any level deeper than a mud puddle. It floated her away from all thoughts of her mother's forked tongue, her ex-husband's lies, and Sheriff Harrison's all-knowing eyes.

The dry grass crunched under her feet as she detoured off the gravel road and cut through a few empty campsites toward the front of the General Store. Sun dappled shadows danced under the old cottonwoods as a comfortable breeze rippled through the R.V. park.

At some point last night, she remembered dancing with a cowboy who had looked vaguely familiar at the time. Actually, it was more like she had stumbled about, tripping over her own boots, while he held her up. She couldn't quite remember his face, only that his breath smelled minty and his eyes were light, light green. Oh, and he kept giving her weird advice about how to take better care of herself. The oddest thing was a warning that he made her repeat several times: "Watch out for the husky and the polar bear."

At the time, she had laughed at him and buried her nose in the buttons of his shirt. But in the skull piercing light of morning, she questioned if he had been a figment of her imagination.

Pausing at the bottom porch step leading up to the General Store, she looked around, noting Natalie's pickup, Kate's car, and Mabel with her shiny coat all within view. She had seen Ruby's old Ford parked around the back next to Mac's truck.

Good ol' Mac. She remembered him carrying her from his pickup into the Skunkmobile and lowering her onto the bed. Then Claire was there, pulling off her jeans and tucking her in.

Katie might have been there, along with Natalie, now that she thought about it. She groaned and covered her face. There was nothing like having the whole family there to see her at her worst. Thank God their mother had not been around to witness it, too. She would never have let Ronnie forget it.

Lowering her hands, Ronnie stared out at the soft browns and sage greens of the desert, soaking up the calm of the quiet morning. It was time. She needed to face her past decisions head on, to hold herself accountable for her choices and then figure out where to go from there.

Last night's wake for Veronica Jefferson was over. From now on, Ronnie Morgan ran the show, and she had no problem with being a general fuck-up, proper posture and perfect dinnerware placement be damned.

First things first, though. Ronnie needed to find Claire and tell her about the watch.

She climbed the stairs and opened the screen door. The cash register sat abandoned, no Jess or Gramps or Ruby in sight.

"Hmmm." That was weird.

Grabbing a can of iced tea from the cooler, she dug in her pocket for a couple of bucks and came up with lint and a phone number scrawled on a piece of paper. Whose number was that? She had pulled on a new shirt and underwear when she crawled out of bed, but these were the same jeans as last night. Had there really been a dancing cowboy? Or had there been someone else there who she could not remember? Much of the time after Grady left did not exist in her short term memory, so for all she knew, a tiny car full of circus clowns could have come along. She needed to ask Claire if she remembered someone slipping Ronnie a phone number.

Ronnie looked up as Katie walked through the curtain from the rec room. She was dressed in her work shirt with her purse and keys in her hand.

Katie jerked in surprise when she saw Ronnie standing near the counter. "Oh, good, you're here. You need to go around behind the counter and watch the store for a bit."

"Why? Where's Jess?" The kid usually covered the morning through early afternoon shift on weekends.

Katie jabbed her thumb behind her. "Over at the laundry building with her mom." She grinned at Ronnie. "You missed all the excitement."

Ronnie squeezed the bridge of her nose. If it involved a lot of yelling between Ruby and Jess, she was glad she had not been present. "What happened?"

"Sex happened."

Ronnie did a double take, frowning as Katie walked past her toward the door. "What do you mean 'sex happened'? Did Claire and Mac get busted down in the basement again?"

Katie turned around, her back to the screen door. "For once, Claire and Mac weren't the busy bunny rabbits."

"Did Natalie bring someone home last night?" She'd been having a lot of fun with that guy on the dance floor, but nothing beyond some flirting from what Ronnie remembered. Hot and heavy had not been Natalie's game last night. Although, there was that blackout portion of the evening that Ronnie could not account for ... yet.

"Nope." Katie giggled. "It was Mom."

Time stopped for a couple of seconds while Ronnie tried to decide if she'd heard that right. "Did you just say our mother had sex? Were there pigs flying, too?"

Another giggle burst from Katie's lips. "Yep. And Claire walked in on Mom right in the midst of her doing the wild thing."

Ronnie stepped backward, her butt bumping into the counter. "Sex?" She was still struggling with the concept of her mother allowing a man to come within touching distance of her nether regions.

"With Manny," Katie whispered loud and clear.

Something in Ronnie's skull splintered. She held onto the counter while the room spun for a second. "Our mother had sex with Manny Carrera?"

Katie covered her mouth, doing a rotten job of stifling her giggles. "Yes. You should have seen Claire's face right after she caught them in the act." She laughed harder, trying to talk between it all. "And now ... Claire says ... her eyes are ... broken."

Ronnie chuckled and then winced and then chuckled some more, confusing images flapping around in her head. Poor Claire. There was no returning from that sight, Ronnie was sure. "Is there anything else I need to know before I head back there?"

Katie sobered. "Yeah."

"What? It can't be worse than Mom having sex."

"Yes and no." Katie glanced toward the curtain. "I'm pregnant."

Ronnie leaned toward her. "Did you just say you're—"

"Shush." Katie silenced her.

"Wow." Ronnie's head throbbed behind her right eye all of a sudden. She held her palm to her forehead. "You and Claire both, huh?"

Katie shook her head. "Claire started her period last night. I'm in this alone." Katie's eyes watered around the edges. "Butch doesn't want kids."

Still holding her hand to her forehead, Ronnie closed the distance between them and hugged her little sister with one arm. "You're not alone, Katie. I'm here for whatever you need from me—a birth partner, a babysitter, a doting auntie, you name it."

A sob escaped Katie's chest. "Damned hormones keep turning me into a crybaby."

Ronnie chuckled and pushed her sister back. "Does Mom know?"

Katie shook her head while dabbing at her eyes. "I don't want to tell her yet."

"Okay," Ronnie said. "My lips are sealed."

"Claire, Mac, and Natalie know, though." Katie backed out through the door onto the porch. "I have to go to work.

I'll see you later today at The Shaft?" There was a hopeful note in Katie's question.

Ronnie nodded, even though the thought of alcohol made her gag and burp up baking soda.

"Good." Katie waved and left.

When Ronnie stepped through the curtain, she found Claire sprawled out on the couch with an ice pack covering the upper half of her face. "What are you doing?" she asked.

"I broke my eyes."

"Yeah, I heard." A snort of laughter escaped before Ronnie could stop it.

"It's not funny, Ronnie." Claire lifted the ice pack off long enough to shoot her with an angry glare. "That image is branded into my brain for eternity."

"Or until you die."

"If I'm lucky." Claire replaced the ice pack. "What if I can never have sex again without thinking about Manny's bare ass or Mom's boobs?"

Ronnie looked away, trying not to let Claire hear her laughing and failed. "I'm sorry, Claire," she said between jags, wiping at the tears leaking from her eyes. "It's just so damned funny."

"No, it's not," Gramps said from the kitchen doorway, his face scrunched in a scowl. He reached in his pocket and pulled out the keys to Ruby's truck. "Here." He tossed them to Ronnie.

She frowned at them. "Am I going somewhere?"

"Yuccaville."

What? No! Grady was there with his internal radar that seemed to pick her up every time she got near. He was the last person she wanted to run into today. "Why me?"

"Because your mother is still drunk, Claire has work to do on the new restroom, and I can't drive yet."

"Fine." But with the way her stomach felt, crawling behind a wheel was not the wisest move. The motion of the car might make everything come up in spite of the handful of antacids she had chewed for breakfast. She stood up and pocketed the keys. "Let me grab some coffee first."

"There's none left."

"What happened to it?"

"Your mother dropped the pot. The glass shattered and the coffee spilled all over the kitchen floor." He turned Ronnie around and pushed her toward the green curtain. He stuffed a wad of cash in her hand. "We need a whole new coffee pot along with more coffee. The stuff Ruby has in the General Store isn't good enough for your mother."

"Yet she has no problem with tequila, whipped cream, refried beans, and horny old men," Claire said from the couch, then groaned and covered her mouth.

Gramps frowned at Claire, then he pulled a few more bills from his wallet and handed them to Ronnie. "Buy me a case of shells for my shotgun while you're at it." He stuffed his wallet in his back pocket. "I'm gonna fill Carrera's ass full of buckshot for sleeping with my daughter."

Chapter Nineteen

Ronnie was standing in line to pay at the Piggly Wiggly grocery store in Yuccaville when she finally got to meet the infamous Mindy Lou Harrison.

The twenty-something platinum blonde with dark roots had pulled out her wallet and set it on the little check writing counter while she dug through it for money.

Ronnie was flipping through the latest glad rag about a scandal involving some distant member of the Royal family, mostly minding her own business, when she heard, "Well, damn, I must have left the rest of my cash in my other shorts. Can I come back later and pay what's left?"

That lured Ronnie's nose out of the magazine. She glanced from the frowning cashier to the bottle of whiskey, two packs of cigarettes, and two candy bars waiting to be bagged.

"Sure, hon," the cashier said, tucking some strands of gray hair back up in her bun. "I'll just set it to the side here until you get back."

Ronnie smirked at the makings for a fun, private party for two. All that was missing was the box of condoms. Oh wait, there they were on the other side of the whiskey. Well then, let the *fiesta* begin.

"I meant I'd take it with me and bring you the cash later."

"Let me get this straight, hon," the cashier said, crossing her arms over her chest. "You want me to let you walk on out the door with this and trust that you'll come back with the money later?"

"You know I'm good for it. My uncle is the County Sheriff."

That's when Ronnie's gaze had swung to the brassy blonde's face, noting the cherry red lipstick, long swishy eyelashes, and smoky eye shadow. So this was Grady's niece. She vaguely recognized her from the bar a few nights back. She couldn't see much resemblance to Grady, but maybe if Mindy Lou would quit dying her hair, the genetics would show through. Ronnie's focus dropped to Mindy Lou's hands. Sure as sunshine in the desert, there on her left ring finger was Ronnie's wedding set.

"I know who your uncle is, Mindy Lou." The cashier shook her head, disgust loud and clear in her sneer. "But I'm not gonna risk losing my job for you to go get your rocks off with some loser. If you want this stuff, I need to see cash or a check or a bank card." She snickered. "Or your uncle and his wallet."

Mindy Lou's face flared bright red, matching her cherry red lips. Ronnie's heart went out to her. She knew the burn of humiliation well. The way it started high in the cheeks and then burrowed deeper and deeper, smoldering clear to the core. Had she not known Mindy Lou's history, she would have been snickering along with the clerk. But thanks to Grady cluing her in last night, she wanted to see Mindy Lou fight her way out of the depths of self-loathing. She wanted to help her somehow. Guide her out of that cesspool of insecurities and self-doubts.

"I'll cover the rest," Ronnie said, and pulled out one of the twenty dollar bills Gramps had given her. She handed it to the cashier, who frowned from the bill to Ronnie, then shrugged and grabbed it.

"It's your lucky day, Mindy Lou."

Ronnie's gaze drifted down to Mindy Lou's fingers again as she tried to zip her wallet around a receipt caught in the teeth. She had wondered how it would feel to see her wedding set on another woman's finger. Wondered if she would feel sad or angry, if she would want to yank it off the other woman and run away while mumbling to herself about getting her "precious" back.

In the end, empathy weighed down her heart. Ronnie knew how Mindy Lou went about getting that wedding set from the greasy pawn shop guy and then wore it when she was with Jess's dad. Figuring Mindy Lou was about to go out and score a drunken afternoon-delight session with yet another loser, something other than the self-confidence she so needed, Ronnie wanted to shelter the young woman. She considered ways of taking her away from the prying, judging eyes in this rinky dink town.

"Nice ring," Ronnie said.

Mindy Lou looked down at it like she was surprised to see it on her finger. "Oh, thank you. My … ah … boyfriend gave it to me."

"He's a lucky man to have you."

The cashier snorted.

"Thanks," Mindy Lou's neck flamed. She scooped up her groceries. "And thanks for helping me out with this. I owe you one."

"Pay it forward," Ronnie told her.

"Huh? What's that mean?"

"Never mind. Have fun."

With a nod, Mindy Lou walked off with Ronnie's ring.

The cashier rang up her groceries. "That was a nice gesture you did there, but Mindy Lou has a problem."

"I know."

The cashier paused. "You know about Mindy Lou being a tramp?"

Ronnie winced at the cashier's lack of a filter with a stranger. She handed the woman two more twenties and tossed aside her years of practiced propriety. "I know Mindy Lou had her heart broken by her rat bastard fiancé who called her 'fat' and then left her for a skinny bitch. Now her self-esteem is in the shitter and she's seeking her self-worth in the arms of any man who will show her an inkling of affection, even if it costs a bottle of whiskey."

The clerk stared at her like she had grown a horn in the middle of her forehead.

Grabbing her bag of groceries, Ronnie smiled. "You have a nice day now. I hear we're supposed to get a bit a rain tonight. Lord knows this place always needs more water."

Swinging her bag while whistling "It's Raining Men," she stepped out the supermarket door in time to see Mindy Lou go past. She was sitting in the front passenger seat of a familiar Cadillac belonging to one Steve Horner, aka Jessica's father, aka the no good, cradle robbing, slick son of a bitch. Crap! She'd assumed Mindy Lou had moved on to her next fix.

Ronnie watched the taillights brighten as Jess's dad slowed to let a slew of pedestrians pass in front of him. Where was he headed with Mindy Lou? Then she remembered that she had just bought their party supplies with Gramps's money and cringed.

"Oh, shit!" She ran to Ruby's Ford, dumped the grocery bag in the back, and climbed inside. She made it out of the parking lot in time to see Horner take a left two blocks ahead. She followed, keeping her distance so that he might not notice the pickup. With Mindy Lou in his car, she had a feeling he was probably a little distracted. At least she hoped so, anyway. She grimaced. Or not, being that it was Mindy Lou.

Jeez-o-petes! This is what she got for wanting to help someone. Every time she put herself out there, she got kicked in the knees.

"Damn it, Mindy Lou! You're supposed to be having self-loathing sex with some stranger, not Jessica's father."

Wait. That didn't really sound right.

She followed them another half mile until they turned into the parking lot of The Sundown Inn, a two-story, sleazy looking motel a block off Main Street that had seen its heyday back in the late 50s. The honeycomb concrete walls, flat roof, and outside entry doors had the look of something that belonged up on old Route 66. All that was missing was a big, campy ... she passed a ten-foot tall, sun-faded jackrabbit.

Never mind, this place had it all. She drove on by so they wouldn't notice her and came to the cross streets right down from the library.

By the time she had circled back around and parked across the street, Steve was leading Mindy Lou up the wrought iron staircase. With his arm around her shoulders and the sleazy grin on his stupid face, Ronnie's chest ached for Jessica. That was her dad, the man who was supposed to set an example for her.

Ronnie thanked the stars for her father, even if he had let Deborah run ram shod over him more often than not. At least he hadn't partied with young girls when he was in his late forties. He had ended up leaving their mother for another woman—but she had been even older than Deborah. After spending thirty plus years with her mother, though, it was a wonder he hadn't joined the monks over in Tibet.

As Ronnie watched, Steve dug out his room key. Mindy Lou glanced around, then grinned and slapped Steve's butt. He grabbed her and put a sloppy lip-lock on her, then backed into the room while his mouth was still fastened to her face. It was like some creepy, alien, face-sucking foreplay.

Cringing, Ronnie leaned back and closed her eyes, wondering what she should do. Mindy Lou was no kid. She was in her early twenties, which was plenty old enough to be having sex with whomever she pleased. But having sex in seedy motels in the middle of the day was like the first stop on the road to drugs, prostitution, and at the least, a few vaginal yeast sores, as King Louie could probably attest.

Should she go up there and interrupt their party? Would that do anyone any good or just humiliate Mindy Lou even more? Ronnie certainly hoped it would embarrass the hell out of Jess's dad.

Maybe she should call ...

The sound of the passenger door creaking open made her sit upright, wide eyed.

A familiar tan uniform, complete with shiny star, cowboy

hat, and chiseled-faced man, slid onto the bench seat next to her. He closed the door behind him, taking off his hat and setting it on his knee.

Ronnie sputtered out a few words before she could clearly ask, "What are you doing?"

Sheriff Harrison leaned forward and peered up at the room where his niece was going to be bonking Steve Horner any minute, if they weren't already doing the bare-skin boogie. Ronnie really did not want to think about what was going on behind that door too much. It was too soon after hearing Claire talk about their mother and Manny's good times.

"The same thing as you," Grady said, sitting back with a frown. "Spying on my niece."

"I'm not spying."

"Really? Then what are you doing? Are you into voyeurism? Did I interrupt your kinky fantasy?"

"Gross!" Ronnie slugged Grady in the shoulder without thinking, and then realized she had just hit the Sheriff of Cholla County. Could he arrest her for that? "That's my aunt's dad up there with your niece," she explained and hoped they could conveniently forget that she had just assaulted a cop.

"Your aunt's dad?" His face paled. "Jesus. She's sleeping with some old guy now?"

"Well, he's not that old. Probably in his late forties is all."

Grady's face got all wrinkled as he looked over at her. "My math is a bit rusty these days, but I know you're thirty-five according to your driver's license, so that doesn't add up right."

"My grandfather married Ruby, so Ruby's sixteen-year-old daughter, Jessica, is now my aunt. Your niece is up there having sex with Jessica's dad, who is in town to try to get custody of her." At least that was Ronnie's conclusion on the reason for Steve's visit.

Not a muscle moved on Grady's face. "You do realize that sounds like a running joke from that old show, *Hee Haw*, don't you?"

She grinned. "I was thinking it sounded like something from a seventies country song, but I didn't mention anything about a pickup or a hound dog, so your idea is more fitting."

His gaze drifted down over her shirt, making the pulse in her neck kick it up a notch. "You aren't dressed right, though, for *Hee Haw*. Not enough skin is showing, and you need to be wearing Daisy Duke shorts, not jeans."

Was that an observation or a complaint? She was not sure she wanted to know the answer with the way the smell of his aftershave alone had her hormones hopping around like Mexican jumping beans. She looked out the window at the hotel room. "I followed them because it's my fault that she's here," she returned to their earlier subject.

"Your fault, huh? Are you acting as Mindy Lou's pimp now?"

"Not quite." She shot him a sideways glance. "But I paid for the whiskey and condoms."

His eyebrows shot up to his hairline. "You what?"

"I didn't realize it was going to be for sex with Jess's dad."

"Did you send her off with plastic bags full of heroin and meth while you were at it?"

"Of course not."

"Damn. That would've given me a good reason to break up the party." He sighed. "Shit. There's nothing either of us can do. She's well over the age of consent."

"That doesn't mean we shouldn't go up there and stop this."

"And say what? 'Mindy, we'd prefer you stop having sex with this asshole because it makes us uncomfortable'?"

"Maybe." Ronnie clasped her hands together in her lap. "I feel bad for her. She's in a tough place mentally. I've been in that hole. I know how deep and dark it is. I want to help her out of it and get her back on her feet again."

"Are you back on your feet again, Veronica?" He stared at her with those piercing whiskey-colored eyes, making her feel naked, exposed.

She thought about her answer for several seconds. "Yeah, I think I am."

"Good." The hard lines on his face softened into a smile. "But I still think you're a little nuts."

She chuckled. "Where's the fun if I'm completely sane?"

His focus drifted south to her mouth, his smile flat-lining. The air in the cab thickened, making it harder for Ronnie to breathe. She clasped her hands tighter together.

"What happened to you?" he asked.

She shrugged, knowing exactly what he was referring to. "He lied."

"About what?"

"Pretty much everything." She looked at the fading tan line on her ring finger. "And omitted the fact that he was still married to someone else."

"Damn. How did you find out?"

"The Feds told me when they were interrogating me regarding the missing laundered money."

"Christ."

Ronnie's laugh sounded hard and brittle. She couldn't help it. "Yep. It was good times in that interrogation room. They filled me in on several other details, too. I guess they figured it was their job since they already had Lyle behind bars."

"What details?"

She glanced at him, not sure why she was baring her soul about this to the Sheriff of Cholla County when she hadn't even leaked a drip to her sisters. Maybe it was because she was used to feeling naked in front of men with badges and uniforms and suits. Or maybe it was because he hadn't known her before when she was trying to be Veronica Jefferson, the high and mighty hostess of the rich. She didn't have as far to fall off her pedestal in his eyes.

"Lyle had been paranoid for a long time. He'd hidden surveillance cameras throughout the house without my knowledge."

Grady grimaced.

"The Feds thought I was keeping secrets from them. They tried to get me to break by showing me videos of Lyle with other women in our bed."

They'd all been blondes. Every single one. Young, curvy blondes. Lyle was a cliché through and through. Ronnie had tried so hard to live up to those clichés.

"When that didn't work," she continued to pour out her ugly tale, "they showed videos of me."

"You had an affair?"

She shook her head. "In spite of my husband's lack of physical attention the last year of our marriage, I found ways to …" She turned her face away, staring out at the motel room door. "To satisfy my needs in what I thought was the privacy of my own bedroom and shower."

He inhaled a breath through his teeth.

"Yeah. There's nothing like watching yourself get off on a little black and white television in a room full of strangers." She laughed again, still brittle, still hard. "I don't quite get the allure of the whole sex tape business."

His hand warmed her shoulder. "I'm sorry you had to go through that."

Her smile felt wrong, like a shoe that was too tight. "That wasn't the worst." She turned back to meet his eyes. "Lyle warned me that someone would be coming after me."

"Like the FBI or ATF?"

"No. Someone he stole money from. He said I needed to watch my back, because even though he'd told 'them' multiple times that he had spent all the money that he'd stolen, they didn't believe him. They may think that I have the money stashed somewhere and come looking for me to collect what's theirs."

God it felt good to let this out, to confide in someone other than the scared, angry face in the mirror.

He cocked his head to the side. "Do you have something stashed away?"

Only a golden pocket watch, but that was not what he was

referring to, nor any of his business.

"No." She gripped the steering wheel, her knuckles whitening. "On the contrary, Lyle had everything mortgaged and maxed out, so not only do I have no money, I have no savings to fall back on. Did I mention his cocaine addiction?"

"Damn, Veronica."

"Lucky for me, he kept everything in his name only, so the bankruptcy doesn't affect my credit. That doesn't exactly help pay my bills, though."

"That's why you were trying to pawn your jewelry?"

"Yes, but it turned out that was all fake, just like my marriage and everything else in my life." When she saw the sad expression come over his features, she held up her hand. "No, do not look at me like I'm some orphaned, flea-bitten kitten tossed in a dumpster behind the grocery store." She lifted her chin. "I made my life into this Superfund site and I'll clean it up. You just happened to come upon me in the midst of the decontamination. In a few months, I'll have my shit back together and be moving forward again."

"What about the men who might be looking for you?"

She puffed her cheeks and blew out a breath. "There isn't much I can do about that except keep watching over my shoulder."

Her thoughts returned to the cowboy dancing with her last night and his warning about the husky and polar bear. If he hadn't been a figment of her drunken imagination, maybe he was working for the mob guy hunting her down. Maybe he was toying with her, not warning her. Maybe he liked to play with his prey before going in for the kill. She shivered in the warm pickup, rubbing her arms.

"Veronica." Grady's voice sounded velvety, deeper than normal.

"What?" she looked over at him, blinking at the warmth radiating from his eyes.

Her heart tripped over itself.

He started to reach toward her, but then his gaze reverted

to the motel. "Mindy Lou."

Ronnie followed his eyes, watching as Mindy Lou leaned on the railing while she smoked a cigarette. The door to the room stood open behind her.

"Get down," Grady said, tugging her low so that their heads almost met in the middle of the bench seat. "If she catches me watching her, she may leave town, and neither my sister-in-law nor I want her to go to Tucson or Phoenix. We want her here where we can keep tabs on her while she gets through this."

If she gets through it, Ronnie thought. That dark hole was not easy to climb out of, but with enough will power, Mindy Lou could do it. In some ways it was nice to reinvent oneself, put away past inhibitions and show a new side to the world. She turned her neck, her face inches away from Grady's, tempted to take another daring step forward and touch his cheek, feel the contours under her fingertips.

Her eyes lifted and found his. The hunger reflecting back at her made her toes tingle. Or maybe she had a nerve pinched in this awkward position. Whatever it was, she definitely wanted to kiss the Sheriff of Cholla County. Crap, what was wrong with her? Was this some twisted version of the Stockholm syndrome, only she was getting all gooey brained about the lawman with the shiny star instead of her captor?

Grady peeked out the window. "She's gone back in the room." He sat up.

Ronnie followed suit, wondering if she had shown him her cards in those few seconds. She hoped not. The last thing she wanted was Grady knowing she had the hots for him. She preferred his animosity to his kindness. It was more pokey, less likely for her to get comfortable around when they were alone together, like now.

She rubbed her hands together. "Now what?"

He watched her, his expression unreadable. "Well, first of all, this."

His hand wrapped around her arm and tugged her toward

him.

"What are y—" she started.

"Shut up, Veronica," he said, cupped her jaw, and kissed her full on the lips.

He tasted salty and sweet at the same time, intoxicating her with the combination. His tongue teased, brushing along the line of her lips. His fingers spread wide over her cheeks, positioning her mouth for better access.

He lifted his lips, his breathing quickened. His eyes searched hers, for what, she didn't know, didn't particularly care.

"I'm sorry, Veronica. I just—"

"Shut up, Grady."

She grabbed him by the back of the neck and pulled his mouth back to hers, wanting to taste him more. He groaned when her tongue tangled with his, then traced his lower lip before she captured it between her teeth. His hand slid down over her shoulder, squeezing.

She grabbed his lapels and tugged him closer, a need for more of him, so much more, flaring white hot from out of nowhere.

"Grady," she gasped as his mouth trailed over her cheek and found her earlobe. "This is so wrong." She closed her eyes as his fingers traced her collarbone. "I piss you off."

"You definitely have a knack for it," he said, his voice a low growl against her neck.

"I'm the last person you should get involved with," she repeated his words from last night at the bar.

"Yes, you are." He pulled the neck of her T-shirt aside and kissed a line along her shoulder blade. "Your skin tastes like honey."

"I don't want you to stop," she whispered to the ceiling of the pickup. She caught his hand and moved it to her ribs. "Touch me."

A sharp knock on the passenger side window made them both gasp and jerk apart.

Aunt Millie's face was pressed against the glass, her dentures showcased in her wide grin. "What are you two doin' in there?"

Grady groaned and leaned his head against the back window.

Aunt Millie held up the brooch that Ronnie had traded for computer time last week. "We miss you at the library, Ronnie. Come visit us again soon. We have more German to teach you." She winked and looked at her nephew's profile. "Grady, if this is a new interrogation technique of yours, I have a couple of girlfriends who might want to have you over for tea and questioning."

With a cackling laugh, Aunt Millie and her red walker squeaked off down the sidewalk, probably heading toward the library.

"Shit," he said under his breath. "This is going to get a lot of laughs at the Thanksgiving table this year."

Ronnie adjusted her shirt, fanning herself. "I didn't expect it to go like that."

"Me either. That's what I get for going against my better judgment."

Her, too. Lesson learned. Don't play with fire. Her fingers and lips were still burning.

The silence in the cab reminded her of prom night when she caught her date masturbating under the bleachers while watching their Spanish teacher do the tango with the basketball coach—sticky and awkward.

She cleared her throat. "Was there something else you wanted to tell me?"

"Oh, yeah." He pulled a crinkled piece of paper from his pants' pocket and handed it to her. Then he grabbed his hat from where it had fallen onto the floor at some point and shoved open the pickup door. Leaning inside, he looked her over once more, pointing at the paper. "You need to tell me what's going on with that."

With a nod, he closed the door, planted his hat on his

head, and strode off.

Ronnie watched his backside in the rearview mirror until he climbed into an unmarked sedan and cruised by her without even a wave.

She looked down at the paper in her hand, smoothing it out on the bench seat next to her.

"Fuck," she whispered, grasping the steering wheel until her world stopped swirling toward the drain.

The article on the German castle and stolen pocket watch tried to crinkle back into a bowl shape. The Sheriff must have found it last night while he was at The Shaft. She should have picked it up before drinking all of that gin. If only her mom hadn't ... no, she was not going to play the blame game, anymore. This was her fault.

Now what?

With one last glance at Mindy Lou's love nest, she started up the Ford and took off for home. Maybe Claire would know what to do to get Ronnie out of this mess.

Chapter Twenty

Mac's Sunday evening with Claire was not going as planned.

Not even close.

It had all started this afternoon when Jess's dad had called and cancelled movie night with her because of a migraine.

Ruby had taken one look at Jess's teary eyes and decided to take her to the movie in his place. "A movie with my baby girl is exactly what I need right now," she had told Mac, who was down in the basement office going through a bunch of records and information he had collected on Ruby's mines over the last couple of months.

"You do remember the movie is about zombie hunting vampires, right?"

She placed a plate of lemon bars in front of him, one of his favorites since childhood. The smell alone made him swoon a little.

"I know it's not exactly some fancy mother-daughter tea," Ruby ran her finger over the part of the desk not covered with copies and maps, frowning at the dust she found. "But any bonding time at this age is good, don't ya think?"

If Ruby was taking Jess to the movies, that meant Claire was his for the night. Sweet. Mac picked up one of the powdered sugar crusted lemon bars. It was still warm. His mouth watered, thinking about lemon bars and Claire—naked. Maybe he should dust her with powdered sugar, too.

"I need a favor," Ruby said, interrupting his thoughts of Claire. He bit into the bar and groaned in appreciation, then looked up at his aunt. "Name it."

"Well," she hesitated, which made Mac's shoulders tense. "Since I'm fixin' to go to the movies, the boys are gonna need a fourth player for their usual Sunday night Euchre game."

No way. Mac grabbed another bar. "Isn't there somebody else who could fill in?"

She held up her hand and began ticking off her fingers. "Natalie left."

Claire's cousin had loaded up her pickup after lunch, passed around hugs goodbye with promises to return again soon, and headed back home to South Dakota. Claire had watched Natalie's dust trail until it dissipated in the breeze, then she had turned to her grandfather and told him he'd better buck up because she couldn't finish the restroom on her own.

"Claire can't because Kate needs her help at the bar—Gary is out sick still with the flu."

"What about Ronnie?"

"She's already at The Shaft, coverin' for Arlene. It's her night off."

Butch needed to get his ass home soon before the Morgan sisters took over the bar and ran him out of town.

"Deborah can play," Mac said. "It's about time she came out of her bedroom and faced the music." Claire's mom had been hiding away since "the incident."

Ruby grimaced. "I don't think that's such a good idea. Those boys will fight more if she's there, and I sure don't need Harley reinjuring that leg."

Mac shoved the whole lemon bar in his mouth. Fine. Maybe he could play a few hands and then head up to The Shaft and spend the night keeping Claire company while she worked.

One of these days he was going to learn how to say "No" to his aunt, damn it.

A few hours later he found himself sitting at the Euchre table as agreed, holding a lousy hand containing only two trump cards in a rec room full of Chester's cigar smoke and

Manny's liniment fumes.

Harley was off cigars still and now beer, too, thanks to some new pain medication he had started yesterday, so he had no vices available to soften his current cantankerousness. Mac was playing it smart and keeping his mouth shut and fingers back. After the last week or two of being on the receiving end of some of Harley's teeth gnashes, Mac was happy to let Manny hold the chair and whip for a while.

"Hearts is trump," Chester declared, leading with the Ace of hearts.

Mac had no hearts, so he tossed out the ten of spades. He waited for a smart-assed remark from one of the three musketeers, but none came. Conversation had been at a minimum so far. Manny's romantic romp with Harley's daughter had left the atmosphere in the room unstable at best. Mac was beginning to believe his aunt had more reasons for choosing zombies and vampires over Euchre tonight than bonding time with her kid.

Manny sat on Mac's left, following his turn of play. He frowned down at his card while twirling the end of his moustache.

"Any time, lover boy," Chester said around his cigar and puffed smoke at his partner. "Don't mind me; I'm just dying a slow death over here."

Manny touched one card, then another.

Gramps drummed his fingers on the table. "I sure wish you'd thought that hard before weaseling your way into my daughter's bed."

"I did not 'weasel' as you say." Manny threw down the Jack of diamonds, the second highest trump card. "I was invited, not that it's any of your business."

Harley slapped the Jack of hearts down on top of Manny's card, winning the round with the big daddy of trump cards. "Of course it's my business. She's my daughter and young enough to be yours."

"Be careful, *viejo*." Manny had an old West one-eyed squint going on. "Your new bride is not much older than your daughter. There's not a lot of room at this table for you to talk."

"Personally," Chester rolled his cigar in the ash tray as he spoke, "I think Carrera here is my new hero. I didn't think a man could tame that shrew without losing a testicle or two." He raised one bushy eyebrow at Manny. "You do still have both *huevos* after mating with her, don't you?"

"*Sí*. How do you say it—her bark is worse than her bite."

"So she does bite in bed then." Chester grinned. "I win that bet. You owe me a six pack."

"Keep in mind that it's my daughter you two are running your mouths about." Harley's cheeks had darkened since Mac had last looked at him.

Much more of this teasing and Mac might be calling 911. Ruby needed to install a defibrillator on the wall next to the phone if these guys were going to keep having sex in the house.

"What are you shaking your head at, sweet buns?" Chester asked.

Mac had not missed hearing that nickname. "Nothing." He looked at Harley. "It's your turn."

Grumbling under his breath, Harley tossed out the Ace of clubs.

Chester and then Mac followed his suit.

Manny trumped it with a low heart.

"Now you're just being an asshole," Harley said.

"I'm just following your lead, *hombre*."

Chester grunted. "Would you two quit pillow fighting and get back to playing the game like grown men?"

"He started it," Manny said, leading the next round with the King of diamonds.

"You started it when you climbed into my daughter's bed." Harley threw down the Ace of diamonds. "In your old age, you seemed to have forgotten the golden rule—family is off limits."

"She invited me into her room," Manny said.

"You should have said, 'No.'"

"And reject her?"

"Yes."

"Are you blind to your daughter's pain?"

Chester trumped Harley's Ace with the ten of hearts. Mac slid the Queen of diamonds across the table, really wishing they would change the subject to something other than sex with Claire's mother.

"She needed a man to make her feel better."

Chester grunted again while pulling in the pile he won. "Carrera has a point. You should have heard her last night, Ford. Jessica's dad's rejection cut 'er deep. The way I see it, Carrera took one for the team. We should be thanking him for smoothing the edge off her." He tossed out the Queen of clubs to start the next round.

"Nobody asked for your opinion." Harley glared at his cards.

Mac followed Chester's lead with the King of clubs. It had been nice not to have Deborah flouncing around all day, speaking her mind when nobody had asked her opinion, bossing Ruby around in between chastising her. Mac took a drink of his iced tea. Maybe Manny should continue with his tequila and whipped cream therapy sessions, at least until Mac headed back to Tucson Tuesday night.

"Besides," Manny said, twirling his moustache again. "Maybe I'll make an honest woman of her someday."

Mac swallowed a laugh along with his tea, coughing into his hand as his eyes watered.

Chester laughed and swatted Mac on the back a few times. "You got sweet buns all choked up on that one."

Harley shot Mac a glare. "He shouldn't be laughing, not with Claire in her situation and no ring on her finger."

Mac took another drink to clear his throat. "What situation?"

Harley's blue eyes widened for a moment, then he looked

down at his cards. "Never mind."

Claire's grandfather was suddenly focusing way too hard on the few cards left in his hand. Mac turned to the other two clowns. "What situation?" he asked again.

Chester covered his mouth as if he were going to whisper. "The baby," he said loud and clear.

Mac blinked, unable to make things add up in his head. "What does Kate being pregnant have to do with Claire and me getting married?"

"What?" Harley's forehead crinkled like a squeezebox. "Kate's pregnant, too?"

Too? "What do you mean 'too'?"

Chester snorted. "There must be something in the water around here getting everyone knocked up."

"Claire's pregnant?" The cards fell from Mac's fingers, drifting to the floor.

"Shit," Harley said. "There is too much sex going on around this place. Reminds me of a bunch of damned rabbits."

Chester chuckled. "It's like the Great Jackalope Stampede of '58 I read about while waiting for you at the doctor's office the other day."

How could Claire be pregnant? She said she was on her period.

"*Dios mio!*" Manny covered his heart, his face paling.

"What's got your knickers all twisted up?" Chester asked, stubbing out his cigar.

Mac raked his fingers through his hair. Why hadn't Claire told him she was pregnant? Was that why she had been acting so funny last week each time they had spoken on the phone? And here he had thought it was something to do with the damned pocket watch that she was not telling him.

"All this talk about *bambinos* reminded me of something."

"What now?" Harley said.

Manny gulped. "I didn't wear any protection last night."

"Why is this place so freaking busy tonight?" Claire asked Kate, who stood at the cash register at The Shaft ringing up orders. "It's Sunday for crissakes. Don't these people have to work tomorrow?"

"Sure," Kate said, impaling an order on the sharp pointy metal holder. "But Sunday is our third busiest night after Friday and Saturday. People come here to try to forget that they have to go back to work tomorrow."

When Claire had agreed to help Kate at The Shaft after a long afternoon of sanding and painting, she'd expected to be pouring a beer or three an hour. Not struggling to keep up with Ronnie and Kate, who kept bringing her drink orders and dirtying up all of the glasses she kept washing. Butch needed to quit fooling around with buying old cars and get his butt back here. Claire much preferred to be on the other side of the bar when hanging out at The Shaft.

Ronnie dropped onto a bar stool and blew her hair out of her face. "Here's another one." She held out an order to Claire.

Claire frowned down at it. "This has food on it."

"I know. Let the cook know."

"My job is drinks only."

"Don't be a putz. You're right there by the kitchen window."

"You want me to go around and take orders for you, too, lazy bones?"

Ronnie rolled her eyes. "Quit your whining and just take care of it."

"Knock it off, both of you," Kate said, coming over and taking the order from Claire. "You two are acting like some of my students used to." She called the food order back through the kitchen window. "Next you'll be shooting spit wads at each other behind my back."

"Sorry," Claire said, grabbing two glasses and filling them

with beer. "What's that third drink?"

"Gin and tonic," Ronnie said. When Claire shot her a suspicious glance, Ronnie held up her hands. "It's not for me, I swear."

Kate had made it clear that if either of them drank on the job, she would cut off their hair while they slept. Her inability to sleep through the night at the moment made her threat all the more real.

"I'm going to run to the bathroom," Kate said.

"You okay?" Claire asked.

She nodded, fanning herself. "Just need to take care of business and cool off my face."

When Kate left, Ronnie leaned on the bar, her expression earnest. "Claire, I need to tell you something."

"If this is about you stealing my favorite mohair sweater back in high school and burning cigarette holes in it, I know already. Natalie told me about it last week while we were listening to an oldies station on the radio while working."

"That tattletale," Ronnie muttered. "It's not about the past. Well, not about our past anyway."

Claire poured the gin and tonic. "Spill."

"It's about the pocket watch."

She put the drinks on a tray and set it down in front of Ronnie. "What about it?"

"I took it."

"You what!?"

"I took the watch. It's not stolen."

"What ... why would you do that?"

"Because I found something out about it that puts you at risk."

"Me?"

"You and everyone else in the family."

Claire frowned. "I already knew we were all at risk because of it. I've been telling everyone that for weeks but nobody would listen to me."

"I know, I know."

"Then why would you take it and let me think it was stolen?"

"It's complicated."

"I'm waiting."

A sharp whistle from over by the pool table caught their attention. An old cowboy was waving Ronnie over.

"I'll be right back," Ronnie said and took the tray with her.

While she waited for Ronnie to return, Claire busied herself with trying to come up with an explanation why her sister would steal the watch from a secure safe in Ruby's basement and think that would keep the family safe. For the life of her, she couldn't come up with a legitimate reason. Then she remembered the article Ronnie had tried to show her last night. She looked around on the floor, searching the shelves and drawers behind the bar, and wondered where it had gone.

"What are you looking for?" Kate asked, back from the bathroom.

"Did you see a wrinkled piece of paper on the floor back here last night?"

"I put it next to the cash register. I figured someone must have dropped it and might come back for it."

"Did they?"

"Must have. It was gone a little later."

Ronnie returned with another order and handed it to Claire.

"Did you pick up that paper you were trying to show me last night?" Claire asked her.

"You mean this?" Ronnie pulled a folded piece of paper out of her back pocket. When Claire nodded, she said, "No."

Claire scoffed. "What do you mean? You're showing it to me right now."

"I know, but I didn't pick it up. That's what I'm trying to tell you. We have a problem."

Kate moved in closer. "What's going on?"

"Ronnie took the watch out of the safe," Claire explained.

"She's about to tell me why, and it better be good."

Ronnie smoothed out the paper on the bar. "This article talks about how the watch was stolen from this German castle."

Claire stared down at the picture of the castle, a memory of another article she had found in the file cabinet down in Ruby's office flickering in her head. "I think Joe has something on this castle in his old files down in the basement. It was in German, too, so I couldn't read it."

"When did you learn German?" Kate asked Ronnie.

Ronnie shook her head. "That's not important right now."

"So you agree with me then that someone is probably coming for it and we're in danger," Claire said.

"No." Ronnie chewed on her lower lip. "Well, I don't think so anyway. Not yet."

"Then why did you take the watch? And where is it?"

"It's in a safe place." Ronnie looked over her shoulder like the grim reaper might be eavesdropping. She wiggled her index finger for Claire and Kate to lean in closer. "The problem involves Sheriff Harrison."

Kate groaned. "Oh God, that man is the bane of my existence. He almost always makes a point of asking me if I have new crashes to report whenever he sees me."

"You do have a bit of a record," Claire said, and then jerked when Kate pinched her on the back of her arm. "Ouch! Brat."

"The Sheriff knows about the watch," Ronnie said.

Shit! He was the last person Claire wanted to know about this. Then she thought of whomever Joe had skimmed it from and changed her mind. She crossed her arms over her chest. "What did you do, Ronnie?"

"It wasn't on purpose and it's not my fault."

Kate laughed. "That's been your story since we were kids and you rode through Mom's prized flower garden with Claire's bike."

"What did you do?" Claire asked again.

"The Sheriff has been on my ass since I got to town, following me around, looking for trouble."

"Really? The Sheriff just saw you and decided you looked like trouble right off the bat. How come I have difficulty believing that?"

"Well, maybe I was speeding once."

Claire raised one eyebrow.

"And I might have tried to bribe my way out of the ticket with fake jewelry. Then I insulted his niece by insinuating she was a tramp. And there was that one night when I was a little drunk and sort of took my shirt off in front of him in order to get him to drive me home."

"You what?" Kate burst out laughing, drawing several stares.

"Shhh," Ronnie said.

Her eyes watering, Kate smothered her laughs in a bar towel.

Claire had an icky feeling swirling in her gut. "What did you do, Ronnie?"

"I think I kind of clued in the Sheriff that we have the stolen watch in our possession."

"Oh, Christ." Claire threw her hands up in the air. "What were you thinking?"

"I had bigger problems at the time."

"Such as what?"

"That's not important right now. What I need your help with is what I should do to fix this."

"Have you thought about taking off your pants in front of him?" Kate said in between giggles. "Maybe you could do the hokey pokey with him and turn this all around." She laughed harder. "Because that's what it's all about."

"Not funny, Katie."

Claire chuckled. It kind of was.

Ronnie turned her glare on Claire. "Stop it right now, both of you."

"Okay, okay," Claire said, sobering again. "So we have a

problem, but at least it's just the Sheriff of Cholla County who is onto our secret, not the guys Joe stole this from."

"Why don't we just contact whoever owns the castle and tell them we have their watch," Kate suggested.

"No way," Ronnie beat Claire to the answer. "That will bring the Feds down on Ruby, and that is the last thing we want, trust me."

Claire noticed how rigid Ronnie's face had gotten all of a sudden. "You sound like you have some experience with this."

"Maybe a little." When Claire continued to stare at her, Ronnie shook her head. "I don't want to go into that tonight."

"You're going to have to find out what Sheriff Harrison really knows."

"Or thinks he knows," Ronnie said.

"Exactly. Once we know that, we can figure out what to do about him."

Ronnie nodded. "Okay, I think I can figure out a way to do it without making things worse."

"Good," Claire said, "because we—"

"Hello, ladies." Mac broke up their three-ring circus by sliding onto the seat next to Ronnie and shouldering his way into their conversation.

Claire blinked in surprise. She'd been so focused on Ronnie and the problem with the watch that she hadn't seen him come in.

"Hi," Claire said, shifting out of neutral. "You want a beer?"

"Sure, Slugger." He leaned his elbows on the bar, his hazel eyes boring holes into hers. "And while you're getting that, maybe you can explain to me why your grandfather and his buddies believe you're pregnant with my child."

Chapter Twenty-One

Monday, October 8th

The road up to the Lucky Monk was very bumpy.

So was the mood inside the cab of Mac's pickup truck as Claire rode with him up to the mine. She had hoped that a night of sleeping on the news of her pregnancy scare would turn Mac's frown from last night upside down. As busy as The Shaft had been, she had not been able to step outside with him and hash things out until after closing. By then, he'd told her he was too tired to talk and drove her home in silence, which was broken only by George Jones singing on the radio yet another song about drinking away his broken heart. Kate would probably toast her soda water to good ol' George these days.

"Are you still pissed at me?" Claire asked, staring over at Mac's stiff profile. She wanted to bridge the distance between them but was unsure that she could reach that far.

His quiet demeanor at breakfast had given nothing away. Mornings were not usually chatty times for Mac. He had smiled at his aunt and cousin, shot a wary look at Gramps, and dropped a kiss on Claire's temple, but something was off. His chakras were misaligned or his aura was darker than normal or his vibes were not rippling right—whatever. In short, Mac was not Mac at the moment, and Claire did not want to spend the day tramping around inside of a pitch black mine with his cold shoulders.

"I was not pissed." Mac slowed for a strip of washboard in the dirt road. "I told you that when I dropped you off at the

Skunkmobile last night. Surprised? Yes. Disappointed? I guess that, too."

"About me not being pregnant?"

"No. That was all too new for me to digest yet, and you confirmed what I had believed before I even walked in the bar—that you weren't pregnant."

"Disappointed in me then?" That was nothing new for Claire. She had grown up disappointing her mother on a weekly basis. But Mac feeling that way about her was very different. The cut went deeper because he had believed in her from the start, and letting him down stung like the dickens.

"I'm not disappointed in you." He glanced over at her, his lips flat. "I'm not Deborah." He swerved to avoid a deep rut. "But you are who you are, Claire, and I know that commitment in any shape or form scares the shit out of you."

She stared out at the desert with its barbed outer layer of cholla, barrel, and prickly pear cacti. Why did she get such stomach flutters at the idea of letting someone come close? Mac was so careful not to push her too fast or ask too much of her. While her brain insisted that settling down and spending her life growing old with him might not be such a bad deal, her adrenal glands pumped like a firehose whenever the word "marriage" was uttered.

Maybe it was because her parents' marriage had sucked. After three decades of staying together through yelling and fighting, they'd ended it with more pain and anger.

Her grandparents on the other hand had seemed to be happy throughout their wedded life. But now Claire knew that while her grandmother may have made a good wife, her mothering skills had been lacking. Had Grandma given all of her attention and devotion to her husband, ignoring her daughters in the process? Claire should probably ask Gramps for his version of the past before painting any pictures on her own.

"You must have been stressed out this last week," Mac's voice interrupted her commitment phobia therapy session.

Her laugh held no humor. "Having a baby is some serious shit."

"I know." Mac pulled to the side of the dirt road and killed the engine. "I should have been here with you." He frowned out the front window, nodding his head at the mountain that held the Lucky Monk in its belly. "Someday, I would like to be one of the people you lean on. Like you do with your family."

"What are you talking about? I lean on you."

"Ha!" He grabbed his backpack from the seat between them and shoved open his door. "When have you ever leaned on me, Slugger?"

"How about Sophy and all of the crazy stuff that went down with her?"

He bent down and peered inside the cab. "You weren't leaning on me. You were confiding in me." He shut the door and waited outside for her.

She grabbed the flashlight and hardhat he had insisted she bring and joined him out on the path that led up to the mine. "How about when I needed your help back in August, figuring out who was trying to take Ruby's mines away from her?"

He ducked under a mesquite tree and held the thorny branches back for her to follow unscathed. "You didn't ask for my help with that; Ruby did."

Oh, yeah. Hmmm.

Now that she thought about it, Ruby had been turning to Mac for help since Claire had met them both. Was that why he wanted her to turn to him for help? To be more like *his* family? She thought of Gramps and his grumping and growling since he had broken his leg. Now it all made sense. He saw Ruby always asking Mac for help, too. Gramps wanted to be the one she turned to for help, just like Mac wanted Claire to lean on him.

"You were going to figure out on your own who was trying to screw Ruby out of her mines," Mac said over his shoulder. "You're doing the same thing with that pocket watch, figuring it out."

"That's not true. I asked Kate to help me."

"Exactly." He turned around, walking backward for a couple of steps. "You asked your sister, not me."

"That's because you thought I was making a big deal out of nothing."

He held onto his rebuttal until he made it to the base of the path leading up to the Lucky Monk where he waited for her to catch up. "That's not what I said."

Claire closed the distance. "That's what I remember."

"You remember wrong, then." When she frowned up at him, he grabbed the brim of her Mighty Mouse cap and tugged it sideways a little. "My concern from the beginning was that you were nosing into something that would get you into trouble again. Judging from what you and Ronnie told me last night about Sheriff Harrison and that article about the watch being stolen from a German castle, it appears I was right to worry. Trouble is on its way."

She straightened her hat. "Not if Ronnie can fix this mess first."

His eyebrows tipped down in the middle. "You really think she can figure out a way to convince the Sheriff to overlook this?"

"I don't know. Ronnie is different these days. I have faith in her ability to dig herself out of a mess. She claims to have gotten out of worse during her divorce."

"Worse what, I wonder." He grabbed her hand and tugged on it. "Come on. Let's get you up this hillside."

She scoffed. "You say that as if my legs are wet noodles."

His grin warmed his eyes. "I've hiked with you before, Slugger. You aren't exactly outdoors material."

"Kiss my ass," she said, passing by him on her way up.

"I'll take a raincheck on that," he replied about sixty seconds later when she slowed, huffing, and he cruised on by her.

Dust coated her throat and skin as she climbed behind

Mac, taking his hand whenever he offered it. Her pride took a back seat to a heart attack. Under the warm sunshine, sweat ran down her back, soaking the waistline of her jeans and top of her underwear. Mac on the other hand had barely broken into a dew. The bastard.

When they made it to the mouth of the mine, he paused to let her catch her breath.

"Isn't there ... an easier way ... up here?"

"Not on two legs."

She needed to hire a mule.

"Take off your shirt, Slugger."

She frowned up at him. Had she heard that right? "Did you just tell me to flash you?"

Chuckling, he unzipped his bag and pulled out one of his T-shirts, holding it out to her. "Yes, but for honorable reasons. Your shirt is too sweaty to wear for long in there. You'll be shivering in no time. As much as I enjoy your body's reaction to cold ..." His gaze lowered to her chest and hovered there for a handful of heartbeats. "I'd rather have you dry and comfortable."

"Oh, good point." She shrugged off her T-shirt and took his shirt. "What about my bra?"

"I like the blue polka dots," he reached out, running his fingertips over the mound of flesh just above the bra. "What do they look like on the inside of the bra?"

She watched his hand explore her flesh and then looked into his eyes, her body tingling from the current crackling between them. This was what had been missing since last night, his flirting and teasing.

She caught his hand. "I'm not asking for your opinion of my bra. You made that loud and clear when you tore it off a few weeks ago on your way down to my underwear. I'm asking if I should take it off as well since it's damp?"

Mac grimaced. "As much as it pains me to say this, leave it on." He pulled back and jammed both hands into his front pockets.

Claire pulled his T-shirt on over her head. It hung down to her thighs, so she wound it and tied it at her hip. She took off her Mighty Mouse cap and slapped on her hard hat.

"Okay, let's go." She led the way inside the mouth, pausing to turn on her flashlight.

He came up behind her, wrapping his arm around her waist and pulling her back against him. "How do you feel about having sex in a mine this morning?"

"I bet you say that to all the girls."

He kissed the back of her neck, his lips soft and tickling, and then chuckled all warm and husky in her ear. "Kissing you after that hike up here is like licking a salt block."

She pulled away and wrinkled her nose at him. "A salt block? You could have lied and said I tasted sweet."

"Why?" He grabbed her hand and pulled her along. "I like licking salt, especially off of your skin."

"That's a little better."

They walked in silence for a way, and then she remembered something he had said back in the pickup. "What are you disappointed in, if not me?"

"I don't want to talk about it." He let go of her hand and pulled out a folded map of the mine.

"Why not?"

He paused, using the light on his much fancier hard hat to spotlight the map, and traced one of the lines on it. "Because it will sound stupid if I say it aloud."

"Try it."

Folding the map, he took off again, walking faster, pulling away from her in the darkness. "I'm disappointed in us, Claire," he said quietly, his voice almost blocked out by the sound of their boots on the rock floor. "I thought we were farther along with all that has gone on between us." He rubbed the back of his neck, turning to her. "See, sounds silly, right?"

Silly? More like a little gut squirmy. As much as commitment made her antsy, she wanted Mac to remain strong and steady in her world. He was kind and smart and witty, and he knew all of her bells and whistles in bed, and in the shower, on the kitchen table, and ... she was digressing.

She caught up to him, catching his hand and squeezing it. "I told you last night at the bar, I planned on telling you as soon as we got a moment alone. But lately it's been hard to steal any time away from everyone else with the new restrooms going up and all of my family hanging around."

"I don't know if you realize it, Claire, but it's always like that now." His beam of light landed on her for a moment before he turned forward again. "I practically need to kidnap you in order to get you to myself these days. I'm looking forward to the day when you come home without Ronnie in tow."

A squeaky moan leaked out from her throat before she could catch it.

"What?" he asked, slowing.

"Well," she winced as she spoke, "you know how Kate's pregnant."

"Yes."

"I sort of offered to let her stay with us in Tucson until she has the baby and gets back on her feet."

Mac stopped. "You did what?"

She shielded her eyes in the light from his hard hat. "She needs me, Mac."

"Don't we all," he said and did not sound a bit happy about it. He walked away, shaking his head, his light beam moving side-to-side on the walls.

"I'm sorry," she called after him. "It's your house and I should have talked to you about it first."

"It's *our* house, Claire. But it would have been nice to be able to offer an opinion in the matter." He looked down one of the side drifts but kept moving forward. "For once."

"Hey," she caught up to him. "You're the one who invited Ronnie to stay, not me. I knew better."

"You're right." He looked down at his map again. "What

was I thinking?"

"I'll tell you exactly what you were thinking if you'd slow your ass down."

He stood and waited for her, his arms crossed. "I'm all ears."

She walked up and grabbed him by the shoulders, pulling his mouth down to hers. Their hats clacked together. She tipped her head sideways and kissed him hard on the lips.

"You were being a nice guy who was helping his girlfriend's sister because he wanted to help her family like he always helps his."

"Wow." He trailed his finger along her jawline. "I was thinking more along the lines of me being a big sucker, but I like your version better." He leaned his hard hat against hers. "I'll do whatever it takes to get you to come home with me, Claire."

She took his hand and kissed his knuckles. "Thanks."

"But I draw the line at your mother. She can stay with Manny."

Groaning, she clapped her hand over her eyes. The images of Manny and her mother were waiting there for her every time she closed her lids, still crystal clear twenty-four hours later. She prayed her brain did not decide to reformat the film and start showing it in 3-D.

"God, don't remind me. I'm afraid I won't be able to have sex again without thinking of them. All of that whipped cream and refried beans." She groaned again.

Mac pulled her hand away from her eyes and kissed the back of it. "I'll give you some really good therapy, Slugger." He flipped her hand over and rained kisses up the inside of her wrist, like Gomez Addams. "Lots of therapy. We'll get through this together. Now come on. The chamber I told Dr. García I would take a look at is up ahead."

She fell in behind him, careful not to trip over the rusted ore cart rails leading the way deeper into the mine. Several twists and turns later, he came to an abrupt stop. Claire ran into his back, knocking her hard hat off.

"Oops," she scooped it up, fitting it back on her head.

She joined Mac, staring down at the four foot wide hole in the mine floor with several one-by-six wooden boards boxing it in. "Is this part of what you wanted to check on?"

"No."

"Then why are we looking at it?"

"Because of that rope."

Claire followed the beam of his hard hat and saw a strand of black nylon rope tied to a spike tucked behind one of the boards. She took a step closer to get a better look.

Mac locked onto her arm. "Be careful, Claire. Never get too close to a shaft."

"I know." She had learned that lesson the hard way with Jessica up in one of Ruby's other mines a few months back.

She peeked over the edge of the shaft, shining her flashlight down into the dark inky depths. A rickety looking ladder was bolted to the side, leading into the blackness beyond where Claire's beam reached. The rope hung taut down along the ladder. Whatever was at the other end was beyond the light.

Goosebumps crept up her arms. She stepped back and grabbed Mac's hand. "What's with the rope?"

"That's what I'm wondering." He tucked her behind him, shielding her. "It wasn't there the last time I was back in this area."

What was at the other end of the rope?

She peeked around his shoulder. "How long ago was that?"

"Last week."

The red pickup was back.

It was the same pickup Ronnie had seen here and there—The Shaft, the grocery store, the library, parking lots. The driver was keeping back, following her from a distance but following nonetheless.

She had not seen the black sedan in over a week, but she should have known she couldn't duck her troubles that easily. Claire had helped beat back the goons for a bit, but now they had returned. Only this time it was just one goon, and Ronnie was pretty certain she had been dancing with him the other night when she was wasted on self-pity and gin.

Purposely taking a few extra turns around the side streets in Yuccaville, Ronnie watched to see if the red pickup zigzagged after her. She wanted to make doubly sure she was not being paranoid.

The good news was he stayed on her tail.

The bad news was he stayed on her tail.

Grabbing the binoculars Ruby kept under her seat, Ronnie paused at a stop sign and used the rearview mirror to focus in on the pickup's license plate one block back. The numbers were backward, but she figured them out and scribbled them on the inside of a gum wrapper she found in her purse. Now she had to figure out what to do with this information.

But before she tackled that, she had another problem to fix.

For the first time in ... ever, there was a parking space open right in front of the library's double glass doors. She pulled into it and cut the engine. Grabbing her purse, she stepped out and straightened her jean skirt while letting the sun warm the top of her head. This morning had been cool, smelling crisp and fresh, reminding her that fall had made it to town, even way down here in the Sonoran Desert. The heat soaked through her black sweater and fitted cotton blouse.

One of the library's doors swung open as she approached. Ruth, Aunt Millie's second in command, ushered her inside.

Ronnie nodded. "Morning, Ruth." She waited for the older lady and her cane to join her in the foyer. "Those earrings look marvelous with that sapphire scarf and your hot pink lipstick."

Ruth's very bright lips curved into a wide smile. "Thanks, sweetie. You have great taste." She cupped her hand over her mouth as if passing a secret. "In more ways than one."

What did that mean?

"Millie had me hold that parking spot for you this morning."

Ah. That was why parking was a breeze today. It paid to have friends in the library ... or rather fellow gang members. "Thank you. I appreciate that."

Ruth winked. "We haven't had this much excitement since Millie locked horns with that bitch over at the senior center." Ruth grabbed Ronnie by the arm and led her toward their usual hangout by the internet computers. "Come on, Millie's got everything ready for you."

Ronnie allowed Ruth to lead her to where Aunt Millie stood outside the women's restroom, her red walker blocking the door. Before anything was spoken, Ronnie offered a handful of tennis bracelets and rings, opening with her usual gesture of bribery. She was getting close to the bottom of her stash, so she hoped the ladies would be pleased with these as payment.

Aunt Millie pushed away Ronnie's bribe. "Put those away. Save them for another day."

"But I said I'd pay you for your help." Ronnie looked over at Ruth and the other ladies sitting in their usual spots, their knitting needles clicking away.

Greta waved a single needle at her.

"I know you did," Aunt Millie said, "but this one is on me. You have no idea how much fun we've had this morning preparing for your visit."

Uh-oh. That could not be good. "Oh, really?"

"It's amazing what us old babes can do when we put our minds to it." Aunt Millie eyed her up and down. "Nice choice with the skirt and boots, but let's get rid of this."

She grabbed Ronnie's sweater and tugged on it. Ronnie shrugged out of it. Aunt Millie inspected her outfit again with a critical eye, then she undid the top button on Ronnie's blouse, clearing the way for a peek-a-boo of cleavage.

"There we go. Now you're ready." Aunt Millie moved her walker from in front of the restroom door and pushed Ronnie backwards through it.

"Wait! What are you ..."

Aunt Millie waggled her fingers at Ronnie and then pulled the door shut in her face.

"I should have known you were behind this," Grady said.

Ronnie whirled around. Sheriff Harrison sat on the sink counter down by the feminine napkins dispenser. He was dressed in full uniform, hat and star included. His long legs hung over the edge, his toes almost touching the floor. On the counter next to him was a sleep mask.

"I didn't intend for this meeting to take place in here," Ronnie told him, moving to the opposite end of the counter. "But it makes sense now that I think about it."

This was where all of the old girls' important meetings took place—good or threat-filled.

One of his black eyebrows lifted. "Why does it make sense for my aunt and her posse to abduct me from my office, force me to wear a blindfold, and keep me holed up in a women's restroom until you arrived?"

Ronnie covered her grin with her hand, not wanting to irritate the man whose help she needed.

"It's not funny, Veronica."

"You have to admit it's kind of funny."

His expression did not admit any such thing.

"Why on earth would you allow a posse of old ladies to do this to you? You're a big man in this town, Sheriff," she added that last line in a deep, John Wayne voice and then giggled into her fist.

His jaw tightened. "Aunt Millie blackmailed me."

Ronnie pointed at the sleep mask. "And how exactly did she blackmail you into wearing that?"

"She asked me what I thought the busybodies down at the

YWCA would think of the Sheriff of Cholla County necking in an old pickup outside of a seedy motel."

Ronnie winced. "Sorry about that."

"It's not your fault. I'm the one who started it."

"I didn't exactly push you away." She had practically suctioned onto his face. If they hadn't been interrupted, who knew how far things would have gone.

"No, you didn't." Grady removed his hat and set it on the counter, then slid to his feet. "And that sort of troubled me during the night."

Her, too. It was not something she wanted to think about while stuck on the couch in the Skunkmobile with her two sisters sleeping one paper thin wall away.

He crossed his arms. "So, what brings me to the women's restroom today, Veronica?"

"This." She pulled the gold pocket watch out of her purse and dangled it between them.

His gaze narrowed as he stared at it. "Is that what I think it is?"

"I believe so."

"Why do you have it?"

"That's a long story I'd rather not get into today."

"Then why are you showing it to me?"

"I need your help."

"This should be interesting."

"And your promise of silence."

Both eyebrows lifted. "You're asking a lot already."

"I know." She set the watch on the counter and took a deep breath. "I want this watch to go back to its rightful owner."

"You don't need me for that."

"That's true." She shoved her hands in her back pockets. "But now you know that I have it and you know that it's stolen. As an officer of the law," she nodded at the star on his shirt, "you have an obligation to investigate this further."

"Correct."

"I need you not to do that."

He stared in silence, his face as rigid as always.

"If you open an investigation on this watch, it will draw attention to my family. I don't want to see their lives torn apart and dissected like mine was."

She paused, waiting to hear if he had anything to say about what she had told him so far.

When he remained silent, she continued. "If you feel morally that you need to pin this on someone, please put the tail on me." She drew circles on the countertop around the watch, unable to hold his stare any longer. "What the hell, you know. I'm already on the Fed's shit list. They've done a bang-up job totally fucking me over by invading my privacy, trashing my dignity, and hosing my future to the point that I'll be lucky to get a job washing cars. While orange jumpsuits are not my favorite, I can probably benefit from the job training in the big house. Do they still make license plates and furniture in prison? I've always wanted to learn how to reupholster a chair. Going back to college for something more practical than Liberal Arts would probably be a good idea, too. Spanish might be a logical choice if I decide to stay in Arizona when I get out."

"Veronica." He interrupted her nervous rambling.

Her finger stopped circling. She looked up at him.

His gaze remained steady, detached. "Where did you get the watch?"

She wanted to lie. To say she found it somewhere inconspicuous. But Grady would smell that lie from a mile away, and since he stood only a couple of stalls down from her at the moment ... "Ruby's dead husband had it stashed."

He nodded ever so slightly.

"I don't want the Feds to mess with my family, Grady," she appealed, trying not to sound like she was begging. But she would, if it came to it. For her family, she would do whatever it took. "We have enough problems as it is."

He stepped two stalls closer, removing the breathing space

between them. "Let me get this straight, Veronica. You want me to smooth a path for you through the paperwork that will be required with this watch turning up?"

His aftershave lured her even closer, but she held her ground. The last thing she wanted him to think was that she was willing to use her body to secure her family's secret. Although, knowing how his kisses made her pulse rocket, her body probably would not object to the sacrifice.

"I guess," she whispered, and then cleared her throat. "And whatever else it takes to keep my family's names clear of this. It's not just the Feds that I'm worried about. They may be rat bastards, but when they come looking for more from where this came, they won't plan to kill if necessary. Someone else might."

"That's the silence you want me to promise?"

She nodded.

"Is there more from where this came?"

Now there was a sticky question. "I'd rather not answer that in a public restroom."

"Fair enough." The Sheriff grabbed a tissue from the box on the counter and used it to shield his prints from the watch when he picked it up and stuffed it in his pants' pocket. "Let me think about this, Veronica."

She nodded again, afraid to open her mouth, afraid of what might pour out in her moment of desperation.

He scooped up his hat. "Is there anything else you want to tell me before I leave the women's restroom?"

She had pretty much summed up the watch favor request, so not really.

Hold up! There was something else.

"Yes, actually."

He waited, watching her mouth. "I'm all ears."

"There is a cowboy in a red pickup following me around. He's been doing it for several days. I think I may have danced with him the other night at The Shaft after you left, but I was pretty drunk and can't remember his physical description very well."

His head cocked slightly.

"Except for his eyes. They were light green."

"Do you often dance with strangers when you're drunk?"

"No. And I usually don't get drunk, just tipsy. But that night was extra special, including the drinking and dancing."

"You think he's stalking you?"

"I think he's planning to kill me." She pulled the piece of paper with the plate number from her back pocket, along with the phone number she'd found in her pants pocket the morning after the dancing. "I'd appreciate it if you could look up his plates and see if he has anything on his record that I need to be concerned about." She handed Grady the papers. "I think the phone number might be his as well, but I'm not positive of that."

He frowned down at the two pieces of paper. "What makes you think he wants to kill you?"

"Because he warned me to beware of the husky and the polar bear."

Chapter Twenty-Two

The way Mac figured it, he had two options.

He could either back away from the shaft and lead Claire out of harm's way into the warm sunshine, and then return on his own to see what was tied to that rope; or ...

Claire peeked around from behind him where he had tucked her for protection from whatever it was that had spurred his adrenaline. "Let's pull up the rope and see what's there," she whispered.

... or they could do that.

"How do you feel about playing it safe?" he asked.

"What's safe?"

"Going back down to my pickup and waiting for me there."

"You know me better than that." She stepped forward, peeking into the shaft. "It's much more exciting to see what someone is hiding down there."

"I don't know if 'exciting' is the word I'd use." He pulled her back from the edge again. Taking as wide a berth from the hole as possible, he moved around to the side where the rope had been secured. "If we're lucky, it's just a six pack of beer someone wanted to keep cool."

"Why lower it down there? Is the air temperature cooler?"

"Because this shaft has water in it."

"How can you see that far down?" She leaned over the hole, shining her flashlight down in the mine shaft.

"Claire," he said with a growl. "Would you stop getting so close to the damned edge?"

"I'm not going to fall in, Mac. I know what I'm doing."

He snorted. "When have I heard that from you before?"

"I don't know. When have we stood at the edge of a mine shaft and argued about me falling in before?"

Maybe he was going about this all wrong.

"Claire, you're making me nervous. If you accidentally fell into this shaft and got badly hurt or worse, my life would go to hell. Will you please do me this one small favor and go stand over there." He nudged his head toward the opposite wall about eight feet away from the hole, his hard hat beam showing her the way.

"Well, when you put it that way I'd be happy to move away from the shaft." She walked over and leaned against the rock wall. "But I'm coming back for a closer look as soon as you pull up that rope."

"Of course you are." He lowered to his knees, wincing when he came down on some hard pebbles. Spreading his legs wider for a sturdier base, he began slowly reeling in the rope.

"Is it heavy?" she asked.

"I don't know. I think it's still in the water right now."

"You never answered me."

"About what?"

"How do you know there's water down there? Your light can't be that much better than mine."

"I know the drifts and shafts of this mine. I re-mapped it last month because the old maps were inaccurate. I also took water samples from the two shafts that had flooded during the monsoon season and measured the water's depth so I could check back periodically and see if the content or levels are changing. The water level in this one has been going down slowly. I figure it'll be dry again in another month at the rate it's draining."

He continued bringing up the rope, circling it on the floor next to him.

"So that's what you've been doing in the mines when you disappear for a day."

"It's all part of the maintenance that goes into mine

ownership. It's Ruby's responsibility to know what she has up here and to keep others out. The last thing we want is to have someone come in here and do something stupid like fall down in a shaft, break their neck, and drown down there in the dark."

The rope was now wet in his hands.

"That's horror show material." Claire's flashlight beam bounced around behind her, further down the main adit.

"Exactly. It's my job to make sure the mines are securely blocked off from unauthorized visitors, like teenagers, spelunkers, vagrants, and whatever other animal wants to come in here and get into trouble." Parts of the rope were slippery, like it had been down there long enough to get a little slimy. "Remember that pregnant *javelina* you stumbled across last April?"

"I remember her fangs."

He did, too. And her rancid smell. That was the closest he had ever been to a wild *javelina* before. "I come across a lot of animals back in these mines."

"Alive or dead?"

"Both." Rats especially. And porcupines.

"You're creeping me out," she whispered. Her flashlight beam whipped around toward the front of the mine. "Did you hear that?"

"Hear what?"

Claire took a couple of steps back the way they had come, leading with her light. "I thought I heard something scraping across rocks down that way."

"Like I said, lots of animals."

She stood there listening for a few more seconds, and then returned to the shaft, moving a little closer to him than before. "I don't think you should be coming out alone on these maintenance runs anymore. It's too dangerous."

"I take precautions." The tension in the rope increased. He was almost to the end of the line.

"Not enough."

His grip on the rope slipped, letting it slide back down several inches before he stopped it. The payload felt as heavy as a watermelon now, as off balance, too.

"It's a necessary job so long as Ruby owns the rights." he said, wiping his hands on his pants one at a time. "She has liability insurance to protect her financially if somebody gets hurt and tries to sue her, but these mines have seen enough death." He thought of the skeleton of the trapped miner he had found further back, near where Dr. García's crew was working.

"I agree," Claire said.

"Me, too," a deep female voice spoke from the shadows beyond Claire.

Claire let out an "ack" of surprise that made Mac jump and loosen his hold on the rope. It slid through his fingers again too fast this time to stop. He let go to avoid a rope burn or getting tugged into the shaft and watched the loops of rope unravel as whatever was at the other end tumbled back down. Seconds passed, and then a splash echoed up through the darkness from below.

"Damn it," their visitor said. A bright halogen floodlight flashed to life, blinding Mac in brightness. "Way to go, Romeo."

Mac heard the unmistakable clicks of a hammer being cocked.

"I hate to do this, but if you both don't do exactly as I say now, I'll have to add you to the body count."

Jessica was sitting in the passenger seat of the old Ford when Ronnie climbed inside after leaving the library.

Ronnie did a double take. "Where did you come from?" She distinctly remembered driving alone to Yuccaville this morning while being followed by a red pickup.

"School." Jessica sniffed and stared out the passenger side

window.

"Why aren't you there now?"

"I called in sick."

Ronnie peered closer. The girl looked fine and dandy to her. Although in her opinion, Jessica had gone a little over the top with her fruity scented perfume this morning. Ronnie could taste it on the back of her tongue, and it was way more bitter than any berries or cherries she had ever eaten. "You can't call yourself in sick. You're a kid."

"I'm almost an adult."

"Yeah, but you're not." Ronnie stuck the keys in the ignition. "How did you know I was here?"

"You drove right past me outside of my school."

"I did?"

"Yeah. It was like you were lost or something."

It would be impossible to get lost in Yuccaville. That must have been when she was leading the red pickup around town.

"I ran after you, hollering for you to stop, but you must not have heard me."

"Sorry. I was a little preoccupied." Ronnie fired up the old Ford. "Where am I taking you?"

Jessica swiped at her eyes. "You mean you're not going to make me go back to school?"

"Do I look like a truant officer to you?" Did they even have such a position anymore? If so, what were the qualifications? Would a Liberal Arts degree with absolutely no experience in hunting down kids cut it?

"I want to go back to the Skunkmobile," Jessica whispered, dabbing at her eyes with her shirt hem.

"Really?" Ronnie could not think of a single reason to want to hang out in that stinky R.V. any more than necessary.

Jessica nodded, sniffing. "Please don't tell Mom."

"I'll leave that to you when you're ready." She shifted into gear.

Jessica stared out her window, silent except for the occasional popping of her bubble gum.

They made it past the outskirts of Yuccaville before Jessica's bubble of silence burst. "My dad is a liar."

He was also a letch and a cradle robber, but Ronnie would leave the name calling to his daughter.

"He didn't have a migraine Sunday night," Jessica explained.

Ronnie had figured that. After all, she had spied on him while he was bonking his "migraine" yesterday.

"He was with some girl."

Yep. Mindy Lou Harrison was her name, and looking for love in all the wrong places was her game.

Jessica planted her pink canvas shoes on the dash. "I skipped out of class during my second period study hall to go see if he was feeling better."

Ruby was not going to be happy about that.

"I walked to his hotel and looked in his window."

Wincing, Ronnie glanced sideways. Jessica was twirling her shoelaces around her finger, her eyes watery.

"He wasn't sleeping alone in his bed."

No shit.

"He was with some woman with long black hair."

What? Ronnie frowned across the seat. Mindy Lou was a platinum blonde. "You're sure it was black?"

Jess nodded. "I think she's the girl who works at the mini-mart where we got gas last week."

Holy crap. Steve Horner wasted no time planting his seed all around town. Ronnie wondered if Mindy Lou knew she was not his only sex buddy.

"I was on my way back to school when I saw you drive by," Jessica said and then sighed.

Ronnie did not know what to say to cheer her up. She settled for: "That sucks, Jessica."

Several fence posts passed outside the window while Charlie Rich sang on the radio about things that go on behind closed doors. Ronnie hummed along, thinking about what had just transpired behind the women's restroom door.

What was Grady going to do with the watch? Would he be able to find out anything about the cowboy in the red pickup?

After Ronnie had told him about the warning she had received on the dance floor, his eyes had narrowed, but that was it for reactions. His game face gave no clues. He should play Euchre with Gramps. They would make a killer team. Chester and Manny would not have a chance in hell.

His parting words had made no promises. "I'll see you around, Veronica."

Did that mean he believed her?

Or that he believed her to be nuts?

Aunt Millie had been disappointed they had not taken longer for their meeting, but Ronnie assured her all had gone as planned.

"Yeah, but your blouse is still buttoned," Aunt Millie said.

That was when Ronnie realized Aunt Millie had been thinking a different kind of rendezvous was supposed to take place in the women's restroom.

"The Sheriff is not interested in *that*," Ronnie told her, slipping on her sweater.

"Grady is still a young man. He's always interested in getting a little bit of *that*," Aunt Millie replied, pointing at Ronnie's chest.

With no wish to discuss that topic any further with Grady's aunt, Ronnie had thanked Aunt Millie and exited the building.

But damn it all if she did not hold a flame of hope that Aunt Millie was right.

Logically she told herself that getting involved in any capacity with the Sheriff of Cholla County was stupid. Really stupid. Like the biggest-mistake-of-her-life stupid. Yet she really wanted to see what was under that badge. If Grady was as much of a hardass as he pretended to be. If he treated women like they were trophy objects or like they were made of flesh and blood. If his passion in bed was as intense as it was for the law. If he liked to …

"Ronnie?" Jessica's voice derailed her train of thoughts.

"What?"

Was the heat on? Ronnie checked the heater settings. Nope. Whew! She fanned her blouse.

"Are you going to stick around here for a while?"

Ronnie hit her blinker, slowing at Jackrabbit Junction to make the turn toward Ruby's R.V. park. "I don't know." A lot depended on Grady's next move. "Why?"

"I was just thinking of something Claire said."

"What's that?" Turning the corner, she glanced over at The Shaft and saw Katie's car in the lot. Maybe she should drop off Jess and swing back by the bar and see if her sister needed some help with opening. Ronnie had heard Katie stumble outside early that morning and throw up behind the camper. The poor girl was not taking to pregnancy well.

"She said that when you weren't bossing everyone around, you were a lot of fun."

"Claire said that?"

"Yeah. And between you and me, this place definitely needs more fun. So will you stay?"

Ronnie chewed on her lower lip. Since she'd arrived, she had thought only of getting more cash so she could escape this place and hide somewhere else. But maybe this was as good a place to hide as any with its wide open valleys and small town neighborhoods where strangers stood out like sharks in a school of tuna.

"That depends on you," she told Jessica. Well, her and Ruby and Gramps actually. And the Sheriff.

"What do you mean?"

"Are you going to stay living with your mom? Because if you're thinking of moving in with your dad, I'm not sticking around."

Steve Horner saw only one thing when it came to his daughter—dollar signs. Jessica might be blinded by his shiny promises, but Ronnie had a crystal clear view of the situation. While Steve had gotten away with using Mindy Lou for his own benefit, Ronnie would be damned if she was going to let him use Jessica, too.

Jessica returned to twirling her shoestrings again as Ronnie drove over the bridge into the R.V. park and rolled down the drive toward the Skunkmobile.

She pulled up in front of the old R.V. and cut the engine, turning to Jessica. "Well, what's it gonna be, kid? Am I staying or going?"

If Claire had a buck for every time someone had pointed a freaking gun at her these days.

"Move over there by your boyfriend," the voice behind the bright flashlight said. It sounded female but scratchy. Vaguely familiar.

Whoever it was kept the handgun level with the flashlight and aimed squarely on Claire as she slipped around the mine shaft and stood next to where Mac still knelt.

Claire searched her memory for where she'd heard the voice before. It was fairly recent. Was it at The Shaft? She'd come across a lot of people there lately while tending bar.

Mac started to rise to his feet.

"No." The gun dropped to Mac. "You stay right where you are and pull up that rope again."

Mac nodded, moving slowly, taking up the rope. He angled his elbow so that he bumped Claire's leg and nudged her behind him without making his action obvious.

Shielding her eyes, Claire tried to see who it was that had them in her sights. "Who are you?"

"None of your business."

"Well, it sort of is since you're trespassing."

"I'm also the one holding the gun."

Mac glared up at Claire, still pulling. "Stop poking the bear."

Claire quieted, waiting for Mac to get to the end of the

rope. When he did and it came up with nothing attached, she grimaced. That probably was not going to go over well.

"Son of a bitch," said the voice. "Now we have a bigger problem."

"Bigger than you holding a gun on us while you hide behind that light?" Claire asked, still trying to figure out where she had heard that voice. Was it during Ladies Night last week?

Mac grunted and elbowed her kneecap.

"You got a smart mouth, girl."

"I can't help it," Claire said. "It came with my brain."

"Great. Then you can take the two of them and climb down that ladder and bring up what you two nincompoops dropped."

Claire looked down into the dark hole and gulped. "Down that ladder in there?"

"Do you see any other ladders around here?"

"I'll climb down," Mac offered. "I'm the one who dropped the rope."

"That's very Prince Charming of you, but that ladder won't hold your weight. She goes or she gets shot."

Claire hesitated.

"How about I go back out to my truck and get my climbing gear." Mac said. "Then I can rappel down."

The woman laughed. "I don't think so. That ladder will hold her, trust me. I've been down it."

When Claire still didn't move, the gun raised, pointing at her head. "What's the hold up?"

"I'm trying to decide if I'd rather be shot."

Mac reached down and grabbed the top of the ladder, trying to wiggle it. It creaked a little, but held steady. "Get on the ladder, Claire."

"Can I take my flashlight?" she asked the woman.

"Of course. How else are you going to see to swim down and fish the stuff out of the water?"

"Wait a second." Claire crossed her arms. "You didn't

mention the swimming part before."

"Claire." Mac squeezed her calf. "Get in the hole, sweetheart."

That was easy for him to say. He wasn't the one about to climb down into a pitch black throat in the earth with freezing cold water waiting in the bottom.

"You'll be fine," he added.

She disagreed. The last time she had tried to climb out of a shaft on a rusted ladder, it had given way and dumped her back into the water. Now she was supposed to climb down however far and splash around in the dark water at the bottom. She had seen way too many horror movies about creepy things in the bottom of wells to handle this with grace and dignity.

"I'd like to hear what's behind door number three," Claire said to the gun.

"There is no third door."

"Things always come in threes. It's the Rule of Three, even for doors."

"No, they don't. There are only two showcases on The Price is Right. Not three."

"Yeah, but there are always three contestants on Jeopardy and The Wheel of Fortune."

"Fine! Behind door number three is your boyfriend here with a bullet in his head. Now which door are you going to choose?"

"Damn it, Claire." Mac's voice was tight with tension.

She yanked off her hard hat and threw it onto the floor. "This is bullshit!" She stuffed her flashlight in the back of her pants, glaring at the gun-toting bitch. "Next time, pick a better hiding spot when you stow your contraband."

"Just get your ass down in that hole." The gun pointed toward the hole.

Claire grabbed onto Mac's shoulder and swung her leg over the edge of the shaft. He clamped onto her hips, holding her steady as she tested her weight on the top rung of the ladder. It creaked, but held, feeling fairly sturdy under her tennis shoe.

"Here goes nothing," she said and put both shoes on the ladder, her head level with Mac's.

"You can do this, Slugger." His gaze bore into hers. "Get on down there and hold on tight."

She took two steps down, wondering why he was so can-do all of a sudden. Then she realized what he was doing—getting her out of the way.

"No." She frowned up at him. "Mac, don't—"

He leaned down and cupped her cheeks, kissing her silent.

"That's enough kissy face," the voice said. "Get your hiney moving."

Mac let her go, dropping a final kiss on her forehead. "You heard her, Claire. Go."

"I don't like this," she told him.

"You made your choice," the woman said, thinking Claire was talking to her. "The sooner you get down there, the sooner you and your boyfriend will be on your merry way."

Claire didn't believe her. Her multiple experiences of being on the barrel end of a gun had taught her otherwise. However, she did trust Mac, and with trembling knees she followed his bidding and stepped down into the darkness.

Inside the throat of the shaft, things sounded muffled. Below her, water dripped slow and steady, like a leaky faucet. Claire's heart pounded in her ears, lobbying its complaints about the dire situation she had gotten into yet again. She tried to slow it down, sucking in deep breaths of musty, earth-scented air into her lungs.

It didn't work.

And it didn't stop the trembling that had now spread up her legs and torso to her shoulders.

She climbed down, darkness swallowing her more with each rung she counted.

Five rungs down, she could still see her hands.

Ten rungs now, her fingers were barely visible in the

shadows.

Fifteen rungs down, she was going by feel alone.

She was on number twenty-one when she heard the boom of a gunshot overhead.

Her breath wheezed in her lungs. She wrapped her left arm around a ladder rung and peered up toward the lighted circle above her.

A beam of light bounced around up there, hitting the ceiling above the shaft and then disappearing.

"Mac?" she called when she found her voice. She could hear the panic edging her tone and dry-swallowed it down. Twenty rungs deep in a dark hole was not the place to lose her cool.

She tried to hear what was going on up above, but the only sound was the water dripping below her. Then even that stopped.

"Mac, what's going on?" she called, her voice high with fear.

A bright light appeared above her like the sun, shining down, blinding her.

"Keep going," the woman with the gun hollered down.

Claire flipped her off. "Where's Mac?"

"Don't go wigging out on me. He's alive, just incapacitated at the moment. You will be, too, if you don't get moving."

Fuck this.

Claire pulled her flashlight from the back of her pants. *Move this, bitch!* With all of the leverage and thrust she could manage, she whipped it up the hole in an underhanded fast pitch.

The flashlight arced on its way up, ricocheting off the wall of the shaft. She heard a clinking sound, and then the bright light shining down started coming closer, getting even brighter, really fast.

Claire pulled close to the wall. She grabbed onto the ladder with both hands and tucked her head down, wishing she hadn't thrown off her hard hat.

The light bounced off the ladder three rungs above her, glass crunching. All went dark in the shaft as it splashed below.

A hollow sounding crack rang out above. Claire looked up, but her eyes were still blinded by that damned bright light.

She heard a thump and another crack. Then a scream rang out overheard, echoing down the shaft, zinging through her like a lightning bolt.

Wincing, she hugged the ladder even tighter. Something bounced off the wall on her left, then splashed into the water below. What was that?

Then there was a thump followed by a cringe-inducing crunch. Another scream blasted her, this time right over her head.

Holy shit! Someone was falling down the hole!

She plastered herself against the ladder, waiting for the impact of a falling body.

A gut-wracking cry of pain rained down, but that was it. No body. Just silence.

"Claire?" Mac called down the hole.

A beam of light rippled over the ladder in front of her.

"I'm okay," she yelled. "What happened?"

Something dripped onto her wrist. Something dark.

"She fell in," Mac called down.

The drop ran down her forearm toward her elbow.

"What did you do?" she asked.

"I didn't do anything. You hit her with something."

The flashlight!

Claire looked up and gasped at the mangled mess of a leg entangled in the ladder partway up. From what Claire could tell, the woman had gotten caught on her way down. She now hung upside down, her arms dangling over her head. Blood dripped down her forehead onto Claire's arm again. The beam of Mac's light flickered over some khaki colored material, and Claire suddenly placed the voice.

The rattle of the woman's breath made Claire shudder. "She's still alive."

"Hold on, sweetheart and I'll figure out a way to get you out of there."

Something popped up above.

There was a clink and then another.

Then a screech rang out that went on way too long for comfort.

"What was that?" Claire asked, praying it was Mac doing something up top to get her out of there.

"It's the ladder," Mac said. "Hold on tight, Claire. I'll try to secure it with the rope, but I think it might—"

After another echoing screech, the ladder shuddered under her hands. Claire squinted up toward the light in time to see the ladder bend and twist between her and the hanging woman as if some huge hand was wringing it out.

"Oh, fuck," she whispered, stepping down as fast as she could go.

A loud groan rang through the shaft.

Something cracked and scraped.

Pebbles and stones clattered down around Claire's head. She tucked under as best she could while clinging to a rung, bracing for a big stone or piece of the ladder to come down on her shoulders.

Everything went still around her except the dust, which filled her throat.

She coughed and looked up. Something partially blocked her view of the top. She tried to move to see around it and a flashlight shined down, the light thin and dispersed by the time it reached her.

"Claire!" Mac yelled down. "Please tell me you're okay."

"I'm so *not* okay." That word was at the other end of her spectrum at the moment. "I'm scared shitless down here. But I'm not hurt."

"The ladder gave under her weight."

"I noticed." She cleared the dust from her throat. "Mac?"

"What?"

"You know how you said I don't lean on you?"

"Yeah?"

"I could use your help here."

"Got it."

"Make a note—this is me leaning on you."

"I'm going to lower down a flashlight with the rope."

"I'd rather you lower down a firefighter to carry my ass out of here."

A beam of light bounced off the walls around her. She huffed as he lowered the light along the wall, coughing through the dust and fear clogging her throat.

The flashlight snagged on the broken piece of ladder that had tipped and gotten jammed against the opposite wall overhead. Mac wiggled the rope and threaded the light down between the rungs.

Claire held onto the ladder with her left hand and reached out to grab the flashlight as it drew closer.

"A little farther," she yelled.

A groan above her made her freeze. A human groan.

The flashlight bounced off her fingertips.

The sound of cloth ripping filled the shaft.

Cloth ripping ... ?

The woman's body slipped from the ladder's hold. It slammed into Claire and knocked her off the ladder.

Screaming, Claire fell down through the dark, dust-filled air.

Chapter Twenty-Three

Ronnie was debating the wisdom of having brought Jessica to the Skunkmobile.

Since they'd stepped inside the door, Jessica had not stopped talking, not even while Ronnie had hidden in the bathroom for a few minutes, plugging her ears. Apparently, Jessica needed to talk things out, and talk, and talk, and talk.

"... and that was when Jacquie told Sherry to try the passion fruit lip gloss," Jessica went on, following Ronnie into the back bedroom. "I told Sherry not to use it because it would stain her shirt. You should see her shirt, it's really cool. It has these cute pink roses all around the ..."

Ronnie tuned out again. She glanced around the bedroom, noting the unmade bed, the clothes piled everywhere, the litter of cups on the nightstand, and Claire's tool belt tossed into the corner. What a sty! It reminded her of when they were kids and had to share a bedroom. No matter how much she tried to pick up after Claire and Katie, the room was always trashed. She sniffed, picking up the scent of fresh air, and noticed the window was open. She watched the curtain move in and out, as if the R.V. were breathing. Thank goodness it smelled better than it looked.

After five years of sterile living with Lyle, where she made sure every room in her mortgaged mansion was dust free and spotless, and perfectly perfumed, the untidy bedroom made her smile. It felt good to be home, back to her roots, even if they were messy. She scooped up a folded pile of Claire's T-shirts and opened the tiny closet door, stacking them on the shelf over the rack.

"You know I have a boyfriend, right?" Jessica flopped onto the bed. "He works with the archaeology crew. He's majoring in Anthropology."

"I know about your boyfriend, Jessica." Ronnie grabbed a basket full of clean clothes Katie had brought back from the laundry a couple of nights ago and dumped them on the bed next to Jessica. "I worry that he's a little old for you."

"He may be older than me, but I'm more mature. That's what he says, anyway."

After listening to Jessica's extensive views on how important it was to match her lip gloss to her nail polish, Ronnie wasn't sure that was saying much. She had a feeling Jessica's boyfriend would say whatever it took to get Jessica to plant some of that lip gloss on his mouth. Ronnie hoped that was the only place he had in mind for lip planting, or someone might need to show him the error of his ways with a baseball bat. She preferred solid wood ones herself.

In her experience, college boys wanted to do a lot more than kissing. Hell, even high school boys got bored with the light touching according to Claire and Katie. They had both explored the opposite sex more in depth from the start compared to Ronnie, who had waited until college to jump into sex. After saying goodbye to her virginity, she'd had two milquetoast monogamous relationships in her twenties before meeting and settling down with Lyle. Maybe if she'd been a little more curious about men before getting married, like Claire and Katie had been, she might not have been fooled so easily by Lyle's charm.

She folded a pair of Claire's jeans. On the other hand, her marriage had taught her some important lessons. The next time she got involved with a man—IF there was a next time—she would not be so naïve. The home video of her satisfying her own needs in what she thought was the privacy of her bedroom flashed through her head, lighting a fire in her chest all over again. Not so damned stupid either. If the sex sucked from the get-go, she was out the door.

"He asked me to come visit him in Tucson after they finish at the dig site." Jessica sat up and crossed her legs pretzel-like, looking every bit of her sixteen young years. "Do you think Mom will let me go?"

Hell no. "I don't know. You'll have to ask."

"She probably won't. I don't think she likes him much. But Dad might let me go." Jessica sighed. "Wouldn't it be awesome if I could go see him at the next dig site Dr. García has lined up for them during my spring break? It's somewhere down in Mexico in April, I think." She blew a bubble. "A week in the jungle would be so romantic."

Romantic? A Mexican jungle full of mosquitoes and snakes and who knew what other icky things? Ronnie would rather spend a week alone on a lifeboat with her mother and a German U-boat commander.

"He said most of the crew will be going down there, even the volunteers. Hey, I could sign up to be a ..."

Carrying the stack of Claire's jeans and shorts over to the closet, Ronnie nodded her head, tuning out Jessica's voice. Claire kept a stash of clothes at the R.V. park now permanently. Ronnie debated on emptying out her luggage and settling in, too. Jessica hadn't made her choice about staying with her mom yet, but Ronnie was getting sick of living out of her suitcase.

Screw it, she thought, and pulled out her luggage, dumping it on the bed next to Jessica.

"Now that you don't have a job or a husband," Jessica said, "you should volunteer to work on a dig site. You may not make any money, but you get to travel and eat for free. You could be like those two old ladies who keep bugging me to help."

Ronnie thought about walloping Jessica upside the head to see if it stopped the stupid shit from pouring out of her mouth. Instead, she unzipped her bag, shaking out a blouse and hanging it in the closet. That one would need ironing again. "Jessica, I highly doubt they are doing this for free."

"They are."

Ronnie paused. Traveling around to different dig sites would be the perfect opportunity for a woman on the run. She wondered how much education and experience was necessary to be hired to help chart their finds and do whatever other busy work was required. Would she be qualified?

"There must be a little money in it for them, Jessica."

"I don't think so. My boyfriend said they were down in Mexico at some Maya site before they came up here. He said they are like a traveling circus group that way."

Ronnie pulled out one of her knit skirts, brushing off a layer of dust that had somehow gotten inside her suitcase. The desert had to get its dirty fingerprints on everything down here. "Even traveling circus groups make a little money."

"He said they pay their own way, insisting the university uses their funding on the students and dig site stuff. It's even their own camper. The only thing the university pays for is their campsite."

How could those two afford to travel all over the place without making a dime for their efforts? Had they come from money? Were they widows living on their dead husbands' retirement funds?

It was too bad Lyle hadn't kicked the bucket. Although that life insurance he claimed to have was probably just another work of fiction. Oh, wait, she wasn't even his real wife, so the money wouldn't have gone to her anyway. Damn, so much for putting a contract on his head while he was serving time.

"He said they live up in Sedona in a huge, fancy house they are having totally remodeled while they travel." Jessica lay back and stared up at the Skunkmobile's ceiling. "I wish we had a fancy house in Sedona. I hear it's really cool up there."

Ronnie had heard that, too. It was also expensive as hell according to that real estate channel her mother kept watching on Ruby's television. The housing prices were some of the highest in the state.

She unzipped the flap of the inside pocket in her luggage where she kept her jewelry. Opening her purse, she fished out the bracelets that Aunt Millie had refused this morning.

"What's that?" Jessica asked, rolling over to get a closer look at Ronnie's jewelry. "Can I see them?"

"Sure. There are more in that pocket. Have at it."

Scooping up a stack of her shirts, she took them over to the closet and made room for them next to Claire's stuff.

"Ew!" Jessica said. "Why do you have an eyeball in with your stuff?"

Crap. Ronnie had spaced on that darn eyeball. She took it from Jessica and palmed it. "It's a good luck charm," she lied.

"That's just weird."

"So is a dead rabbit's foot."

"My boyfriend has a lucky beer bottle cap on his key chain."

Ronnie was liking this boy less and less the more Jessica talked. She rolled the eyeball around in her palm, warming up the glass, noticing a ridge on the surface.

"He asked me to wear his college ring." Jessica slid on Ronnie's zirconia studded ring Lyle had given her after coming home from a business trip to Florida. "But I told him that my mom would totally freak out if I did."

Jessica was probably right. A ring meant commitment.

She rubbed the pad of her thumb over the ridge on the eyeball again, noticing something scratchy on it.

"Is this a real diamond?" Jessica asked.

"No." Ronnie opened her palm and took a closer look at the eyeball. The ridge was chipped.

"It sure looks real."

"I know." Ronnie had certainly been duped by Lyle and his fancy ring.

She scraped her fingernail along the ridge. Claire was wrong. She'd thought they were glass eyeballs. But would a glass eyeball have a scratchy ridge like this? Ronnie remembered one of those Antique Roadshow episodes she had watched with her mom about an antique doll. Hadn't the buyer told that lady the best doll eyes were made of blown glass?

This must be made of something else. The workmanship on it was not as detailed as the doll's on that show. The irises looked pretty real, but there were no red veins.

"What are you doing?" Jessica sat up and moved next to Ronnie.

"Trying to figure out what this is made of."

"Where did you get it?"

"It was given to me as a gift." Sort of.

"If you aren't too stuck on it, you could break it open."

She stared at Jessica's freckled face. What would Claire say when she found out Ronnie had broken the eyeball? Maybe she need never know. Ronnie could always go get another one from the box under the khaki ladies' camper without Claire ever knowing.

Besides, after hearing that the camper had been down in Mexico recently, Ronnie had an idea about the eyeball. During all of those years stuck in a lonely marriage, she had often watched romantic movies while left on her own for much too long. One of her favorites was *Romancing the Stone*, with Michael Douglas acting as her inspiration for her one-on-one moments with Raphael, her now-famous vibrating pal.

"Grab that hammer out of Claire's tool belt," she told Jessica, moving over to the desk. She knocked the pile of clean underwear and socks onto the floor.

Jessica handed her the hammer. "You're really going to smash it?"

"Sure. Why not?" The ridge on the eyeball kept it from rolling off the desk. Ronnie shielded her eyes with her left arm and swung with her right.

There was a crunching sound that was definitely not glass shattering.

Ronnie stared down at the smashed eyeball. "Damn," she whispered. "Would you look at that."

Jessica reached out and knocked aside the pieces of ceramic. "Is *that* a real diamond?"

Picking up the tiny, cool stone and holding it up to the light coming through the bedroom window, Ronnie frowned. "God, I hope not. Because if it is, we've got a big problem."

Claire had a big problem.

She was stuck in the bottom of a mine shaft with a dead woman floating facedown in the water next to her. At least she was pretty sure she was dead. The beam of light shining down from the flashlight Mac was still dangling overhead shed plenty of light for Claire to see that there was no sign of life in her body.

"Claire?" Mac yelled down, his voice tense. "Claire, are you okay?"

She coughed, sputtering in the mineral laden water. "I think so," she called and dog-paddled over to where the ladder rose out of the water.

Her whole body trembling, she placed her feet on a rung and willed her legs to hold her weight. She climbed out of the cold pool, which turned out to be only about ten feet deep judging from the length of time it took her to reach the surface again after shoving off from the bottom.

"What happened?" Mac asked.

"She fell on me and knocked me into the water."

The body floated toward her, like it wanted to come, too. Claire didn't want to touch it, but she had to be sure the woman was dead. Catching the wrist, she pulled it up and checked for life. The woman's hand flopped limp, her skin cold to the touch. There was no pulse.

Tremors racked Claire, her own pulse fluttering on wings of panic. She sucked in several breaths, swallowing the fear climbing up from her chest.

"Are you swimming in the water or can you climb out on the ladder?"

"I'm on the ladder."

She poked the woman's body in the ribcage, double-checking for any reaction. It floated over to the wall, bounced off, and came back toward her. She climbed several more rungs up the ladder to get away from it.

"You have to stay out of the water or hypothermia will send you into shock."

"Good to know. Exactly how long were you thinking I was going to hang out down here, because I'm thinking I need to get the hell out of here *now!*"

"I have to run to my pickup."

"I'm sorry, but I could swear you just said you have to leave me stuck down here with a dead body and go down to your truck." Claire used the toe of her tennis shoe to push the body away from her again.

"Are you sure she's dead?"

"She's been floating face-down since we popped up."

"Can you turn her over?"

Can I turn her over? "I'm not flipping goddamned pancakes down here!"

"Claire." His voice was steady, strong. "You have to keep calm."

She sighed. It came out ragged. "I can try to turn her, but

it's fucking cold down here." She climbed back down the ladder, close enough to snag the body with her foot. Latching one arm around a rung, she grabbed the wet, khaki vest and tried to lift the woman to turn her face up. Claire's wet arm slipped, almost dumping her back in the water on top of the body.

"I can't do it, Mac," she hollered up.

He didn't reply.

"I can't see my own lips, but twenty bucks says they are pretty freaking blue right now. If I go back in that water, I'm not sure I'll make it out again." Maybe she was exaggerating a little, but she wasn't going to go swimming with a corpse unless there was a really damned good reason.

"Okay. Try to conserve your body heat."

"Throw down my spare parka, please." She took a deep breath, trying to slow her shivers. "Can't you use the rope the flashlight is hanging from to get me out of here?"

"There's no way it will hold your weight."

"Is that a crack about my MoonPie addiction?"

"No, Slugger. You know how much I love your curves."

"Good save. Get me out of here and I'll reward you with the best sex you've ever had."

"Even the kinky stuff?" She could hear the laughter in his voice.

"Especially the kinky stuff."

"Damn. I'll be back before you can change your mind. Stay put."

"Where in the hell do you think I'm gonna go?" she called up, but he didn't reply.

Mac was gone.

She was alone with a dead woman.

Claire stood there shivering, watching the body, waiting for the woman to turn into some sort of zombie and start reaching up the ladder for her feet.

When that didn't happen, she spent a couple of minutes having a grand ol' pity party. When the party ended, she climbed up closer to the flashlight, snagging it, and struggled with Mac's knot. Her cold fingertips were stinging by the time it finally came free.

After inspecting the broken ladder above her and figuring out the safest path through the tangled mess, Claire shined the light down into the pool. Enough time had passed that the ripples had dissipated, leaving still, mostly clear water with a few murky spots.

She shined the flashlight around the body, noticing a cloud of pink in the water. Blood. The woman must have hit her head on the way down the mine shaft, and not just her head judging from the odd angle of the left leg below the knee.

Something green further down in the water caught Claire's eye.

"What's that?" she whispered.

She climbed down several more rungs until the water almost touched her shoes. Gently toeing the body aside, she shined the flashlight into the water. There were several green things littered on the bottom of the shaft, all close to the same size except one, which was bigger and seemed to be partially wrapped in something black.

These must have been what the lady was hiding down here. What were they? Where had she found them? Were they from one of Joe's stashes?

Claire peered up toward the shaft opening, looking for any signs of light from topside. How much longer was Mac going to be? Would he be willing to swim down in the water and grab one of them? No, wait. That would mean he would need to climb down in the shaft and she didn't want him coming down. With her luck, the rope would break and they would be stuck, left to die next to the dead woman.

She nudged the body away again, leaning down with the flashlight until it almost touched the water. There was one of those green things directly below her, close to the wall.

The water would be so cold.

But she was already wet and shivering.

No, she should play it safe and wait for Mac.

She shined the light around, counting the green pieces. Twelve plus the big one.

Looking up again, she saw nothing but darkness. How long had it been? What if something happened to him on the way down? What if he fell down, broke his leg, and got eaten by vultures.

Okay, that was the panic talking, trying to rise to the surface again. Claire beat it back down by bonking her head lightly with the rubber flashlight.

Rubber flashlight. She stared at it. Of course, it was one of Mac's waterproof flashlights.

She shined it back in the water on the piece of green directly below her. She could be in and out in less than ten seconds with whatever that was.

That would be stupid. What if something happened and she got hung up and drowned all because she wanted to see what the dead lady had been hiding—what she had been willing to kill for down here.

Claire stood there waiting, thinking, wondering, shivering, waiting, listening, dripping, counting the seconds, waiting, peering into the water.

If she had that green thing in her hand, at least she would have something else to look at while she waited.

"Mac?" she called up and waited some more.

"Oh, screw it." She gripped the flashlight tight, took three short breaths, held the fourth, and stepped off the ladder.

Chapter Twenty-Four

Mac couldn't scramble back up the hillside to the Lucky Monk fast enough.

While Claire was able to get out of the water, he knew the temperature in the mine and how fast the combination of cool air and the cold water would sap her heat and energy. Trembling muscles made it twice as hard to hold onto a ladder, let alone climb one, which was what she was going to have to do to get back to the surface.

He shifted the tactical nylon rope ladder he had grabbed from his pickup, carrying it with his left arm for a while. She needed enough strength to climb twenty-five feet or so up the rubber rungs, which should be doable for her so long as she had conserved her energy.

Sweat rolled down his back as he jogged through the mine, wondering if Claire was freaking out about the body floating down there with her. Her love of horror movies might be coming back to bite her in the ass right about now. Christ, why had he dragged her up here? She would be safe at Ruby's right now if he hadn't been so hell bent on getting some time alone with her.

As he made it closer to the drift with the shaft, he thought he noticed a sweet hint of flowers in the musty air. He slowed, sniffing again. After racing down the side of a big hill, grabbing thirty pounds of gear, and chugging back up with it, maybe his synapses were misfiring, screwing up his senses.

He rounded the last bend and skidded to a stop.

No. They were not misfiring after all.

In front of him stood another khaki vested woman,

peering over the edge of the shaft.

She looked at him, her eyes widening. She reached down, digging in the backpack at her feet. When her hand came up, she held what looked like another .38 Special.

"Don't move," she said, raising the gun.

Mac threw the rolled up ladder at her, all thirty pounds of it, as hard as he could. It slammed into her chest, knocking her hand with the .38 aside, but she hung onto the gun. She stumbled backwards away from the shaft. Before she could fully regain her balance, he rushed toward her.

She lifted the gun again in her right hand, her aim wobbly. He swung his arm around, slamming into her wrist, trying to break her hold on the .38. But her grip was strong, her face pinched in determination.

He clamped onto her wrist with his left hand, forcing her to point the gun away from him. "Drop it!" When she refused, he raised his right fist. "I said drop it now!"

Shielding half her face with her other arm, she said, "You wouldn't hit an old woman, would you?"

Mac's gaze narrowed. He had heard that one before. His hesitation when wrestling the dead woman below for her .38 had given the bitch the opportunity to plant the toe of her hiking boot solidly into his nuts. He'd dropped to his knees, which had allowed her time to retrieve her gun and aim it at him again.

His balls still ached from that error in judgment. There wouldn't be a second mistake.

"If she's carrying," he said, "hell, yes." He nailed her with a hard right, his fist smashing into her cheekbone.

She crumpled to the floor at his feet.

Huffing from the adrenaline flood, he waited for her to get back up and come at him again. When she didn't move, he squatted next to her and rolled her over. She was still breathing but out cold. Her cheek had an angry, purplish-red mark already. She would live, but she was going to have a big shiner come tomorrow.

He took her gun, made sure the hammer was down, and shoved it down his sock on the outside of his calf. Then he dragged the woman away from the shaft and tied her hands and feet together with some of the rope he had carried up to the mine along with his ladder.

When she was safely tied up, he leaned over the shaft. "Claire?"

The sight of a flashlight moving around below the tangled mess of the ladder made his limbs feel rubbery with relief.

"What took you so long?" she called up.

"I stopped for a beer on the way back up." He flexed his right hand, his knuckles beginning to throb from that punch. "I'm going to lower down a tactical ladder. When you're ready to grab onto it, let me know so I can secure it up here."

"I thought I requested that you bring a big sexy stud to carry my ass out of here."

"They were all out of big sexy studs at Creekside Hardware." He started unrolling the ladder down into the shaft. "As for carrying you, I thought with women's lib and all, you'd want to haul your own ass out of there."

"You thought wrong."

"Darn. How about when you get topside, you take off your bra and we'll burn it together."

"You said you liked the blue polka dots."

"I like you better without them." He threaded the ladder around the twisted mess below.

"The ladder is here," she hollered up.

"Count to ten, and then climb on."

"Are you sure this will hold me?"

"Positive. Make sure you take one step at a time, no rushing. This is not part of a timed obstacle course."

"When was the last time you saw me rush for something involving physical exertion?"

"True. Exercise is not really your style." He shined his light on the bent ladder, making sure there was nothing sticking out that might snag her on the way up. "I'm going to be a few feet away holding the other end of the ladder, so I can't help you over the edge."

"What ever happened to chivalry?"

"I think I saw it at The Shaft the other night."

"Ronnie probably threatened to hogtie it." He felt her tug on the ladder. "I have a surprise for you when I get up there, Mac. You're gonna love this."

"I have a surprise for you, too." He frowned over at the woman tied up over by the wall, her eyes still closed. "Hurry up and start counting."

There was another tug on the other end of the ladder. "Don't let go of me, Mac."

"Never, sweetheart. Trust me."

He took several steps back as she counted, unrolling as he went, giving himself more leverage. Then he slipped the ladder over his head and one shoulder, bracing his foot against an outcropping in the mine wall.

"Here I come," he heard her yell, and the ladder jerked and pulled.

He held steady and counted the seconds. The sight of the top of her head could not come soon enough.

Her hand showed up first, then her crown, then her brown eyes, bright with determination. Those were the eyes he wanted to look into every day, morning and night, until he keeled over. One of these days he was going to tell her that, but not yet. It was still too soon.

"You were right, Slugger." He tightened his hold on the ladder as the leverage shifted with her reaching the top. "Your lips are blue." Which was one of the signs of shock, but he didn't want to alarm her until he saw how severe her injuries were.

"It's my new Star Trek look. Blue is the new green." She hoisted herself up out of the shaft very ungracefully, rolling over the broken two-by-six and coming to a stop on her back a few feet away from the shaft. Her breathing didn't sound shallow or rapid, even though she had just climbed up twenty-plus feet. "Captain Kirk would find me hot, I bet."

Mac reeled in the ladder enough so it wouldn't slide down into the shaft, then lowered to his knees next to her. She hadn't acted injured at all when she'd pulled herself up and out. He scanned her clothing, her head, her arms. There was no evidence of blood that he could see. No cuts either, only a small bruise on her forearm.

"You sure know how to show a guy an exciting time," he said, brushing wet tendrils off her cheek. He picked up her wrist and checked her pulse. Under her cold, wet skin, it felt strong and steady. Good. "Want to come back and do it again next week?"

"Only if you go down first."

He chuckled and stared into one eye and then the other, checking her pupils. Nope, not dilated. Another good sign. "I'm always happy to go down first, but only if you have your tool belt slung low on your hips again and those pink lacy panties on."

"You're incorrigible." She swatted weakly at his chest. "I almost d-died down there and you're flirting with m-me."

"I can't help it, Slugger. I'm nuts for you." He leaned down and kissed her cold lips, trying to warm them up.

He ran his hands over her shoulders, feeling her body begin to tremble under her wet shirt. He was no doctor, but from what he could tell by her other checkpoints, she was not going into shock ... yet. But here came the shakes anyway, which could be just a delayed response to the prolonged exposure to the cold water and air. Add to that the psychological trauma of spending time stuck in a mine shaft alone with a dead woman, and a release of the stress was inevitable. He had seen it before. A person made it through something traumatic without a hitch only to collapse afterward, shaking and crying uncontrollably.

"We need to get you out of these clothes," he said. More importantly, they needed to get out of the mine and into the sunshine with its heat and brightness. But one step at a time.

"I know I agreed to k-k-kinky sex if you rescued m-me, but I don't think I can get into the m-mood to do the wild thing with that woman floating d-d-down there."

"I'll take a raincheck." He helped her into a sitting position. "I need to get you warmed up, Slugger. This shirt is cold and wet."

He tugged the shirt she had borrowed from him over her head, and then wrapped her shoulders in a threadbare but dry towel he had found stuffed under his pickup seat. He helped her crawl further away from the shaft to be safe. Dropping down next to her, he pulled her onto his lap and wrapped his arms around her. She snuggled in under his chin while he rubbed her arms and legs, alternating.

With a little more time and friction, his body heat might warm her enough to slow her shaking. It probably wouldn't hurt to keep her lucid and talking while he was at it.

"I'm s-s-s-so c-c-c-c-cold." She burrowed into him, her whole body racked with shudders. Her coolness soaked through his shirt and jeans. "Who's th-th-that?" She nodded toward the tied up woman.

"The other half of our problem. She's that surprise I mentioned." He pulled her closer, rubbing faster. "What's your surprise?"

She shifted, reaching into her back pocket, and came out with a green stone about half the size of her palm. "This is w-w-what the other one s-sent me down to g-g-get."

Taking it, he frowned down at the piece of jade, inspecting the carving on it. "No shit. What's this design?"

"It looks like s-s-something from the Maya c-c-culture to me."

"Maya? Here in Arizona?" Still warming her skin with one hand, he ran his finger over the jade. "Something tells me these ladies have been busy getting into trouble elsewhere."

"There are twelve of th-th-these, and one bigger piece that I think is a s-s-skull."

"You think?"

She nodded, burying her cold nose in his neck and her hands under his shirt. "They're all still under the w-water,"

Her breath warmed his neck while her freezing hands on his bare chest stole his breath.

"And where did you find this one?" He had a feeling she had not been doing her best to conserve her heat while he went to get the ladder.

A tremor traveled through her. "I had time to kill while I w-waited for you, so I took a quick swim."

Mac shook his head. "Do you ever do as I ask, Claire?"

"Sometimes."

"Like when?"

She pushed away enough to look him in the eye. "Ask me to kiss you."

"I'm serious."

"So am I."

Actually, that might not be a bad idea health wise. "Kiss me, Claire."

"You're supposed to ask."

"Oh, for Christ's sake. I—"

"Okay." She leaned forward and kissed him. "See, I did as you ordered. Happy now?"

"No, that was too fast. I meant like this." He tipped up her chin and kissed her, slow and soft, tickling her lips the way that usually lit her inner fire. Her mouth seemed clumsy under his at first, but he continued to take it easy, teasing and tasting, yet tender.

Her response grew warmer, her shivers waning. When he pulled back to adjust his sitting position, his lower spine starting to ache where a sharp rock pressed into it, she stared up at him. Her brown eyes had that dreamy look that always turned him inside out.

"Is that it?" she asked. "I was hoping for a little more than just a kiss before we headed to your pickup."

He knew that teasing smile too well to take her seriously. "Oh, yeah? Like what?"

"I don't know. To start with, maybe some proclamations of your everlasting adoration."

"You've had that since the first time you stood in front of me in your tool belt and panties."

"You mean the time with or without my bra?"

"Yes."

A moan came from the woman he had knocked out.

Claire threaded her fingers through his. "The woman over by the wall is waking up."

"I noticed."

"I think I can walk out of the mine on my own now."

"Good." He really wanted to get her into the sunshine and the rest of the way out of those wet clothes.

"What are we going to do about her?"

"Take her with us to see Sheriff Harrison. She can ride in the back."

"What about the jade piece?"

"We can't keep it."

"Maybe Dr. García will know where it's from," she said, struggling to her feet.

Mac stood and steadied her, re-draping the towel around her shoulders. "You sure you're ready?"

"As much as I'm going to be."

"Hold on." He checked the bonds of the other woman, making sure they were tight enough to hold. He planned to lead Claire outside and have her wait for him in the warm sunshine while he came back for the woman.

Claire stumbled a little at first as they started out of the mine, but once she got going she had no problems walking on her own.

As they drew near the mouth of the mine, she squeezed his hand. "The next time you want to spend some time alone with me, let's rent a seedy motel room in Yuccaville, order a huge pepperoni pizza, and rent a sci-fi movie starring a nasty monster from some dying planet."

He grinned. Her stuttering had stopped. Her shakes

seemed to have eased as well. "I love it when you get all romantic on me, Slugger."

Unfortunately, thanks to the two troublemakers back in the Lucky Monk, he had a feeling it was going to be a long time before they could slip away to that seedy motel room.

He led her outside, pulling her around behind an outcrop that shielded her from view and from the breeze but not the sun. The temperature was about twenty degrees warmer thanks to the heat coming off the rocks.

Claire handed him the towel and unbuttoned her jeans, wiggling out of the wet denim. She stood before him in her lace panties and polka-dot bra and a lot of bare skin. "Will you help me get this bra off, Mac?"

Right words, wrong setting. Damn!

Tuesday, October 9th

The parking lot at The Shaft was empty when Ronnie got there. She parked Katie's car close to the front door and shut off the engine.

Yesterday had been a trip. Between the diamond she had found stashed inside of that eyeball and Mac and Claire's adventures up at the mine, The Dancing Winnebagos R.V. Park had been a whirling dervish long into the early morning hours.

Extracting Katie's keys, Ronnie headed to the front door. The Shaft needed to be ready to open in a couple of hours for the lunch crowd. If she was going to accomplish every task on the list Katie had written for her, she didn't have time to sit around reminiscing about yesterday in the warm sunshine and fresh desert air.

As she stepped inside, she could still smell the bleach water Arlene had used to mop up last night, mixed with a hint of stale beer, perfume, and wood—ghosts of scents lying in wait for the party to crank up again. It was no wonder Katie had dreaded coming in here. With her over-sensitive nose right now and constant state of nausea, especially in the early hours, she must spend as much time leaning over the toilet as getting the place ready for the day.

It was a good thing Butch was supposed to be back later today. She had a feeling that was as much the reason Katie begged Ronnie to open the joint as her morning sickness. The big turkey should have told Butch about the baby already.

Ronnie dropped the keys on the counter after locking the door behind her. She grabbed her phone and plugged in her ear phones, cranking up her Favorites playlist. Then she pulled Katie's list from her skirt pocket and got to work.

A half hour later, the bathrooms were sparkling and ready for stocking and Ronnie had a sheen of sweat on her face. She washed her rubber gloves and then took them off and scrubbed her hands for good measure. When she was done, she rinsed off her face in the sink, glad Katie had suggested she wear the short-sleeve shirt, skirt, and Claire's flip flops. She would be sweating like crazy in her jeans and boots.

Fixing her ponytail and fast forwarding past a slow love song to another upbeat dance tune, she headed back to the supply room to get some toilet paper, tampons, and condoms.

The cook would be in around ten-thirty, Katie had told her, along with Arlene shortly after. That left Ronnie an hour to prep the bar and get the kitchen grill warmed up and some lettuce washed and chopped.

Singing along under her breath, she pushed through the swinging doors that led to the back, flicking on lights as she went.

The supply room needed an air freshener to get rid of the cardboard and old grease smell. She grabbed a box of tampons and stuffed a handful of condoms in her pocket. Would that be enough? She had no idea how many prophylactics the men in this town went through in a night, but based on Katie's predicament, more might be needed.

Flipping up the hem of her T-shirt, she filled her makeshift kangaroo pocket with more condoms—mostly the regular sized ones, keeping in mind the gargantuan pickups many of the men drove. Those guys had to be overcompensating for something with those huge rigs.

She turned to grab a couple of rolls of toilet paper from the other side of the room and almost ran into a six foot four wall standing behind her.

Ronnie screamed.

Condoms flew everywhere; the box of tampons crashed to the floor, spilling the mini-rods all over Grady's boots.

Yanking her ear buds out, she glared up at him, too ticked at nearly being scared to death to be embarrassed about handling such intimate items in front of him. "You scared the holy hell out of me, Grady."

"I hollered for you, but you didn't hear me."

He stood there in his Sheriff's uniform with his hat in his hand and the star crooked on his wrinkled shirt. His face was more lined than usual, his eyes red-veined, his shoulders drooping. His whole body painted a picture of exhaustion.

Ronnie hadn't seen him since their women's bathroom meeting. She wondered with all that had gone on up at the mine if he'd been up for most of the night dealing with the dead woman, or the live one, or both.

"You look tired," she said, and then wished she hadn't pointed out the obvious when he pinched the bridge of his nose as if her words had hurt.

"I haven't been to bed yet."

"You're not wearing your gun." Sheesh! Was there anything else stupid she could come up with to say? How about something he didn't already know?

"I'm off duty. I was on my way home but wanted to talk to you first." He rubbed his eyes and then blinked a few times. "Your sister said I would find you here."

"How did you get in?" Had Arlene or the cook come in early and let him in?

"Butch gave me a key years ago." His gaze drifted down to her feet, a hint of his smile showing. "You look ten years younger dressed like that."

And he looked about ten years older after the day and night he'd obviously had. Ronnie wanted to go to him, smooth away some of the lines, make things easier for him somehow, but she didn't know how. All she had to offer was complications and goons.

"I looked into your dancing buddy in the red pickup," he told her.

"It was one dance and I was drunk."

"Right." He worked a muscle in the back of his neck. "Anyway, he's not out to kill you."

"Did you talk to him?"

He nodded. "He's actually been assigned here to keep an eye on you."

Keep an eye on her? "You mean the Feds are actually protecting my life now instead of destroying it?"

"Not quite."

She jammed her hands on her hips. "Why else would he be watching me?" Then it dawned on her. "Am I being used as bait?"

His wince said it all.

"Those fucking, cock-sucking bastards!" She looked around for something to throw or smash or kick.

"They're expecting some heat to come your way thanks to your ex-husband. It seems he was doing quite a lot of double-dealing over the years to support his expensive cocaine habit, amongst other big ticket vices."

"If you're pussy footing about his high-priced mistresses, Grady, you don't need to. I told you, the Feds had a hell of a good time showing me what Lyle was really up to during our non-legal marriage. They were sure they could get me to roll over on him." She glared at his crooked star, remembering that hard aluminum chair, the bright lights, the one-way glass mirror. "Unfortunately, I was as clueless as they were on all fronts. That didn't stop them from giving it their best shot, though."

"Aren't you concerned at all about who they think might be coming for you?"

"You mean the husky and the polar bear?"

"Yes. He confirmed that, by the way. Those are the nicknames of two hit men preferred by one of the bosses."

"Is that the best those two could do? What happened to cool names like Richard 'The Ice Man' Kuklinski and Joseph 'The Animal' Barboza?"

"You joke, Veronica, but these men may try to kill you. Or worse."

"I joke, Grady, because it's all I can do. What do you want me to do? Cry? Cower? Throw myself at you and beg you to keep me safe?" She squatted down and began to box up the tampons. "You aren't paying attention. I'm being used as bait here. The only thing I can do is keep living. The other option involves a coffin and men in somber suits."

"What about the Witness Security Program?"

"If these guys really want to find me, they will, no matter where I live or who I pretend to be." She closed the lid on the box and placed it on the shelf beside her. "If that guy in the red pickup is good at his job, maybe I'll luck out and he'll spot the hit men before they corner me. I should start giving him my daily itinerary, make this easier for him."

Grady dropped down on one knee, helping her pick up the condoms and pile them on the shelf next to the tampons and jugs of bleach. "I don't like this going on in my county, Veronica."

Pausing, she shot him a raised brow. "You gonna run me out of town, Sheriff?"

His forehead wrinkled in a series of Vs, like those Russian dolls, one inside of the other. "No. That wouldn't solve anything."

"It would keep the trouble from coming to you."

He stared at her for a few beats, his amber gaze loaded

with raw hunger. "She's already here."

Lust zapped down through her core leaving her tingly, breathless, and burning for more.

Her eyes lowered to that star pinned to his chest, her brain trying to regain control of the ship, reminding her that he was one of *them*. Besides, throwing herself at him would only leave her embarrassed, even humiliated from his rejection. Just because he found her attractive didn't mean he wanted it to go anywhere. He had said it before—she was the last person with whom he should get involved. Nothing had changed with her situation. Things had only gotten worse.

She picked up the last three condoms. "What about the pocket watch?"

"What pocket watch?" he stood, moving over by the door.

"The one that I gave ..." she looked at him. "What did you do with it?"

"Sent it back."

Claire might not be happy with that, but Ronnie was glad to have it out of her hair. "Will someone be contacting me?"

"Nope." He peered out the supply room window. "We have enough trouble in Cholla County. The last thing we need is a few more money-hungry criminals swinging their guns around."

"I don't understand." Why was he looking out the window? Was there someone out there?

"I took a long drive last night after things cooled from the mess up at Ruby's mine." He turned around and leaned back against the door, crossing his arms over his chest. "The watch is going back to its rightful owners in an anonymous package shipped from Phoenix."

"You went clear to Phoenix?" That was about four hours away.

"Yep."

"Why?" She stood, brushing her hands off on her skirt.

"The way I figured it, Joe stole that pocket watch. You and your family were left to clean up his mess. Since none of you were trying to gain financially from it, it was a matter of returning it and wiping your hands of it. Now nobody knows where to come looking for more." His eyelids narrowed. "Unless there is more."

Not gold pocket watches, no. Just a diamond hidden in an eyeball, and maybe a few more in that little box she had snatched after convincing Jessica to go back to the General Store yesterday afternoon and tell her mother about skipping school.

"Thank you, Grady." She clasped her hands together, tempted to touch him, show him how much she appreciated what he had done for her family. She glanced at the star. *He's one of them.* "Thanks for all of your help with the watch and the Feds."

He nodded slowly, seeming to study her. "What is it, Veronica?"

"What is what?"

"What is it that is keeping you from coming over here and kissing me?"

She felt her eyes widen, then tried to hide her surprise with a quick laugh. "You think I want to kiss you?"

"I can see it in your body language," his focus drifted downward. "But something is holding you back."

She thought about denying it, but he'd probably read that lie on her, too. "They teach you that at the police academy? Lust Detection 101?"

"It's something I picked up on the side." He placed his hat upside down on a shelf half filled with folded bar towels. "So, is it the hat? You frown at it a lot."

"I do?"

He nodded. Then he reached for his star. "But not nearly as often as you do this." He pulled it off and dropped it in his hat. "That piece of metal really irks you, doesn't it?"

Hells bells, yes! "It looks sharp and pokey," which defined her experience with lawmen in general up until now. She watched him unbutton the top two buttons on his shirt. "Are you going to strip down to your birthday suit in front of me, Sheriff?" she jested, sort of.

He unbuttoned several more, revealing the white T-shirt underneath it. "Maybe."

"Isn't that against some ethics deal for you guys?"

"Us guys?" he shucked the shirt and draped it over the supply room window, hooking it on the metal corner joints in the molding. "I'm just an officer of the law in these clothes, Veronica." He reached for his belt buckle. "I'm not out to hurt you." He pulled his belt free in one tug and placed it next to his hat.

"You're not?" The lust simmering in his gaze made her want to do wicked things with him. Things they absolutely did not teach in her etiquette classes.

"Not unless you want me to," he said with a grin. "But I promise I'll kiss it better."

Holy shit! It suddenly registered. Grady was stripping for her. No man had ever taken his clothes off in front of her, not even Lyle when tipsy on his expensive wine. She wasn't sure where to look, what to say, or what to do with her hands at that moment.

"What's next?" he asked.

He was giving her a chance to stop him. Did she want him to stop? This was Sheriff Harrison, the hardass in uniform who had given her a speeding ticket she still hadn't paid.

But damn if she didn't want to see more of what he had to offer.

"Your T-shirt," she told him, holding out her hand for it. She wanted to breathe him in while she ogled.

He pulled it off and tossed it to her. "More?"

She buried her nose in the warm cotton, filling her lungs with the heady scent of his skin.

"Are you sniffing my shirt?"

"Yeah."

"I've been wearing that since last night."

"I know. It smells like you." She sniffed again, shivering.

"I don't think I've ever had a woman want to smell my clothes before."

"Their loss."

"It makes me want to do things to you." He stared at her mouth. "Things that will make you quiver even more than my shirt."

Her smile felt wicked on her lips. "Did you bring your handcuffs, Sheriff Hardass?"

Surprise flickered over his features. "Hardass?"

"Handcuffs?"

He pulled them out from his back pocket and held them up. She moved closer, reaching for them. His hand snaked out and captured her arm, spinning her around, backing her against the door. She felt the cold metal on her right wrist just as she heard the click of the handcuff. There was another click, but she didn't feel that one. She looked down and saw why—he had the other handcuff on his left wrist.

He raised their wrists as one and pressed his palm against the door next to her head, his face almost touching hers. "Now did I or did I not hear you call me 'Hardass'?"

His question reminded her of a line from *Two Mules for Sister Sarah*, so she responded in kind. "I suppose a man might hear just about anything after being awake for almost two days straight."

He lifted his non-cuffed hand, running his knuckles along her jawline. "You have a sassy mouth, Veronica Morgan."

"What are you going to do about it? Arrest me for protesting too much, Sheriff Hardass?"

"Only if you're trespassing."

She grabbed him through his pants. "Is this trespassing?"

His mouth came down on hers hard, demanding. She didn't back down, meeting his tongue in the middle, matching thrusts.

"Veronica." He reached down and covered her hand with his, showing her how he wanted to be touched.

Passion boiled over, melting everything inside of her,

steaming her brain. She fumbled with the button of his pants, wanting to feel the real thing. After years of faking orgasms with Lyle and finding her only release with a vibrator, she needed to touch the real thing, stroke him, feel him inside of her.

"Take off your pants," she said against his lips.

"Are you sure?" he asked, blinking down at her as if he were shocked to find them handcuffed together on the verge of sex against the supply room door.

"Yes, Grady. I want you inside of me."

"I'm not carrying any protection."

"You mean these aren't standard issue with the hat and star?" She pulled a handful of condoms out of her pocket. "Now take off your pants."

He looked at her for a moment.

"Unless you don't want me ... or this," she said, feeling a blush start to crawl up her throat. Jeez. Had she taken things too far too fast for him?

His gaze softened. "Of course I want you and this," he kissed her, lowering his forehead so it was touching hers. "I just had something different in mind when I imagined taking you the first time."

He had fantasized about her? That made her knees feel wobbly. "Like what?"

"Fewer rolls of toilet paper in the room, for one."

She smiled. "You mean you didn't picture us handcuffed in a supply room?"

"Not in a supply room, no. But we were handcuffed."

She laughed, deep and throaty. Wow, where had that come from? She had a James Bond sex kitten thing going on for a second there. "Grady?"

"What?" He ran his tongue along her collarbone, making her writhe, her hips tickle.

"Why am I still wearing my underwear?"

His groan sounded almost painful. "Let me fix that for you." He yanked up her skirt and tugged down her panties, dragging her cuffed hand along with his.

"Now about those pants," she said, her breath coming faster as his palm slid up her inner thigh.

"Hold your horses. I'm busy."

"My horses are long gone." She tugged on his handcuff and unbuttoned his pants with both of her hands. "Get them off," she said, trying to tear open a condom with her free hand and teeth while he dropped his pants.

"Give me that," he said, taking the condom from her and frowning at it. "Small? You're hard on a man's ego, Veronica. I'm going to need a bigger one."

She held out the others. He grabbed one and ripped it open.

"I want to put it on." She had watched a porno once where the woman made the guy all hot and bothered with her technique. Ronnie had watched it over and over. It was that or rearrange her walk-in closet since Lyle had been out of town on business yet again.

"You can do it next time," Grady said.

There was going to be a next time?

"If you touch me now," he continued, "I may not be able to last long enough to even get inside of you."

Knowing he wanted her that much was some heady juju. She watched him slide the condom on, admiring what he had to offer. When he finished and looked up at her with a questioning brow, she lifted her leg and wrapped it around his thigh.

"Now, Grady."

He took her at her command. The first plunge gave her goosebumps, the path slick with her need for him.

"Veronica," he breathed in her hair. He tugged on her other thigh. "Wrap both of your legs around me."

He lifted her, positioning her against the door, then drove into her again and again.

Her one hand was pinned against the door with his, her other clutched his shoulder, squeezing tighter the higher she spun. "More Grady," she whispered. "I need more of you."

"Like this?" He buried himself inside of her.

"Oh, God!" she cried, digging her heels into him. "Yes! Do it again!"

He did, and then didn't stop, at least not until she shuddered around him, her limbs losing all strength. He slammed into her a couple of more times before groaning through his own release. When it was over, he leaned his forehead on her shoulder, his breath heating her skin through her T-shirt.

"Damn, woman." He grabbed a towel from the shelf, lowering her to the floor. "You bewitch me."

Her toes tingled when they touched down. Grady made her feel light and airy, warm all over. Nothing with Raphael had ever come close to that, nor Lyle for that matter. That was troubling. Sex with the Sheriff of Cholla County could quickly become addictive.

"I think I'm going to want to do that again," she said, pulling her skirt down.

"You think?" He chuckled. The deep, happy sound made her heart swell. "It wasn't supposed to be this good."

"Why not?"

"Because you're you and I'm me, and this thing between us might cause problems."

"Oh." Yeah, there was that star of his.

"But knowing that hasn't stopped me from wanting you, even when you said I'd need tweezers to find my dick."

She laughed. "Yeah, I was sort of wrong on the size."

"Sort of?" He shot her a mock glare while pulling up his pants.

"My memory is growing hazy now." She looked around for her underwear. "You may have to show it to me again."

He pulled a key to the cuffs from his pocket and held it up in front of her. "I was right. You are a handcuffs kind of girl."

She snatched the key from him. "That's only because I figured Sheriff Hardass would get off on locking me up."

"Next time—"

Someone pounded on the door, twisting the locked knob.

"Oh, crap!" Ronnie whispered and hopped away from it.

"Who's in there?" a male voice demanded from the other side of the door. She knew that voice.

"Damn it." Grady tucked her behind him. "It's Butch."

"Harrison!" The pounding grew louder, faster. "If you're in there messing around with Kate, I'm gonna kick your ass! I don't care if you're the goddamned Sheriff."

"He's not joking," Ronnie whispered. She could hear it in Butch's tone. "What are you doing?" she asked when Grady grabbed the knob.

"Opening the door." And he did just that. "Hi, Butch. How was Phoenix?"

Ronnie peeked around Grady's shoulder.

"What are you doing in my supply room with the door locked, Harrison?" Butch asked, his mouth tight, his tanned face more ruddy than the last time Ronnie had seen him. "Where's your shirt? And why in the hell does it smell like sex in here?"

Grady stepped back, pushing Ronnie, too. "Calm down. It's not Kate." He pulled his left wrist, which was still attached to Ronnie's right wrist, out from behind him.

"Welcome home, Butch," Ronnie said, trying on a bright smile for size and feeling like an idiot wearing it.

Butch stared at her for a few seconds, then snorted. A smile eased onto his face, adding laugh lines around his dark blue eyes. "You've got to be shitting me."

"It's not what it seems," Grady said.

"It's not?" Butch smirked, his gaze darting from Grady's bare chest to Ronnie's mouth to their locked wrists. "So you weren't having some kind of kinky handcuffed sex with my girlfriend's sister in my supply room?"

Ronnie's face sizzled.

Grady sighed. "Yeah, that's pretty much what it is."

His grin now ear to ear, Butch backed out of the room.

"Ronnie, I think you left your underwear on that shelf behind you. Harrison, come by my office and catch me up when you're done." He shut the door on his own laughter.

Ronnie blew out a breath and peeked up at Grady. "So much for keeping that our little secret."

He dragged his hand through his hair. "Yeah. My Aunt Millie already suspects as much."

Ronnie wanted to adopt his Aunt Millie as her own. She unlocked his cuff and then hers. "You could always lie to Butch."

"How's that?" He took the handcuffs from her.

"Tell him you were trying to arrest me and I distracted you with my body."

Grady's eyes twinkled. "With our history, that wouldn't really be a lie, now would it?"

Chapter Twenty-Five

"What's with the jeans?" Claire asked Mac from where he had left her spent, sprawled out and naked on the sheets. They had the Skunkmobile to themselves for another half-hour, her family warned to stay out. What was his rush to get back to the chaos? She wasn't done with him yet.

"I forgot about Dr. García." He grabbed his shirt from the floor, shaking it out. "Damn, Slugger. You ripped two of the buttons off."

"It's your fault."

"How's it my fault?" He pulled on the shirt and buttoned what he could, staring down at her chest.

"My eyes are up here, big boy." She pointed at her face, redirecting his gaze from her bare chest. "It's your fault because you did that thing you do with your tongue. You know what it does to me." She pushed up onto her elbows. "What about Dr. García?"

"I asked him to meet me outside his camper this afternoon to talk about securing the dig site." His focus drifted south again. "I meant to tell you; he mentioned yesterday when Sheriff Harrison was here that he's pretty sure he knows the origin of the jade pieces."

"Did you tell Gramps about this meeting?" Knowing how frustrated her grandfather had been lately with taking a back seat to Mac, she could see him getting all growly and pissy over this if not.

"He's the one who suggested we talk to Dr. García." Mac's hand inched toward her breast but she laughed and rolled away before he made contact. "Get back here, woman."

"No way. Don't think you can start something and then leave." She swung her feet over the edge of the bed. "Besides, I'm coming with you."

"You sure you don't want to get some rest? You were still staggering around late last night after all that went down and then over inhaling paint fumes at the restroom first thing this morning with the boys. You're not Superwoman, you know."

"That's not what you were saying a little while ago." She grabbed her underwear from the foot of the bed. "Have you seen my bra?"

"I was overly smitten when I said that." He walked out into the hall and came back with her bra dangling from his index finger. "I still think we should burn all of these."

"They're too expensive to burn. Did you leave a hickey on my neck? I vaguely remember some biting going on at one point." She peered in the closet mirror, lifting her chin. "As for the good doctor, I'm the one who swam down in the shaft and got that jade piece. If anyone deserves to know the story of its origin, it's me."

"I left a hickey on your hip, not your neck, and you were the one doing the biting."

Oh, right. That was his fault, too. He smelled so fresh and yummy, like the sun-warmed desert in the morning. He should try not to tempt her like that if he didn't like being bitten.

He sat on the edge of the bed and pulled on his socks and shoes. "If you're coming, we need to leave here in the next five minutes."

"No problem." She fastened her bra and then combed her hair with her fingers.

He came up behind her and pulled her back against him, staring at her in the mirror. "Have I told you how crazy I am about you?"

"Yes, in the hallway right after I tore off your shirt, remember?" She stopped his hand as it headed south into her underwear. "When Sheriff Harrison confiscated the camper that belonged to those women, did he mention anything to you about finding something odd underneath it?"

"No." Mac's reflection frowned at her. "Why do you ask?"

"Oh, nothing," she said, turning in his arms, pressing into him, making his eyes go all dark and sexy again. "Are you sure we need to leave to talk to the doctor right now?"

Mac pushed her back a step. "Claire, did you snoop inside that camper?"

She couldn't outright lie to him. "I might have sort of gone inside of it one day when I was patrolling the area after realizing that they had gone off to the dig site and left the door unlocked." But she could fudge the truth a little.

"Claire," he said, following it with a heavy duty glare.

She kissed his Adam's apple. "That's not important, though."

"How is breaking and entering not important?"

"Because I had no intent to commit a crime." She grabbed a clean T-shirt from the closet. "I just looked around and left."

"Which is illegally trespassing, another misdemeanor to add to your growing record."

"What Sheriff Harrison doesn't know won't hurt anyone." She pulled her Zombies Love Girls with Big Brainnnsssss T-shirt over her head. "Besides, the Sheriff did inform me recently that he has spruced up the jail cell for me."

"My anxieties are not at peace knowing that, sweetheart." Mac crossed his arms over his chest. "Why did you ask if the Sheriff found something odd under the camper?"

"Because I found something under there. Ronnie has it hidden somewhere in here."

"I thought you said you didn't take anything when you snooped."

"I didn't. Not then. But a few days later, Henry's leash got caught up under their camper. When I crawled under to unwrap him, I found a little box tucked up in the back bumper. I just wondered if the Sheriff found that box." She went out in the hall, where Mac had peeled her jeans off and given her the hickey, carrying them back to the bedroom.

"Now that I think about it, the Sheriff had Deputy Dipshit with him yesterday. That incompetent fool wouldn't know where to find his ass if it weren't attached at his waist."

Mac watched her tug her jeans up over her hips. "Did you open the box?" He didn't even let her react to his question before saying, "What am I thinking? Of course you did. What was in it?"

Her Mighty Mouse cap hung on a hook inside the closet. Claire could tell Ronnie had been in the bedroom cleaning. Her older sister had always picked up after them when they were kids. Time had not changed some things. She grabbed her cap and pulled it on her head. "Eyeballs."

Catching her arm, Mac turned her in his direction. "Eyeballs?" When she nodded, his brows wrinkled. "Human?"

"You've been watching too many horror movies with me." She looked around for her flip flops, not seeing them, and grabbed a pair of canvas slip-ons. "They were round glass eyeballs, I think. A bit smaller than human eyes, but not small enough to be doll's eyes."

He dropped onto the edge of the bed, resting his elbows on his knees. "That's weird."

"And creepy." She walked over to him and tipped his chin up. "You ready?" She kissed him on his wrinkled brow.

"I worry about you, Slugger."

"Don't let the eyeballs mess with your head."

He pulled her closer, resting his forehead on her sternum. "I don't want anything to happen to you, and I can't always be around to keep you out of trouble."

"Is this about you leaving tomorrow morning?" She tugged him to his feet. "I swear, I'm just gonna paint the restroom and help Ruby with some stuff Gramps can't do right now until you get back Friday night. No chasing gun-toting older ladies or harassing Deputy Droopy."

He followed her down the hall. "Promise me you won't go up in the mines while I'm gone."

"I promise. It's way too spooky when you're not there

with me."

Holding the door open for her, he caught her hand on the way outside, kissing her knuckles. "I can't wait until you come home to Tucson with me. It sucks there without you."

She smiled at him. She missed him, too, but she wasn't looking forward to returning to her job search and rattling around in their big house all day, waiting for him to come home. Life here in Jackrabbit Junction had much more to offer—only it didn't have Mac. Looking away before he could see that struggle in her eyes, she dragged him outside with her into the afternoon sunshine. "Time will fly until you're back here again."

She kept hold of his hand as they strolled along the drive toward the new restroom and the archaeologist crew's setup beyond it, not quite ready to leave the land of bliss they had slipped away to enjoy. Reality had way too many barbs and left a mess in its wake. Take her mother, for example, and her bitterness toward just about everything.

Deborah appeared in front of them, as if she'd stepped out of Claire's thoughts onto the scene. Damn it. That's what Claire got for even thinking about the woman.

"Claire," Deborah said.

Claire couldn't look at her mother, the scene with Manny still too fresh. "What?" she asked her mother's feet.

"Oh, would you stop with this silly business and look at me."

Wincing, she did as her mother demanded. Deborah had forgotten to put on lipstick this afternoon.

Or maybe Manny had kissed it off.

Oh, blah. Claire's stomach curdled at the image that thought brought with it, along with all of the others that tumbled after. There had been so much whipped cream—ugh.

"I'm human, Claire." Deborah said, shoving a plate of cookies into her hands. "I have physical needs, just like you and MacDonald. Manuel was able to … to help me find some release for the time being."

"Jesus." Mac covered his face. "Somebody please wake me up."

Claire tried to focus on the cookies and not remember the sight of Manny's naked stress reliever. "Is this thing with you two going to keep happening, Mom?"

"Well," Deborah hem-hawed. "Manuel is a very generous lover."

A sickly sounding groan came from Mac. "This isn't happening in my world," he said and left them in his dust. Claire watched him go, surprised he didn't break into a sprint.

"And," Deborah continued, "he makes me feel attractive again for the first time in a long time." She tittered. "You should hear the things he says to me when he—"

"Mother, stop!" Claire interrupted before her stomach turned inside out and dumped her lunch on the ground. "It was a simple question to help me prepare mentally for future visuals."

She heard Gramps shout and watched Mac veer off toward the new restroom, joining Gramps and Manny who were both holding paintbrushes.

"Yes."

Claire turned back to her mother. "Yes?"

"I enjoyed having sexual relations with Manuel." She looked over at the man of the hour.

The old sex god glanced their way. His new hearing aid must have started ringing. When his gaze settled on Deborah, his smile widened, making him look like a lovesick Don Juan. He waved his paintbrush.

Deborah lifted her chin and turned her back on him. "But I'm not going to make it easy for him."

"Mother," Claire waved at Manny in Deborah's place. "That's rude."

Deborah patted Claire's cheek. "No darling, it's called playing hard to get. You could use a lesson or two. You make it way too easy for MacDonald. Did he even offer to marry you when he thought you were pregnant?"

They were not going to have this discussion again right then and there while Claire held a plate of cookies. "Why am I carrying cookies?"

"Ruby made them for the men." Deborah glanced back at Manny again, fluttering her eyelashes.

"I don't think he can even see you do that this far away, Mother."

"You'd be surprised what a man can see when he wants to. That reminds me, I need you to take me to the beauty parlor in Yuccaville tomorrow for some highlights." She took a closer look at Claire's hair. "You could use a haircut and maybe some highlights, too. I see some gray strands poking through. If you want to keep MacDonald coming back for more, you need to work harder on looking good for him. Let's get a mani-pedi while we're at it, and then we can see about getting you a pretty dress to make MacDonald pay a little more attention when he comes back next weekend."

No freaking way. This was not happening. Damned Kate for being too sick to do this shit with their mother. And where in the hell was Ronnie? She used to love this mother-daughter bonding crap. Didn't she?

Claire grabbed a cookie and crammed it in her mouth to keep from screaming in terror. "Gotta go," she said, spitting crumbs on Deborah, who frowned, clearly disapproving.

Sidestepping her mother's reprimand, Claire jogged over to where Mac stood listening to Gramps.

"... so I've been a little more crotchety than normal," Gramps finished as Claire joined them.

Just a little, she thought, jamming another cookie half into her mouth so her tongue didn't decide to speak up and agree with him. Ruby had doubled the chocolate chips today. Was there a reason for celebrating Claire didn't know about?

Manny patted Mac on the shoulder. "This is Ford's way of saying he's sorry for being such an asshole lately."

Gramps glared at Manny.

"Apology accepted," Mac said, stealing the other half of

the cookie sticking out of Claire's mouth. "If Ruby asks me to help her with something in the future, I'll refer her to you."

"Good," Gramps said, glancing at Claire under his bushy brow.

"But," Mac continued, "if she tells me something in secret, I won't break her confidence."

"Fine." Gramps took a cookie from the plate. "Same goes for me with Claire."

Claire gulped down her mouthful of cookie. "What?"

Manny grabbed two cookies. "Your grandfather is promising to keep your secrets from Mac."

The squint Mac was giving her made her want to go back and discuss more beauty ideas with her mom. She smiled. "I'm an open book, baby. I swear."

Gramps snickered, not helping her win her case.

"Did your mom say anything about me?" Manny asked, sidling up next to Claire.

He was standing too close, especially now that she'd seen him naked and her mother had talked about his generosity under the sheets. She shoved the plate of cookies at him.

"She said ..." Claire thought about how her mother had actually smiled at her—a real, honest-to-God smile—before cutting into her about her hair. Maybe Chester was right, Manny was a hero. He had taken the edge off her mom. "She said that you look handsome in blue, but she didn't know if you were going to be man enough for her."

Manny glanced down at his blue shirt covered in paint splotches. His eyes twinkled when he looked back up at her. "*Ay yi yi.* That sounds like a challenge to me." He walked off whistling, carrying the cookies over to where Chester stood in a holey T-shirt and ripped overalls, painting while a cigar hung out of his mouth.

"You owe me for that, girl," Gramps said, his whole face scrunched in a scowl. "Now I'm gonna have to listen to the fool moon over my daughter all afternoon."

"Hello," a voice said from behind Claire.

"Dr. García," Mac said, shaking the other man's hand. "We were making our way down to you."

The doctor looked tired today. His brown eyes drooped at the edges and his thick salt-and-pepper hair was mussed like he'd been running his hands through it, but his smile held strong. "Good to see you again, Mac, Claire," he nodded at each of them and then Gramps, "Harley."

Gramps shifted his paintbrush to his left hand, balanced without his crutch, and shook the doctor's hand. "How is your crew holding up?"

"Well, they're still shocked, but we're keeping busy so there isn't time to let their tongues wag too much." He turned to Claire, squeezing her shoulder. "Once again, I'm so sorry you had to go through what you did."

She waved him off. "I've been through worse."

The tender look in his eyes made her feel warm and happy inside. It was no wonder his crew was willing to work so hard for him, including Sundays.

"You remind me of my daughter, Angélica. She runs her own dig site down in Mexico." He sighed. "I spoke with her on the phone last night about all of this. She confirmed my suspicions—the jade pieces were stolen two years ago from a dig site near her own. She was able to describe the pieces to me from memory. Her brain is much sharper than mine these days."

"I can relate to that," Gramps said, glancing at Claire.

Was that a compliment from the old buzzard? Was the world coming to an end this afternoon?

"Angélica remembered seeing our two thieves at that site when she visited it years back. They'd pulled her aside and spoken with her about joining her crew, but she had no need for them at the time."

"Lucky for her she didn't, it sounds like," Claire said.

"Yes. She's had enough trouble lately." His lips tightened for a moment, making Claire wonder what kind of trouble. *Like drug cartel trouble?* "Anyway, she mentioned that they may be responsible for thefts at several other dig sites where valuable Maya artifacts have disappeared over the last decade, including a few rare gold pieces. I will need to contact the Sheriff and see if they found anything inside of their camper."

Like a box of eyeballs?

Mac shot her a frown.

She had kept that thought in her head, hadn't she?

She focused back on Dr. García. "Do you think they were selling pieces through some black market?" Claire asked. Was the black market for archaeology finds the same one Joe had dabbled in with his stolen treasures?

"Yes, I was thinking that, but Angélica suggested they might merely have been mules."

"Mules?" Mac asked. "You mean like a drug mule?"

Dr. García nodded. "They could have been working for someone here in the States. We have been warned by customs to watch for these 'mules' since we cross borders with artifacts."

Claire glanced at Mac. What were the chances of these two women ending up at a campground that used to be owned by a man who stole high-priced treasures from other thieves? It was too much of a coincidence for Claire's gut to let it go. Had they been here before? And if they had, did they know he had stashed treasures up in his mines? If the eyeballs were Joe's, then they had known, and they might not be the only treasure.

"Dr. García," Claire said, "how did these two women end up working for you here? Did they come to you looking to volunteer?"

He nodded. "We had worked together before at a site up on the Navajo reservation."

"Did they request this site in particular?"

"Yes, as a matter of fact, they did. We had another site the university was considering at the time with more area to cover and I offered that one to them, but they wanted to join me here."

"What are you getting at?" Mac asked her.

She didn't want to spell it out in front of Dr. García. She shrugged. "I find it interesting that they may have been acting as mules over the last decade and that they knew of this place." Hint, hint!

His eyes widened. "That is interesting."

Gramps grunted. He got it, too. "Well," Gramps patted Dr. García's shoulder, "in spite of the most recent problem, we've appreciated your crew staying at the campground."

"It's been our pleasure." García nodded back toward his group of campers. Jessica stood there talking to Beanpole, her smile too wide to be flirty. She hadn't mastered the art yet, thankfully. Claire would have to keep her away from Deborah and her new man-catching agenda. "I see that one of my kids has taken a real shine to your girl. If you need me to curtail that, let me know."

"He's been a gentleman so far," Gramps said, "but I have my shotgun handy just in case."

Dr. García grinned. "I'll let him know you're watching."

"You mentioned you were concerned about vandals," Mac said. "Is there anything we can do to help secure the dig site?"

"Mac works for a company that builds retaining walls," Gramps explained. "He could help you guys out."

"I'm thinking *we*," Mac pointed to Gramps and then himself, "could put up something to secure the opening when your crew isn't up there."

"That would be excellent. We have to be cautious about taking care of our equipment as well as our finds."

They needed to be cautious, period. If those women knew about Joe and his skimming, whether acting as his mules or fellow thieves, Claire's fears about the pocket watch and what it meant to Ruby and Gramps's welfare—hell, to all of their lives—had a solid base. This might be just the beginning of the flood of trouble flowing their way. If Joe had left a piece like the pocket watch where it was relatively easy to find, what things had he gone out of his way to hide? And where?

She glanced at the bluffs surrounding them. Joe was no

idiot. He must have come back to Jackrabbit Junction on purpose. Here, out in the open amongst the creosote and sandy bluffs, in an open valley ringed with mountains full of excellent hiding places, he could have made a stand, if needed. Unfortunately, he had keeled over and left his widow alone with the shotguns and stolen loot, a mound of debt, and an R.V. park in shambles.

Lucky for Ruby, Gramps had come along, dragging his family and friends with him.

Mac squeezed her hand, bringing her back to the present.

Dr. García apologized again for her ending up in a mine shaft, then he and Gramps headed off toward the golf cart.

"Where are they going?" she asked Mac.

"To the store to discuss their options over a cold drink."

"Aren't you going with them?"

"They don't need me right now." He took her face in his hands, his gaze full of a warm tenderness that made her knees loosey-goosey. "What about you, Slugger? Do you need me?"

"Careful, Claire," Chester called out from over by the cans of paint. "I hear sweet buns there isn't afraid to hit a woman."

"Even old women," Manny piped in. "Maybe we should change his nickname to Rocky."

"Slugger and Rocky," Chester puffed his cigar in thought. "Yep, I like that. Reminds me of a pair of mud wrestlers I saw up in Reno years ago. They looked a lot like men in the face, but once you covered 'em in mud, that didn't matter so much. All of the bumps were in all the right places, and that's all I cared about three beers into the match."

Claire stood on her toes, wrapped her arms around Mac's neck, and kissed him, long and slow. She did her best to make him forget about eyeballs, Deborah, and the two dirty birds heckling them.

When she pulled back, she smiled up at him, feeling all sloppy inside with love. "I need you more than ever, Mac."

Especially if Jackrabbit Junction was about to recreate the Alamo.

Chapter Twenty-Six

Later that night ...

Claire sat on the top porch step of the General Store, waiting for Mac to finish his game of Euchre with Gramps and the boys. She had left the porch lights off so she could see the stars. She could still smell the scent of burned cedar chips in the air from the fish Gramps had smoked for dinner.

A cool breeze tickled Ruby's wind chimes, making them jingle and ping.

Henry growled from his perch behind her on the porch swing. He pushed up onto his front legs, eyeing the drive.

Something moved in the darkness.

Her heart stopped to see what it was. She peered into the shadows and then chuckled. "Relax, Cujo," Claire mocked. "It's just a tumbleweed."

He barked at her.

Flipping off the ornery mutt, she returned to star-gazing.

It was the perfect night to drive out into the desert, lie down in the back of a pickup, and look for constellations. That had been Mac's romantic suggestion, anyway, for his last night before heading back to Tucson for a few days.

Claire had another idea. "Or we could have more sex on a soft bed inside a stinky R.V."

"The stars are overrated," Mac had returned, his gaze already undressing her.

Looking up now, she was reconsidering his idea. The stars were out in abundance tonight, celebrating in the moon's absence with all kinds of twinkling. Maybe they could consolidate the two notions—have sex under the stars. That might be fun, so long as they didn't get busted again. A third time would not be a charm.

The sound of a car engine reached her long before headlights came over the bridge. Claire shielded her eyes as Kate slowed to a stop and killed the lights and engine.

She waited for both of her sisters to climb out and shut their doors, realizing Ronnie was driving instead of Kate. "How did Butch take the news?" she asked.

Kate sniffed. "I think he's in shock."

"You think?" Ronnie asked with a dose of sarcasm. "When you said the word, 'pregnant,' the man turned chalk white."

Claire scooted over, making room for Kate. "So what's next?"

"She's going to keep working there," Ronnie answered, leaning against the railing.

"Really?"

"I have to." The porch step creaked as Kate settled onto it. "At least until I find another job."

Henry hopped down from the porch swing and planted himself on Kate's lap, his butt toward Claire. The little shit.

"I'm sure Butch had no problem with that." Claire had a lot of doubts about many things in Jackrabbit Junction but not Butch's feelings for her sister. The little smile he got whenever he watched Kate move around the bar gave away too much.

"I don't think he heard a word Katie said after she dropped the baby bomb."

"So did you actually break up with him?"

"Yes."

"More like 'sort of,'" Ronnie said.

"What do you mean sort of?" Kate asked. "I clearly explained that I didn't expect him to want to have any part in this baby's life."

"First of all, as I already said, I don't think he heard a word you said after you told him about the baby. Second, you didn't actually say, 'Butch, I'm breaking up with you.' It was much more garbled than that, with a bunch of half sentences in between your sobs."

"I didn't sob."

"You did."

"It's the damned hormones."

"Right," Claire said, not believing that for a moment.

"I'll be sure to make it all crystal clear when he gets back from his brother's later next week."

"He's leaving again?" Claire asked.

"Yes, but this is just a short trip to attend a couple of meetings and sign off on some more paperwork. After that, he'll be around for a few weeks."

For a man who owned a bar in a dusty pit stop, Butch had a lot of shit going on in his life. "Kate, are you sure he won't want to be part of this kid's life?"

"I told you, he said kids were not in his future. There was no 'ifs' or 'maybes' in his tone when he said it."

"There were none at that time, Katie," Ronnie emphasized. "He might change his mind now."

"I'm not trapping him like that. An old girlfriend tried to do that to him, only the baby turned out to be a lie." Kate hugged her knees. "I want him to want this baby and me out of love, not obligation."

Ronnie snorted. "You've been reading too many romance novels. Real life doesn't happen that way. Look at Mom and Dad."

"I am thinking of Mom and Dad. I don't want Butch to hate me two years into the relationship and spend the next thirty miserable, eventually leaving me for another woman when I'm too old and bitter to pick up the pieces."

"There's always that chance with any relationship." Claire understood Kate's reasoning. It was part of the reason a long-term commitment scared the shit out of her, even with Mac.

"Besides," Kate continued, "this new business of his will probably involve more traveling than ever. I doubt he'll want a wife and baby tagging along everywhere."

"He has a nice house, though," Claire said. She and Kate had snooped around it a couple of months ago and spent the night in jail because of it. Damn Sheriff Harrison and his stinky cell.

"Trust me," Ronnie said. "A fancy house and cars won't make her happy if he doesn't love her."

Kate sighed. She sounded weary and much too old for her age. "I'll figure something out."

Claire put her arm around Kate, hugging her close. "We'll figure something out, spaz."

Henry looked over his shoulder and growled at Claire. She glared down at the rotten mutt. "Keep it up, and I'll dress you like a girl dog for Halloween."

"I have something that might help us," Ronnie said and dug in her pocket.

"What?"

"Hold out your hand."

Kate did.

"What is it?" Claire asked, seeing something sparkle despite the shadows.

"A diamond."

"What?!" Kate said.

"Where did you get it?" Claire had a bad feeling about this clear to her toes.

"The eyeball we took. I broke it open. This was inside of it."

Oh, crap. "I thought the Sheriff hauled those away with the camper."

"Nope. The box is in the Skunkmobile under the bathroom sink."

"We have a problem," Claire said, thinking of the phone call Ruby had received from the Sheriff this evening.

"Nobody saw me take it."

"You taking the box is not the problem. Sheriff Harrison called today for Ruby. The other woman in the mine had mentioned something to him before clamming up and demanding an attorney. Something that made the Sheriff pretty sure she knew Joe."

"You mean Ruby's dead husband?" Ronnie asked.

"Yeah, that Joe." Claire rubbed the goosebumps that had popped up on her arms, which had nothing to do with the desert breeze rippling past them. "Sheriff Harrison asked Ruby if she remembered meeting either woman back when Joe was alive."

"Did Ruby?"

"No."

"What's the problem then?" Ronnie asked.

"Dr. García's daughter has a theory that those two women were mules, hauling stolen treasures across the border for someone else. If they knew Joe, I'm wondering if he was their boss."

"They were his mules," Ronnie said. "Interesting. Did you tell Grady about this?"

"Grady?" Claire said. "We're on a first name basis with the Sheriff of Cholla County now?"

Kate giggled.

"Shut it, Katie," Ronnie said.

"What?" Claire poked Kate in the ribs. "Spill."

"Ronnie had sex with the Sheriff in Butch's supply room this morning."

Claire blinked. She must not have heard that right. "You did what?"

Kate was outright laughing now. "They were handcuffed together when Butch caught them."

Claire grinned. "Shit sticks, Ronnie. Is this about the watch? I told you to take care of the Sheriff problem, not get all naked and kinky on his ass."

"We weren't naked."

Kate shook with laughter between them. Henry tried to lick her nose.

Claire chuckled in spite of this new mess. Poor Butch. He

could share the therapist's couch with her. "Did you tell the Sheriff about the eyeballs?"

"No. But while we're airing my dirty laundry, I have some bad news to share."

Claire sobered at the tension in Ronnie's voice. "What? Something worse than having the Sheriff sniffing around you even more now?"

"Yeah." Ronnie blew out a breath. "The Feds are here watching me."

"Feds?" Kate asked, her laughter petering out.

"Lyle got into some bad shit. He stole from the wrong guys, and now the Feds think these not-so-nice men will be coming for me because I know something about where Lyle hid the money."

"Do you?"

"There is no money. Lyle blew it all on cocaine, high priced whores, and who knows what else."

"Holy crap," Claire said.

"Yeah. Grady knows about this. He also knows about the Fed who has been following me around since Claire blew the cover on the last two guys."

"You mean those two assholes at the bar? They were Feds?" Claire shook her head. "They need to learn a lesson about how to go undercover."

"What are you going to do?" Kate asked Ronnie.

"I don't know. I was originally going to leave, but then Jessica asked me to stay and I sort of made a deal with her that I would stay if she did."

"She isn't going to live with her dad?" Claire asked. That must be why Ruby was smiling and laughing so easily this afternoon, adding extra chocolate chips to the cookies, even complimenting Deborah on her shoes.

"Yeah. She figured out he lied to her the other night and ditched her for sex with Min ... with some woman."

"Poor Jess," Kate said.

"But if I stay," Ronnie continued, "that brings the

potential for the goons paying a visit to Jackrabbit Junction."

"You're staying," Claire said.

"I don't want to put my family at risk. I need to talk to Gramps and Ruby about this."

"Gramps and Ruby will agree with me—you're not going anywhere. Jackrabbit Junction is as safe as anywhere else."

"Plus, there seem to be a lot of guns around this place," Kate added, scratching Henry between the ears.

He wagged his tail, smacking it against Claire's arm.

Claire scooted away from the damned dog and grinned up at Ronnie. "Smart move, by the way, using your body to hook a man who carries a gun for a living."

"It's not like that with Grady."

"What's it like then?" Kate asked.

"It's ... I don't know. It's more complicated."

"You've got to be kidding me," Claire said, nudging Kate. "She likes him."

"I do not."

"Sex in a supply room?" Kate snorted. "Liar."

"Well, maybe I like him a little."

"You don't have sex on a whim, Ronnie," Kate said. "That's more Claire's style."

"Hey!"

Ronnie groaned. "Fine. You're right. I like him a lot, even if he is a cop. He's just so big and gorgeous with that deep, deep voice of his."

"I know that voice too well." Kate said, dryly. "It's read me my rights before. You don't forget something like that."

"Yeah. I've come to associate the sound of the Sheriff's voice with the smell of a urine-laced jail cell," Claire added, which brought her back to the eyeballs. "Do you think all of those eyeballs are full of diamonds?"

"Maybe," Ronnie said.

"You think they were from another one of Joe's fence jobs?" Kate asked.

"Maybe. They could've been from a job involving his

mules that he was sitting on to let cool for a bit and then he died. They also could've been another skimmed treasure." Claire stared out into the dark desert. "The problem is that they aren't only our secret. That other beige bitch is going to prison, but she knows the eyeballs are out here somewhere, and maybe other stolen pieces, too, like the watch. And she's most likely not the only one."

"You've been preaching this for the last month, Claire." Kate said. "We got it."

"I know, but everyone thought I was paranoid before."

"You are paranoid." Kate dodged Claire's elbow.

"But now I have a legitimate reason for it."

"I have one more confession," Ronnie said. "I gave Grady the watch."

"Ronnie!" Claire cursed. "Now he's going to open an investigation and bring even more attention our way."

"No, he's not. He sent the watch back to its rightful owner in an anonymous package."

"No shit." Claire chuckled. "Did you use some magic love potion on the man to wrap him around your finger?"

"Trust me, he's not the kind to fall for any potions or finger wrapping schemes. All I did was tell him the truth. He was kind enough to help us out instead of making everything worse."

"You need to sleep with him some more," Kate said. "Get him to stop calling me 'Crash.'"

"There is only so much I can do with my body, Katie." Ronnie said, tongue-in-cheek. Then she sighed. "I'm worried about you."

"Why?"

"You're pregnant. What if something happens to you and the baby because of all this crap with Lyle?" Ronnie asked. "Because I stayed here and made things worse?"

"Listen," Claire said. "We could stay here all night and come up with all kinds of 'What ifs' for every one of our problems. But we can't spend our lives waiting to see which of the scenarios might pan out."

"Easy for you to say," Ronnie said. "You're not on someone's hit list."

"Or pregnant."

Henry barked at Claire.

She frowned at each of them, especially the dog. "Come on you guys. If we all stay here, we can deal with whatever comes our way together."

"Like we used to when we were kids," Kate said.

"Okay," Ronnie pushed Kate toward Claire, joining them on the porch step. "So what do we do in the meantime? Enjoy desert life under the stars?"

"Yes." Claire watched a satellite racing across the night sky. "And keep an eye out for strangers."

The screen door creaked.

"Uh-oh," Mac said, coming up behind Claire. "The three of you together out here in the dark? That can lead to nothing but trouble for all mankind."

"No, only for you, Mac," Kate said. "We're focusing all of our evil powers on torturing you at the moment."

Ronnie chuckled. "You'll rue the day you stole Claire from us."

Claire smiled up at him. "And you thought spending time with my mother was tough."

"I still do. She's in there flirting with Manny. I had to escape before things got too graphic." Mac held out his hand for her. "You ready to see some stars, Slugger?"

Did he mean the ones in the sky or the ones he lit up inside of her? "Yes." She grabbed onto him and let him pull her up and lead her down the steps.

"Don't do anything I wouldn't do," Ronnie called after them.

"Without handcuffs, that shouldn't be a problem," Claire called back.

"Zip it, brat."

Kate giggled. "Don't forget a condom. Ronnie has plenty

to spare."

Ronnie's curse was followed by Kate screeching in fake pain.

"Is it always going to be like this?" Mac asked, sliding his arm around her, dropping a kiss on her head.

"No." She stuffed her hand in his back pocket. "It'll probably get worse."

"Excellent. I'm a lucky man."

Claire chuckled, low and husky. "Not yet, but you will be as soon as I get you naked."

She wasn't kidding, either.

The End ... for now

* To read a bonus scene from *The Great Jackalope Stampede*, download the PDF from the hidden page on my website using the password: **Claire**

http://www.anncharles.com/?page_id=991

Connect with Me Online

Facebook (Personal Page):
http://www.facebook.com/ann.charles.author

Facebook (Author Page):
http://www.facebook.com/pages/Ann-Charles/37302789804?ref=share

Twitter (as Ann W. Charles):
http://twitter.com/AnnWCharles

Ann Charles Website: http://www.anncharles.com

About the Author

Ann Charles is an award-winning author who writes romantic mysteries that are splashed with humor and whatever else she feels like throwing into the mix. When she is not dabbling in fiction, arm-wrestling with her children, attempting to seduce her husband, or arguing with her sassy cat, she is daydreaming of lounging poolside at a fancy resort with a blended margarita in one hand and a great book in the other.

Ann's Five Fun Research Facts
(Learned while writing The Great Jackalope Stampede)

Sheriff's Posse: Arizona is one of the few states that allows sheriffs' offices to form semi-permanent posse units which can be operated as a reserve to the main deputized force under a variety of circumstances, as opposed to solely for fugitive retrieval as is historically associated with the term. (Source: http://en.wikipedia.org/wiki/County_sheriff#Arizona)

Artificial Eyeballs: Sources vary on when and where artificial eye manufacturing originated, but there is evidence that the craft can be traced to the late Renaissance when Venetian glassmakers started creating glass eyes. The art flourished primarily in France and Germany where carefully guarded fabricating secrets were handed down from one generation to the next. In the nineteenth century German ocularists began to tour the United States, making glass artificial eyes on a national circuit, setting up for several days at a time in one city after another. Glass stock eyes were also fit by mail order and out of drawers. Eye manufacture in the United States began about 1850. Eyes continued to be made of glass until the onset of World War II. German glassblowers were no longer touring the United States. Most German goods were being boycotted which compelled the development of an American technology for fabricating artificial eyes. Since World War II, plastic has become the preferred material for the artificial eye because of its durability and longevity. The plastic used in eye making is a high optical quality acrylic (Methacrylate resin), similar to the material used to make dentures. Although it is a common misconception that artificial eyes are made from glass, most artificial eyes produced in the United States are fitted and fabricated by ocularists from Methyl Methacrylate plastic. Source: (http://www.artificialeye.net/history.htm)

Sonoran Desert Cacti: The Sonoran Desert's eastern border is Arizona's Route 191, which runs right through the middle of my fictional town, Jackrabbit Junction. This desert is one of the largest and hottest deserts in North America, with an area of 120,000 square miles. It is an incredibly beautiful place with the greatest diversity of vegetative growth of any desert in the world, including 60 mammal species, 350 bird species, 20 amphibian species, over 100 reptile species, 30 native fish species, and more than 2,000 native plant species. (Source: http://www.newworldencyclopedia.org/entry/Sonoran_Desert)

The Devil's Highway: The Arizona section of U.S. Route 191 (which cuts through Jackrabbit Junction in my story) used to be U.S. Route 666 just a decade or so ago. The road earned its nickname, The Devil's Highway, due to more than four hundred curves in the 90 mile stretch between Alpine and Clifton. It is listed as a National Scenic Byway and is now called the Coronado Trail Scenic Byway, as it approximates the path taken by Francisco Vásquez de Coronado between 1540 and 1542. Travel writer James T. Yenckel, in an article in *The Washington Post* on December 29, 1991, commented: No structural evidence of Coronado's passing remains, but the verdant countryside, abloom in summer wildflowers, is largely untouched, and it must look now as it did when he struggled through. An almost empty highway to nowhere, U.S. 666 climbs to above 9,000 feet along the Coronado Trail in a cliff-hanging series of twists and turns so sharp the speed limit often drops to only 10 miles per hour. The reward for this little test of nerves is a picture-postcard panorama of pine-draped ridges leap-frogging across the horizon. (Sources: http://en.wikipedia.org/wiki/U.S._Route_191 and http://www.fhwa.dot.gov/infrastructure/us666.cfm)

The Fusee (in relation to Pocket Watches): The fusee is a cone with a spiral groove in its surface that accommodates a cord or a chain, attached at one end to the barrel containing the spring and at the other end to the cone. As the power of the spring decreases, the cord on the fusee unwinds, engaging the fusee at a point of greater diameter and thus evening out the force transmitted. This invention probably had its origins in about 1400 in the technology for winding crossbows. By 1600, most timepieces made by watchmakers outside the boundaries of German-speaking Europe employed the spring-and-fusee device for watches. It would be the preferred mechanism for a long time to come. (Source: http://www.metmuseum.org/toah/hd/watc/hd_watc.htm)

Made in the USA
San Bernardino, CA
17 July 2014